Also by Michael Carin

Five Hundred Keys
The Neutron Picasso
The Future Jew
The Anti-Trump

Churchill At Munich

a novel

Michael Carin

The Métropolitain Press
Montreal

Published in 2018 by
The Métropolitain Press
1117 Sainte-Catherine Street West
Montreal, Quebec, Canada H3B 1H9
metropolitainpress@gmail.com

NATIONAL LIBRARY OF CANADA CATALOGUING IN PUBLICATION DATA

Carin, Michael, 1951-, author
    Churchill at Munich / Michael Carin.
ISBN 978-0-9688569-5-6 (softcover)

    I. Title.
PS8555.A735C58 2018   C813'.54   C2017-907804-6

First Edition 2018

Cover and Text Design: Karen Cross Landon
Author Photo: © Laszlo Montreal

www.churchillatmunich.com

PRINTED IN CANADA

For Cielo

Whose love is my life;
whose wisdom, goodness, charm
and confidence live in this book

Sometimes it is necessary
to change the truth,
in order to remember it.

Santayana

Contents

Introduction
by Maxwell Brian Lowell

I am the eldest son of the late Elizabeth Heidi Lowell. Shortly before she died my mother revealed to me a collection of letters that had been written to her in the 1930s. She asked me to publish the letters after her death. She had kept them hidden for over four decades.

After arriving in the United States in the fall of 1935 my mother began receiving these letters from Mr. Joffrey Pearson of London, England. The earliest of them she destroyed for fear they might fall into the hands of my father. "Some of Joff's first notes," she said, "were true moans from the heart."

In January of 1936 my mother began preserving Mr. Pearson's letters. To the best of my knowledge my late father was not aware of the correspondence while it took place and never subsequently learned of it. Inquiries in England have yielded no trace of my mother's part in the correspondence. None of her own writings appear to have survived.

I share my mother's conviction that the letters of Joffrey Pearson form a valuable document of the period and cast essential new light on the events they encompass. Indeed, as she said to me, "Joff saw, heard and played a personal part in an historic moment, one that no history book has yet made known to the world."

Boston, Massachusetts
September 1981

1

A Note on the Text

The letters in this book have been reproduced word-for-word from the originals. Where spelling differs from American usage, the author's British form has been preserved. Editing has been restricted to the correction of minor grammatical errors and the deletion of ellipses. Joffrey Pearson indulged a pronounced weakness for the ellipsis (...), a form of punctuation indicating a brief pause or omission of words. He used the ellipsis to such excess that publication required a significant culling. The only other change to the text has been the replacement of Mr. Pearson's underlined expressions with italics.

PART ONE: 1936

Probably the battle of Waterloo was won on the playing-fields of Eton, but the opening battles of all subsequent wars have been lost there.

George Orwell

Saturday
11th Jan. 1936

Dear Heidi,

Father and daughter are just back from the zoo. Vicky was so eager to see the lions you can imagine her disappointment when she found them prostrate in their winter pen. They lay there like drunken yobs, tongues hanging out, occasionally blinking with tremendous apathy. The alpha male, the one with the biggest mane, was dozing … oblivious. You could have offered him a succulent gazelle on a platter, he would not have budged. The fearsome predator turned slumbering lamb!

"That's not proper," Vicky said in her most accusing voice.

"What isn't proper?"

"Lions sleeping."

I explained to my plum that lions have to sleep like any other living thing.

"I know that, Daddy," she puffed, "but they should sleep when nobody sees them."

I told her she was absolutely correct and that I would take up her complaint with the keepers.

By the way, Heidi, my heart missed a beat when a black-haired woman in a red scarf and tightly belted coat swept by outside the aquarium. The impression of you was startling. More so since the woman had a tall, doting, American-looking fellow on her arm. I caught no sight of her face, but her resolute bearing and cascade of hair instantly brought you to mind. Did I say my heart missed a beat? I lied. It missed two, possibly three. The gods should not torment your admirer in such a way when he's with his daughter.

Damon still has not called. Consider me puzzled and hurt. He is yet to defend himself for missing our customary tipple at Christmas. He may have run off to Paris again for his illicit pleasures, but why no word?

The hour grows late. I will soon be comatose, like those forlorn lions. I send you a hug and all my best,

Joff

Wednesday
15th Jan. 1936

Dear Heidi,
Thank you for yours of the second. Yes, I promise to take from the new year everything it has to offer. Reprimand also noted. I do apologise, but things are rather gloomy. Have you forgotten the parks full of vagrants? The newspapers say things are improving but a quarter of coal miners are still out of work and conditions are worse among the iron and steel men. We have a desperately poor family tucking in above us with the spinster, including a couple of kids who don't sound the least underfed while stomping on our ceiling. I'm being cruel, I know almost nothing about the family, just that a neighbour mentioned seeing a means inspector come by.

The general gloom is not helped by today's news of the King. He has taken ill at Sandringham and his time may have come.

As if things are not depressing enough, some predict another Great War, more shiploads of boys grave-bound to Europe. You should hear the debates in the lunchroom, each side hot-blooded. Curious how the prospect of war seems at once near and unthinkable. People talk of it like a cloud on the horizon while life carries on, unwilling to believe a new storm may come … but here I am shovelling more gloom.

Sneaking this note on Whitehall's time. Tremayne is home with the influenza that has felled half the Foreign Office. Why is it I work more effectively when the bully is off sniffling in bed?

Now well over a month since Damon last called. I am growing uneasy.

Mary has gone to Scotland on a recruitment drive, Vicky's rubbing shoulders with patrician swells at her pricey school, and your admirer is stuck at his humble station dreaming of your … yes, he knows, such reveries are out of bounds. He will post this on his way home.

Missing you. As always,
Joff

Thursday
23rd Jan. 1936

Dear Heidi,
I see the King's passing has drawn huge attention in America. Curious how your new countrymen fancy an institution they threw off centuries ago. What is it they miss? Dukes and princesses without a useful thought in their heads making cartoons of themselves at paddocks and lacy banquets?

You can imagine the sombre mood here. The bunting of grief hangs everywhere and newspapers carry black borders. Both the high and low dress in mourning, and people are shedding tears in public. Did we love old George half as much when he was still breathing? We had been expecting word but it still came as a shock. During the final hours we were all glued to the wireless as bulletins issued every fifteen minutes. The final announcement said the King's life was drawing peacefully to a close.

My dear spouse adored George. Not just for his love of Empire, which Mary so unflaggingly shares, but because she met him once at an Auxiliary function and found him 'effortlessly charming'. I remember she came home aglow because the King said a few kind words about women in police work and specifically complimented her on the increasing number of recruits.

"We may not see his like again," said Mary. Then she surprised me with, "Edward is not exactly the mixture as before." Surprised me, because the soul of my Mary is made of the toughest British fibre, spun on the loom of loyalty and knotted with tradition. She would certainly be saying 'the King is dead, long live the King', save for having reproached Edward so often for the trail of gossip he creates. The man is a determined pleasure-seeker, unquestionably a womaniser, but still, in my view he deserves his chance.

Offering an olive branch on Edward's behalf, I said, "Maybe he'll bring a breath of fresh air into things."

"Like his grandfather did?" Mary replied. My spouse has never allowed a good word about loose morals. Sometimes I think she longs for the resurrection of Victoria and the canons of a stricter time. You will remember it was Mary who insisted on our daughter's name.

Government offices and schools are closed today for official mourning. Mary and Vicky have gone to King's Cross for the arrival of the coffin from Norfolk. A gun carriage procession will then make its way to Westminster Hall. The body will lie in state for four days.

"I want Vicky to see the affection of the people for their King," said Mary. "You'll come of course, Joff?"

"I am all for Vicky and you going, darling," I said, "but you know my dread of crowds. Besides, I have a bit of writing to catch up on."

This brought a frown but no quarrel, thank heavens. Mary knows my phobia for mass gatherings is not entirely fictional. And look, here, I've caught up on that writing ... or almost.

Yours of the seventh wounded me, I must say. True, I have been marking time at the F.O., but 'drifting aimlessly'? I am compelled to wonder if America has changed you, made you less gently critical. Or is it the other new aspect of your life, married respectability? Careful, or this sensitive soul will stop admitting his flaws if you judge them as defects!

You ask if I know what I want. I would guess very few people know what they want. Our friend Damon would be one, he has always known, and you are another. You knew in the womb what you wanted and to hell with what anyone else suggested you should want.

The lunch club meets tomorrow, first time without you. Will tell all.

Yours as ever,

Joff

Saturday
25th Jan. 1936

Dear Heidi,
Prepare to be amused. Or disgusted, I am not sure which!
My day started with a scuffle. I had just left the flat at my usual early hour when a man called to me, or rather shouted at me, from across the road. "Sir, you must see this. Look!"
On the gate of a house someone had painted a swastika. The thing was black and glistening, and skilfully done. Under the light of a streetlamp I could see it was perfectly proportioned save for a dribble deforming one of the arms. Brought to mind newsreel footage from Berlin of vandalised Jewish shops.
"The ugly nerve," said the man, whom I could see now was an elderly gentleman. He was wearing a buttoned-up mac with a regimental pin and a tightly wound muffler. "Who would do this?" His hands rose in fists. "What filthy beast would dare?"
I offered, soothingly I thought, "These things are not uncommon, sir. It's likely the prank of a foolish boy. I wager it will be scrubbed off by noon. Good day to you." As I turned to go, however, the man seized my arm.
"If you don't mind," I said loudly.
"If YOU don't mind," he bellowed, spraying me with spittle. "Do you think this is just litter in the ROAD?" The man must have been a horse handler in his day, he had a grip of iron. I was frankly frightened. I tore my arm free and fled, in a damn hurry. Wiping the spit from my face I looked back and saw my assailant cough up some phlegm and aim it at the cause of his distemper. I almost laughed, though I was still trembling. My dear sweet émigré, do you have barmy pensioners on your side of the pond?
You are missed, sorely missed. Our lunch club tried a new spot off the Haymarket. The hock and claret were quite good, but I hardly participated in the talk. I had to fake joining the toast to your new life. Down in the cataclysm you have dug for me, I sat stricken.
Received yours of the twelfth, thank you. I know my declarations aimed at your heart are sinful, but I will show no remorse. After all, my musings are valid only for a place beyond an eternity of obstacles

9

and an infinity of walls … an other-lifely place.

Your house sounds simply fabulous, the garden … enchanting. I assume 'Beacon Hill' is Boston's challenge to Mayfair. If so, my hat is off to That American. We can almost begin to pardon him for stealing you from England. You say you have adjusted, but have you really? Where is your studio? What friends have you made?

This morning's weird grapple has already receded into the stuff of dreams, though the bruise on my arm proves it did indeed happen. I mentioned the encounter to Tremayne, who gave me a mocking glance and naturally judged me in the wrong. "Englishmen don't attack each other in the street with no reason," he said. Still dripping from the influenza of a couple of weeks ago, he put a silk handkerchief to his nose and sniffed, "You must have provoked him."

Tremayne's comments often leave me speechless, since they are often foolish. You would not think him stupid at first glance. He has a fine straight nose and a good sweep of sandy hair. People often think he's Ronald Colman. Once in Hyde Park a smitten young lady mistook him for the film star and without so much as a how do you do planted a kiss on his cheek. Tremayne has dined out for years on that possibly true story. Unfortunately he squanders his leading man's likeness the moment he opens his mouth. His lower lip curls when he speaks, which is to say when he condescends to lecture and enlighten.

He was sitting at the gunmetal table which Jenkins and I call his schoolmaster's desk. His chair faces our own desks and he presides over us like a teacher at the front of a classroom. He has a real desk, a large oak thing out of our sight in an alcove. Jenkins and I call the alcove Tremayne's broom closet. Which is where our dismal department's single telephone roosts.

About that swastika . . . on my way back to the flat I walked by the besmirched house (fully alert for dangerous codgers, I don't mind telling you). The gate has been scrubbed, but a ghostly outline remains of Herr Hitler's fangy emblem.

Please write the instant this reaches you, my dear. Tell me everything you know I want to know. Your adoring,

Joff

P.S. Knocked on the door of Damon's flat yesterday and passed by the studio. Both shuttered. I have been thinking back to the last time I saw him. He seemed under the weather, pale, a bit hollowed-out, very unlike him. But miss our champagne at Christmas? Utterly unlike him. Maybe he has plunged deeply into work somewhere and forgotten the world. Which would be a welcome thing, if he has become the prolific hermit again.

Saturday
1st Feb. 1936

Heidi dear,
This is how the gods taunt me, by planting your lookalikes in my path. You appeared again last night. This time she was a younger you, a good ten years younger, and dining unaccompanied. I would have stared, but that would have been reckless. I was with Mary and Vicky at The Ivy.

She was your junior twin, I swear. Slender to the point of peril yet still formidable. With your icy alertness too. I suspect that early in life men are taken by a certain type of woman, then struck down and made wanton whenever she materialises in their path. I favour serene knives of women, bold glinting reeds. If I had been alone I would have found a pretext to address your black-haired, vaguely Italian double if only to hear the sound of her voice. She was wearing a neck-hugging black dress and a necklace of green stones. If I had been alone and unmarried I might have done something foolish like instruct the waiter to bring her a glass of champagne.

Instead I chatted with wife and daughter as if your doppelganger behind them were no more interesting than a painted pillar. Mary was just off the train from Birmingham, Vicky on furlough from her swish school. We were over-spending before the cinema. Remember the significance of yesterday's date? Vicky is an astonishing eight now. *Eight!*

I took a last wistful glance at your twin as we left. She was conserving a glass of claret and carving a chop, splendidly aloof.

Some mild weather has arrived and carried a bit of optimism into life, even mine. Leads me to dream of escape from these dreary years. We enjoyed the night air on our stroll to Leicester Square, man and wife, arm in arm, child in tow. Our film was *Birds of a Feather*. George Robey plays a nouveau riche merchant who moves his family into the castle of a destitute nobleman. Coming out of the theatre Vicky said in her most serious voice, "People with pots of money are no different from anybody else, and neither are people with *titles*." Mary and I looked at each other, then collided in the rush to hug our delicious prodigy. Surely no finer description of a film has ever been uttered by

12

an eight year-old. Comes of her love of books, no question.

Received yours of the twentieth with the tale of the sleigh ride round the Common. You seem taken with the pleasures of winter. I liked your ode to the marvel of icicles hanging from eaves.

I am always flattered by any interest you take in my work, or are you just aiming to deflect my forbidden declarations? Fact is, the F.O.'s demand only grows for information about what is happening in Germany, so I expect my position in Translation, German Section, will remain secure. Tremayne's little fiefdom, including himself, now numbers four whole-timers. A young man named Kenneth Retinger joined me and Jenkins in the trenches this week. Retinger is in his late twenties and seems a pleasant enough fellow. When I pointed out the diabolical location of our two windows, which attract less than an hour of sunlight per day, he said, "We can call it the sunroom then!" His good cheer won my instant liking. I am yet to ask him, but I suppose his mother is English and father German, the reverse of my own inheritance.

A good thing Retinger has come. Jenkins is showing his age and should retire soon. He still translates accurately enough but can no longer work at speed. Watching his decline I sometimes wonder about my own fate. Jenkins' career has never taken him beyond his desk, yet he suffers no regrets. Should I adopt his view of the world and stop expecting advancement in life?

Even with the addition of Retinger we are feeling understaffed. The Berlin embassy is sending documents in greater and greater number. They come in belted parcels, and in rare instances we see documents in the form of photographs stamped MOST SECRET. This always stirs a moment's frisson because it connects us, however remotely, to the black arts, agents in the field – espionage! It particularly thrills Jenkins, who will take excitement where he can and often sees intrigue where there isn't any. The excitement quickly palls, I assure you. The work can be a bore. Last week I was handed a sheaf of cuttings from the *Frankfurter Zeitung*.

"Don't bother translating," said Tremayne, his tone back to full annoyance after the 'flu. "Summarise. Give me the meat, in notes."

Pity me, my dear. An article on winter camping written by a fifteen year-old Hitler youth. One about a Munich house burglar sentenced to hard labour. Another about a bronze statue of Bismarck erected in a Dresden park. What possible advantage for statecraft could my superiors pluck from these trifles? Mostly written, I might add, in atrocious German.

Compensations are few, but they do arrive. This morning I laboured over a confidential memorandum evidently pinched from the innards of the *Reichspressekammer*, the German Press Chamber. Dispatched to the editors of newspapers, it tells the troops on the journalistic front lines how to behave during the Olympics.

"The eyes of the world will rest on our labours, often with intent to defame. While the struggle of the German nation can neither cease nor slow, foreigners cannot be expected to grasp all of our Fuhrer's goals." One must admire the ingenuity of 'labours' where the writer means repressions, and the cunning use of 'struggle' to denote the works of a tyranny-in-progress.

"As the uniqueness of the Reich's social project excites corrupt criticism (*korrupte Kritik*), our efforts must focus on emphasising, to the exclusion of negativity (*unter Ausschluss der Negativität*), Germany's resurrection, thriving economy, and the avid roar of our optimism."

One cringes at 'avid roar'. A turn of phrase like that could only issue from a Nazi functionary. Can you and your Yankee friends read between the lines, or is America remote from German guile? Unter Ausschluss der Negativität happens to be code. In advance of the Olympics, the Nazis are lowering the temperature on diatribes against the Jews.

Still no word from Damon. My worry deepens. Your comment about Paris and rent-boys was extremely mean. He would forgive you, however ... and so do I.

Missing you terribly, Heidi. Are we never to lunch, stroll, debate and tease each other again? Give up forever the elation of baring our minds? Please be reminded of my adoration.

Joff

Saturday
8th Feb. 1936

Dearest Heidi,
Half-day in the trenches behind, home to yellow notepad and escape
hatch. Mary is out on her usual Saturday drill. All would be calm
save for the little horrors above. They have made a playground of
the spinster's drawing room. They might be amusing themselves with
hammers. Either that, or they are running about in metal shoes.
Received yours of the twenty-fourth. Thank you for not doubting
my fascination with your new life. You make the winter Common
sound enchanting. Less so the wives of your husband's associates! And
thank you again for the pat on the back about my work, but I deserve
no applause. I happen to be naturally suited to the rigours of my niche.
My skills reflect no achievement, but rather a condition of birth. Think
of the porcupine fending off predators by virtue of the quills evolution
gave him. That's me, sustaining life with what quills nature, primarily
in the form of my mother's instruction, has given me. I see now the
clever pun in 'quills', but it was unpremeditated!
The new man in our department started the week badly when he
unwittingly goaded Tremayne. We had a bit of pathetic theatre for
which I blame myself. I should have warned Retinger about our
Section Head. Tremayne was sitting at his schoolmaster's desk leafing
through a batch of documents when he commented on the Winter
Olympics in Germany. "Apparently the organisation is exemplary,"
he said. "People are finding Germany's not the horned beast many
claim it to be." If Tremayne had stopped there we might have avoided
the drama, but then he added, "I think once the Games are done we
shall see Chancellor Hitler moderating his approach to international
dialogue."
The neophyte Retinger was taken aback by this. He innocently
piped up, "Do you think there's a moderate bone in Hitler's body? His
regime is loathsome from tip to toe."
Tremayne looked at our new colleague as if he were an insect
emerging from a crack in the floor. "How long have you been with us,
Retinger, all of six days?"
"That's right, sir, but – "

"Perhaps after six *years*," said Tremayne, getting to his feet, "we will be interested in your judgment of what may, or may not be, *loathsome*." With that he turned on his heel and repaired to his palatial broom closet. Jenkins and I shared a cheerless smile. Later I apologised to Retinger for not prepping him on our short-tempered lord and master. Different shades of opinion about the Nazis compete at the Foreign Office. Tremayne's view has always been 'anti-war'. I explained the spectrum at lunch in the cafeteria.

Those on the anti-war side are inclined to overlook Nazi sins, because they simply cannot bear the idea of another ghastly bout with Germany. For the Tremaynes in the Foreign Office, if lesser evils must be tolerated to forestall war, then so be it. On the opposite side we have 'the belligerents'. They abhor Hitler and advocate a hard line against him. The Foreign Secretary, Anthony Eden, and the Permanent Under-Secretary, Sir Robert Vansittart, are certainly belligerents, but their views really do not matter much.

"Eden and Vansittart do not decide policy," I said. "All they can do is try to influence the ultimate decision-maker, the Prime Minister."

"No need to tell me which side Baldwin's on," Retinger replied, in a tone that signalled I should not take him for a naif. "I'm surprised he hasn't run up a white flag over Number 10. Hitler shrieks, and Baldwin cowers."

I decided at that moment to never again talk down to my new colleague. "Aren't you being a little rough? I think Mr. Baldwin sees Hitler as a convenient counter-weight to Stalin."

"True enough. Baldwin marches on the leash of our aristocrats, who hate the Soviets more than they distrust the Nazis. The toffs look at Mussolini in the same way, as another useful buffer against the Bolsheviks."

"By the way," I said, "we have no shortage of toffs upstairs. They like it here. Messing about with international issues suits them."

"So I've joined an Old Boys' club," said Retinger, with mock pride.

"You are in a cellar of the club, toiling in one of the engine rooms."

"I'm a grease monkey, then."

"Now you're getting it!"

I came back to my little lesson about Tremayne. "So remember, our Section Head takes the view that Germany is undergoing a revolutionary ferment or an historic transformation. Mumbo-jumbo like that always lets him give the Nazis the benefit of the doubt."

"Wait, don't tell," said Retinger, "but at some point he has grandly declared, 'To make an omelet, you must break a few eggs.'"

I threw my head back and laughed. I was liking this fellow more and more. "One of his favourite eggs," I said, "is the Treaty of Versailles. Tremayne will argue that all the punishments loaded onto Germany after the War only caused resentment, and that's how the Treaty-bashing Hitler came to power in the first place."

Retinger asked where I myself stood, with the anti-war crowd or the belligerents. I told him I was firmly in the grey centre.

"So you take comfort in being a cynic?"

I didn't hear a drop of malice in his voice, the comment was made in good humour, but it brought me up short. "Yes," I said, looking into space, "I suppose I am a cynic."

"Not unlike half the world these days," he said.

"You won't find me debating you, but I repeat … you must watch yourself with Tremayne. He lives with the illusion that he has a keen intellect. Steam will rise in him quickly if you contradict him in public."

"If by 'public' you mean Jenkins and yourself, you may be in for some steam."

"Please listen to me, Kenneth." (My first use of his given name caught his full attention.) "Tremayne regards anyone who disagrees with him as a pleb, a fool, or a communist. I understand there was once money in his family. Imagine the comedown of requiring a post in the civil service. Add to that the indignity of overseeing a trivial department in a gloomy little room. He is a proud and easily malicious man. He can make life miserable for you. Do *not* go to war with him."

Retinger saw how serious I was and thanked me for the warning. "Righto then, I will remain the soul of cordiality and poke fun at the blockhead without him knowing. Otherwise *I'll* boil over."

"Just be careful."

"I have a wife and two little ones to feed. Do call me Ken, by the way."

"Once you call me Joff."

Seems I have a new friend! Meanwhile, still not a peep from my old friend. What is to be done? Damon's only family is a senile aunt up in Dunblane, so no help there. I called Maddy Kloff at the Walter Gallery, but she is also in the dark. Damon has been her biggest earning artist for years. At what point, we asked each other, do we involve the police?

Write again soon, Heidi. Remember the extent to which you are involved in my thoughts and, please, you must tell me … is it true I'm a cynic?

Joff

Saturday
15th Feb. 1936

Dearest Heidi,

The mystery of Damon's whereabouts has gone beyond the circle of his friends. It has now reached into Billy Colman's tittle-tattle in the *Evening News*. William 'Billy' Colman is a little alligator of a man we occasionally see crawling about at The Squire's Arms. I would slip in the cutting, but I must save it for Vicky. She meticulously collects all the ink about her famous godfather.

Wanting to be celebrated as a rebel is not exactly a plausible formula for remaining anonymous, but somehow he has done it for over twenty years: shunned publicity, kept out of the public eye, forbidden all photos, while earning a reputation as one of Britain's most subversive painters. Good on him, but now he seems to have pulled a vanishing act. The erstwhile *enfant terrible* of British art has not answered his telephone in months. Nor has he been glimpsed at his local of late. I know because I have been ringing him, and his pub happens to be mine. Has anyone seen Damon Chadwick?

I myself have put the same question to everyone in my circle. Nobody has heard a thing. Maddy and I have decided that if another week or two go by, we will make a formal report to the police.

Remember the first time you met Damon? I took you to an exhibition at the Walter. He had done a series of portraits of cabinet ministers, none of them solicited, and none of them flattering. It was fifteen years ago, and you were wearing a certain dress. If you asked me the colour of the dress, or whether it had sleeves, or if it allowed a peek at your knees, I would not be able to say. There is only one thing I remember about that dress … it hung on you like a provocation.

The things that stick in our minds.

You were the woman for whom I would have swum the Channel with my legs in shackles. You were The One. Whatever obstacles stood between us would eventually vanish, I was certain. This while you conducted torrid affairs with half a dozen suitors. We never had a concentrated, sustained, pinnacle-reaching moment together. It might have made our bond but it eluded us, and I blame myself. I should have pitched a tent at your door. I should have orchestrated one grand gesture after another. But I was a coward. I was paralysed by the possibility of alienating you or, even worse, disappointing you. And so I lost you, without ever making the supreme attempt to win you. Ancient history? Not quite, I seem to be recalling it like yesterday.

This recalling, is it tantamount to adultery? I think not. Here is the simple fact: it is with you I am unguarded. You are the person in the world to whom I tell my secrets. Ironically, you must now remain one of them.

Received yours of the fourth. My darling Mary is fine, thanks for asking. You shock me when you ask if I still love her. You know very well she is my anchor. Besides, how could I survive without her giggle in my life? The sound enchants me, that abrupt gulp of joy from her deepest self, exposing the policewoman's uniform as an incongruity, a career appendage. Seriously, I revere my Mary as I do my life, as I do my country. I wish I could be more like Mary, I wish I could *deserve* her.

Yes, if she learned of this correspondence she would consider it infidelity. She would not accept an explanation, and possibly put a match to our wedding photo. But how many times must I declare to you, persuade you, that my motive is not in any way a betrayal of Mary. I am buoyant in this space, weightless. You free me, and that is what unbreakably connects us. Am I justifying myself? Very well then, I am justifying myself.

At work I have been steadily rowing my little boat, and the new man Ken has been providing some amusement. He bows and scrapes whenever engaged with Tremayne, diligently affixing 'sir' to every utterance. He does it so artfully that Tremayne fails to notice the mockery. The other day our dimwitted Section Head was incensed over an article in the *Telegraph*. "Look at this," he said, addressing no one in particular. "The daft old warmonger keeps beating on his drum."

"What have you got there, sir?" said Ken.

"The usual rattle and doom from Churchill. Now the sky is falling because Germany is building too many planes."

"Winston the warhorse was stamping his feet just as angrily, sir, back when the Germans left the League, and he was galloping to the front again when they pulled out of the disarmament talks. Last year he got red in the face when they introduced conscription. Always griping and growling in the Commons as if a hurricane were approaching and the government not bright enough to get inside and close the shutters."

"A panic-monger is what he is," said Tremayne. "Churchill's so disgruntled at being left out of Cabinet, he pours dirt on his own party."

"One must understand as you and the Prime Minister obviously do, sir, the martial impulse of the Germans. They must have their army to feel equal again. They must have their submarines and fighter aircraft to feel properly respected again. As soon as Germany regains its strength it will be a satisfied country, a country ready to reconcile with the past. Churchill simply does not understand that about the Germans, does he, sir?"

"Quite," said Tremayne, looking like a man unsure of where he put his spectacles, and reminding Jenkins and myself that we have an amusing new reason to come to work.

I received something of a compliment from our lord and master the other day. Still, Tremayne being Tremayne, the praise had to be diluted. "I understand the Permanent Under-Secretary was pleased with our work on the Goering speech," he said. "We did well with the accompanying notes."

The work is always 'our' work when it comes to applause from above. Tremayne can effortlessly assume responsibility for work he never touches. That is his unique talent, believing his own inventions. He made zero contribution to the Goering translation, and I wrote the accompanying notes. Not that I mind sharing the glory, since career advancement is not an issue. To where would I advance?

The Goering speech had interested me. The Air Marshall is regarded as Germany's *Nummer Zwei*, Number Two. Evidently the man is a hedonist and monstrous glutton. Also rumoured to be a pervert and sadist, the whole kit. They say he preys on kidnapped gypsy boys and takes his pleasure in an upholstered torture chamber. Jenkins swallows these fairy tales whole, and annoys us with his 'where there's smoke, there's fire' nonsense. You would think he was channeling my father, who has taken to blaming Hitler and his gang for everything from summer rain to the cost of tea …

I like doing rants.

Goering's speech rated as one, a tirade delivered at an *inoffizielles* meeting of bigwigs in Hanover where he was guest of honour. Meant to be off the record but a stenographer of the National Socialist Party innocently took the whole thing down. The transcript found its way to our embassy in Belgrade, a bit of a howdunit that delighted Jenkins no end; he does love the cloak and dagger. He was disappointed when Tremayne gave the file to me.

Maybe they put something in the Hanoverian water that day. The fat Air Marshall had a veritable fit. Seems an increasing percentage of state funding is going to other branches of the German military at the expense of his beloved Luftwaffe. "They're stripping us naked and feeding us birdpiss and Jew dung." (Forgive my faithful translation!) "We get sticks and rocks when we need engines and machine-guns. Soon they will be ordering us to frighten off the enemy by wagging our *Schwanzen* at them!"

Loose cannon stuff, obviously never meant for publication. The buffoon wanted to present himself as an expert on modern military doctrine but sounded more like the village pornographer. His speech was mainly a stew of scatalogical invective directed at *them*, the unnamed, ignorant, 'shit-coated insects and tiny-cocked rats' in the economic planning apparatus of the Reich. As I say, wacky stuff.

My notes pointed out the speaker could not be translated precisely. His use of language was too sloppy. The stenographer may have been to blame, but we have never encountered an instance of amateur shorthand on the part of a German steno. I ended with conjecture to the effect that the Air Marshall, reputed to be an alcoholic when not suspected of being a drug addict, might have been intoxicated when he rose to expel his steam. I considered 'fart out his resentments' but my departmental decorum prevailed.

Let my superiors upstairs, those professional tea leaf readers, unravel the significance of the speech. That is what they do up there, they read tea leaves. I can see them scratching their heads as they weigh what the *Nummer Zwei*'s outrage says about Germany's military preparations. Then again, my betters on high may regard the document with disbelief. Is it an invention, a plant? Ah, the byzantine alleys and labyrinths of the great game, Heidi, papered with miles of tea leaves. A few of which peel off and float about and find their way into His Majesty's embassies and then by diplomatic pouch to your admirer's desk, his sunless perch in the world, where he transforms them from his mother's tongue into his father's, the dull thankless task of his days. From time to time he offers observations, extracts a bit of fun, and thereby reminds himself that curiosity can still move him, the weirdness of the world still fascinate him. Maybe he is not, after all, just gears and levers – pop in a penny for your programmed reflex! – not yet, anyway.

Missing you. Be well, and please write.

Joff

Saturday
22nd Feb. 1936

Dear Heidi,
Damon has surfaced, thank the gods. But not yet in the flesh, and not yet in London. This comical proxy arrived at the F.O., postmarked Paris:

My Dear Joff,
You have been denying me exposure to your excellent self, which leaves me bereft in two respects. First in regard to missing the rare energy of your character, and second on account of being singled out for such cruel neglect. I am thus doubly blackened by your wilful inattention.
Your servant,
Damon

It gave me a hearty laugh, Damon writing like an Edwardian dandy and blaming me for his vanishing. My cackle caused Tremayne to look up and bark, "Some childish diversion, Pearson?" Our new colleague, Retinger, simply caught my eye and winked. Ken's a bit of a rough diamond, bad-tempered at times, but never less than likable. Have I told you we are firmly on the path to friendship?

Can't begin to tell you how relieved I am about Damon. A few dark possibilities had crossed my mind. Will let you know his story as soon as I hear it.

Thanks for yours of the twenty-third. You flatter me, dear. My ramblings hardly deserve such tribute. I will take your praise as incentive, however, not that I need any. I enjoy playing with language, and that is only half of my motive. I enjoy telling you things.

Must tell you the latest about my delicious plum, who is growing up far too fast. She decided the name 'Vicky' is not quite right for her, and I must call her Victoria. I told her this was unexpected, bewildering, and probably difficult. Was she sure?

"Perfectly sure," and her mouth settled into a grim line.

"This is a weighty matter. Can I take time to think about it?"

The determined mouth opened and closed summarily, "No."

"Can you tell me why you have suddenly come to this decision?"

"The name Vicky is for a frivolous and idle person," she said. "I am a Victoria." End of discussion because she walked dramatically from the room.

Eight years old and already Regal Woman winning debates. Vicky is the greatest compensation of my misbegotten life. You can imagine how I fought against sending her away to school. I would have preferred the neighbourhood comprehensive and the chance to see her safely into bed every night. Mary, however, was adamant about the benefits. An infinitely better education to start with. "Vicky will have her chance to the extent any woman is allowed," she said.

Only rarely does Mary chafe against the injustices of patriarchy. She was once an eager suffragette, but that battle at least has been won. Lately she has never accepted restrictions because of gender and usually dismisses talk of career limits. She believes no rung in the police hierarchy is beyond her. She is now aiming for a transfer to the Metropolitan Force and sees no reason why she cannot be Head of Recruitment there one day.

Speaking of patriarchy, I visit my father next Saturday. I still lack the talent to prevent his senile harangues. He has become more single-minded than ever and his obsessions crawl under my skin. Wish me luck.

Must run, Heidi, but may I tell you once again that you are an uncommonly attractive woman? Having nothing else of you to embrace, I embrace the facts. You attract, Madame. To your fingertips, you attract. Do you know I used to secretly watch your fingers? They beguiled me. I tried to imagine how they would feel interlocked with mine, to the very tips. Has any other man ever thrown himself at your fingers? How about That American? I would doubt it. Husbands rarely behave like fawning suitors.

Forgive me.

Joff

Wednesday
26th Feb. 1936

Heidi,
Looking out into fog, third straight day of it. Our lifeless windows might as well be cement blinds. Jenkins called in ill, and Tremayne is attending a meeting of Section Heads. Invoking a pretend seniority I sent Ken home after hearing a nasty cough. I shall leave in a moment myself, but first this reprimand: No letter from you for over a fortnight. Have you forgotten the power you hold? A word from you can leave me euphoric, whereas silence makes me fear losing you. I will say no more. The prosecution rests.
  Your devoted,
  Joff

Sunday
1st March 1936

Dearest Heidi,
Your letter came on Friday, healing me instantly. I had a wonderful laugh from your salutation. I should have expected it after my atrocious pun on 'quills'. Should I inform Vicky that this is the name I now prefer? She would probably adopt it in a heartbeat, and I would be a spiky rodent for a relentless month or two.

Amusing also, your run-in with the Boston brogue. *War-shington*? How do they slide an 'r' in there? The curmudgeon in me would gape with incredulity, maybe fall about laughing.

Thank you for those comments about Mary and our marriage. I feel now you understand me. If you ever doubt my feelings for my spouse, think back to our courtship. On one of our early days she came to see me directly from the Old Bailey, where she had testified in a gruesome wife battery. This was long before she became Head of Recruitment at the Auxiliary. She looked official and stern in her uniform, but also uncharacteristically sad. I asked her why the gloom on such a perfect face, and she burst into tears. That is when the pillars within me shook and shifted. I looked at the formidable policewoman crying her eyes out and realised I loved her. From that moment on no words were needed, we simply knew. Do you remember the whirlwind? I was a bachelor in May, in heavy courtship in June, betrothed in July, and married in September. You were delighted to have me off your case …

I visited the pater yesterday, with predictable consequences.

Did my morning at the F.O., then took the train to Bury from King's Cross. The overheated carriage had me sweating. Last month the heating died and I read my newspaper wearing gloves. On both occasions, I need not tell you, roasted or frozen, my fellow passengers and I sat like a pack of sheep. Complain to British Rail? Might as well take the case to God in heaven.

Walked from the station to the shabby little house in which my father inhabits a shabby little room. Two former army chums of his have similar deluxe lodgings there. The landlady of the trio, Mrs. Stockton, is also their cook, nurse and plenipotentiary. She was wearing her customary dull blue smock. Mrs. Stockton is an abnormally large woman with bloated ankles, yellow fingernails, and absurdly non-existent breasts. The fearsome battleaxe smokes black foreign pungent things and wafts about like the stink from an ashtray. My father's helpmate! Why he consigned his old age to the succour of this woman and her so-called carer home (more of a vestibule to the grave) remains something of a mystery. I would never have agreed, but he made it a fait accompli, arguing that his chums were satisfied with Mrs. Stockton's kitchen and household ministrations. "She serves us Welsh rarebit every Thursday night," I remember him telling me. "Once a month we have roast beef and Yorkshire pudding. I tell you she's a good woman." Furthermore, he pointed out, the cost would not destroy the pittance of an inheritance I have coming. He also once claimed, outrageously, that Mrs. Stockton had been one of my mother's protégés. That was a sheer invention and I told him so, to his rage. My mother throughout her life taught her German classes and went home and read her German novels and passed on the language of Goethe in all its precision and unlovely force to her two children and never, ever, took a personal interest in a single one of her students. Besides, I have never heard so much as a syllable of German out of Mrs. Stockton. As for her nursing, I doubt if she ever learned anything but the rudiments of it. But I digress.

It seems my father's decline has entered a new phase. Mrs. Stockton buttonholed me at the door with the latest direness. "I must speak to you, Mister," she said, waving me in with her malodorous cigarette. The 'Mister' affectation comes from the American gangster films she faithfully watches at the local Odeon. She has a weakness for that wise-cracking little hoodlum, Jimmy Cagney.

"Yes, Mrs. Stockton?"

"It's about 'is confusion."

"What do you mean?"

"'e's become an 'andful. Bloody nightmare is wot."

Apparently the pater often forgets who, where (and especially when) he is, and confuses Mrs. Stockton's attentions for affection. Lewd comments erupt, suggesting a roué from late Victorian days. Worse, his gropings imply paws that can no longer distinguish between a shapeless old carer and the charms of a chorus girl.

"I will raise the matter with him right off," I assured Mrs. Stockton in my best solicitor's voice.

I hate to think he might have had something to do with her in his days of nature. The mind recoils from certain images. Mrs. Stockton has probably been a hag since her twenties. She looks in her late-fifties now. I have no idea of her first name. None would suit unless plucked from the deeper reaches of Dickens. Etheldreda? Maybe something Viking, like Gunnilde. I don't think my father ever strayed. He loved my mother in his martinet's way. But again, I digress.

"Joffrey!" my father roared. Actually his voice has weakened and taken on gravel. The greeting came out more as a raspy croak than a roar. You might not recognize him now. You met him in his prime when he was a real yacht of a man. Remember the fastidious moustache and perfect placement of every hair? Those were props to go with the sartorial get-up of the diplomat. You could have cut through sheet metal with the crease in his striped trousers. Remember the supercilious attitude that coated his every remark? Back then he would pit mother England against any comer. Oh, he's a ruin of a boat now. The great prow of his head is bald and cadaver-like. Steel grey hair grows out of the tips of his ears. He looks like some great white monkey.

"Dad, what is this about you interfering with the help?"

He paid me no heed, immediately swung his attention to the newspaper I had under my arm. "What's that you have there, *The Times*? The bleeding *Times*?"

I should tell you, the pater's days are taken up with two principal activities. First come the newspapers; they represent his daily mass. He reads the often errant but still sainted *Telegraph* and scans two or three others. This consumes his mornings. After lunch he and his chums sit together playing draughts, talking about the War, and solving world problems. On many of my visits I have found the trio in the small drawing room, huddled in parliamentary session. Half of the solutions these former trenchmates, these saviours of Empire, prescribe for the majority of difficulties on earth involve the fist of the British navy, and the other half involve the boot of the British army. And none involve agreement with the hated *Times*.

"That bleeding rag will be the death of England! Did you see what it said about the enemy yesterday?"

29

It never ends. His year in the trenches and loss of his leg created the obsession. After the War he never called Germans Germans or Germany Germany; they were always 'the enemy'. He never realised he might be offending his Bavarian wife, and she never gave him reason to think he was offending her. Nor is he shy about letting off steam about the enemy in my presence, because he has never regarded me as half-German. His loathing has boiled regularly for going on twenty years now, often with good cause since Hitler came in. He finds *The Times* 'too easy on the enemy' or 'in the pay of the enemy', and on particularly egregious occasions 'in stark raving congress with the Hun enemy'. Being my father's son I have been known to react with some hot blasts of my own.

"When it comes to my mother's country, your wife's place of birth, you are an obstinate, irrational man and I would take it as a favour if you would make talk of Germany *verboten* between us."

The pater simply ignores my disgust. Same way he ignored his colleagues through the '20s. The general view in the F.O. was to regard the restrictions placed on Germany, and the reparations extracted, as excessive. Yet with every ounce of his being my father supported Germany's punishment at Versailles. It hurt his career. Who could want a bitter zealot as a colleague? He made serious enemies. That, and his natural incompetence as a diplomat, kept him on the lowest rungs.

It took adulthood to teach me the pater was a diplomat in name only; a role-filler and not the power-broker I had childishly imagined. He dressed the part and was adept at make-believe, but he never made it beyond the backwaters. The closest he came was his posting as Third Secretary in Tunis, and then only because he had a basic command of French. He certainly never learned a word of Arabic. He left the F.O. in '27 when he was passed over yet again for a minor opening in the First Eleven.

I hear Mary in the hall. She's talking to a man who has a voice like a foghorn. He must be the father of the ceiling stompers. The family seems to have bunked in with the spinster for good.

At long last seeing Damon on Tuesday night, to resume our regular pint at The Squire's. Will tell all. Soon,

Mr. Porcupine

Tuesday
3rd March 1936

Close to midnight, dearest Heidi. Mary left this morning for Nottingham, attending to some new recruits, so I can entertain you with abandon. I am just back from seeing Damon at The Squire's. Our friend is looking his robust self, much better than when I last saw him. He made amends for missing our Christmas tipple, insisted on ordering champagne. He said he was in Paris the whole time, working, which I found odd because he has never been known to paint anywhere but in his Kensington studio and I thought Paris was mainly for … you know.

"For three months? Where did you stay?"

"With admirers."

"Of your art, or your – "

"Both!"

"Why didn't you drop a line?"

"I do apologise. Couldn't be helped."

"What the hell do you mean, couldn't be helped?"

"I am sorry, I should not have said that. Of course it could have been helped."

"Jesus Christ, I was about to bring in the police."

That earned me some scrutiny. "I admit guilt, Joff, and beg forgiveness. In my defence, I was completely immersed in work and refused myself even the slightest distraction."

"Maddy will be thrilled. Her gallery thrives on you. But your insensitivity has reached a new low."

He acknowledged as much with a contrite bow of his head. Forgiveness granted, he was soon boasting about a stunt he pulled the other night at the Anvil Club on his first day back from Paris. He was a guest of one of his wealthy patrons, a City banker. Damon had heard the club was ferociously off-limits to Jews. When they sat down in the hushed dining room known for its ultra-starched decorum he asked the waiter – in a contrived quarrelsome voice – if he would be so kind as to bring the kosher menu.

"Precious, the look on the face of my host," he laughed. "Worth every lost sale in the years ahead."

"Why did you do it?"

"The plaster mouldings in the place are atrocious."

"A perfectly good reason to torment your host."

"I also wanted to pull down the monstrous gilt-framed mirrors. Horrid things."

"Chadwick, kindly – "

"I did it because the smug, useless toff could not say the first intelligent thing about any of my four paintings hanging in his Mayfair home. He had no interest in talking about my work. He was showing me off like a prize bit of horseflesh he bought at auction. I hated myself for being there."

Damon insists his antics have a point, but I am not always persuaded. Remember his appearance at Birmingham City Hall, when the Lord Mayor publicly thanked him for painting the mural in the Council Chamber? He showed up in disguise wearing a long-haired wig that made him a bohemian redhead, and a fake goatee and moustache that made him even more ridiculous. The money he spent to make it authentic! He was also wearing thick-rimmed spectacles. No one at the event had ever met Damon or knew what he looked like, because he had never allowed the press to take his photo. So no one suspected the redheaded Damon Chadwick, who by the way affected a thick Scottish burr that day, was looking any different than he normally looked. He does love a lark, the bigger the better.

As usual I played the taciturn listener to Damon's raucous raconteur. You have always resented my playing second fiddle to him, haven't you? On that score you have an ally in Mary. She says I have mistaken myself for Damon's little brother. How can I explain it, such is our way. He swings through my life like some great trampling guide, but mostly like a showman for a privileged audience of one. Would you have me try to top his stories or contradict his polemics? I would be the damp squib to his bundle of firecrackers. Match his prodigious intake of alcohol? I would be taken to hospital.

Remarkable, is it not, how Damon can enter a room and dominate it? Something in the genes no doubt. His personality sweeps all before, while mine prefers a private kip. You must stop thinking he has some kind of hold over me. He is my best friend and has never once played the renowned painter with me, never held anything over me but friendship.

I stopped by the studio after our pint and he showed me some pencil studies for a series of oils. Something new is emerging from his old fixation with trains (yes, trains again). A different riff on his theme of mankind's mastery over nature, vistas of countryside stitched by train tracks, the human factor lurking in symbols. Attention-grabbing stuff like all his work, but I found the studies … meagre.

"You say you were working in Paris for nearly three months, and this is all you have?" The remark brought him up short. He turned away.

A cagey Damon? That's akin to a timid daredevil. The only thing more improbable is a prudish Heidi, but such is the voice I have been hearing in your letters. What is the world coming to? My dear, your pen has grown shy. Your choice of words hardly recognise me, certainly never goad me. I should not expect otherwise now you are married, but you cannot expect me to forget your rebellion against 'the old, the common, the ordinary and dull'. How I loved hearing you chime off that refrain. Trade anxieties for liberties, you also used to say. What has become of your war against the prudes? Forgive me if I continue to subscribe to all your former dictums. You may not be wearing them on your sleeve in your new home, but surely they endure in your heart, which is the place I will go on addressing until you command me to stop.

Please write again soon. Your admiring and devoted,
Joff

Tuesday
10th March 1936

Dear Heidi,
Please join me in cursing the Rhineland. I suppose the name of that
tiny strip of geography is on everyone's lips in America too. You might
think a giant earthquake has struck. The tremors are rattling every
capital of the world. Try to imagine the walls of bricks that have
shaken loose and tumbled onto my little corner of the F.O. This is
what Germany's march into the Rhineland means to your admirer:
piles of work marked URGENT. I'm at the flat now. I abandoned ship
after lunch. Tremayne could hardly object. He was also on the verge
of collapse.

A box of press notices, speech transcripts and newspaper cuttings
arrived by special flight from Berlin on Sunday morning. Tremayne
called in the three of us, the lord's day be damned, and we worked past
midnight. Yesterday we did much the same, working long into the
evening. Tremayne was in his element, conducting us like an orchestra.
"The Foreign Office never sleeps," he gushed. In his miniature brain
and bloated ego the man fancies himself an indispensable servant of
His Majesty.

In all the rush Retinger forgot himself for a moment. Within earshot
of His Majesty's indispensable servant he voiced astonishment that the
French army has not budged from its barracks. "Hard to believe,"
he said. "A provocation of this magnitude and the French are simply
standing by. If Hitler re-militarises the Rhineland, then the League of
Nations will have to declare Germany guilty of aggression."

Tremayne's nose went up the instant he heard the word 'provocation'.
"Sounds like you're in favour of starting a war, Retinger," he said,
and followed with an observation I have since heard from others and
which Tremayne surely borrowed. "Seems to me Herr Hitler has
simply walked into his own backyard."

"Oh, I agree with you, sir," Ken replied, "war must be avoided at all
costs. The French insistence that a part of Germany, no matter how
small a part, be kept demilitarised has always been nothing more than
plain stubborn revenge." Then he added indignantly, "The French
should suck it up, sir, and forget that the Rhineland was the jumping-

off point for Germany's invasion in '14. Bygones should be bygones, sir, you are absolutely right."

Jenkins and I adore Ken's sneaky eviscerations of Tremayne, but sometimes we think his scalpel cuts dangerously close. Tremayne may be ignorant and credulous, but not entirely stupid … or at least not always.

Tremayne's position on the German gambit clings to the line the Prime Minister has taken. Simply put, it is to abstain from reacting. Pretend the provocation is something other than a provocation. Baldwin knows the vast majority of the British people are against risking a confrontation. On this aristocrats and commoners agree: *no more war*. We all live with the appalling knowledge of what a new war would bring. Aerial bombardment of our cities, and quite likely gas attacks on civilians. No matter the aggression inflicted upon some old Treaty – a piece of paper! – we must avoid sending our boys into another European quagmire.

The Foreign Secretary, Mr. Eden, has been inclined to take a tougher line with the Nazis, but he has been held back by Cabinet solidarity. We hear he is particularly chafing at the moment. Not only have our people made no demands on Germany to withdraw, all our signals to France have insisted on restraint. In other words, best let marching dogs lie.

I can appreciate the view of the Edens and the Retingers. The Germans may indeed have walked into their own back yard, but when they arrive with thirty-five thousand troops and thereby dynamite one of the pillars of Versailles … excuse me, the telephone is ringing.

My dear Heidi, I am just back from a one-sided shouting match. Can you guess with whom? My father rarely bothers Mrs. Stockton for use of her telephone, but when civilisation is on the brink of disintegration he must do what he must do. He shouted over the line, "What the bloody hell are you doing at the flat?"

"Father, I – "

"Did you see the bloody *Times*?"

"What about it?"

"The Rhineland! We have given up without firing a shot."

"Given up what, Father?"

"We are doing bloody *nothing* about the invasion."

"Father, we can hardly call what happened an invasion."

"Am I talking to my own kin? Are you as blind as the rest of them?"

"You're over-reacting. As you have for years."

"The cowardly French are as much to blame as the lily-livered Baldwin. Hitler is *bluffing*, and here we are holding our pricks in our hands."

I sighed. "Father, calm down. Hitler has no ships on the Thames."

"And how long before he bloody does? Is there no one but Churchill who *sees*?"

It went on for some time, until the pater changed course, though not volume. Even at the best of times, when civilisation is secure, my father mistrusts the telephone to carry his voice. "When am I going to see you?" he shouted. "Months have gone by."

"I saw you three weeks ago, Father."

"Months! And you must bring Vicky. Will you bring Vicky?"

I promised to bring Vicky and the line went dead. He may have slammed down the telephone. Back soon, Heidi, I must go out for a few things …

Good lord, what is it about this day? I am being haunted by old men. Remember that crazed codger who spat in my face one early morning? I just saw him at the grocer's. The regimental pin on his mac was hanging by a thread. There was something sad about his shuffle, the grim resignation in his face, the tins of sardines and jar of marmite in his fishnet little bag … I paid quickly for my things and scurried out before he noticed me.

Now if you don't mind, Morpheus is calling, one old haunter I'm glad to embrace. Until soon great lady.

Your devoted,

Joff

Saturday
21st March 1936

Dear Heidi,

Received yours of the fourteenth. What a candid question! Makes me think of the bohemian sculptress of yore. The answer is yes, Mary and I still harbour a healthy attraction, occasionally even an eruptive one. I should qualify that. We are now a long-married couple, which is to say we practice our union as residents rather than explorers. But you have made me think … The key to our eruptions is Vicky, she ignites them. Not long ago, when we celebrated her birthday, Vicky said something extraordinary and Mary and I rushed to hug her, our little girl, our wonder, our glue. Can it be a coincidence that our regard for each other later that night was … healthy? In fact, I don't mind telling you, it reached the uncommonly eruptive.

Curious, your comment about the Rhineland, that your new friends showed almost no interest. Are they typical Americans? It was taken as a giant quake over here. Happily though, the tremors have ceased rattling the sunroom. Life goes on. One thing I do sense is a change in Germany. Herr Hitler's prestige has soared. His newspapers are portraying his march into the demilitarised zone as a victory. They say he has erased the dishonour of 1918. Of course this is predictable porridge from the Nazi-controlled press, but as I told the tea leaf readers upstairs in my accompanying notes, the anthems of praise for the Leader no longer appear motivated by pure obedience. Authentic respect has entered the tone.

My colleague Ken said to me yesterday, "We've allowed the despot to win a battle without firing a shot."

"I don't see where a battle has been won. Last time I looked there were no armies locked in combat."

"We had a chance to humiliate the nasty rat. The man who never rose beyond the rank of corporal has amazed his generals. They are much less likely to stick a knife in him now. As Churchill said yesterday in the House, we have suffered a terrible defeat."

Ken would make an ideal son for my father. They could join forces and build a shelter against the enemy. I frankly do not see Armageddon coming over the ridge. Evidently neither do your new countrymen.

The newspapers speak of an 'isolationist mood' in America. Is it a passing craze, or something deeper?

You ask why I cannot get along better with Tremayne! My dear, you force me to surmise that your exposure to Yankee culture and Boston beans has fiddled with your memory. Have you forgotten what ticks at the heart of Ye Olde Countrie? I doubt if a single American of your acquaintance would understand why Tremayne regards me as he does. Why after eight years it is still "Good morning, Pearson" or "Pearson, you're running late on the so-and-so file." Not once has he stooped to my given name. The little man clings to ancestral glory, insists on recognising an aristocrat when he looks in the mirror. He is not only my departmental supervisor but my life superior. Last week he berated Jenkins over a minor mistake, lacing his meanness with dreadful humour. "I say, Jenkins, are we slowing up inside the cranium?" An earlier episode had him taunting, "Next thing you know, Jenkins, we shall be dressing you with a bib." Bad enough that Tremayne finds it witty to remind Jenkins of his age (at 71 the old dear should have long since called it a day), but ascribing his occasional lapse to senility is simply foul. The thing is, Tremayne has the ability to feel persecuted by the authority he has over us. He takes the attitude that every error we make reflects on him, taints his name, slows his earned ascent. Stuff and nonsense, of course. He has nothing but his name, propped up by some university German which he polished with a stint as a graduate student in Hamburg (an heroic overseas exploit according to his frequent reminiscence). His principal credential is a mysterious connection that oiled his way into our humble department in the first place. He continues to hold the belief that our gloomy little room can be his steppingstone to something brighter. If only he toes the correct line long enough and lords it over his worker bees diligently enough, the reward will come. He will go upstairs in some capacity and participate in the great game. The notion is cringe-worthy, Heidi.

Where was I?

You were wondering why Tremayne and I can't be chums! Here I am wasting ink on that ass when I really want to tell you about Damon. Our friend has finished five new paintings. He poured me two inches of Glenfarclas before letting me have a look … and I still felt ambushed. Something seems to have altered him. A new goal seems to be driving him. That said, his quest for drama remains obsessive. He continues to toil over every inch of canvas as if he were a watchmaker, or a diamond cutter.

Five oils, each about five feet by five.

In one a sleek train from a remote place in his imagination races across undulating farmland on a track that connects jewels of villages. Not a person to be seen except as blurred images through the windows of the otherworldly train and you have the distinct impression of human mystery at work. In another you are inside a train furnished with luxuriant seats and opulent lighting and the countryside outside is the moving blur. I had the eerie feeling that Damon and I were in the paintings ourselves. Must tell you, Heidi, this signature effect of his has grown so powerful it caused me to grip his arm in congratulation. "Well done, Dame. Well done, indeed. What do they mean to say?"

"Can't you tell? Take a look at these."

Three canvases were propped against the wall and draped in sheets. He uncovered them one at a time. He had not shown me any sketches for these; I frankly was not prepared for them. Two of the three will make little old ladies recoil. They depict city rot. One shows a row of houses, or former houses. The houses are not in ruins but in a kind of terrible, depraved decay, as if collapsing from malicious flaws in construction. Another painting features a more pronounced tableau of destruction, blocks of flats seemingly flattened by a hammer from the sky. The irony is that both pictures convey a strangely exquisite beauty. Then came the third of the lot. Which will cause even strong young men to flinch.

At first you see a panoramic scene of shattered and tangled cars, lorries, motorbikes and train carriages involved in some kind of tremendous accident. The carnage extends to the horizon. The vehicles are not on a road but in a valley thick with trees. Then you notice the punctuation of severed limbs and strewn corpses and you realize with a start that the splotches of crimson you might have taken for bursts of tightly packed roses are little pools of blood. The ghastly havoc disturbs, again, mainly because it's all made so damn … beautiful.

"Good lord, Chadwick!"

"No cause to call on a deity, but still the response I want."

I was not about to quiz him about his purpose, fearing I would sound silly or blind. I also held back for another reason. As impressed as I was, as fine as the paintings are, I did not want to tell him how they finally struck me. How can I put it … the paintings seem to be trying too hard. Maybe it was unconscious on Damon's part, but he appears to be making a deliberate effort to get back on top. As you know, prices for his work have been plummeting in the last few years. He blames the economic situation, but I know better. His name no longer carries the clout it once did. The movement into cubism, expressionism and other variants of so-called modernism has seduced the big-spending collectors. They are putting their money elsewhere. We must face it, Damon Chadwick is passé.

"Have you considered doing any abstracts?" I asked.

He looked at me sharply. "If I go that route, have me arrested for high crimes."

"Have you shown these to Maddy? I think she'll be thrilled."

"These beauties are going abroad. A dealer in Munich wants them."

I asked him if he was joking.

"Have you ever known me to joke about my art?"

"Why Germany?" I said. "Better prices?"

"Money is not the point." He said it was time he went seriously international. All of his works hanging in other countries were originally purchased in England. Exhibiting new works abroad will generate greater attention and enhance value for his foreign collectors. He already has several patrons in Munich and Berlin who have urged him to exhibit there. They believe his art can attract a huge audience in Germany. This news struck me as … unsettling. "Well," I said halfheartedly, "here's to success in *Deutschland*."

He winked, and we drained our glasses. His fourth or fifth; my first and only. Write, great lady, and tell me all your news. As ever,

Joff

Saturday
28th March 1936

Dear Heidi,

Your letter of the fifteenth … an amusing suggestion. It never occurred to us to muffle the stomping by asking the spinster to lay a carpet. Sounds like a solution an American would suggest. Build a thicker floor! Mary went up to have a word the other day and learned the spinster has gone to Edinburgh. She was met at the door by the stompers' mother, a grossly overweight woman smelling of cabbage, wet woolens and tobacco. The fat lady apologised for the noise and said she would try to control the wild cubs. The relief since has been patchy.

Damon and I met for our regular at The Squire's. I found him reading a story in the paper about a house fire in Leeds. A little boy was seen waving frantically from a second-storey window, and a passerby rushed into the burning building. The good samaritan rescued the child, his act was heroic, but he himself later died from smoke inhalation. "Boldness and doom," said Damon. "The most ironic thing about the story is that this good fellow was taking a different route home than he usually took. If he had kept to his usual route he would be alive today."

"How long have you been drinking?"

"I'm right as rain. *He chose that day to take a different route.* But at least the little boy was saved. Remember that … the child was saved."

Our friend, when blasted, has lost none of his capacity to irritate. I censored his ravings by going to the loo.

Curious, your asking about my enjoyment of life. Is that another American thing? With a spouse, a child, a croaking father, a tedious job and an awful man for a Section Head, life is all about duty and carrying on. Besides, they never taught the skill of enjoyment in any of my schools. That would be unEnglish. But you have made me think.

I adore watching Vicky grow. There you have my principal satisfaction. My marriage follows in a close second, it's like Gibraltar, and Damon's friendship is pure gold. Occasionally I take pride in my work, but no, there is no serene joy in the everyday. I do occasionally look closely at the man in the mirror and into his eyes. What is the result? The inquiry skims along the surface, abstains from the deeps.

In the end, as so many times before, I retreat into a daydream and conceive intimacy with a woman in America.

Don't forgive him, for he knows exactly what he does. As ever,
Joff

Saturday
4th April 1936

Dear Heidi,

Your admirer anticipates Saturday afternoons at his writing desk as some men await assignations in dusky parlours. A kind of self-hypnosis overtakes him here. He finds that sharing himself brings you to him.

Do they sell *Tatler* in Boston? Make all speed to your newsagent and seek out the April number. Damon seems to have forgotten the need for discretion. He invited a photographer from *Tatler* to his studio. The four pages of fawning photos are a scoop for the magazine, but goodbye to anonymity for Damon Chadwick.

"What's this about, Dame?"

"Fitting on my part, don't you think," he said, "to add a bit of culture to all those photographs of society balls, fashion events and shooting parties?"

"Are you striking back at the boffins for putting you out of fashion?"

"You misjudge me, old friend."

"You could at least have visited a barber before revealing yourself to the world. You look like a grubby savant."

"I *am* a savant," he said, twirling the hair on his collar and sporting it like a Jew's ringlet. "My goal is to address the stupidity of our time. Someone must reverse the plunge into madness and lead the people to understanding. *Lecture* the people."

"You just want to lecture the collectors on what they ought to be buying, and what prices they should be paying. Which is fine, but what if the press gets on your trail? What if they start prying into your … Paris trips?"

"There is that," he admitted, "but I will not allow a condition of birth to limit my public life."

First time I ever heard him, or anyone for that matter, describe his sort as a condition of birth. As for the idea of a public life, that sounded distinctly unDamonlike. His behaviour baffles, but why should I be surprised? People say and do strange things. They oddly zig when you think they should zag. Look at our lunch club, which met last week by the way, and of course toasted our expatriate in America. Graham's passion, his precious fleet, goes forward like an arrow on target. He is not simply responding to the need to make a living; *he wants a fleet of lorries*. Take our poor Catherine. We love the woman, but she is obviously bonkers, going from perfectly good man to perfectly good man, and finding each less than perfect. Result: misery, childlessness, probably terminal spinsterhood. As for Patty, in her case no one would have predicted domestic bliss and complete surrender to motherhood. Back in the day, when she was lead researcher for the Balfour Committee and could talk your ear off about the sorry state of British exports, a distinguished career in the civil service was hers for the taking. Some of us saw her destined for the Commons. Now she mothers two little commoners, is planning a third, and nary a word about public policy ever passes her lips. Then we have Seamus, a roiling muddle of stresses, short-lived fanatical hobbies, and an endless appetite for sweets. He holds on at the lab, but shows no sign of initiative or a wish for promotion. I expect him to announce he has been discharged (cause: inertia) every time I see him. At this very moment he's watching dogs run themselves to death in Bournemouth. Two weekends ago he went on a birdwatch at crippling expense in Norfolk. He saves the sedentary life for his career!

I do not exempt myself from the ranks of the odd. After all, who writes these letters? An obsessed man, addressing a lost, inaccessible, never-had love even while she is married to another and he as well. I might be the oddest of all as I tread water in career, life, spirit. Will the day arrive when your admirer recognises what kind of fleet *he* wants to build?

Incidentally, Damon insisted I join him Tuesday night for an opening at the Clement Gallery. "Why?" I asked.

"I shall need moral support," he said.

"Why?"

"You'll see."

We love him, but at times Dame can be maddening.

I finally met the father of the ceiling stompers. Ran into him on the stair and we had a chat. Martin Nellis is his name, voice like a foghorn which comes out of a long reedy frame so brittle-looking you might think somebody could put him over a knee and break him in two. When the fellow became animated I stepped back … an instinctive retreat from the shocking blast of his voice. Picture the business end of a tuba on the stem of a flute. He tells me he trained as a chemical engineer and worked at a plant in Manchester for years. When the plant closed he could find nothing in his field and now he's having some kind of wrangle with the Labour Exchange. His worker's insurance benefit of thirty shillings a week has been exhausted. His older sister, the spinster, is supporting the family, while Nellis is intent on finding another position in his field.

I mentioned the encounter to Mary, who takes the view Nellis is a whining wretch who should accept any kind of job he can find. "No matter how menial?" I protested.

"Of course!"

"Mary, the poor man is a chemical engineer."

"Yes, but only if he can afford to be one," said my spouse. "If the chemical engineer must sweep the streets to feed his family, then he ought to sweep the streets. Did you remind him to keep his boys from jumping up and down on our heads?"

I had to confess negligence in that regard. The noisy brats are at it again even as I scribble. Impatient for spring's flowers, and yours as ever,

Joff

Thursday
9th April 1936

Dear Heidi,
This yellow paper is what we use in the sunroom for notes and drafts. Tremayne has gone out so I can answer your tongue-lashing of the twenty-second while my wounds are still fresh. What have I done to deserve such a tirade? Sounds like you had a fit of hysteria. The accusation that I'm 'cheerfully decaying in a minor cavity of the Foreign Office' stings (though I applaud your attempt at metaphor). When I say similar things about myself I am half joking, but when you attack ... I feel on trial.

I admit, I have overstayed my time in this airless hutch, but please remember my circumstances. I have a home with wife and daughter, and a posh school for daughter. There may be some surrender involved in working where I work, but it comes with a decent pay packet.

What really bites is your comment about my apathy. True enough, I have grown largely indifferent to the vile news out of Germany, but that hardly makes me guilty of 'wearing a blindfold'. Dearest Heidi, my work makes me feel like a doctor examining a nonstop parade of terminally ill patients. Must I feel sadness and wrath every hour of every working day? I hope you are answered. Wait. One more thing. A curious last dagger you slip in, that I am "living unconsciously". Where did that come from? Have you taken up eastern philosophy?

I am done, I am done. When I write again on Saturday I promise to forget this little quarrel of ours. Love you as ever,
Joff

Saturday
11th April 1936

Dear Heidi,
The unpredictability of the Atlantic mail occurs to me. You might receive this letter before my note of a couple of days ago. Only to say, your broadside hit me hard and I dashed off a miffed reply. Let's put it down to intimate friends taking a smack at one other. I am now turning the page …

Double dose of Damon this week. I was sure his appearance in *Tatler* would prove an exception and he would return to his senses, but I was wrong. On Monday the *Standard* published a photograph of him wearing his absurd deerstalker. A seriously upset Maddy Kloff telephoned the next day and asked if Damon has undergone a personality change. "Hell and damnation," she said. "What does he think he's doing?"

I myself had been thumbing through the paper on the tube when I came across the photo. Lucky I had a seat; I might have fallen down from disbelief. His deerstalker! No article accompanied the shot, just a caption headlined THE CELEBRATED ARTIST with this quote:

> I paint to assert, to protest, to celebrate, or to dream. I paint with cause. I paint with reason. I implore the viewer, I demand of the viewer, to seek out meaning in my work. There is always, *always* meaning, and my aim is to deliver it like a thunderclap in the mind.

When I showed the thing to Mary, she replied with her usual Damon-inspired frown, composed chiefly of reluctant tolerance. At least one member of the family, however, had no qualms over this folly. Vicky was home from school with a wretched cough. Damon's picture in the paper worked on her like strong medicine. She brightened like a sunburst and insisted I go out at once to purchase a dozen copies for her friends. She also insisted on telephoning her adored godfather. In a most ladylike fashion ("Uncle Damon, this is Victoria Pearson calling") she let him know how thrilled and proud she was. My delicious and amazing plum, growing up faster than I can possibly keep up.

That was Monday. On Tuesday I did as requested and accompanied our friend to the opening at the Clement, where he made a different kind of spectacle of himself. As things turned out, so did I …

We met on the steps of the Clement. He came in a long camel hair coat and a rakish black fedora. I remarked that I'd seen a preview of the exhibition in *The Times*. "They say we'll be taken to the frontiers of modern art."

"Which is why I require your support," said Damon. "We are entering the realm of *l'avant-gardisme abusif.*"

He removed his fedora and I saw he had ignored my advice about visiting a barber. "The coat may be Savile Row," I said, "but from the shoulders up you look like a dustman on his rounds."

"Democracy on two feet!" he boomed.

No other dustmen challenged the uniformity of the crowd. The male art lovers on hand were all in double-breasted tweeds and loud ties; acquisitive types from the City determined to make a small bohemian sound while holding fast to respectability. The women were underweight to the point of willowy, and painfully self-conscious. They wore sharply tailored suits, small hats, and precariously high heels. A few had opted for evening wear and showed a daring amount of back. Not for the Clement your doddering greybeards or stuffy matrons from country castles. In their stead were these animated specimens of affectation.

"The catalogue says we are about to see a few experimental works," I said.

"Ho! I wonder if their creators would care to be 'experimented' upon by a doctor."

"Come again?"

"Should an artist be any less professional than his doctor? Ah, what mutiny against the lucid and cogent do we have here?"

The show's first work consisted of a host of triangles, all of them yellow, quite yellow, explosively yellow, and arranged in a circle to give the effect of a flaming sun. I found it striking, and said so. "That's a good yellow," Damon agreed, "but does it stop you for more than a moment? What is it telling you? Is it trying to say anything?"

"Maybe it's trying to show me the colour yellow."

"Capital! There's a high and noble purpose for you."

"Why drag in purpose? The effect of the yellow is quite … effective."

"Precisely. The thing provides a momentary sensation, nothing more. It's a poster. A bagatelle. At best decoration. So sell it in a furniture shop, not an art gallery."

I was scanning the catalogue. "You'll love this quote from the painter. Asked what he dislikes in art he replied, 'I don't like what I understand'."

"I rest my case," said our friend.

The second work was by the same artist, triangles again, this time each a different shade of green. The triangles were dangling by their vertices from a thick purple line against a pink background. Damon was grinning broadly. "Put a tail on the frame," he said, "and we can call it a hanging weasel."

As we continued through the show I had to admit that most of the works shared a depressing sameness. Only one painting stood out, as Damon was glad to confirm. It was the single figurative piece in the lot, a portrait of an elderly lady squinting with a mixture of anger and incomprehension at a book in her lap. "This is almost good," said Damon.

"Why 'almost'?"

"Well, look. Examine the woman's face. All very well to capture her likeness and render her real, but her features are inactive. We sense no thought churning behind her eyes. Her attitude is set and done, totally congealed. The thing is good up to the point achieved, but a portrait should indicate the mind in motion. That's not me talking, but Leonardo."

"Must we all paint like Leonardo to earn the approval of Chadwick?"

"Not at all. I would never say that. Even Chadwick doesn't paint like Leonardo."

"Surely you wouldn't mind painting like Leonardo?"

"Well, he's done what he's done, hasn't he? I must aim still higher."

Ah, the modesty of our friend.

We came to the final piece in the show which featured a heap of black trapezoids atop a bright green rectangular platform. I liked the effect, frankly. To tease our friend I looked for ammunition in the catalogue. "'Mason has juxtaposed his colours to simulate clash and conciliation. He creates emotional resonance that defies purely intellectual response. Look closely and you will see terror here, and infinite kindness.'"

Damon guffawed. "Look for half a second and you will see concealed horseshit here and someone imagining it's tuna salad. You might think a gallery owner with half a brain would know it by *smell*."

"Your reaction has impressed that little boy."

A few steps away a boy in spectacles and bow tie was standing at attention beside his mother and gaping at Damon. Our friend's off-colour remark had fallen on the boy's ears like blasphemy in church. His mother hadn't noticed, her nose was in the catalogue.

Damon stepped over, bowed deeply, and said to the boy, "They've stopped telling stories, haven't they?"

"Mummy!"

The little boy grabbed his mother's arm but kept his eyes on Damon in case the attacker moved closer. He seemed about Vicky's age or a bit older. I wanted to kick myself for prompting this silly diversion.

"Davy?. . . Oh, hello!"

"I do apologise for startling you, Madame," said Damon in his most courtly manner. "This young gentleman seemed to be interested in what I was saying, and I took the liberty of addressing him."

Luckily the mother was no dry stick. In fact she recognized Damon, probably from *Tatler*. "Goodness, Davy," she said, "I do believe you have made the acquaintance of the famous painter, Mr. Chadwick," and she extended her hand. She was wearing a pillbox hat at a jaunty angle. She seemed a sister of yours under the skin, dear Heidi, a daring modern woman storming the boundaries of gender. To my discomfort our friend swept into a role I have seen him play too many times before: the ingratiating great man, slavishly at the service of his admirers.

He lowered himself to the gallery's floor to be eye-to-eye with little Davy, actually sat and extended his long legs in a 'V' to capture his latest acolyte. Meanwhile other gallery patrons were shuffling about us with murmurs of annoyance. I stood there like a lamppost, the muted bystander as always. Please, please, remind me never again to go out in public with him.

"To a certain extent, my young friend, we should all be policemen in life," he was saying. "When we see something we know is wrong, we should act, we should speak out. That is what I was doing when you overheard me, I was speaking out. I do regret if any unfortunate language reached your young ears."

The boy may have been impressed, but it was hard to tell from his paralysis. He was wide-eyed and clutching his mother's wrist with both hands. Damon might have been a film character come magically to life. At least little Davy would have a good story for his friends, this collision with a wild-haired eccentric. Meanwhile a buzz of recognition had made its way round the room. I heard someone whisper *That's Damon Chadwick on the floor*. At the same moment a large, very large red-haired man in a short-sleeved shirt and perspiration coating his face materialised with a camera slung round his neck.

"Righto, Mr. Chadwick…" The fat interloper must have considered permission a formality. He raised his camera and the flash went off, blinding me for a moment.

A sudden rage came over me. Maybe it was a protective instinct gone haywire. I abruptly found myself warding off the slovenly tub. With a hand on each of his shoulders – repulsively moist, squishy, sponge-like shoulders – I was *shoving* him away.

"What the bloody – ?"

"Joff!"

Damon had shot to his feet and grabbed my arm. "Have you gone mad?" He swung me about easily (Damon is *strong*) and squinted into my face like it was something inscrutable. Then I heard him making amends while his hold on my arm grew tighter.

"Mr. Tatchell, I do apologise," he said to the quivering obesity. The increasing pressure on my arm told me to stay still and keep my mouth shut. Apparently Damon knew this Tatchell creature and was expecting to be photographed, had planned to be photographed, a bewilderment in itself.

"Please take my card, Mr. Tatchell, and telephone me first thing tomorrow. We shall arrange another encounter at your convenience."

Turning to little Davy and his mother, Damon bowed to the pillbox hat. "Madame, I congratulate you on your son's composure and ask your forgiveness for the disturbance." He said a final kind word to the boy, acknowledged with a statesmanlike nod the gaping stares of gallery patrons, then marched your numb admirer out of the Clement, his fist only intensifying its iron grip …

Never think that I keep anything from you, Heidi. I remember the event like a bad dream but proof of it remains in the bruise above my elbow. To bed now for this humiliated, blundering oaf. Goodnight, sweet lady.

Joff

Saturday
18th April 1936

Dear Heidi,
Must tell you the latest from my precocious darling. "Daddy, what do you want written on your tombstone?"

"Good lord, my plum, what has that got to do with the price of beer?"

"I was reading about Sir Christopher Wren. Did you know he designed St. Paul's Cathedral?"

"I probably learned it at your age."

"Did you know he's buried there?"

"I have stood at the very spot. We should vis– "

"Do you remember what it says on his stone?"

She had me there.

With genuine solemnity she said, "'Reader, if you seek his monument, look around.'"

Which prompted me to say that my daughter would certainly be my monument. "You will become so famous throughout the British Empire that on my tombstone will be written HERE LIES THE FATHER OF VICTORIA PEARSON." That won me a delicious hug, especially since I remembered to call her Victoria.

In the principality of Tremayne the usual tide has been lapping our shores. The end of the week washed up a confidential file from a shadowy Reich department, the *Sonderabteilung zur Forderung der jüdische Auswanderung* ... the Special Department for Facilitating Jewish Emigration. Jenkins gave a little whoop when he saw the file's documents. They came in the form of photographs, which always leads him to speculate about our agents in the field. The file contained confidential directives about implementation of the Nuremberg Laws, now six months on the books and being strictly applied, coming Olympics or no. The Germans are turning the screws ever tighter on the Jews, creating a *dis*-emancipation in the name of blood and honour.

"Germany has ceased to be a civilised country," said Ken, with Tremayne safely out of earshot. He held up a photograph of a memorandum. "This thing was written by a so-called Jewish expert in the German civil service, to bring attention to a situation in Berlin. Wealthy Jews – "

"Keep your hair on, Ken," I said, "we've been seeing these things for years."

"Excuse me, *formerly* wealthy Jews, stripped of their businesses and prevented from practising their professions are now renting their houses to foreign diplomats. They are moving into the cellars, garages and attics of their own homes. Factory owners, bankers, former *judges*. But this is not cruelty enough. Listen to the memorandum: 'These scurrying Jews have exercised the cunning of their race but have not escaped the notice of the Reich. Property regulations which overlook continued Jewish owership of land and real estate in the Fatherland will shortly be amended in accordance with Reich policy affecting public health and security.'"

"The Nazis clearly mean to drive all the Jews out," Jenkins said. "But I understand passports are available to them. Why don't they just leave?"

This angered Ken. "Yes, naturally, uproot half a million people with a snap of the fingers. A fully *assimilated* people, as proudly German as any other community of Germans. Let them be Frenchmen! Let them learn Swedish!"

"That would be possible," I chipped in, "only if France lets them be French, and if Sweden invites them to learn Swedish, which largely isn't happening. The Jews are lining up at embassies in Berlin, begging for visas, and mostly getting doors shut in their faces."

Ken's eyes were still flashing. "That allows Hitler to crow, 'Look, nobody else wants our Jews either, so let the world shut up about how we treat them.'"

At that moment Tremayne returned with his trademark what's-all-this-about look on his face and the discussion promptly ended. Ken volunteered brightly, "We were just trading guesses, sir, on the date of King Edward's coronation. Nothing has been announced as of yet. When do you think it will take place, sir?"

Tremayne replied impatiently, "Not until next year, Retinger. These events require long-term planning. Are you so eager to see the King crowned?"

"Oh, that *will* be an event, sir."

Jenkins and I hid our smiles. Our colleague Retinger is that rare bird in England, a republican. He would prefer to see the crown abolished rather than parked on another hereditary head. In regard to our new King, he might have a case. Lunchroom whispers about Edward suggest an intellectual lightweight. Apparently he never picked up a book at Oxford. Some say his conversation does not extend beyond the juvenile. Others whisper that in the early days of Mosley, before everyone saw the barbarian Oswald for what he is, the Prince of Wales sent him a cheque. The worst gossip is that Eddie's a bigot who makes repulsive comments about negroes, but ... who knows? If I run into the fellow at a garden party and he tells me in heartfelt fashion the natives of Tanganyika are no smarter than monkeys, I shall go over to Ken's side. Until then the new King gets the benefit of my doubt.

The benefit of your news, please. Have you any hint of spring over there? The grey drizzle as you can imagine has been endless here.

Be well and happy.

Joff

Saturday
25th April 1936

Dear Heidi,

Your letter of the eleventh gratifies. You may call me any names you wish, accuse me of any crimes, so long as nothing between us changes. Thanks for feeling the same. I ask your forgiveness for the comment about hysteria. I remember hesitating and giving some thought to tearing up that letter. My apologies!

Delighted to hear your work has taken flight. The scale you are pursuing sounds grand. I must assume America has caused you to think BIGGER. Any idea when your first show might be ready?

Yet more folly from Damon. It simply does not stop and in fact has gotten worse. With this latest piece of madness I genuinely fear he may have blown the gaff. We are having our weekly at The Squire's and he inquires casually if I have seen the item in the news.

"What item?"

He pulls a cutting from his billfold and I think, here's some amusement. Then I see by 'news' he means *News of the World* and something distinctly unamusing happens in my stomach.

A few weeks ago at the behest of one of his collectors he donated a series of pencil sketches to an organisation called The Rural Community Buildings Loan Fund, which backs the construction of village halls and the like. The sketches went up for auction at a fundraising event; sketches of nudes, groups of nudes, all of them men in idealized forms resembling classical statues, broken classical statues, some with arms missing, others with stumps for legs, all lying about as if some exhausting effort just felled them. Startling enough, amputee nudes, but then something becomes obvious in the sum of what you see, in the arrangement of forms, the relation of the men to each other … The sketches stirred whispers and the bidding went high. Charity mission accomplished and all that, but the item in the *News* described the sketches as 'Grecian' and our friend as a 'confirmed bachelor'.

"Dame, this is fucking dangerous."

He waved me off.

A few days earlier I had run across a court brief in *The Times* about a married solicitor prosecuted under the sodomy law. A Bow Street magistrate sentenced the man to two months of hard labour. *The Times* published the convict's name, no doubt destroying both his marriage and career. Mentioning it to Damon would only enrage him. I said instead, "You have never looked for noise in the press to make your name. Now you seem to be running a campaign for election."

"We must all play our proper role in the great events of our time," he replied with a remote gleam in his eye. "How else am I to play mine?"

He delivered this rubbish in a level voice and showed offence when I threw up my hands. At least he didn't repeat his tripe about the gullible masses requiring education lest they be misled.

Must tell you, Ken Retinger continues to have fun with Tremayne's thick skull. An opportunity arrived last week when a sheaf of articles from *Der Sturmer* came in. They were all about Jewish corruption in far corners of the globe. Are you aware that monopolist Jews bear direct responsibility for malaria deaths in the Sudan? You should know too that cancer is a Jewish disease, its parasitic origins recently found to be Hebraic in nature. The competition is obviously heating up between *Der Sturmer* and the *Völkischer Beobachter* for the rabid anti-Semite readership. Tremayne distributed the poisonous comedy among the three of us.

After sifting through his lot Ken asked, his voice respectful, "Sir, why do you think Hitler hates the Jewish people so much?"

There are moments when the conceit which richly flows through our Section Head rises to his face and lends him a look of imperial hauteur. I first met the look not long after I joined the F.O., when I suggested we and our wives might enjoy a Saturday night dinner together. The transformation in his face combined umbrage, wonder, pity and amusement. It telegraphed that I had no idea what schools he had attended or who his great-grandfather was. His comeback was quick, probably well practised. "An idea, Pearson, an idea," he slithered, sounding almost sincere. "Leave it with me, would you?"

Here's another idea, Heidi. You should do a bust of the awful man. Can the genius of your clay expose a fool and failure beneath film star looks? Think of the challenge. With what magic would you carve his face to reveal a soul that sneers?

"Quite clearly," Tremayne said, reacting to Ken's question about the Jews with a flick of a wrist and his lip curled, "Hitler requires a whipping boy, and the Jew has been chosen." He smiled, showing his perfect teeth, delighted with his felicitous play on words.

"I believe, sir, it may be a little more complicated than that," said Ken, his tone remaining deferential.

"I don't know why you should think so. It's obviously a temporary measure, a – "

"After more than three years, sir, temporary?"

" – a letting go of steam," said Tremayne, impatience expressed in a sigh as he leaned forward to remedy and instruct. "Hitler is not a religious man. The fact that some Jews dress like medieval relics happens to be a convenience for him. To siphon off German anger and frustration, who better to target than those who are alien, and whose power and influence happen to far outweigh their numbers?"

"That is a widely held point of view, sir. It holds that the Jews have grown too big for their britches and the Nazis will stop their persecution once the regime achieves its nationalist goals."

"Precisely," said Tremayne, and sat back well pleased with himself. Ken's game, however, had only reached the interval.

"If I may express another view, sir, it is that the persecution will never stop. In Hitler's mind the Jews are carriers of the most potent weapon feared by men like him."

"My dear Retinger, the Jew may have wrapped his paws around economic and intellectual levers, but he is a meek timid pacifist, most conspicuously lacking weapons."

"Of course, sir, but if there is anything Hitler hates more than Jews, it would be what he calls the flabby futility of democracy. He has said clearly that democracy undermines a nation, cripples its capacity."

"That is as may be, but what are you trying to tell me?"

"Well, sir, the story of the exodus from Egypt, slaves revolting against tyranny, there lies the central myth of the Jews. The story is also a pillar of the Bible. For Herr Hitler, destroying democracy is not enough. He must destroy the people who invented its foundation."

Glimmering to the realisation he had been lured into water over his head, Tremayne said, "Are you a Jew, Retinger?"

Our colleague Jenkins had been leafing through his share of cuttings, listening with one ear, but at this he raised his eyes. A moment of hush settled on the sunroom, the sort of moment you experience now and then in the human zoo which always leaves you less impressed with your species. The bully, challenged and thrown for a tumble, kicks out a hind leg to mock the slate clean. *Are you a Jew?*

Vain spiteful imbecile, Tremayne. I was embarrassed for him. I was embarrassed for all of us.

Ken did not miss a beat. He answered the question as if it had been meant kindly. "Oh, sir, I can only claim a Jewish great-grandfather on my father's side." Then in his real voice, hard, unforgiving, "No, I am not a Jew, not even under Nuremberg."

At lunch later I asked him if he ever trained as a surgeon, his skill in amputation seemed flawless. "You removed his intellect so efficiently," I cheered, "he wasn't even aware of it."

He took a bow and said there was no better way to treat bigots and other adult children. I like Ken, we have hit it off famously, I wish you could meet him. I wish you could meet me, in stealth, out of time. How about in mid-Atlantic, in the Azores? Pardon my lunacy but there are so many things I want to tell you, thoughts that occur to me, secrets locked in my mind. Why is it that I wish to share myself with a woman lost to me and now forever beyond reach? A woman possessed by a tall, doting American who is considerably wealthier than myself? I ask, dearest Heidi, only because I wonder if you know the answers as well as I do. Forgive me. As always,

Joff

Sunday
3rd May 1936

Heidi,

The insanity continues, takes new forms, *proliferates*. The latest madness happened yesterday. Vicky was home for the weekend. "Daddy, Uncle Damon telephoned."

"Yes, my plum, what did he want?"

"We must listen to the wireless tonight."

"I beg your pardon?"

"Uncle Damon is going to be speaking with Mr. Clifford Ward. He says we should all listen in."

He once needed to be, *enjoyed* being, the faceless famous Name. Now he is becoming not only a household Face but a national Voice. Vicky stayed up long after her bedtime to hear him. You know how she worships her godfather. Ward started with a fair enough introduction, but Damon vexed him from the get-go.

"We have the pleasure today to welcome Mr. Damon Chadwick, who became the bad boy of British art some twenty years ago, when he was not yet old enough to vote. He has since kindled wide debate with exhibition after exhibition. Mr. Chadwick, even while the content of your work has charted new ground, your allegiance to representational form has been stubborn in the extreme. Many reviews have branded you a diehard conservative. One critic has called you a reactionary rebel. You are quite the paradox in British art, and all these years you have stubbornly kept away from our microphones. We are privileged to have you in the broadcast booth. Welcome!"

Damon was supposed to reply at this point or at least utter a polite hello, yet he said not a word. The gap made for an awkward moment.

"Mr. Chadwick, your many admirers throughout Britain are eager to hear your views on the latest trends in art and your own current work."

It happened again! The silence was audible, like a remembered moan. People must have been cringing all over Britain, half a million listeners wondering if the famous painter was deaf and dumb.

"Well, perhaps we should begin by asking you, Mr. Chadwick, if we can expect any new works from you in the near future?"

"Ah, a question at last," said Damon. "No, not in the near future, Mr. Ward. Perhaps in several months. You may know that I recently exhibited some new works abroad. Call it my diehard conservatism if you will, but I believe in putting thought and rigour into my work. This is one reactionary rebel who will never peddle the slapdash."

"That sounds like a thinly disguised attack on some of your colleagues in the modernist movement."

"Then I apologise, because I don't mean to disguise any of my views."

"Can we take it then that your comment was indeed an attack on some of your colleagues?"

"Only those who have abandoned the responsibility to paint intelligibly. Some of them specialise in baffling us with their detonated objects and soulless geometries. Should we not protest the absence of meaning in their random gloops and glops?"

"I would never presume to speak for your fellow artists, Mr. Chadwick, but many of them are exploring expression beyond mere representation, and beyond the natural world. They are investigating what can be done on canvas with colour and emotion alone."

"Well said, Mr. Ward, audaciously played! I am put in my place. The ability to interpret the unexplainable, or rather the sorcery involved in finding meaning where none exists, and to give it such vivid metaphor, is a skill not granted to many."

"My dear Mr. Chadwick – "

"When fidelity to the material world and its splendid complexity, its infinite labyrinthine depths, becomes 'mere representation', we know that we are in the hands of an able conjurer. You may shortly be hired as chief apologist for the new and impenetrable. Or have you already been taken on?"

The half million listeners experienced another moment of dead air. Many of them probably wondered if the redoubtable Ward, stung by his mocking guest, would bite back, as he is well equipped to do. Instead he gave a mirthless titter and turned the other cheek.

"Mr. Chadwick, I should not like to think of myself as your adversary. Your views are as abrasive as your paintings. Is it not a fact that the War had a profound effect on art? Painters saw the world drained of reason and smashed to pieces. They naturally sought out new forms to reflect what they'd seen."

"If the world is smashed to pieces, Mr. Ward, your job as an artist is not to reflect it, but rather to help put it back together. The response of your *soi-disant* modernists was precisely the opposite – they went on smashing. They chose to emulate the shattered mess when they should have pulled on their boots and walked over the rubble to a better place."

"Mr. Chadwick, how far does your tar brush extend? Do you paint the impressionists black as well?"

"On the contrary, I applaud the impressionists. They invented a new optic on reality and never abandoned the actual world. Their successors took that dreadful step. Their successors made *un*reality the new religion."

"Mr Chadwick, would you – "

"Meanwhile the credulous collectors have clapped and bought, feeding on counsel from art critics who have made themselves eloquent in a new vocabulary of profound twaddle. The collectors have clapped and bought to such an extent that it is no longer possible to call the hoax a hoax, not just because so many people are invested in it but because our *museums*, our temples of culture, have also succumbed to the cheapjacks and fraud."

"Surely the term 'fraud' goes too – "

"But what do I know? I have spent only a thousand hours learning to draw a simple line, and five thousand solving shadow, and after twenty thousand hours at the easel I am still not satisfied with my sunlight. So nothing I say should carry any weight whatsoever. Your guest is a mere technician, Mr. Ward, an unfeeling *illustrator.*"

Mr. Ward managed a full sentence at that point and steered the discussion to calmer waters. He asked Damon about his methods of work and how he chooses his subject matter. Our friend subsequently behaved himself and gave a relatively polite account of his approach, going on at some length (and not altogether understandably for this listener) about physical modelling, brush technique, and modulation of colours. Vicky adored the performance from beginning to end and pretended to understand every word. My precocious peach! She promised to draw a card of congratulations for Damon in her next art class.

I may be wrong Heidi, but it seems to me our friend is guilty of hypocrisy. He remains furious because his work has fallen out of fashion. Don't get me wrong, he makes good sense to me, and he is certainly proving adept at being a publicity hound. Still, if he treats others as disrespectfully as he did the mighty Clifford Ward, who will think of inviting him on air again?

Enjoyed your letter of the twenty-second, thank you very much. No, I never apologised to Damon for the little event at the Clement. Was I not acting on a gallant protective reflex? Your plan for my new career as a vigilante sounds about right; someone must perform this public service. Henceforth I will hunt down camera-toting anarchists and shove them from the public square at every opportunity.

Damon was good enough to let the matter be until his third pint. "By the way," he said, "I made it up with Aubrey."

"Aubrey?"

"Tatchell. The gentleman you assaulted at the Clement."

"That was no gentleman, and my defence of you was no assault. I still cannot believe you *invited* that fat heffalump of a waster."

He laughed. "Aubrey happens to be overweight, but he does not deserve contempt."

"As a matter of fact he does. The man is a quivering pile of blubber. He sweats and waddles about like a menace on two feet. He should be incarcerated and fed a diet of dried apricots. He – "

"All quite amusing, Joff, but please belt up. Aubrey is an accomplished photographer."

"Where did you meet the dashing 'Aubrey' with whom you seem on such amiable terms?"

"He did the *Tatler* shoot as a freelancer. I thought I would reward him for a job well done. These people make very little money."

"In other words, invite more exposure? Put your photo in various other magazines?"

He was now on his fourth pint and he lit up what must have been the evening's tenth cigarette. He did me the courtesy of pretending to take my questions seriously, but then made one of his fatuous observations which gave me no reply at all. "I have achieved everything in art I want to achieve, but have I done any *good*?"

In a bad temper I downed the dregs of my one and only pint, got to my feet and bid him goodnight. He grabbed my sleeve! He was by no means smashed, not nearly; it takes six pints to take him over.

Holding tenaciously to my sleeve he said, "Most people stumble through their lives without any idea what is happening in the world. They give no response to the times. They act like luggage on the cart. Only individuals with great souls and great daring influence the times."

"Indeed," I mollified the babbling genius. "You are a madman with a great soul, and the world will salute your daring. Was it Shelley who said something about artists legislating the times?"

"Good for you, Joff! Good for you. It was Percy Bysshe Shelley. And thank you for those words of tribute."

"May I go now?"

"You may, you may. My love to she who stands guard."

"Mary will … value the tribute."

"And a big kiss for my goddaughter!"

"There you have an unquestioning devotee."

At least it was only the sleeve of my jacket, which looked none the worse for his clutching. The bruise on my arm from his herculean grip at the Clement is still showing.

I send you a herculean hug. As ever,

Joff

Saturday
9th May 1936

Dear Heidi,
I have no idea why but during the last couple of weeks a dread has latched onto me. When I cross the street I imagine automobiles hurtling from the unseen. On stairways I fear tripping and tumbling. I can be sitting peacefully at home, alone, and for no reason envision – abruptly – a cricket bat smashing upwards into my chin. Exactly that, a cricket bat swung with full force into my chin.

A few minutes ago I was actually relieved to reach the flat and close the door behind me, shut out the world, take refuge from … what? Nothing in particular has been pre-occupying me, so why this apprehension? I should be relaxed in the middle of my life, don't you think? My wondrous Vicky is doing her best to conquer her school and consume half its library, or at least everything in it about the glories of British conquest. Mary loves me no less than the day we married, an extraordinary truth that puzzles as much as it sustains. Furthermore, and this is not a small thing, I can tell one of the most famous painters in England that he is a roaring madman. These are riches, I should be *basking* in them and taking serene joy in the everyday. Yet I am unable. My mind reverts to the disappointment of yesterday or the deadline of tomorrow or the irritation of the moment. Kindly enlighten me, my dear. Act the psychologist. Tell me where I have gone wrong.

As ever yours,
Joff

Saturday
16th May 1936

My dear Heidi,

I take back my last letter, there is no need for worry. The black mood ate me alive for a few days, then left as mysteriously as it came. Now it seems almost an abstraction, like last year's toothache.

I dropped by Damon's studio for a drink and a look at his new oils. Jesus Harry Christ, something has super-charged our friend. He must be painting with the word INVINCIBLE stamped on his brain, with a destination in mind called PINNACLE. If the latest works have a common theme it would have to be … conquest. They have nothing to do with war or fighting of any sort but you get the sense of wars already won, of vast enemies defeated. The paintings focus on heroically posed figures, all larger than life, bestriding vistas of cities or mountains – or whole geographies. He seems to be playing with ideas of vast revival and colonisation. Somehow he keeps the effect entirely realistic, so the impact becomes … intimidating.

"Chadwick has become Caesar," I said. "Or is it Alexander the Great?"

The remark was casual, but he answered in a cold voice, "What would you have me do in these times? Go to Cornwall and paint seascapes?"

I laughed it off, and the odd moment passed. I will not pretend to know what on earth he was on about. Did I mention that his figures wear the implacable gazes of classical statues? He has always worshipped classical statues, our Damon. Except these creations of his come with extra confrontation in their attitude. You see pent-up anger in their eyes, epic resolve in their gestures. I find them a little scary, frankly, but they will certainly find buyers. "I predict a return of the collectors," I said. "Maddy will have these sold ten minutes after she hangs them."

"Maddy has been a dear, but these beauties are going with me to Berlin."

Will his surprises never cease? Apparently the five oils he shipped to Munich last month were snapped up at absurdly high prices. Now he has been invited to meet collectors at the Weinhauf Gallery, one of the most prestigious art dealers in Berlin.

"Selling your paintings to rich Germans is fine and dandy, but do you actually want to *go* there? Hitler has his people decked out in brownshirts and jackboots these days."

"I am going to the land of Goethe, Schiller, Beethoven and Bach."

"You don't have to tell me about the greatness of Germany. My mother did a thorough enough job of that. She was talking about another time, however. The Germany of today has become something rather different."

He told me about the currency restrictions. Foreigners are forbidden to take deutsch marks out of the country. His sales in Munich earned him the equivalent of several thousand quid, but he must spend the money in Germany.

"Now I get it," I said. "The filthy lucre is the point. You will be staying at a luxury *Gästehaus* and dining on gourmet *Kassler mit Sauerkraut.*"

"*Nein! Ich würde viel lieber etwas Schweinebraten. Vielleicht mit ein Haufen von Kartoffelpuffer, und eine Schüssel Spargelsuppe zuvor.*"

You could have knocked me over with a batted eyelash! We had been drinking liberally from Damon's excellent Dalwhinnie, but this could not account for what I had just heard. In quite serviceable German our friend said he preferred pork roast, perhaps with a pile of potato pancakes, preceded by some asparagus soup. "You've been learning my mother's tongue!"

"Oh, I poked into a guidebook or two."

"You astound me, Chadwick, you astound me."

Damon has always been a quick study, but no number of guidebooks can endow a tolerable accent and respectable fluency. He does astound.

As I was draining the last of my scotch he asked: "Joff, I leave London late next week. Care to join me for a pipe before then?"

"My answer to that question, my dear friend," I said, while rising to leave, "must remain what it has always been. Thank you, but no thank you."

At the door, with his hand on my arm, he said, "I was thinking of the safety of the shore, and how you never let yourself push off. You ought to take yourself out, beyond your usual boundaries."

I thought of revealing to him the sinful yearnings I regularly post to Boston. Fortunately I controlled myself. My enduring adoration of a lady who is not my wife must remain a secret, even from Damon.

Instead I answered him with a salute and said flippantly, "Yes, sir," which elicited heavy disappointment – his eyes fell. At times I can be thickheaded, obtuse, and ever so swiftly stupid. I wondered later about that awkward moment. I think he was going somewhere too private, and I did not want to follow … Adieu for now, my American secret.

Your adoring,
Joff

Saturday
23rd May 1936

Dear Heidi,
The spring Bank Holiday approaches, thank the lord. Vicky will be home for the long weekend. Her latest obsession is the Olympics which are still two months away. She talked of nothing else during our Wednesday night chat. She has it in her head Britain ought to win the most medals.

"Why do you think that?"

"It is only proper," she said. "England has built the greatest empire in the world. We have the best people. We also have the best doctors and best health."

My precious plum absorbs notions of British primacy from her mother, but I never heard Mary saying anything quite so boastful. By the bye, I was reading about a possible boycott of Berlin by the Americans to protest Hitler's treatment of the Jews. Is there anything to it?

Ran into the stompers' father, the unemployed engineer Nellis. He seems to be growing thinner by the month. I asked him if he was quite well and he lied, said he couldn't be better. The man looks like someone on the tramp. All the boiled cabbage upstairs must go into his wife. That would be Martha, whom I finally met the other day at the grocer's. She is a full six inches shorter than Mary and maybe twice as broad, a remarkably *wide* woman who swayed over like a low-gliding blimp. "You must be Jeffrey," she wheezed, "I seen ya out the winda with your Mary."

"It's *Joffrey*, actually."

We exchanged a few words as one of her little stompers tried to break away on a leash. Apparently Martha's on tick for all the tinned meats I saw her heap on the counter. Not to shatter Vicky's illusions, but the Nellis couple certainly make a rum portrait of the greatest empire in the world.

Eagerly awaiting your news. Missing you as always,
Joff

Saturday
30th May 1936

Heidi,
Received yours of the eighteenth, many thanks. A 'phonographic' memory? Never heard of it. Surely you would have known back in our salad days if I possessed such a mental ability. Interesting that you suggest it though. Mary rewards me with her precious giggle when I recall, almost word for word, conversations from our courtship. Vicky used to fall over laughing when I regaled her at bedtime with my father's lectures on correct comportment for the children of a British diplomat. (Shrieks of delight when I aped her grandpapa's snooty manner!) Nowadays I am subjected to the gentle letdown of "Daddy, I am too *old* for stories at night," and she takes two or three books to bed, tales of swashbuckling adventure from British history, and lately anything she can get her hands on about the Spanish Armada. I can only try to fascinate her at the dinner table, which is far too seldom now she's away at school.

My work went underwater this week. A report about U-Boat construction arrived with the Jenkins-thrilling stamp of MOST SECRET on it. Apparently the Germans are turning out two U-Boats per month and have the means to double that output. My translation involves parts specifications and the Reich's intricate supply lines. My work will probably be read by half a dozen analysts in the naval bureaucracy, then filed in an underground storage bin in Portsmouth. We must have a spy in the *Kriegsmarine*. Otherwise how do we put our hands on these documents?

It occurs to me that these letters of mine tell you things I should probably not be telling anyone. Kindly reassure me that you are putting them to their deserved incineration.

Mary and Vicky arrive any minute. We have our precious darling until Monday, thank goodness for Bank Holidays. We join Graham and his family today for a boat ride on the Thames, and tomorrow Vicky wants to hear the imbeciles at Speakers' Corner. I send you good cheer and some ripening English summer.

Joff

Saturday
7th June 1936

Heidi,
I have been proven wrong once again. I thought our friend's rudeness to Clifford Ward would exile him from the airwaves, but I should have known better. Every scribe and presenter in England is after him for an interview. He said to me the other day on the telephone, "I'm giving up answering the bloody telephone." I happened to call him back an hour later and he answered the bloody telephone. He knows damn well the media jackals adore a short temper and eloquent effrontery. The collectors may have abandoned Damon, but he remains something of a National Institution. Can you imagine him on *Personalities in the Spotlight* with Christopher Burns, who has always been keen on ferreting out scandal?

"Why in heaven's name are you going on with Burns?"

"He invited me," he said. "You forget I have an obligation to my public."

"The comment of a third-rate comedian."

"You know my *armoire*, it holds hats of many different colours."

I'm not sure what kind of hat he was wearing when he sat for the interview. Maybe a *Pickelhauben* because he was leaving for Germany a couple of days later. Can you picture our friend as a Prussian general in a spiked helmet?

Burns began with a question about the purpose of Damon's work. Our friend replied, harmlessly enough, "People like seeing things they know, but rendered in ways they have never conceived. That is exactly what I give them, because what interests me most is to create realities that never existed."

A fine phrase that, 'realities that never existed'. I started hoping he would stick to his craft and avoid dangerous detours. Soon after, however, answering a question that had nothing to do with matters of the spirit, our friend declared that many of his works represent the futility of belief in God. Burns, his nose always alert for controversy, sensed a pongy fish on the line. "Are you an atheist, Mr. Chadwick?"

To which Damon replied that the plainly observable absence of God can be taken as evidence of His non-existence. It only got worse from

71

there as Burns began to reel in his catch. "What of the church and religion, Mr. Chadwick? Have we missed in your paintings an attack upon faith and the foundations of our morality?"

Damon could have slipped the bait with some innocuous diversion, but it was as if he preferred heading straight into the cooking pot. "You mention church and religion, Mr. Burns. I have nothing against either, but we should recognise them for what they are, namely places where the meek wallow in false hope, and where the timid relieve their anxieties with dreams of an after-life."

Burns began to interject, but Damon rolled on. "And faith? Faith is the mistake human evolution made when it turned off Primitive Lane and found itself on Messiah Boulevard … a path that has led us into the arms of charlatans selling make-believe and soothing fantasy."

Madness. Our former attention-shunning Damon revealed his ungodly thoughts to about two million God-fearing listeners. He has been a big-headed iconoclast since he first dipped his brush into paint, but always and only with the brush. His hates were always consigned to snobbery, corruption, and the special brand of elitist stupidity that has the Union Jack stamped all over it. I never heard him say a word about religion. As for attacking the Almighty? I have no idea where that came from.

I rang him up a few hours before he boarded his train to Dover and asked what the anti-religion stuff was all about. He said it came of meeting Bertrand Russell.

"You met Bertrand Russell? When?"

"Last Wednesday. He invited me to tea."

"And you talked about God?"

"Not quite. If you must know, when I was on the air with Burns I trotted out my usually dormant atheism as a kind of *chapeau* to Bertrand. I knew he would be listening."

"What did you talk about with dear old 'Bertrand'?"

"Pigments. Wood as a surface to paint on, vellum as another. *Brushes.* The great man is interested in fundamentals. Also dead painters, and a few that should be dead. I thundered about the rubbish of Nash, Piper, Nicholson and that lot. He wanted to know what I think of the Futurists and I told him they strike me as Cavemanists."

"I'm delighted that Bertrand Russell invited you to tea, and I want to hear more about it, but have you gone mad? When you go on the radio, you're talking to the very fickle public that buys your paintings."

"Fuck the fickle public." He let out a terrific laugh. "The fickle public be fucked."

"Christ, what have you been drinking? How did Bertrand Russell come to invite you to tea?"

"He admires my pictures. He sees reason and order, even hope, in them." Then, with a sly humour in his voice, "And he saw my photograph in *Tatler*."

"Surely he's not – ?"

"Silly boy, I'm teasing you. Not long ago he married for the third time, a sweet young pup who used to be governess of his children. The man is a randy bugger."

"*Bon voyage*, Dame. Stay clear of those brownshirts."

"*Danke*. Expect a postcard of the Tiergarten. My suite, I am told, overlooks it on the Unter den Linden."

The next day in *The Times* two letters appeared about his ravings on the Chris Burns show. One was from a deacon in Littlehampton who expressed outrage at the BBC for putting blasphemy in a public window. The other was from a declared admirer of Damon's wondering if the painter was trying to commit career suicide.

At this moment my dear I have nothing more to say to you. Except that my mail is desolate without you, and I miss your voice. Please catch up!

Yours as ever,

Joff

Saturday
13th June 1936

Dear American,
Received yours of the second. The land of the free has clearly stolen our Heidi's heart. I was wondering if she misses England, but her story of lunching on the lawn with her tradesmen persuades me she has turned Yank. Did I ever tell you my mother's fondest wish? She hoped my father would earn a post in America, any post. The pater could have been assistant tea-fetcher in the Milwaukee consulate for all she cared. She had the notion that America is different, open, inviting. I became aware at a young age of her loathing for the ubiquitous calibration of British life. She once saw a mill-hand in overalls take a seat beside a lady on a train. The mill-hand offered the lady a perfectly courteous word of good morning, which caused the lady to stiffen as if an arctic gale had swept in. She thawed only when the train had the good sense to reach the mill-hand's stop. My mother told the story to me and Irene more than once. Class arrogance and class shame, both ends of the national banger, gave her indigestion. She called it the British disease.

Did her Bavarian town regard the high born and low with equal deference? I doubt it. Germany before the War with its goose-stepping Prussians and revered Kaiser probably suffered a divine-right pecking order much like our own. So who knows where her views came from. Maybe from the mushy Karl May novels she loved. All I know is I owe my egalitarian impulses to my mother. I am so glad you met her that one time you visited Shimpling.

Must tell you how much I enjoyed your description of the dinner party with Matt's colleagues and their frumpish wives ... you were obviously the rose among bloated nettles. But then you always did stand out no matter the level of competition. Pardon me dear, but I had a difficult morning in the sunroom and I crave the horizontal. All my best,
    Joff

Saturday
20th June 1936

Dear Heidi,
Well done, great lady! Received yours of the ninth with the cutting
from the *Boston Globe*. The lunch club had its quarterly feast and we
were all cock-a-hoop with your triumph. The cutting went round the
table to suitable exclamations and a great roar of delight from Seamus.
His weight has become dangerous by the way. He huffs and puffs
when he walks, and his buttocks spill over his chair like sad balloons.
Patty announced she's pregnant again, Graham's company has added
another lorry, and our Catherine professes to a new love interest, an
estate agent from Lincolnshire, or is it Leicestershire?

Graham said the critics have always adored you, and now New
Englanders can boast the same refined taste. He quoted from the
cutting in his Shakespearean baritone: "'Elizabeth Lowell, an émigré
from England to our shores, gives diverting life to stone with the
dramatic lines in her busts, and most strikingly the expressions in her
subjects' eyes. Those eyes! Do not sit for Mrs. Lowell if you shelter
dark secrets; she probes deeply and exposes all. Join me in welcoming
this gifted sculptress to Boston. Her art reflects the variety and depth
of personality, and does so with unique brio.'"

"Bravo, Heidi," said Patty, tapping her tummy and smiling serenely.

"'Unique brio'?" Catherine teased. "Has Mr. Lowell purchased
the newspaper?" (Our Catherine cherishes the notion that your tall
handsome Matt is wealthy as Croesus.)

"No need," boomed Seamus. "Liz charmed the critic out of his
boots."

I sternly reminded the group that our divine friend's works fly on
their own wings, as their arresting execution provides catnip for the
discerning. Well, I may have said words to that *effect*, and probably
not sternly, but I do recall earning another bravo from the voluminous
Patricia.

You are not the only triumphant artist among my friends. A postcard
from Damon speaks of his being feted and flattered. All the paintings
in his Berlin exhibition sold within hours. We should not expect him
back quite yet because he has pots of deutschmarks to spend and he

finds the city fascinating.

Must tell you the latest fascination to issue from my little darling, home for the hols. We were out strolling yesterday evening and saw a fellow running backwards. Vicky asked if he was a silly person.

"I would think so," I replied.

"Is he going to the Olympics?"

"I wouldn't think that, my love."

My eight year-old let out a hoot, then declared, "Maybe he's leading the government!"

I had to grab her for a hug. And I send another to America.

Joff

Saturday
27th June 1936

Dear Heidi,
You find me sitting at my desk in a sentimental sulk, lamenting that I never met my paternal grandfather. I'm sure I would have loved him. Burnett was his name. He died a few years before I was born, apparently a terrible death from lung disease. The last thing Burnett Pearson ever built was the desk I am sitting at.

I adore it.

A twin pedestal, they call it. Dignified, regal, possibly even valuable. You will not find a single nail in it, the joinings are something miraculous. The lion-head brass handles on the drawers, they say, make it unique. This desk is the one grand thing passed down to me. I have a man who polishes it every year with a waxing trick from Victorian days. Did I tell you I adore it?

Heaven knows what Vicky will write on this desk when she's an admiral in the Royal Navy, the latest occupation she has decided to conquer. When she first walked, she used to trundle over and ignore me as she petted the lion-heads. This is where I install myself when I compose my reports to you, my long rambles and poems. (Poems? she asks. What poems?) My grandfather spent forty years at Morgan and Sons in Nottingham, and they let him build himself a retirement gift. He scoured the firm's concession in Sherwood Forest to find the perfect walnut. When he left they gave him a silver watch as well, which my egregious sister took and eventually lost, or so she claims. I think she sold it for a wretched pittance.

Another note from Damon, a postcard from Munich, written in tolerably good German. He says he will be home in a few days and needs a favour. I have no idea what the favour involves, but I look forward to his impressions of Hitlerland.

Some fiery summer heat has finally arrived. I send you its warmth. As for those poems, give me time dear lady, give me time.

Joff

Saturday
4th July 1936

Dear Heidi,
Damon has returned. At least I think it was Damon.

Except for the short-clipped back and sides which he blamed on a Berlin barber, the man who met me at our usual table in The Squire's did appear to be the Damon I have known all my life. Same easy, dominating manner. Same pronounced cheekbones and intent grey eyes. His relaxed posture could never be imitated; long legs in khaki stretched out and crossed at the ankles as if locked, a traffic hazard for itinerant drinkers. We had not been sitting long when a gawky student who claimed a place at the LSE asked our friend for an autograph. (This business of Damon being recognised in public can be a royal pain in the rear domain, pardon my iambic pentameter.) The LSE chap braved his approach with shy reverent eyes and a pen at the ready. Damon obliged with his usual aristocratic air. The signature he grandly gave the little pest was the same violent slash he has used forever and which nobody could mimic. So yes, *yuh can be sure*, as they say in American films, it was our Damon down to his fingernails.

Except it was not.

The stuff that issued from his mouth confounded me. It sounded like … infatuation. He was utterly thrilled by what he saw in Germany! "The energy, Joff. The speed at which things are getting done. The order, the coherence, the planning. New construction everywhere. Flawless transportation systems. Streets clean as laboratories. People crowding the stores, the cafés, the parks. A society blooming. I was staggered. I was swept away."

As you know, on the one hand I am dismayed by the Nazi project and its brutal racism, and on the other appalled by my father's demented loathing of the Germans. Let the opposing sides slug away at each other, but leave me out of the ring thanks very much. But Damon taking the side he was taking?

"You may have to excuse me for saying this, old friend," I said, "but it seems to me somebody has kidnapped the Damon I know and sent an imposter back in his place."

"Why do you say that?"

"I have some knowledge of what has taken place in Germany over the last few years. I am also familiar with the political views expressed by a certain British painter since he was a schoolboy. How is it I am not hearing a single negative word about the Nazis?"

"Have you gone to Germany since the present government came in?"

"You know I haven't."

"Then your impressions have all come through a telescope. You are ignorant of what is happening. Or misled."

I stared at him. "Were you treated like royalty, by any chance?"

He admitted he had been. His gallery provided him with a car and driver. He did a tour of various artists' studios. Collectors laid out the red carpet, competing for his attention, introducing him to powerful people …

When he began describing the flattering reviews his work had received in German newspapers, I cut him off. "The posh treatment obviously went to your head. You arrive for the first time in a foreign country and are promptly taken up by elite circles. They wine and dine you. They make you feel like a celebrity. I wager you failed to see much of the real Germany at all."

Damon was smiling. "You are wide of the mark by a country mile."

"Furthermore, those elites were probably allowed to make you a celebrity, perhaps they were *instructed* to do so. After all, the art of Damon Chadwick, well known anti-modernist, would be approved by Dr. Goebbels, am I right?"

To this he said, "You mustn't judge me, Joff," but that damned smile stayed on his face.

"Do you think the German people will ever again vote for a leader?" I said. "Ever again in their lives?"

"A vote to be won by one or another competing interest? While the interest of the nation as a whole is ignored? Tell me the benefit of such a vote."

"Something called democracy? A little benefit called choice?"

"A choice of yoke, one way or another. Germany is now a country united in its energy. This is something new in the world."

This humbug is something new in Damon, and not to my liking. He was turning a trick I might not have thought possible … awakening my father in me. I glared at him.

"Why are you looking at me like that?"

"I'm thinking of a mess of pottage."

He threw his hand up like a stop sign, splayed fingers quivering in mock horror.

"It seems you have taken some bad bait," I said, "and the worm is corrupting your judgment."

"My dear Joffrey! Insults to my integrity are one thing, but I will not forgive that atrocious metaphor." His voice was still jocular, but at least the damned grin gave way to something embattled. When I mentioned Hitler's treatment of the Jews he shot me a look of exasperation.

"You know I could never be anti-Jew. The bullying of the Jews is obviously a mistake, most likely a reaction against what Germany has suffered since the War."

"You call it 'bullying'?"

"I call it the worst mistake being made in Germany."

"A mere *mistake*?"

"I can't see how they can escape censure for it."

"Yet I hear no censure from you."

"I make no excuses, but revolutionaries can do terrible things."

"Did your hosts among the master race mention the teeming prisons of the Reich? Did your chauffeur take you to any of the bucolic 'camps' where the undesirables are held?"

"Joff, when a movement of such scope enlists the masses and organises science to the degree the Germans have, there may be as many faults as there are advances."

"What the devil is that supposed to mean?"

"It means I can't indict a society that has chosen to change. Germany is undergoing a transition. You have to see it. You have to feel it. You arrive in Berlin and get caught up in the dynamism. You feel a purpose, a unity – a goal. In such circumstances things can be done."

I was up against a stubborn zeal that no reasoning would dislodge. Anyway, my heart was not in it. I hate losing arguments, and when have I ever won an argument against Damon?

"You mentioned you need a favour."

"Yes, I do. We'll talk about it next week, before I leave for the continent."

"Please don't tell me you're going back to Germany!"

"I've been invited to attend the opening of the Olympics."

I could only stare at him.

"Herr Weinhauf is well connected," he added. "Besides, I've been commissioned to do some pictures."

I found my voice. "I will not pretend to be excited about all this. Who commissioned you?"

"Herr Weinhauf has a collector in mind."

"Who would that be?"

"A particular collector," he said, indicating the matter was closed.

Can you make him out, Heidi? I certainly can't. *Defending Germany? Doing pictures in Germany?* But I have no wish to dwell on the madness right now. The Pearson family, with Vicky in the vanguard, leaves tomorrow for the Cotswolds and an actual holiday. Back to you in two weeks.

Joff

Sunday
19th July 1936

Dear Heidi,

Little wonder my chief complaint with the universe involves the speed of time … the calendar tells me the summer is rapidly passing. I do at least have some idea where it has gone. We are back from our fortnight's holiday. Vicky would have preferred a tour of the battlefields of France, but her school fees tie us to a ghastly budget. So we went to the Cotswolds where the father of one of Mary's colleagues let us a small cottage in Gloucestershire.

Bracing, Heidi, well nigh restorative, the long walks on country lanes, and I may have developed a fair palate for goat's cheese. Our landlord, a generous chap by the name of Benson, arranged some free horseback riding lessons for Vicky. It was also good to see Mary out of uniform day after day. She found an oversized denim jumpsuit which made her positively rustic – Vicky chortled! – and she insisted on helping out with the rabbit pens on the adjacent farm.

The riding was a highlight for darling Vicky, but she soon declared herself done with 'trifling matters' and settled down to Robert Louis Stevenson. She had packed *Treasure Island* and *Kidnapped*, and a couple of other Stevensons. I asked if his adventure stories were not more apt for boys.

"Daddy!" The look on her face said I had blundered badly. Since when were buried treasure, piracy and historical action tales exclusively for *boys*? My question was unworthy of a reply. What she did say was, "Do you know I have already read *Dr. Jekyll and Mr. Hyde?*"

"My darling, I hope you never suggest a touch of Mr. Hyde in your poor pater."

"Daddy!" This time the look was coy, wise, concealing and triumphant. The little imp is a knowing actress and skilled subjugator. Eight years old!

Back in harness tomorrow. The Olympics open in Berlin in two weeks and I must expect to be a workhorse. We will be knee deep in speeches and articles that may hint at the Nazi regime's posture going forward. I see the Americans have decided to compete after all. For the best, I assume. Maybe the international glow and warmth of the

Olympic flame will thaw Mr. Hitler's icy heart.

Damon left for Germany a couple of days ago. I never had a chance to see his latest canvases, and he never got round to telling me the favour he wants. You may be sure I still haven't come to terms with our last conversation. I can only hope his flirtation with Germany comes to an early end. His personal situation alone should cause him to steer clear of the Nazis. From what I read they despise and abuse his … confreres, just as much as they hate and abuse the Jews.

My dear Heidi, the basic irrationality of people increasingly reveals itself to me. They do strange and perplexing things. Life follows no sensible order. Except in my case, where strict routine prevails. You are my one extravagance, my one deviation from the straight and narrow. May you remain so, and I,

Yours,

Joff

Thursday
23rd July 1936

Dear Heidi,
A day to circle on the calendar. Have you ever been told, on this special day, that you are a woman for whom any red-blooded man would climb Everest or dive to the deepest ocean floor? Lest no one has done so I make it my duty to be the messenger of Truth. The world is a richer and more charming place for your having been born. Happy birthday, great lady. Many happy returns.

Thinking, as always, of the unique light in your eyes,

Joff

Saturday
1st Aug. 1936

Hello dear Heidi,
Auntie Beeb is impressing me. Tommy Woodrooffe is coming through clear as a bell, direct from Berlin. A spirited *Ode to Joy* played a few minutes ago, not long after Hitler's opening speech. The Germans appear to be putting on a proper ceremony. They even have the airship *Hindenberg* hovering above the stadium. Tommy sounds impressed but I can also hear vexation in his plummy voice. The triumphalism troubles him. Swastikas billowing on giant banners outnumber Olympic flags by about twenty to one, he says. As for the thousands of police, brown-shirted S.A. men, and black-booted military in rigid formations around the stadium, "You might mistake the pitch for an imminent battlefield if you forgot these were Games." When the Leader took his seat, Tommy said, "Ladies and gentlemen, can you hear the roar of this crowd? They are standing and cheering. They are screaming and waving and holding their arms out in salute. Ladies and gentlemen, it is as if a sun-god has entered the stadium."

Good old Tommy. He brought along Harold Abrahams to report on track and field. Remember our gold medal sprinter from the '24 Games? Caused a fine fuss at the time. I wonder how the Nazis are receiving him. Lunchroom talk has it that the *Kauft nicht bei Juden!* (Don't buy from Jews!) signs in Berlin have been taken down. To be a Gypsy, however, remains a challenge. The Gestapo did a sweep and have removed all the beggars from the streets.

The competitions begin tomorrow. Darling Vicky and her friends will be keeping score. My understanding is the British team will be lucky to finish in the top ten. Medals will come in rowing and relay-running for sure, but even little countries like Finland, Sweden and Hungary have us beat in the more obscure sports. I hope Vicky is not too disappointed.

There will be no running or jumping anytime soon for your admirer. The black melancholy I told you about has not returned, but an equally nasty relative of it has shown up. Not what I would call Dread this time, nothing to do with anxiety, but something physical. It started with nausea when I rose from bed a few days ago. As I got up, the inside of my head felt like water heaving in a tub. My first thought was *Why am I drunk?* which was absurd because I had just slept seven hours. My second thought was *Did that just happen?* because the sensation quit me at lightning speed.

The same thing happened in the afternoon when I rose from my desk in the sunroom. Again, for half a moment, the world took a vicious spin. I thought I was losing balance, so I grabbed the back of my chair. Half a dozen times since, the same sneak attack. It comes in the mornings when I hoist myself up, and at various moments when I least expect it. Have I contracted a disease of the little grey cells? Am I getting old?

Apologies for the moaning and grumbling. Asking your pardon, I send an explosion of pink lilies.

Joff

Saturday
8th Aug. 1936

Hello Heidi,

A tropical week here, extraordinary heat. Yours of the twenty-seventh only turned my temperature higher. Kindly retire that old crusade, I beg you. Have you been exchanging notes on the matter with Damon? He too has never relented. I may have been bold and brazen in the past, even wildly ambitious in my youth, but those days are distant memories. Neither of you quite understand, I have very little imagination. I could never tell a story to my darling Vicky without impersonating the morning paper or last night's novel. I am nothing more than a pedestrian reporter, a miner of memory. My ramblings simply plagiarise reality. Passionate? There you may have a point. I have an obsessive purpose after all. It is to seduce the attention of a great lady in America …

Vicky's face has assumed a scowl, courtesy of the standings in Berlin. She and her friends have been spending hours by the wireless and learning to their dismay that Britain does not always prevail. In this case we are limping painfully. Germany is on top of the medals list by a wide margin and His Majesty's team on crutches somewhere in the middle. *Sic transit gloria imperii?* At least your Jesse Owens has deflated one Nazi balloon. Imagine how galling it must be for the master race to see a black sprinter leaving invincible whites in his dust. Take that, Mr. Hitler. Still, we hear no end of ideological boasting from the Germans, seeing as they are winning most of the gold medals. The Nazi press trumpets the ideals of Aryan superiority. As if that were not annoying enough, the Italians too are among the medal leaders and Mussolini is bragging about fascism.

The Olympics have brought less work to the sunroom than I had feared. Our masters upstairs realised there wasn't much to be gleaned about Hitler's foreign policy from the frivolous stories and rhetoric about the Games.

As for the interior of the Pearson cranium, the strange attacks continue. They lie in wait, stagger me at unpredictable moments. I can be sitting in a chair, reading, and all the machinery in my head is functioning routinely, but when I look up and turn my head … there it is, a wave, a wobble, a discrepancy in space and time. No mention of this yet to Mary. She would bundle me into an ambulance and summon half the doctors in England. If the attacks continue, I will make a discreet call on Dr. Cooper.

Spouse and daughter are out shopping and we are to meet later at the cinema. I was fancying Carol Reed's new picture *Laburnum Grove*, about a suburban gardener who's actually a sucessful counterfeiter. Vicky, however, came out enthusiastically for *Captain January*, the latest Shirley Temple film. I lost the fight by a knockout in the first round.

The damned ceiling stompers.

Sounds like the squalor up there is being kicked around with hobnailed boots. We had a long spell of quiet for awhile, not sure why. Recently ran into the emaciated father of the stompers, months since I last collided with him. No more chemical engineering dreams for him. He is now earning three quid a week as an apprentice butcher in the Gloucester Road. I doubt if such a salary can keep Her Corpulence in bacon and kippers. I suppose our lamentably absent spinster (oh, how quiet she was! how we miss her!) remains the family angel. The times, Heidi, the times. Pardon me while I escape the wild urchins and read my newspaper in the park. Wish me a bench in the shade.

All my best,

Joff

Saturday
15th Aug. 1936

Dearest Heidi,
You are quite right, I do deserve credit for remembering your favourite flowers, but the 'shriek of surprise' indicates you failed to take me seriously. Still, the shriek, heard clear across the Atlantic, gratifies me enormously. No, I will not discuss the expense, save to say the telegraph to your Quincy Square florist exceeded the cost of the lilies themselves.

The Berlin Olympics close tomorrow. My darling Vicky refuses to accept the medals count: a total of fourteen for Britain against eighty-nine for Germany. How could this happen? Her young mind assumes that Britain's place is at the top, in the lead. She knows well what Cecil Rhodes once said. "To be born an Englishman is to win first prize in the lottery of life." What can explain Britain finishing ... *tenth*?

"My dear peach," I tried to explain, "some countries devote more time and resources to sport than we do. You should never think the results of the Olympics mean anything about our place in the world."

"What *do* they mean, then?"

"Simply that we avoid silly activities like hurling a metal sphere halfway across a field, or picking up huge weights and holding them over our heads."

She has since turned her attention elsewhere. Blessed childhood.

I thought the tilting episodes in my head would pass, but no such luck, the wretched moments of imbalance keep coming, three or four times a day. I feel stalked by an elusive phantom. Worse luck, Dr. Cooper is on holiday. I pleaded with the nurse who answers his telephone for the earliest possible appointment once he returns.

Consider me disappointed by your news of social distinctions in America. My mother would be appalled. The curse of caste, she would say. These 'Boston Brahmins' of yours, are they descended from the earliest colonists? I suspect they command mountains of inherited money, the spoiled dears. Money isolates, insulates, demarcates ... I wish I had more of it myself so I could enjoy a bit of demarcation. But I digress.

Enjoyed your latest run-in with the local vernacular. Escapes me how people can put an 'r' on the rear end of 'idea' yet *fuhget* it in other places. If the travesty extends unto your high and mighty Brahmins I will be left with a serious conundrum. How in heaven's name can they constitute an aristocracy if they render Harvard Law as *Hawvawd Lar*?

Delighted to hear you hold a place on Damon's postcard list. He favoured me too with a quick note, written in markedly improving German. He has extended his stay in Germany and will return via Paris, where he will likely muck about in his usual way. I would imagine he's keeping his … inclinations, under tight rein in Berlin. He signs off with *Will you do me that favour when I get back?* and still doesn't identify the bleeding favour. I will be happy to do him any favour he likes so long as it includes drinking his excellent single malts.

Bedtime, my dear. I take the train to Bury in the early morning. Wish me luck with the raging pater.

All my best,

Joff

Saturday
22nd Aug. 1936

Heidi dear,

Must say, Vicky being with us for the hols has been a tonic. Having her at breakfast and dinner changes my life. She has enrolled in a summer course at Actonvale's, so Mary escorts her there in the mornings and I swing by in the afternoons to take her home. We have her for another fortnight and I dread the day she leaves.

In the sunroom nothing but the humdrum to report. *Mon nouveau ami* Ken has become more and more of a saving grace. We eat our sandwiches together most days now. Ken's a highly intelligent fellow, though a bit starry-eyed. He would convert your admirer, imagine this, to a faith in humanity. He thinks an epidemic of reason will sweep the earth, and not just in some distant imaginary future. "In our lifetime a global system will come about and contribute to the common good," he says. "Trade will produce permanent peace and lift huge numbers of people from poverty. Dictators will go the way of the dinosaurs. Movements will emerge in the backwater countries to abolish the leftovers of feudalism and insane patriarchy. There will be – "

"Will the lion also lay down with the lamb, Professor Retinger?"

"Just watch. There will be such a thing as an international morality and the means to enforce it. We await only the right juncture between history and a political figure with vision and power."

"You remind me of a friend who smokes opium. I must introduce the two of you when all of us are lounging in the promised land."

My visit with the pater last Sunday was ... different. Sad, actually. I am the adult now, indulging him, protecting him. He complains about headaches, strange twinges in the chest and almost ceaseless exhaustion.

"Are you not sleeping well, Dad? Maybe a light sedative – "

"There are days when I can't keep my food down, I vomit it up. Ten, fifteen minutes after I've eaten, vomit it up."

"We will have your doctor in," I said, "and discuss your diet with Mrs. Stockton."

"The bloody woman gives me only two baths a week now."

"I'll speak to her."

It went on. The prosthetic is giving him pain. He uses crutches to get about. He has become afraid to venture outdoors, even into the yard, for fear of a tumble. The physical complaints were only the beginning. "I have a daughter I never see, that drunken traitor. Is she still with the Nazi arselicker?"

"Dad – "

"I have a granddaughter I adore and want to see but never see. Where is Vicky? I need to see Vicky."

"She's very busy with a summer course, Dad."

"It all slips away," he said. "You keep postponing things, you plan ahead, but then the years pass, the plans come to nothing, and then suddenly you're at the end."

"You still have good years ahead, Dad. You can enjoy your reading and leisure of mind."

"I wanted to take Ulli to Spain. I wanted her to see the cathedral in Seville, the Alhambra in Granada."

What we don't know about the inner lives of our parents probably far outweighs what we do know. My mother had taken Irene and me to Germany before the War to visit our grandparents, and we had spent a few summers with the pater while he was posted abroad, but the two of them had never taken a holiday together. I had never heard so much as a whisper from my father about taking my mother to Spain.

"I'm better off dead now," he said. "I don't know why the body persists, when the mind simply wants an end."

"Maybe the body knows better than the mind."

"Rubbish." Then a light came into his eye and he said, "At least the book will live on. It grows more important by the day for people to read my book."

Oh, Jesus, I thought, please don't torture me with the book. Heidi, I have never told this to anyone, but after the War he wrote a book. It was not a very good book. No publisher would take it, but this did not stop him from fiercely believing the thing was important and must be published. He did a private printing of a thousand copies. Then he found no shops would put the thing on their shelves, and no newspapers would review it. I have a box of them deep in a closet, kept out of filial loyalty but undistributed from sheer shame. My father in his vast naiveté thought that whatever he put to paper was akin to High

Thought. In his mind the rejection by publishers was either timidity on their part or, more darkly, suppression of his ideas. When he was on leave in Britain he would take satchels of copies on strolls through Mayfair, Belgravia, the best streets of Knightsbridge – you have the idea – and randomly leave copies in mailboxes. Why in heaven's name am I telling you this? The embarrassment is excruciating.

I quickly got him off the book by asking about his ankle. "What?" he shouted.

"How is the godforsaken niggle in your ankle?"

"What the bloody hell are you talking about?"

When I first visited him in hospital in '18, he said there was a godforsaken niggle in the ankle of his amputated leg. Ever since, we have regularly joked in those same words about the phantom limb. I have to wonder what other pillars of memory have cracked and fallen in his mind, and whether the decay is accelerating. We know these things are inevitable, and yet …

My Saturday errands call. I will post this on the way. Be well and happy.

Joff

Tuesday
25th Aug. 1936

Dear Heidi,

Just back from a wretched evening. Feeling low and mucky. What I learned tonight is not something I can tell Mary. A good thing she's asleep, otherwise I might blurt it out.

Damon returned a couple of days ago. We met up at The Squire's. Our friend is looking well, too damned well. On his way back from Berlin he gave up his usual detour to Paris. "What have you been doing," I asked, "all this time in Germany?"

"I'm not sure you wish to know."

"If it has anything to do with the wonders of National Socialism, you have that right."

"More like the wonders of chance and fate, actually."

"What do you mean?"

"I've met someone in Berlin. He has become a special friend."

I looked at him. He held my eyes. He nodded.

"Jesus Christ," I said.

That ended the evening, or at least my share in it. Aside from croaking out the name of our saviour three or four more times I don't think I said anything of consequence. I could not wait to get the hell away from our insane friend. I could not *bear* the sound of any details. He remained entirely himself of course, a prince of indifference, like a foolish fucking *child*. He cheerfully accepted I was mortified and left me sitting alone while he swung about the pub and chatted with various acquaintances including, to my horror, that crawling little alligator Billy Colman who writes the scandal column in the *Evening News*. I stayed sunk down in my chair as if a great weight were pressing on me. *Have you shit your goddamn brains out of your bloody poofer's arse?* I looked up at the sound of a smarmy cackle and saw it was the Colman creature responding to something our insane friend had said. *Have you lost your fudgepacking mind?* I don't remember drinking my ale though I must have because I noticed my glass was empty when we left.

The chill of the night helped. So did the rain. Opening my umbrella I felt a semblance of normality, even civility, seep back. Damon put his arm round me in contrition and said, "Don't worry, Joff. You might laugh when I say this, but believe me, I am a very careful man."

"You can't blame me for thinking the opposite. Let's not discuss it any further."

"Done," he said.

"What is that favour you mentioned wanting?"

He let out a hoot which startled some passersby. "Let's talk about it next week." He saw me into a taxi and looked for another, said he was late for an appointment.

"Where the hell are you going this time of night?"

"Seeing a collector in Belgravia, something of a night owl."

My eyes are falling shut, Heidi. I am obviously not another night owl. Maybe I can sleep now.

Joff

Tuesday
1st Sept. 1936

Dear Heidi,
I booked off the afternoon and saw Dr. Cooper. Happy to report my health is nothing to worry about, but we must always have something to distract and trouble us, *n'est-ce pas*? If the anxiety is not a medical thing, it can be an insane friend thing. Damon called yesterday to cancel our pint tonight, said he was too deep into work to sacrifice the evening.

"Sacrifice?"

"Sorry, that came out wrong."

"Thank you."

"That favour," he said, "I'll be needing it soon."

"What is the bloody favour?"

"Tell you what. I shall drop by your little salt mine on King Charles Street next week and take you to lunch. We shall talk about it then."

At least we know he's deep in work and in no immediate danger of being lynched by Nazi thugs. I have to train myself not to dwell on the extreme risk he's taking. The German penal code on these matters makes ours in Britain look like hire and salary. But I was telling you about Dr. Cooper…

He shone a miniature torch into my eyes and asked if my problem affected anything other than my balance. When I replied no, he said I have a simple case of vertigo, likely brought on by infection in the inner ear, and I should cease worrying.

"How long is it going to last?"

"It could end this afternoon, or months from now. Until it tapers off, avoid climbing ladders or peering down from the edge of rooftops."

My dear Heidi, can you picture your fumbling admirer on a ladder? It would be less challenging to imagine him swinging from a vine in the jungle. As I was leaving his surgery, the doctor pressed a leaflet into my hand. "Do read this."

I glanced at the heading and saw it was from the Peace Pledge Union. This surprised me. "I would not have taken you for an objector, Doctor Cooper."

"Not one who marches in the streets surely, but we must all do our part in renouncing war."

I have never encountered my physician except in his surgery wearing a white coat and explaining aches and pains. He is surely entitled to his views, but ply me with a PPU handout? Of course I might feel the same dismay if I saw Dr. Cooper in the park wearing Bermuda shorts and sunglasses.

Remember when our dilettante Seamus briefly took up with the PPU? I vividly recall him making an ass of himself with his white poppy on Remembrance Day. *We must remove from the world all causes of war,* he went about saying like a pompous ass. Right, and at the same time we must abolish volcanos and hurricanes. I deposited the good doctor's handout in the first dustbin.

Now that I know my condition is a temporary nuisance and not a death sentence, the symptoms seem to be retreating. I was off balance only once today. Yes, I will keep you posted, my dear famous Anglo-American sculptress. All my best,

Joff

Wednesday
9th Sept. 1936

Dear Heidi,
Yours of the twenty-fourth arrived. I see now it was a mistake to mention the pater's book. I should have known you would demand to know more. Very well, I consent to reveal the book's contents. On condition you never mention the humiliation again.

He started writing in hospital as he recovered from the amputation, and finished three years later when he was vice-consul in Cracow. The thing is a long childish barely readable conniption. My father spun his fixation on Germany's guilt into a crackpot indictment of the whole history of the German people. The thesis of the book, if it can be called a thesis, and if it can be called a book, is that Germans have forever hungered for conquest because blood-lust dominates their Hun genes. In their view they possess the right to subjugate and rule because they are superior. A whole chapter tries to make the reader laugh at the irony of barbarians regarding themselves as transmitters of light. (This reader wanted to run and hide from the charmless malice of the argument and artless whine of the prose.) If anything clever exists in the book, it's the way my father stretches out his disgraceful polemic to fill two hundred pages. The last lines deliver his prescription for taming the Germans and preserving world peace. *They must be denied heavy industry. Let them farm!*

I hope my mother never read the thing; she would have been horrified. Or maybe not. I never heard her pine for her native Bavaria and never once did I hear her criticise the pater. She loved him in a fully decided, clinging way. Please, no more talk of the mortifying book.

Happy to report not a single dizzy lurch for well over a week. Our friend Mr. Vertigo must be off visiting someone else's cranium. Unhappy to report a huge absence in the flat … Vicky has returned to school. I miss her fabulous chime and energy. Breakfast and dinner have reverted to routine, almost sad things.

A sudden downpour! I send you some fine thumping English rain, and my eternal regards.

Joff

Saturday
12th Sept. 1936

Heidi dear,
Damon fetched me at the F.O., took me to lunch, and told me the favour he wants. Hold on to your hat. He needs photos of himself in the nude and has decided I am the man to take them. "I want to be my own model," he said, "and I can't work off the mirror."

Finding my voice I said, "I have no idea how to use a camera."

"Don't be ridiculous."

"What qualifies me to perform such a task?"

"The eyes given you by patient evolution. And further, the fact you can stand up and look through a lens."

"Why not have a professional in?"

"No, that would defeat my concept."

"Why not that shambling gorilla of yours, Tatchell?"

"Oh lord, no. Aubrey would not be suitable for this."

I was doing my best to find a way out. "Someone in Germany?"

He smiled. "Not possible. We would need a studio for proper lighting, which would involve … complications."

"There's a lot more involved than looking through a lens if you require high-quality photographs."

"Do I detect shyness?"

That shut me down. He overwhelms me, nothing new there. He wants the photos as soon as possible. I am fine with doing it, really, I'm no prude, but the request poked a memory loose of another favour he once asked. This goes back to when we were kids. It was before I knew, and it was probably just after he himself began to know.

It was the year the War started. I was fourteen. We had been friends since we were seven, inseparable mates. I visited him often in the summers at an uncle's cottage outside Bournemouth where his mother sent him for mineral air and the tutelage of a father figure. Those summers were grand. We played pirates, King Arthur's knights, Arabian thieves, desperados in America's wild west. A dense wood nearby had a tiny glade which acted perfectly as a hideout. That was where we plotted train robberies, bank hold-ups and assassinations of enemies of Great Britain. It was also where we planned to hide from the law if any of our conspiracies went wrong. When we were older and beyond childish games we still found use for the glade. We had our first stolen cigarettes there and first solemn talks about life and death. And of course our first ferocious heave after guzzling half a quart of Irish whisky mixed with warm ginger ale.

The autumn of that year was still bright and hot and we were in that special haunt and I was sure I had brought the goods to top all. With keen anticipation of gratitude and approval I pulled out a long forgotten secret of my father's, discovered in an old steamer trunk. The amazing find was a collection of French postcards which had never suffered postal marks or the eyes of my mother. Most were from the 1890s and showed demure young women in fancy underpants and spicy corsets. The scenes all had transparent curtains in the background and showed the women pulling on stockings or brushing their hair. A few of the more dog-eared ones were from a decade earlier and featured big-bummed ladies beguilingly dressed in lacy lingerie and fascinating garter belts. Not a mons *veneris* to be seen, but you can imagine my obsession over the treasure of bare breasts. Those sepia-tinted postcards from the pater's private life were easily the greatest fruits of my boyhood archeology. They had given me hours of solitary transport and I was eager to share.

Imagine my perplexity when Damon recoiled. His face fell and he walked off.

"What's the matter?"

He continued walking away.

I yelled, "What have I done?"

He stopped at the edge of the glade and kicked some fallen leaves. Then he strode back and I could see he had recovered himself. "Joff. . ."

"Yes?"

"Would you do me a favour?"

"Of course!"

"Turn round and close your eyes."

"Why?"

"Just for a moment."

"What's it about?"

"Please, close your eyes and keep them shut 'til I say."

I did as he asked, not remotely alert to what he was up to. As best I can remember no warning at all went through my head. I turned and closed my eyes and a breeze whistled through the surrounding trees as I waited.

"Joff ... "

I turned back round and opened my eyes. He had taken off his clothes. For a few moments both of us were frozen in place. Neither of us said a word. Then he raised his arms in a kind of supplication. His eyelids were fluttering but his face appeared calm. I still have the notion that ripples were running up and down his arms. He breathed in deeply and offered something novel for Damon, a shy smile. He lowered his arms and I could see he was excited. He clawed his fingers down his chest, then slowly across his abdomen, and enclosed his genitals in the cup of his hands. He said, "I just want you to know."

In the quarter century since, I have wanted to ask him when he himself first knew.

He gathered his clothes and dressed. Of course I was gobsmacked. To the extent of my schoolboy awareness I had a grasp of the implications. This kind of thing was forbidden. It was abominable. Oscar Wilde had gone to prison.

My friendship with Damon changed but remained the same. Of course things cannot change while remaining the same, the statement is plainly absurd, but some things can be absurd even while they're true. A space would always exist between us, defined by his different nature, yet Damon had proved we could still share a bond. There were years afterwards when I gave his secret almost no thought. I did not realise it that day in the glade when he revealed himself to me – so much is unconscious in our youth – but I was awed by his maturity. Also by his courage, because I was vaguely aware of all the difficulties and even dangers he would have to face. I felt out of my depth, like a student on a solo outing with a teacher. That feeling of awe mixed with deference has been with me ever since. Of course he has gone on earning the awe, as all England knows. But my innermost sense of him is that he was born to be different, he sees deeper, his fires are hotter, and what makes him powerful is that *he is not afraid*.

Since that day we have discussed his ... nature, maybe half a dozen times. He knows the discomfort of the subject for me. He says the thing limits him, separates him, hunts him. But it most assuredly does not weaken him; he will never allow it to affect his resolve. He considers the predicament of men like him, what he calls 'the insane hounding', one of the last citadels of righteous foolishness in society. "If not for the law I would shout what I am in the streets with no shame. But go to prison? You do not see a martyr in front of you, Joff. Martyrdom is for people too lazy to do battle. And there's penury on top of ruin. The polite and genteel who buy my paintings would stop buying them. The canvases themselves would take on the ugly vice. Let them flail away with their repression, I refuse to be repressed. Do I commit a crime? Here's a better question: do I sin against nature? My dear friend, I embody it."

Damon admits he has needs but none of them desperate. At any rate, he seems to take care of them on a regular enough basis. I remember you always blamed his mother. How many times did you meet the woman? I wonder if anyone is to *blame*.

What I remember most clearly from our childhood is how precocious Damon was, how effortlessly distinct and prematurely eccentric. When he was ten years old he nailed a manifesto to the wall of Mr. Chesney's history class declaring the school to be a CENTRE OF AMNESTY AND CHARITY (amnesty and charity for whom he never spelled out). When the Headmaster told his mother such behaviour could not be tolerated, she severely reprimanded him – the Headmaster! – for wanting to stifle her son's creative instincts, and besides, what in heaven's name was objectionable about amnesty and charity? I think that was the same year Damon gave me a gift of a jade elephant, a dear curio from China his father had picked up during his travels. He never met his father. The legendary fellow died shortly after Damon's birth. Apparently he was an alcoholic of some means and minimal prudence; he drowned after a night of drinking off the shore of the Bosphorous.

Damon put the glittering green elephant in my hands with the words, "I woke up this morning wanting you to have this." That is how he made me his friend when we were seven years old. Imagine a little boy in shortpants and school tie fixing on another and announcing, "We are to be friends for life." That was Damon and exactly what he said, in a tone of unbreakable certainty. He didn't know how much I admired him, envied his easy way with the world. Miraculously, he made me his best friend.

Ever since then he has lifted and broadened me with his spirit, his strongly held views, his easy understanding of things. He was always inclined to be wild. More than a few times he led us into remarkable mischief. Never in his presence, however, have I doubted he knows better than I how to live. Maybe because he has never stopped wanting and pursuing a heightened sense of living, which he has never doubted for a moment is both achievable and rightly his. Same with the heights he has climbed in art. He always sketched with amazing ease while growing up, but never gave painting serious thought as a career. I do believe his talent was inborn, he merely had to exercise it. When I saw him draw as a boy, his skill made me think of birds flying, gardens blooming, ocean tides crashing. The talent came naturally to him. Still, he discounted the talent; it meant little to him; he was intent on the law. That was because he had the gift of speech, he could talk you into the ground. The law would serve as the place to harness his oratorical skills, send them into battle, sway magistrates and juries, save the unjustly accused. No doubt he would have made a great barrister.

The transforming idea arrived when his mother took him to Madrid for his fifteenth birthday. They visited the Prado and the hand of fate reached into him when he saw the great canvases of the central room. He declared then and there what his life goal would be. "I will be the British Velasquez," he said to his mother. You would think it was just a pompous, ridiculous schoolboy boast. Yet his whole being thereafter focused on achieving that level of triumph. He often followed up the puerile boast with the grimly mature, "Nothing is going to stop me."

His mother's aspirations for Damon had tended toward politics. She saw him living at Number 10 with the panache of a Disraeli and the consistency of a Gladstone, but she settled for a newer and better Velasquez and sent her darling to art school. He hated the snobbery and sluggish tempo of the place; he was a man in a hurry. He left after six months, then lived for three years like an industrious monk on the Isle of Skye. His only diversion during those years was single malt whisky for which he developed a connoisseur's taste. When he came home a self-taught artist he arrived with canvases that tore the scalp off convention.

British art had become hesitant, finicky, dark, priggish, elusive.

What Damon did was throw open the doors and windows and let in Mr. Certainty and Madame Bold and their children Liberty, Eros, Vex and Rile. He came with something new and unequivocal and sent the old guard reeling. Remember the fabulous fuss?

No, of course you don't. You were still a teen and didn't meet him until some years later, but try to imagine Damon at twenty when he first exercised the power within and saw his earliest paintings recognised as daringly original, furtively seditious, and suggestive of genius. It was the narrative quality of his work, the tremendous rigour and accessibility that won him attention both within and outside the art world. A hail of print baptized him a revolutionary. His canvases were furiously denounced and just as passionately defended – and bought for princely sums.

Huge sprawling allegations and impeachments they were, and executed with a technical finesse that was beyond most of his contemporaries. Impeachments aimed at the British state and British society. 'Sprawling' was the operative word because the vistas teemed with details both plain and coded that could keep you studying them for hours and make you come back the next day for a second 'did I really see what I think I saw?' look. He was not simply a taste of something new, he was a typhoon of it, and how often do typhoons visit Britain? In coherent visions occupying yards of canvas he would paint a vicious knife fight, a shadowy business deal, a stealthy coupling in a dark alley, and the faces of the killers, the corrupt, the prostitutes and prostituted would belong to characters plucked from history, or heroes taken from ancient myth, or men of the day who were sitting on the front benches of the House of Commons. You might think he was a Mexican muralist with a French soul and a lust for libel.

"This is not British art," harrumphed the critic for the *Telegraph*.

"Thank Christ," Damon said.

If he were a writer he would probably be branded a polemicist. Some of his paintings are pure invective. Remember your first look at his work, the cabinet ministers hung at the Walter? The series was a forty-gun broadside, and precisely targeted. With a cruelly subtle eye he cast the politicians as blind, mendacious, conspiring, poisonously repellent human beings.

The denizens of the rebellious, anti-bourgeois culture of the twenties tried to claim him as one of their own but he disappointed their expectations. He lost most of his potential friends on the Left when he made fun of socialist realism with a series depicting Lenin and Stalin as fishermen in the Sahara, then as a pair of peasant gamblers in a casino, and most memorably as arsonists in a cathedral.

His stock in trade was the arresting image which made his paintings popular with the common man. This of course caused some critics to turn up their noses and denounce him for being 'pictorial'. Respect from the professional commentariat was always grudging, but in the long run they had to grant it for his superb draughtsmanship and hard-won mastery of light and shadow. They learned to discount his habit of finding the worst in people!

I don't think he set out to be a trouble-maker, it came to him naturally. He reveled in the lancing of sacred cows. Politics was not his only hunting ground. He found victims among business magnates, musicians, writers, other artists, and he treated them as mercilessly as he did the politicians. Some critics branded him a high rent cartoonist but the charge never stuck. He went on being grossly impolite and remained widely loved for it, probably because of the targets he chose – the mighty, the super-wealthy, the arrogant, the vain.

The idea of belonging to a group or school or worst of all a 'movement' appalled him. He was not a pacifist, a Marxist, an imperialist, a socialist … he wasn't any ist, unless it was hedonist. He had never fallen for Trotsky or made time for Freud, even when he was nineteen and a wild willing vane in the wind. He once said he had a weakness for Einstein, mainly because he would never understand him and wished he could.

One early review called him a bastard child of Goya. Later the eminent critic Edward Hodge referred to him as Vermeer inoculated with venom or Rembrandt inflated by rage. Damon choked on the associations, not because of the negative connotations (I always thought they were rather positive myself), but because it put his stuff in the same room as others. He wants his talent to be regarded as solitary, unprecedented, *sui generis*. Like Velasquez in the Prado, he wants a room to himself.

Instantly irritated, *tired*, that's me whenever he gripes about having his name linked to dead giants. His wish to be unique seems like a useless organ, the appendix of his egomania. When we share our pints and he starts complaining about comparisons to some of the greatest painters who ever lived, I go piss …

These days, as you know, he aims his harshest fire at the critics. His canvases have fallen out of favour because of what he calls 'the prevailing norms'. Who dictates the prevailing norms in art? The critics of course, and the critics steer the collectors. Who are the collectors? According to Damon, they are wealthy cretins content to be driven about like sightless sheep. The wicked critics and cretinous collectors also influence the artists themselves. Most of our artists are spiritless and purposeless, happily driven in whatever direction those prevailing norms happen to be pointing. The pathology of art à la Chadwick!

The ironic thing is, despite all the stalking and emasculating he does with his brush, Damon calls himself a lover of the human race. Moreover he believes he has a role to play. He must contribute, he must add, he must help build. Our friend is fundamentally twisted of course, but aren't we all in our way? I couldn't give a damn about the destiny of the human race, except as it bears upon my darling Vicky. People could say *I'm* twisted.

Forgive me, I got carried away. Look, eleven pages of scribble! At my grandfather's desk of course, my airfield for taking flight to you. Put me elsewhere and my pen would be wingless.

Photography with Damon next Tuesday night. Wish me equanimity in the presence of nudity. Adore you as ever,

Joff

Saturday
19th Sept. 1936

Dearest Heidi,

For yours of the fourth, many thanks. We have no particular opinion of your Mr. Roosevelt. He appears an honest enough chap, though his patrician air strikes me as troubling. The cigarette holder seems an affectation when I see him cocking it in the newsreels. All in all he gives the impression of having a proper spine. To answer your question, no, hardly anyone here cares about the American election. The name of Mr. Roosevelt's opponent, Alf something, sounds like the moniker of a music hall comedian.

The 'shoot' has been delayed. Damon and I had a drink at his studio and he told me he has arranged to borrow a Rolleiflex, but will have it only next week. Apparently the Rolleiflex has won fame as the Rolls-Royce of cameras. "Press people use it," he said. "It's the best camera for capturing action."

"Action?" I had this notion he would be standing still against a curtained backdrop or reclining on a. . . who knows what.

"The idea will be to capture me in motion. With the Rolleiflex you can focus right up to exposure, even compose during exposure."

"I wish I knew what that means. When did you become an expert in these things?"

He looked away. "We must do this right. I want the sharpest possible stills." Then he poured us some Lagavulin, raised his glass, and said, "Thank you for being my friend."

"Jesus, you *have* become an odd bird."

"Why do you say that?"

"First you rubbish your anonymity by letting your photo be seen by every Joe and wide-eyed Jane in England. Then you go on the wireless and trash the Almighty. Then you go to Germany, where you somehow see and hear no evil. The next thing you did is unmentionable, not to speak of dangerous and insane. And now you thank your oldest and best friend for being your friend. What has come over you?"

"Can't a man thank his friend for not suffering a whit from the single most corrosive force in the world?" he said, ignoring everything I had just said.

"What corrosive force, pray tell, am I not suffering from?"

"Envy, *mon vieux*, envy. Most people carry it on their backs in cement bags, or wear it on their faces. Not you. My reputation means nothing to you. You knew me when I was nobody. Very few people can join me in taunting my fame, or seeing it as a great joke. To use one of your untranslateable maternal words, you would feel no schadsomething tomorrow – "

"*Schadenfreude.*"

"You would not feel a speck of *Schadensigmunde* if I suddenly couldn't paint anymore. Can I say the same for any other friend? No, they all nurse a silent envy. But not you, you would cry with me if I lost my talent, and I adore you for it."

Next Sunday I will at last be acting the role of photographer, emphasis on acting. Must confess to a heap of hesitation. Will tell all, my sweet.

Joff

Saturday
26th Sept. 1936

Dear Heidi,
The shoot was delayed again. The Rolleiflex was unavailable. Damon is set on that camera and only that camera. Maybe next week.

Tell me if these things happen in America … We are having our pint at The Squire's in lieu of the shoot, a couple of friends sitting in their local, engaging in ordinary conversation. All is calm, could not be more civil. Then a certain subject comes up, and you would think war has been declared. The knives come out and the two friends are suddenly stabbing away at each other.

No doubt you think it was Damon and me. We have our rows, God knows, and go at each other hammer and tong, but then we resume wherever on earth we left off and the storms leave no trace. No, this argument took place between Damon and a friend of his from the short-lived art school days. Dame and I were minding our own business, and I was making the vital point that Arsenal's wealth of talent at mid-field is no bleeding use without a gifted striker to convert opportunities … when a shadow came over our table.

"Chadwick! How are you, old man?"

We looked up to see a short, broad, flabby fellow rocking on his feet, grinning from ear to ear and swerving his pint as if he were directing it through traffic. "Good lord, it's Dicky Johnson," said Damon, not unhappily. He got up from his chair and gave the man a proper hug.

"Dicky Johnson, Joff Pearson. Joff, Dicky."

"A pleasure," I said, shaking Johnson's hand.

"Mine entirely," he replied, while looking me searchingly in the eye.

My anxiety over the pointed look was calmed when Damon asked after the man's wife and children. A run of the mill conversation followed about events since the two had last collided. Johnson gushed about Damon's success, said he had seen the splash in *Tatler*. He himself looked back on his art school days as a waste. He had given up his dreams in that line and taken a teaching degree. He was now in his second decade of spoon-feeding modern history into sixth formers at a comprehensive in Shepherd's Bush. His descriptions of classroom antics and the numbskulls among his students were surprisingly entertaining. I almost forgave him his intrusion.

Then.

He mentioned he had recently sat as a judge at an inter-school debating competition. "The resolution before the house was that Germany under the Nazis represents a threat to European peace. The negative took the day. Ran away with it, in fact. To my dismay."

He waved his pint in a throwaway gesture, but Damon asked: "Why do you say to your *dismay*, Dicky?"

"Well, the affirmative had no fire in them and the negative were the passionate ones, fancy that."

"I don't get you."

"Who wants another war? Certainly not our kids, they would have to fight it. So they refuse to see the truth behind current events."

"Who could possibly imagine another war?" I said, sensing an unfortunate turn in the conversation.

"Well, of course," said Johnson. "Peace is the god of gods. Who can argue against peace? The affirmative was the loser before the starting gun went."

Damon had arched an eyebrow. "But why your *dismay*?"

The very thing came over Dicky's face. "Well, old man, the better arguments are with the affirmative, clearly. Seems rather definite to my mind. The Huns are once more becoming a nasty menace. But don't try telling that to the kids."

"Are we down to calling them 'Huns' again? I think the kids have got it right, Dicky, and you have it wrong."

Oh, Jesus Christ, I thought.

Damon started in on his theme of Germany representing a new type of society. Bold directions were being taken, he said. He had just been to Berlin and Munich, had seen it for himself. "These Germans have it in their power to create a genuinely new model for our times," he said. "They are not interested in war."

Dicky's face had lost its high spirits during Damon's little lecture, and his pint had stopped veering. "I don't know what you saw, but have you given up reading the news? Germany is a police state. Nothing can excuse what Hitler is doing."

"And what is he doing, Dicky? There were six million unemployed in Germany when he took office. Today there are less than a million.

The factories are humming, the autobahns amaze, the stores bulge with goods. My dear man, there's a spirit of revival in the country."

Dicky planted his pint on the table, ran a hand through his hair, and shook his head sadly. "Have you noticed that the labour unions in Germany no longer exist? You give credit to Hitler he doesn't deserve. Huge amounts of money borrowed from America, along with something of a rebirth in world industry, have created most of those jobs. For another thing –"

Damon was having none of it. "Dicky, millions of people who voted communist in 1933 would vote for Hitler today. Then they had nothing to eat, now they swim in bratwurst and beer."

Dicky gripped the handle on his pint, but didn't move the glass an inch. "Germany's improvement in the number of employed," he said, "is also a result of Jews and women disappearing from the statistics. Jews under Hitler have become non-persons, and women are being told to stay home and breed a lot of little Hitlers. He needs livestock for his marching columns. Speaking of marching columns, do you have any idea how many jobless Germans have been drafted into the army? Sorry, Chadwick, but what people call a miracle is actually a fraud."

I was looking at the history teacher with a respectful eye. Behind the flab lurked intellect. Meanwhile the cheer at our little table had evaporated, as I feared it would the instant the Nazis were mentioned. The identical thing happens regularly in the F.O. cafeteria. In fact the quarrel over Germany is everywhere these days. It flares up in clubrooms, boardrooms, faculty lounges and dinner parties. Just this past week on the tube I saw a sudden exchange between two complete strangers, sparked by a newspaper headline.

"Oh, Dicky," said Damon, "the vast majority of our countrymen are with me on this. Can you at least admit Germany has become a welcome bulwark against the Bolshies?"

"There's your ticket. Embrace a pestilence to block a plague. In my book the Nazis are a bloody lot more threatening than the communists."

"You miss the larger picture, Dicky. Does that book of yours point out that civilians in our cities, especially in London, have become vulnerable to air attack? Why should it surprise you that people hate

111

the thought of another war?"

Dicky answered this quietly. "No rational person wants another war. But that should not keep us from seeing what Hitler is doing. Namely making Germany the strongest power in Europe, toward what ends we can only imagine."

His tone signaled he was trying to put an end to the unfortunate discussion. But the bull Damon, apparently intent on seeing red, rushed at the conciliatory moment and gave it a special kick. "My dear Dicky, I fear you have been taken in by the likes of Churchill and his ravings."

That darkened Dicky's face and put a swift end to his peace-making. "Ravings? What has he done but recite chapter and verse the armaments production in Germany? Churchill points at facts, and people paint him a maniac. I think you should stick to your easel, and keep your brush out of politics."

One of Damon's advantages in argument is that he can ignore personal insult. He speaks back to provocation like a snob to a servant, occasionally closing his eyes to ward off the sad rays of inferiority and ignorance. This he did now, his eyelids in a flutter. "Dicky, Dicky, your whole argument hinges on believing the Germans want war. Nobody there wants a repeat of the last mess."

"The Germans may not want war, but have you read their dear leader's book? It has a one-word answer to everything. Fight! Fight the foreigner. Fight the Jew. Fight anyone who thinks differently. The man's a crazed beast who has somehow mesmerised his country."

"'Crazed beast', Dicky?" said Damon with a smirk. 'Mesmerised' his country? Really, Dicky, leave that language to the penny dreadfuls."

"Kindly stop Dicky-ing me, Chadwick, it's a bloody pain. I have to wonder what *side* you're on, old man."

"The angels, Dicky, I take the side of the angels."

Our guest drained his pint and got to his feet. "I must also think we have become a nation of *sissies*, if you care to know." He said he had to run, tossed a goodbye at the table, and abruptly showed us his back. His parting comment startled me.

Damon was not the least bit ruffled. Maddening, really, how his equanimity behaves like thick armour. Nothing penetrates. "Sad deluded fellow," he said.

"I wouldn't say that."

I was none too pleased with our Damon, the insensitive Damon, not to speak of the Damon with the off-putting take on the Nazis. I said Johnson had made good sense and had got in the last word.

"A vicious slur more like, but we must excuse him. A moment of tantrum."

We went back to discussing Arsenal's mid-field, but the evening was spoiled. I always feel on a busman's holiday when National Socialism enters the conversation. I know more than most about developments in Germany, but when the two sides go at it I promptly park above the fray. That would be my father's fault, he long ago drove me to neutrality. I refuse to side with his demented claims and hysterical charges.

Speaking of the paternal, I had a call from Mrs. Stockton adding to what I learned on my last visit. My father is now eating very little, moaning day and night over his inability to sleep, complaining of imaginary ailments, and cursing loudly when he glances at the newspapers. She hinted bleakly that he may be becoming too much for her to handle.

More news of your life in Boston, please, and let your admirer know what new works you have on the go.

As ever,

Joff

Saturday
3rd Oct. 1936

Dear Heidi,

You must be thinking, here it is at last, Joff's account of photographing Damon, but the event was postponed yet again, heaven knows why. Maybe *next* week.

At work dull reports burden my desk and threaten to turn my brain to mush, but something interesting came in last week. A memorandum labeled *Geheime Reichssache*, which normally marks information reserved exclusively for top Nazi officials. It was written by Klaus Schumann, head of a creepy section we have run across in the past. I think I mentioned it to you, the *Sonderabteilung zur Forderung der jüdische Auswanderung*. A department specialising in fomenting Jewish emigration. So this Klaus Schumann must be a dyed-in-the-wool Nazi and professional administrator of anti-Semitism. Before I could read the thing Jenkins snatched it for an admiring once-over. He was intrigued because it was that rare beast, a photograph, meaning our chaps in the black arts had somehow gained access to the original document but could not or would not steal it … a further indication of its sensitive and restricted nature.

I had to tug the prize back from my excitement-starved colleague. "I'm recommending you for a post in MI6, Jenkins. Think of the great things you could do for England. Who would ever take you for a spy?"

He gave a rueful laugh and replied, "Work for a much younger chap, I'm afraid."

The memorandum harshly condemns Dr. Hjalmar Schacht, Germany's Minister of Economics. It brands the Minister a fool, and accuses him of being subverted by Jewish poison. Apparently Dr. Schacht, the minister responsible for the growth of industry, had said in a committee meeting that it would not be a bad thing for Germany's economy if entrepreneurial Jews were allowed to exercise their skills.

According to the memo-writer, Dr. Schacht's idea represents heresy of the highest order. "What we have in the Minister's reckless statement is a sinister undermining of Party policy. This irresponsible excretion from his dwindling brain should be taken as argument for Schacht's immediate dismissal from government."

Fascinating stuff, the overwrought language of moronic Nazis. Confidential material like this is always welcome in the sunroom; it keeps me entertained and awake. In my accompanying notes I pointed out the gap between cause and effect. Dr. Schacht's recommendation had not been made on any *moral* ground. He had not in any way rebuked the overall panoply of anti-Jewish policies. He had merely said Jews can be useful tools. I also noted Dr. Schacht's reputation. He has been widely hailed as the chief architect of Germany's economic miracle. In that light, I ventured, we might presume from this little episode something significant about the current temperature of Jew-hatred in Germany. Was it not remarkable that a coldly utilitarian aside from an esteemed minister could ignite such a fiery response from a lower level functionary? I ended my notes with, "This extraordinary outburst leaves us with something of a puzzle. If the Jews in Germany cannot obtain visas to emigrate, and if they cannot even aspire to be useful tools, we must wonder what the Nazi authorities have in mind for their ultimate disposition."

Ken looked at the notes and offered this: "Never rule out slave labour."

Our lunch confabs, by the way, have been cut in half. Ken is wolfing down his sandwiches these days, then heading for the library. One day this week he came back to the sunroom with a stack of Hansard.

"Good lord, Ken, what are you up to?"

"Bedtime reading."

"Have you converted to masochism?"

"We should know what our so-called leaders are saying, and where they're taking us," he replied, almost angrily.

Trust me, Ken is not a twit. Just young. Still young.

An old man sends you his love,

Joff

Saturday
10th Oct. 1936

Dear Heidi,

Yours of the twenty-sixth arrived. You have over-reacted. Damon is our friend and will forever remain so. Turning away from him is not an option, certainly not for me. No nasty winds, not even gale force bad behaviour, can break our connection. Damon is deluding himself for greater fame and gain, that is how I see it. This repulsive romance with Germany is an aberration, it will pass.

Your admirer has become an accomplished photographer. We did the deed last Tuesday night. Damon greeted me with a brisk handshake and a tumbler of Bowmore. He was business-like, commanding. He started by telling me a chimpanzee could operate the Rolleiflex.

"Yes," I said, "but I hope you understand I could never compete with a monkey when it comes to machinery of any sort."

"Unfunny. This is what you do …"

The Rolleiflex, if you have never seen one, and I don't suppose you have, looks like a pair of goggles set in a box and stood upright. It has two huge curvalinear eyes, one atop the other. They glare out blackly like envoys from mystery. Intimidating to a man whose kinship to devices is primitive, and whose dexterity could win him the Nobel for gaucherie.

"We have one roll of film with twenty-four exposures, so you have to keep wasted shots to a minimum."

"Of course."

He took away my whisky, handed me the camera, and put the sling over my head. I felt like I had a robot baby hanging on my chest. Then he stepped back of me to demonstrate how I should hold the little tyke. "Work with it at chest level. Sit it in the palm of your right hand, like this. Let it rest against your chest for support as well. Put your index finger on the release, here. Good! How does it feel?"

"Like I'm ready to become an airplane pilot, or submarine commander. I can do anything now."

"This is the focusing knob on the side. Use your left hand to manipulate it. Just your thumb and index finger!"

"I've got it," I said.

116

"Brave words from the luddite. You look into the reflex finder on top as you shoot. It will show you everything that the photo will contain."

"Spiffing. I'm ready."

"Not quite." He came back round and fixed me with an amiable glare as he unbuttoned his shirt. "A word about releasing the shutter. You want the pressure to be gradual, purposely gentle."

"Of course, child's play."

"Hold the camera as steadily as possible. Please be aware that the tiniest quivers will be writ huge in the enlargements. The shutter speed is pre-set for the amount of movement I expect of myself." He looked me over like a drill sergeant and said, "Place your feet wider apart. That will give you additional stability."

He had arranged a bank of high intensity lamps in the sitting area and had cleared it of furniture. A plush new rug covered the floor, and a silk sheet covered half the rug. He removed the last of his clothes and tossed them out of sight. "No need to concentrate on whether you have a composition. Wait until you see a tension, an inner conflict. Know that your subject is trying to come out of himself and fully into the world."

"Which means what, exactly?"

"I'm aiming at something new with these nudes. It has to do with sharing my privacy. I like that concept, *sharing privacy*." He was naked but addressing me as if he were fully clothed and chatting in a public square.

I backed up and clicked the shutter. It made a swift opening and closing sound like the chirrup of a small bird. He took to the floor and assumed a sitting posture with a hand under his chin. "Not quite Rodin, but good," I said, and clicked again.

"Is this more Chadwickian?" He was langorously splayed on the floor. I clicked the shutter. "Or this?" Now his legs were straining as if he were trying to push himself up a hill. The muscles in his buttocks were pronounced. I took two, three photos.

Then he was on his feet again and moving his arms like a man swimming upward. "Hold your breath as you push the button," he said. "That will minimise any shaking." He wrapped his arms about himself, hugged himself. For a moment he looked like two men. He was aroused and went on as if he were oblivious to it but I felt a rampancy in the room . . . wondered if I should shoot.

"Now!" he barked.

He was holding himself with one hand and running the fingers of the other through his hair and looking directly, directly, into the camera. Vague alarms went off in a number of my cerebral crevices. I activated the little bird call.

Both his arms reached up again, hands straining, seeking, while he pushed upward on his toes so he was lean, leaner … taut. "I'm trying to capture something," he said. "Can you guess what?"

"Enlighten me."

"You are a lazy man."

I clicked, maybe to prove I wasn't lazy.

"The thing I'm after is shamelessness."

"What the hell for?"

"You *would* ask that. To bump up against limits. To be stripped to my truths. Something possible only in company, however. One needs an accomplice."

"I see no candidates in the room."

He was running his hands over his body. "Now!"

I clicked.

"There's a place of personality at the core of each of us," he said. "It's remote, inaccessible to anyone but our own self. A challenge worth taking up, is it not, to make that place accessible to another?" He was looking at me with childlike innocence, a hand over his heart. I clicked.

He crossed his arms so he had a hand on each shoulder. The word archbishop occurred to me the instant before he held his hands out the way a preacher might while offering a benediction. I went down on one knee and released the shutter once, twice.

He struck a pose from Greek statuary. Made me think of a life-sized marble of a boy-god I once saw … nude, smooth-skinned, innocent, beautiful.

"I want sensations related to the feral, but without the savagery, only the freedom. We have all known such moments. Can we be blamed for wanting them again?" He turned full front, hands reaching out in the form of a question, then kept himself motionless. Was he urging me to be a *voyeur*? In my vexation I clicked, though my hand was not

118

entirely steady.

Abruptly he assumed a new position. He was on his knees now, his hands held out in front of him like a prayer book. "When I come to a place of calm in my mind, I think often of … communing. I forget my defences, the usual walls we put up around ourselves."

I was hiding behind the camera, moving from side to side, studying him through the viewfinder, clicking when the moment seemed right. I was a boy with an adult again, our usual configuration, only intensified now.

"I want confession. I want the sound of truth in a voice. That is what I crave. Give me sharp, jagged reality."

"Ultra-honesty," I said.

"Good!"

I clicked while he seized the air in front of him as if he were choking an imaginary foe. Then he kept on doing it … reaching forward with claw-like hands and choking the air.

"What the hell are you doing?" I said.

"Practicing for my statue."

I laughed. Genuinely. It was a relief, a release.

He composed himself, lowered a hand in mock modesty. I clicked and his hand slowly rose, holding himself, pointing.

"You can instruct me, Joff, tell me what positions to assume." He let go, turned to the side, profiled the full arc of his excitement. "We must find ways to venture in, find the wild within." He stopped moving. "I hear no commands."

I mumbled something about the difference between loosening the collar and eliminating it. He would have to be satisfied with my collar undone but still proximate to my neck.

He said sombrely, "If you fail to live your life while alive, when are you going to live it?"

I was only half listening and saw we were up to twenty exposures. "Four shots left," I announced.

He brought his legs together, hunched his shoulders in a strong man's stance – exhibited a raging nudity. Then he turned, leaned, arched his back. I was moving the camera mechanically, my mind veering and careening with the chatter in my head. I thought stupidly of my two fumbling couplings at college; envisioned Damon in Berlin appeasing his demons; remembered our boyhood glade …

He bent over still further, obscenely sharing his privacy. "Now, Joff!" Then he straightened, seemed to flex from head to toe and his voice was a loud whisper, "Again!"

I clicked.

Then, abruptly, "Enough!"

He switched off the lights and went for his clothes. One exposure remained untaken. I looked at my watch. Twenty minutes had passed. He came back with my scotch recharged. "So, do you think me a debauched beast?"

"Of course. Wouldn't have you otherwise."

We chatted about whether a chimpanzee could have done better. I conceded it might not have. My anxieties finally evaporated. Thinking of those anxieties now … they strike me as unfaithful to our friendship. I should celebrate the fact I have a friend who could reveal himself to me the way he did, and the fact I have another, a great lady in America, to whom I can recount such events. I find myself inclined to thank him, and you. Life sends us strange turns and satisfying consolations. The more of each the better, I say.

Damon telephoned yesterday, said the photos were ripping good and I should consider photography if my language skills ever fail. Right. I will take up a paint brush next, or maybe try my hand with your clay.

Another call from Mrs. Stockton. She wonders if she can care for my declining father much longer. I must play doctor and diplomat from a distance to regulate the situation. You may add those professions to my list.

I send you all my skills.

Joff

Saturday
17th Oct. 1936

Dear Heidi,
Remember Penelope Perkins? Hostess of the nation's giddiest hour on the wireless? Britain's fearless guide through the nettles of modern mores? Of course you do. Well then, you can guess what has happened. Yet another reckless foray into the limelight for our friend. It happened last night and he said a few things I have never heard him say before.

After introducing Damon as a renowned artist who for many years has made tongues wag, dizzy Penelope asked him to name his gods.

"My gods? You offer a provocation, Miss Perkins. None to whom I send prayers, I can assure you. I do have a trio of mortal heroes, however."

"Of *course* I meant your heroes," Penny screeched. "Do pardon me."

"I should warn you, Miss Perkins. Not a single one of my heroes, so far as I know, ever laid brush to canvas."

"All the more revealing of your character and life influences, Mr. Chadwick. Do tell!"

"Are you acquainted with Edwin Hubble, Miss Perkins?"

"The astronomer!" rang her delight at not being stumped.

"Precisely. The man who defied conventional thinking and helped us understand nothing less than the immense and intricate nature of the cosmos. A man deeply, deeply into reality, on a sublimely scientific basis."

"And number two?" It sounded to me like the high-pitched hostess had heard quite enough about Edwin Hubble.

"Friedrich Nietzsche could never be regarded as a runner-up, Miss Perkins."

"I *am* sorry. You admire Friedrich …?"

"Nietzsche, Miss Perkins. A fearless philosopher of the will to live. An exponent of the human potential. Nietzsche taught that man, and art, can incarnate boldness. He was – "

"Most interesting," Penelope chimed, betraying a complete lack of interest. "And the third? Whom I will dare not call number three."

"Are you certain you wish to know, Miss Perkins? My third hero is Jack London. He stormed the page with harpoons and bare knuckles.

Have you read *Martin Eden*?"

Penelope responded with a throttled denial which sounded like something was stuck in her throat. "Listeners," said Damon, "I should tell you, Miss Perkins is shaking her head and a scandalised look has invaded her eye. Imagine an educated Englishman exalting an American teller of dog stories and gold rush yarns. Get thee to a library, Madame. You will find assorted amazements in London's work, few of them properly celebrated."

I imagine Penny was near to having kittens, but she found her voice and kept it level. "Mr. Chadwick, you have named two Americans and a German. Are there no Englishmen among your heroes?"

"Actually none top of mind."

"How can that *be*?" said Penelope, her nip and chase reviving.

"In these dangerous times," said Damon, "one is more likely to have favourite villains."

"Villains? How delicious. Who would *they* be?"

I thought I heard Damon take a deep breath. I took one too. I may be his best friend, but that doesn't mean I can always predict him. The salute to Nietzsche came as a bewildering surprise. I had never heard that name pass his lips.

"The men who would meddle in matters that needn't concern us," he said. "Let the continent be. Leave it alone. Let the Europeans settle their own affairs."

"To whom are you referring, Mr. Chadwick?" The 'referring' was vintage Penelope. It issued like a long reedy trill. She was fully restored and genuinely interested.

"The men who would run us straight into another war. The entire pack of those growling wolves. At their head of course is Churchill. He would lead us a nasty chase, that one."

"*Oh, bloody hell!*"

Mary leaped to her feet. Did I tell you my dear wife was listening with me?

"Sssshhhhh, I want to hear," I said, looking with surprise at my usually unflappable spouse.

"Turn off the silly brute!"

I did nothing of the kind, so Mary took herself away and slammed the bedroom door behind her. A bit of domestic drama for you, Heidi, not a frequent occurrence, but there you are. Mary has never been keen on Damon, and not because of his secret nature. In our eleven years of marriage we may have discussed that part of him half a dozen times, and then carefully, like an unexploded bomb, and only because someone may have inquired if our famous friend was still unmarried. No, I would guess Mary shares your jaundiced view of his privileged place in my life. She resents that if Damon and I were numbers in a club of two he would be One and I would somehow be Fourteen. Like you, however, she refuses to own up. Instead she clams up, or changes the subject, the habitually fair Mary who would never say a bad word where none is warranted. She accepts that Damon is my oldest friend. Which does not endear him, does not absolve him, it only preserves him from banishment.

Penny Perkins for her part has never been one for politics. Wisely sensing it would be reckless to follow Damon's lead, she steered him into a discussion of contemporary British art, then to his work habits. I switched off when she poked at his sartorial preferences! Besides, I was anxious to make it up with Mary.

My spouse has her heroes too and when you speak ill of the man with the cigar, well, watch out, you blunder with big feet into Mary's minefield. She adores Winston. A glance at the bookshelves in our bedroom provides the testimony. Mary's literary pantheon is crowded with novelists and campaigners for women's rights. Churchill is the one and only politician and historian represented there. His works are lined up like soldiers and share the most privileged shelf with Mary's current pet Rosamond Lehmann, a prized first edition of Sylvia Pankhurst's *The Suffragette*, and a signed copy of Mary Allen's *The Pioneer Policewoman*.

Mary's attachment to Churchill actually began as a disappointment on her sixteenth birthday. Her father, a retired army man and Lancashire councilman, presented her with Churchill's biography of his father, *Lord Randolph Churchill*. She rebelliously treated it as a pedestal for her desk lamp, spine contemptuously turned toward the wall. (What she really wanted was an overnight stay in London and a show in the West End.) Only months later did boredom drive her to open the silly thing. She was amazed when it planted hooks in her. She became immersed in the grandeur and formality of Victorian life and what she calls the 'dignified intrigue' of its politics. Of course the most important discovery was of this uncharted dimension within herself, the part she had little known could be fascinated by narratives of the past. She gave full credit to the author whom she recognised as a thinker and stylist of special power. The book turned her into a Churchill devotee.

No half measures for my Mary even when she was a teen. On her next visit to London she combed the second-hand bookshops of Charing Cross and went home with all of Churchill's works, from *The Malakand Field Force* to *My African Journey*. After that she loyally purchased his books while following the waxing and waning of his political career. No one needed more than the occasional glance at a newspaper to follow Churchill's long, bendy, often glorious – and equally abortive – political path. Has anyone generated more ink than him this century? At one point or another he has held most of the prominent positions in Cabinet, except the highest. They say he was too bumptious, too intractable, too commanding to ever be allowed the keys to Number 10. Now he has become marginal of course, conspicuously denied a place in Cabinet. Churchill partisans would claim he was left out because of his imposing intellect and breadth of experience. They say Baldwin rightly fears being outshone. Still, despite Churchill's exile to the sidelines, no one can claim to be a more prominent fixture on the national scene.

When I met Mary in 1925 she was reading the third volume of *The World Crisis*. When we married six months later the fourth volume accompanied us on our honeymoon. I guess you can mark me down as the world's most tolerant husband; Churchill shared our bed many a night. I presented Mary with the fifth volume a full fortnight before it went into bookshop windows. My little coup came of cajoling a review copy from a friend at *The Spectator*. The cost was a lavish lunch at Manfredi's, supplemented by a bottle of Talisker. That was shortly after Vicky arrived, so we were often *four* in bed those days: a reader, a book, a baby, and an occasionally useful male accessory.

Your correspondent may be tolerant, but not infinitely tolerant. Mary often attends Mr. Churchill's public lectures, but I resist joining her. I find the chubby icon somewhat irritating. His ability to transform in mid-speech from bulldog to cuddly cherub appeals to Mary, but strikes

124

me as sham. What's more, when he reverts to his most pretentious self and paints the air with baroque language I am rapidly reminded of his well-known weakness for strong brandy. Don't misunderstand me, the sizeable fraternity of Churchill-haters cannot count me as a member, but neither can I side with my father and the Ken Retingers who regard him as some kind of Cassandra. For years now Churchill has been embarrassing the government with inside knowledge about both the speed of Germany's rearmament and the decayed state of Britain's military – a recipe, in his view, for "mortal danger to the life of our island." People wonder where he gets his facts and figures. The speculation is that someone high in the F.O. is passing confidential documents to him.

Churchill would have us believe everyone who decides foreign policy in this country is wrongheaded, and only his prodigious intellect has kept pace with events. At least that is the impression he creates when he rises in the Commons, hooks his thumbs in his waistcoat, and imagines he's orating in the Senate of ancient Rome. He does enjoy the sound of his own rumble! I heard him recently on the wireless, bleating over the need to boost army enlistment, commission new warships and *rapidly* build more front-line fighter aircraft. He keeps poking and badgering in the Commons like a one-man political party. Some wonder why anyone should listen to him. Churchill is the man who gave us the great cock-up at Gallipoli. You can measure his extraordinary resilience by the fact that his career survived such a disaster.

"Your friend's remark about Mr. Churchill," said Mary, "was beyond the pale."

"I agree. Totally uncalled for. He must have had a few."

"Fiddlesticks! He was sober as a judge." Mary was in bed with Huxley's new novel, *Eyeless In Gaza*. She put it aside and gave me a coy smile. "Sorry for flying off like that."

"My love, whenever a friend of mine offends you in the slightest, you may fly off to your heart's content."

"You simply must not attack an elder statesman with such a crude remark when so many people are listening."

"I reckon his purpose was to make them sit up and take notice."

"You can tell him some of us got up and took our notice home."

"Damon has persuaded himself that Germany is being defamed. I suppose he regards Churchill as a principal defamer."

"Your friend is guilty of his own charge then. He has insulted a great man."

"Darling, most people think Churchill is ringing a false alarm."

"It does not sound false to me, and if Mr. Churchill says a thing I should tend to believe it."

"I understand, darling, but in this case he antagonises almost everybody. He says Germany under the Nazis is a wicked place and a danger to the world, full stop. In his judgment Hitler should be condemned outright. He rails against the smallest compromise. How practical is that? Sorry to say, but for quite a large number of people Churchill has become the batty uncle in the attic."

My spouse would make a suitable nominee for Home Secretary, but as she herself would admit she comes unprepared to take over the Foreign Office. She can recite chapter and verse the latest poverty statistics from Wales and unemployment figures from the Midlands, and she can certainly tell you the name of every cabinet minister in recent history who expressed himself honourably on gender equality … but Mussolini's invasion of Abyssinia? The Japanese plunder of China? Civil war in Spain? *Nein.*

Mary picked up her novel. "Tell Damon he should pay attention to his painting and leave politics to the politicians."

"Darling, you are not the first to suggest it. How's Mr. Huxley?"

"Higgledy-piggledy in this one. I like a beginning, middle and end in a story, all nicely tied together."

I have come to the end of this letter, dear Heidi. Heaven knows if it ties nicely to the beginning! Hoping you are well and happy.

As ever,

Joff

Saturday
24th Oct. 1936

Dear Heidi,

Lovely note, yours of the twelfth, thanks so much. I do admire your life and wish I could have one like it. Your country club sounds divine, though the image of you with a golf stick fails to register; you must be pulling my leg. I would never be so crass as to talk about money or inquire after your husband's bank balance, but this pursuit of pleasure and high living comes at an extravagant cost, *n'est-ce pas*?

You tell me nothing about your work. Are you on extended holiday? What is happening in your studio?

Yes, my colleague Ken's heart and zeal do commend him. Would you believe he wangled a lunch with his Member of Parliament this week? He said it took half a dozen letters and as many telephone messages, but he finally extracted an invitation. He was passionately pleased with himself.

"Ken," I chided, "the fellow's a government backbencher, a nobody. He has no power."

"I concede he has no influence on policy. Still, he can raise his voice in the party caucus."

"Kenneth, what did you ask him to raise his voice *about*?"

"Tanks."

"Tanks?"

"The allocation in the last budget for upgraded tank design *has not been spent*."

"And this agitates you?"

Not for the first time Ken gave me an incredulous look. According to Ken, I should understand, all of us in Britain should understand, *people throughout Europe* should understand, Germany is rearming to reach a point where it can pursue aggression with impunity. If we want to save the peace, we have to be prepared for war. Apparently Ken instructed (instructed!) his M.P. to find out why the budgeted monies for new tank design has not been dispensed.

My colleague is an eternal optimist, bless his soul, but I pity him his dreams and ambitions. Before his journey is done he will be in a grand position to write a twentieth century *Gullible's Travels*. Lately he has expressed hopes of promotion within the F.O. He fails to grasp that the four floors above us are packed with sinecures for bluebloods. The place will become a meritocracy at roughly the same time tomcats embrace monogamy. Fools like Tremayne from the privileged classes will rise sooner than smart young chaps like Ken.

Speaking of Tremayne, the photo in the cutting is of the film star Ronald Colman. I had a good laugh when I saw it in yesterday's *Standard*. Tremayne could easily be Ronald's twin, take my word for it. I send it in case you take up the challenge I suggested. Anything to get you into the studio!

Damon was out of sorts this week. When we met at The Squire's, I congratulated him on his performance with Miss Perkins. He answered with a dour grunt, so I spared him the vivid image of Mary leaping angrily to her feet. Instead I said, "You were really quite eloquent."

"My eloquence didn't have the required effect."

"What effect would that be?"

He ignored me.

"Incidentally," I said, "when did you become a fan of Nietzsche?"

"Been reading him for years."

"You have not!"

Up went his glass, down the ale, and our friend got to his feet for another.

"I sense a loafer in my presence," I said when he rejoined me. "Get thee to the studio and pick up a damn brush."

"The idea isn't coming."

"You've told me for years that ideas come as you work. Wait for ideas and the work will never start."

He was watching the smoke from his cigarette curl toward the ceiling. "I need to think," he said. Then his face came alive. "Join me for a pipe."

I frowned. His pipe habit strikes me as a brother vice to his much bigger unmentionable vice. For some reason I have always related the two. Maybe that is why the pipe never appealed to me. There are sides to his life I would prefer not to know about.

His eyes stopped darting about. They were fixed on mine. "Come with me. We shall at last share a pipe."

I told him I was sorry but the pipe was still not my cup of tea. He was not to be denied however. The distracted look on his face had vanished. "How many times must I tell you?" he said. "The pipe offers an experience you must have. See what I have seen. See it for yourself."

Damon was speaking to me in complete candour, much the same way I write to you in these letters. The realisation caught me short. My resistance seemed silly. I said I would think about it. Which brought a smile to his face. "Good for you, Joff. You will go to amazing places in your mind, revisit amazing memories."

"Not so fast. I have questions. Where does the. . . ingestion, take place?"

"Our little circle meets at different homes. The better to avoid inquisitive neighbours and such."

"Your 'little circle'?"

"An eclectic group of associates, not of the variety you may be fearing."

"Am I acquainted with any of these … associates?"

"Not personally."

"You mean I would recognise some of their names?"

"Oh, yes."

"Any in government?"

"I will say no more."

Into my head came a polluting image, unsummoned, of Damon and his unnamed friend in Berlin, strolling between the trees on the Unter den Linden. Rampant are the world's zeals, appetites and hidden corruptions.

"I won't pass out in a daze? Wake up delirious?"

"Myth! You'll have some queasiness at first, so be warned. The impact might be severe, but it passes after a few minutes."

"And after that, what should I expect?"

"Think of the behaviour of your mind while you sleep, its power to remember events or develop new uncommon events. Well, normal dreaming is not in the same league with your waking mind once you take the pipe. You will unlock a tremendous power."

"Will I go home a vegetable to my Mary?"

He sighed. "I can only say again as I have said to you for years, I never look for escape in opium. Rather the opposite. Clarity is what I seek. Lucidity. *Insight*."

"You have weakened my defences."

He raised his pint. "To the audacity of Joffrey Pearson."

"More like the dragooning of him."

I felt we were back in our secret glade, which was a welcome sensation. The last time I did anything this crazy was before I met Mary. Remember the foolishness at Blackpool? At least that wasn't illegal.

Wish me luck.

Joff

Saturday
31st Oct. 1936

Dear Heidi,
We ought to sit in a meadow on a spring day. Hold hands and be witnesses. The sunlight would be a living thing. Our condition would approach awe. I did it. I went with Damon and shared a pipe. Be patient with me, I will try to tell all.

He treated me to Manfredi's first. I was nervous. He saw my tension and told me vulgar stories about German art collectors, none of which I found diverting. It was good however to have him in regaling form. As the waiter cleared our dishes he said, apropos of nothing, "Did you know Picasso is coming to London?"

"Oh?"

"To the Clement, next summer. The gallery has scored a coup. The exhibition will be a batch of new works, cubist stuff and related rubbish."

"Why should it interest you?"

"It has given me something to think about."

"In what sense?"

"There you have my dilemma. I am not quite sure yet." He then announced our liqueur was waiting for us elsewhere.

I felt furtive as we took a cab to Baron's Court. We got out on the high street and walked to a row of flats on Edith Road. "Always more discreet to arrive on foot," said Damon. "Draws less attention."

"Which only reminds me we are about to do something illegal."

"A thing perfectly law-abiding people have been doing for centuries. Be of good cheer, Joff, a new experience awaits."

"Right. Participation in a den of iniquity. A foreign substance introduced into my lungs. Dazed orientals lying about in grotesque postures."

"Have you dusted off your Dickens?"

"Smoke like lethal fog in the room. A den filled with vice and idlers. Policemen coming to arrest me."

He laughed. "Hoaxed by Hogarth! First of all, put the idea of a lurid den out of your mind. We are going to a *home*, with no Chinamen anywhere near. And as I have said to you many times, I do not seek oblivion with the pipe but the exact bloody opposite."

We stopped in front of Number 33. It was a three-storey block of brown brick, bland, down at heels, made invisible by its commonness. Separate concrete steps curled down to a basement flat. I noticed a child's drawing of a bright red maple leaf in one of the basement windows. Damon took me by the arm and ushered me up the stairs.

"Whose house is this?"

"Best you don't know."

The door rapper was gleaming silver in the shape of a tiny book opened at the middle. Damon tapped delicately. We were let in by an elderly woman whom our friend greeted with a double-cheek kiss. The woman said nothing, only smiled to reveal hideous teeth.

I felt a sensation of transport, an impression of … dislocation. Have you ever had an appointment in an ordinary building on a street as common as they come, and then, once inside, felt as if you have suddenly crossed a mysterious boundary? The hag led us into a large drawing room where the light was hazy. As Damon had promised, our liqueur was waiting. A carafe of a colourless liquid on a silver tray with two exquisite crystal glasses. He whispered something to the woman who withdrew without a word. Then he filled the glasses. "To our travels," he said.

I could feel him watching me as I sipped the drink. "Sambuca," he said.

I found it horrid, an oily sticky scum.

I looked about the room. Every inch of wall was covered by tapestries and hanging carpets. The tapestries depicted misty islands on emerald seas. The carpets scowled with intricate geometric designs and dizzied the eye with undulating spiral patterns. The drape over the window featured a goddess-like female with several arms and impossibly long black hair. Scattered about was an unruly assortment of carved wooden chairs and small lacquered tables, oriental cousins all. I was in a Chinese Persian Hindu blizzard of a room. A *bohemian buffoon lives here*.

The sambuca was filthy, clinging to my palate like liquid sand. *I don't belong here!*

"Come," said Damon.

He took the glass from me and led the way up a spacious stairway

132

lined with antique portraits of formal gentry, including one life-sized curio of a bewigged gentleman in a pastoral setting. He held a riding crop and appeared master of all he surveyed. Said Damon, "Behold, a Joshua Reynolds."

"Ah, my annual salary multiplied by ten or eleven."

"True, but an early Reynolds, sadly weak on expression. Hardly worth your time."

"Hardly."

At the top of the stairs we came to a decidedly more contemporary painting of a magnificently flowered garden in which a host of people were … cavorting.

"Christ Jesus," was all I could muster.

"Chadwick Damon, actually."

The crimson signature in the lower left corner, our friend's familiar laceration, gave me a turn. "Christ Jesus!"

Everyone in the picture was naked and joyously coupling, All the men were conspicuously negroid, black as coal and supremely muscular. The women were delicate, even fawn-like, and white as fresh-bloomed lilies. Black and white in vivid colour. I had the impression the abundant genitalia in the picture, the gaping quims, arcing members, tautly quivering testicles, represented another form of earthly harvest, like the ripe peaches, pears, pomegranates and bananas sumptuously drooping from the surrounding trees.

"Good lord, when did you do this?"

"Years ago. One of my uncatalogued works. Imagine introducing it to Penelope Perkins. Come!"

Again, Heidi, the sensation of crossing a bizarre boundary. It was like the sudden sense of remoteness you feel when you dive underwater. Damon led me into a small room lit by candles which stood on a row of stone pedestals. The room was otherwise bare save for three canvas mats on the floor. An undraped window looked out on pitch black. Damon sat cross-legged on a mat and gestured me to do the same. My condition was tame, reflexive, obedient.

"The two of us are alone in the house," he said. "No one else is expected tonight. Zarine is preparing the mixture and will join us shortly."

"Zarine?"

"The good lady who greeted us."

"Is she the mistress of the house?"

"She looks after it. The owner prefers his estate in Dorset. This is a hideaway for a few private treasures, and a prudent address for indulgences."

"The painting on the landing … this Dorset toff is a patron of yours?"

"That charming commission paid for my first motorcar. Remember the burgundy Vauxhall? Please forget I ever mentioned Dorset. I do slip now and again."

"Must tell you, the old woman's teeth gave me a fright."

"Zarine is not nearly as old as you think. She was one of our host's treasures, salvaged from Armenia in 1915. Preserved from murder, actually. Just a retainer now I'm afraid."

"More a relic," I said.

"Be kind, Joff."

At that moment she of the gruesome dentition squatted on the extra mat. Giving no indication of having heard my cruel remark she laid down a tray of long-stemmed pipes. The stems of the pipes were carved from what I took to be jade and silver. One appeared fashioned from petrified bamboo. The little ceramic bowls grafted onto them were decorated with bucolic scenes in blue ink. Even to my untrained eye these pipes were rare artefacts. Damon, forever reading my mind, said, "They came out of China and are probably three hundred years old. The British Museum would love to have them."

Also on the tray were a diminutive spirit lamp, a bowl of gummy black pellets, and metal skewers like extra-long needles. The silent Zarine lighted the spirit lamp and moved it to the centre of the tray. She was not as crone-like as I first thought. With her teeth hidden she shed a good number of years. Best if she sewed her lips shut. A heartless observation, it approaches nasty, forgive me …

Zarine upped and left without a word, closing the door of the little room gently behind her. "Quiet woman," I said.

"The Turks cut out her tongue."

Damon speared a pellet with one of the long needles and with his other hand selected the jade pipe. Reclining on his side he guided the impaled pellet into the bowl of the pipe, then inverted the bowl directly over the flame of the spirit lamp. As the pellet vaporised he sucked on the pipe and clapped his eyes on me. He looked all candour, inquiry and invitation as he drew the smoke in. The pipe made a faint whistling sound as he steadily inhaled. Once the fumes of the pellet were exhausted he ceased sucking. His face swelled as he kept the smoke in his lungs. Finally he exhaled a brownish plume.

"They cut out her tongue?"

The muscles in his face shuddered, refocused.

"At least Zarine's life was spared," he said. "Her three brothers were butchered. Her parents took bullets. History has forgotten the Armenians. I suppose the world is too ashamed to remember."

He placed the pipe back on the tray with the ease of a man liberated from some vast weariness. Then he sat still, gazing inwardly, but seemed to be … emerging. He took a deep breath, said, "Taste the aroma."

An odour more like. Pungent, severely sweet, cloying, not unpleasant but surely no 'aroma'. We, the room, everything seemed abruptly clothed in it.

"A pipe, Joff, choose a pipe."

I was a passenger in one of our friend's imaginary trains. The track would take us wherever the track was bound. Enough new scenery had already swept by to make the evening memorable. I chose the silver pipe. It was not silver, I now noticed, but ivory. I held it tightly for fear of dropping. My lord, what a beautiful thing, an intricate carving of peasants, animals, fields, huts; a feudal moment in China alive on the stem of a pipe made from an elephant's tusk.

Damon was a dear. He directed my initiation with the same fuss he had shown with the sainted camera in the studio. I leaned forward as our friend lanced an opium pill … Heidi, it may be difficult to provide you with the essence of what went through my mind during the next several hours.

Stop.

I am well ahead of myself. I want you to know all. First, I must tell you, there was distress. It came in two waves, a wave of coughs followed by a tide of nausea. This was no mere cigarette. My lungs rebelled at the sting. For a scary interval I coughed horribly. Then came the dizziness, incomparably more intense than those baby-like episodes of vertigo I told you about. I felt violently poisoned. I cringed, quailed, doubled over, almost vomited. But it passed. What a blessing, it passed.

"All is fine," I heard Damon say, his arm about me as I recovered. "You have now paid the price of admission."

His words struck me as hauntingly precise. For a moment I was lost in contemplating the remark as an observation of genius. The bite in my lungs, the blow to my solar plexus, had sanctioned me to proceed. I was experiencing a sensation I can only describe as radical composure. I looked at Damon and swung my eyes about the room. But I was seeing inwardly…

My eyelids have sagged. Wish to tell you more, everything, but not just now, must put it off, must sleep. Until soon my sweet, your done in,

Joff

Saturday
7th Nov. 1936

Dear Heidi,

Thanks for yours of the twenty-sixth, which explains a rumour I heard in the lunchroom about American newspapers coming off ships with pages scissored out. I was wondering if freedom of the press had been abolished without me hearing about it.

No one here would think it troublesome for the King to carry on with a married American. He has already done it with any number of married Europeans. But you say the lady is twice divorced? Now that would be scandalous. A two-timer once again on the rebound sounds novel even for Edward and his saga of mistresses. Your newspapers are free to spread such gossip, ours voluntarily keep silent when it comes to the royals… noblesse oblige turned on its head. But government snoops cutting pages out of imported newspapers! That goes too far.

If the affair continues I suppose the public will have to learn of it. Discretion has limits even in buttoned-up Blighty. I won't much care, but my Mary will be enraged on behalf of the nation, the church, decency and decorum. Who is this Simpson woman? Do send some cuttings. Juicy ones only. Take them from your tabloids!

Almost two weeks since Edith Road, but the experience is still intact in my mind. The sensations endure as if branded in memory. I promised you a full retelling, but beware, some bits may startle. They still startle me.

I had expected drowsiness and lethargy to set in after the inhalation. Happily I was mistaken. After the nausea ebbed I felt no drain of energy, but rather a surge of mental strength. The lamp in my mind glowed bright. It shone on luxuriant Memory. The room was small and bare save for the stone pedestals and candles, yet my sense was of infinite space. You could imprison me, lock the door, no matter … I had Memory.

I was standing on the front steps of the house in Shimpling. I had just turned nineteen. My sister Irene was with me. We were waiting for Father to arrive. Mother had gone with a member of his regiment to bring the maimed pater home from the hospital. He had been invalided out of the army a few months before the Armistice. I was bundled in a coat and scarf against the chill. Irene shivered in a leather jacket, the gin on her breath thick and sour. My wretched sister belonged to the sad, pathetic, very thin ranks of those who believed Britain had had no business fighting Germany. She was muttering inanities about the crime done our family by imperialist Britain, and cursing about the utter foolishness of Edgar Pearson volunteering.

The car drove up. It was flying the pennant of my father's regiment. The driver, in dress uniform and beret, hurriedly came round to help my father out. It would be a long while before he would feel confident on his prosthetic. Mother stood to the side with his crutches. On this day he wanted our first look at him to be as we had always known him. The moment moved me to pride. I could forgive all his extended absences, his career stasis, the lunacy of his enlistment. I could forget my little sister, her perverse grievances and foul drinking, my exams waiting in London and the heartbreak a certain Melissa had recently inflicted upon me. My father had given half a leg to the soil of France on behalf of England and now he was strapped with an oak replacement and coming home under his own power. I went up to him with arms wide and for the one time in my adult life hugged him.

This is good. You belong here.

Damon was wearing a charmer's smile and studying the palm of his hand as if he were about to paint it. It was not he who had said *This is good.* Evidently I had said it to myself. I had the impression then of being two persons, two myselfs. One of the two had said to the other, You belong here. A conundrum that, the seeming reality of two myselfs, but I could not ponder it just then, I had been shunted elsewhere into memory...

Mary and I were in our cups, langorous after making love, indulging in one of our guilty pleasures, guessing, speculating, giggling about the secrets of couples. What is their special glue? Has their initial attraction waned? Can they still surprise each other? Is one allowed to interrupt the other while reading the morning paper? Do they still do it in the sitting room on an intoxicated whim? How often? What in heaven's name do they guess about *us*?

A knife of sound brought me back to the small room where I was sitting cross-legged on the floor. Damon had unlatched the window. The candle flames on the stone pedestals bowed and bobbed in the draft…

Vicky was ignoring me as she petted the lion-head handles on my desk. She was a chubby toddler and had waddled across the drawing room to the little nook where I write. In her other hand she was tenaciously gripping a favourite purple bunny her godfather Damon had given her. "Hello, plum-pie," I said. In truth her face was distinctly apple-like, rosy cheeks bursting with the juice of childhood, but my preference in nicknames followed a strict consonance and stopped at plum, peach and pumpkin. The form of nickname at any given moment was a function of mood and my angel's comportment. I could never be sure what sort of pie Vicky was going to be from one hour to the next. Some matters of child-worship are infinitely complex and defy a father's analytical tools. My angel finally shifted her attention from the brass lion-head and showed me her purple bunny. "Pu'ple 'unny," she said. "Pu'ple 'unny." "Yes, my peach, pu*rrr*ple *bbb*unny."

"Joff, are you well?"

"What? Yes! What is it?"

"You're crying."

So I was. Tears were streaming down my face. I had no time then for the why, though I can explain it now. The tears were venerating the simple and basic, links in the chain … continuity. I felt an elation. Also a surging desire to be *honest*. "I have to tell you something, Dame."

"Yes, dear boy."

"This is a gift. Thank you."

"No gratitude please, it is only what I owe you."

"Having you as my friend is one of the great prizes of my life."

"It delights me to hear that, more than you know."

The next thing I remember was Damon's hand on my shoulder. He was standing over me, helping me to my feet. "Come."

"Where are we going?"

"Across the hall."

To a room with deep cushioned chairs. We spent the rest of the evening sunk in luxurious equanimity, barely speaking. Damon said at one point, "This is the law of the house, to be nowhere and no-when except here and now."

Philosopher Joff, in his speechless wisdom, almost grasping the meaning of his friend's comment, replied with a nod of profound endorsement. At another point, it may have been minutes later – or hours or days – Damon mused aloud, "I seem to be breaking the house law."

"Why do you say that?"

"I find myself thinking about Picasso."

From a distance away I heard philosopher Joff say, "Why? Doesn't he enrage you?"

"Utterly."

"So why think about him?"

"I need a thunderclap," he said.

"You are a lunatic," I replied.

"That may very well be."

Hard to describe how I felt during our time in that cushioned place. For a long period I felt as if a wind had gone through me, leaving nothing but the core me. All the little worries, the daily distracting clutter, were taken away. I was in a kind of void, a pleasant void, I had that distinct impression. Something else. I felt a benevolence. This I remember powerfully. I had no fear for the world with all its struggles, failures, conflicts and catastrophes. It might stumble to the lip of one abyss after another but would always stop short, save itself, begin again. The world is addicted to new beginnings … the bread and drink of insatiable time.

"Come!"

Damon helped me from the depths of the great chair, though I could certainly have managed. I looked at my watch. Four hours had passed.

"Before we leave, another Chadwick hangs in this house, also unknown to the public. Would you like to – "

"Take me directly!"

Down the hall he led me into a room that was obviously the master bedchamber. It contained the largest bed I have ever seen, an expanse of mattress covered with black sheets and framed by a four-poster canopy fitted with an overhead mirror. This charade of a Parisian brothel stood preposterously high off the floor and was flanked by carpeted steps for mounting. The bed ruled the room like some mad flagship.

Drapes covered the four walls. I could not tell the location of the window, or if there was a window at all. Directly across from the huge bed, that island citadel to which my eyes kept returning, Damon drew a drape.

Good lord god on high.

Remember the Chadwick at the top of the stairs, the edenic garden lush with vaginas and flourishing members? Here was a cousin of that painting, or a perverse uncle. Arcadian again, though the setting was not bucolic, but rather blatantly phallic, a place of bare granite platforms ringed by obelisks. The scene suggested depraved Greece, degenerate Rome, primal Vice. There were no women in the painting. The couples on the platforms (and the threesomes, the foursomes) were all men. Each granite divan hosted a different … combination. Clearly the aim was to leave nothing to the imagination. The priapic riot was pure exhibitionism, the effect almost photographic. Think of Beardsley at his bawdiest under a noonday sun. An obscenity, Heidi. A vast, fierce, heaving, deliberate obscenity.

"This paid for the studio," said Damon, and I caught a note of justification.

My voice said, "I assume the Dorset gentleman is a homosexual."

"I haven't shown you the other paintings in the room. He is a … libertine."

"Did you fuck him?" This came out unbidden. It popped from my mouth like a subversive sprite. The surprising thing was, the question didn't embarrass me, much less mortify.

Damon, possibly amused, replied without missing a beat. "One night, years ago, he was at sea and needed a good oar. I brought him nicely to the beach. Come!"

He held my arm as we descended the stairs and guided me from the dark house as if he were a manservant helping an invalid. "I really am capable of navigating these stairs, Dame."

"People have been known to tumble down them. I am only anxious to ensure the occasion is not spoiled in any way."

Outside, walking in the deep night, I asked, "Will you invite me again?"

"If you wish."

"Do you come often?"

"Seven, eight times a year."

"Next month, then?"

He stopped me on the sidewalk and scanned my face under the lamplight. "Can't, Joff. I will be in Berlin."

"Ah, that's fine."

"I think not," he said, seeing right through me. "We will not return soon."

"May I ask why not?"

"You have experienced the fascination. I am not about to lead you into the torment."

"Don't be absurd. What torment?"

He took me by the arm and we continued on toward the high street.

"Take the pipe in a week's time or a month's time and your wish for it will only double. I've seen it. The craving takes over and the descent begins. Ask me four or five months from now, and I'll invite you a month after that."

This made me bristle. I felt he had talked down to me.

"You know it from personal experience, do you?"

"Sorry?"

Like a child feeling lashed, I wanted to lash back. "When you disappeared you were 'drying out', weren't you? Or whatever it's called for addicts of the pipe."

"What *are* you going on about?"

"Last Christmas. We never raised a glass! You disappeared for months, then claimed you were working in Paris. What was it really, a clinic on a Swiss mountain?"

He was scanning my face again, intently, as a scientist might observe a novel organism he had created in the laboratory. What mysterious behaviour would the organism perform next?

"Are you going to answer me?" I said, squirming on his lab bench.

"My dear Joff," he said, maddeningly amused, and more maddeningly dismissive, "I have never needed a clinic. Never been within a country mile of one."

We had reached the high street where a single taxi was waiting in the rank. He saw me into it, said a smiling goodnight and shut the door without getting in. Then he told the driver my address, gave him a pound note, and walked back in the direction we had come.

The moment I was alone in the taxicab I realised I had spent the evening outside the boundaries of my own self. I had strayed, become an unJoff. As for Damon, I had already forgiven him. My foolishness about a long-forgotten escapade no doubt deserved his indifference. What had possessed me? And there's this, Heidi, about the lure of the pipe… I may have denied it to our friend but to you I confess. Best if I stay away for a good long while.

  Much love,
  Joff

Saturday
21st Nov. 1936

Dear Heidi,

Received yours of the thirteenth. It floored me. The handwriting was yours but the voice ... unrecognisable. ('Sucking fantasy like a drunken lout ... indulging weakness ... fleeing from reality.') Good lord. You have rebuked me in the past, at times very harshly indeed, but not like this. The pipe with Damon cannot be what so infuriated you, there must be something else behind your attack. All I did was take in a bit of opium, I launched no missiles at civilisation. Your letter is unfair.

Please know, you start no quarrel with me when you say I should keep clear of dodgy houses and risky doings, but with the verdict of 'guilty man' you go too far. Bringing up the law only confirms your married respectability. Where was the offence? Who were the victims? I am with Mr. Bumble on this. The law is an ass, an idiot.

You are still harder on Damon as the instigator, but nothing new there, he has evolved into an established villain in your book. Your charge of *abomination* in regard to the nancy boys in the painting might be accurate, but remember, it was a commission, and did I tell you there was no signature? A wise bit of discretion, because the depictions in that bacchanalia could have put our friend before a magistrate.

We part company again when you mock what I experienced. I do not deserve to be teased. The evening was one of discovery, not debauchment. You say my thoughts were artificially induced, but they were mine no matter how they came. Absent the opium I might never have had the thoughts, I grant you, but they were still every inch mine.

I will admit the Joff of that evening was not the Joff you know. Didn't I admit having strayed? But I came back to the genuine Joff, the Joff who cannot be changed, lost or assimilated, who will always exist in the form you know him. Should events ever prove me wrong, here is when you will know for certain that Joff has transformed permanently into someone you don't know: *when he stops telling you how much he adores you.* I am quite cross with you today, however, and will refrain from telling you how vast a place you occupy in my admiration. Consider yourself punished.

No rumours have yet surfaced in the lunchroom about the King diddling with a Yankee lady. I await with impatience a packet of spicy articles from your American tabloids. Be well, dear girl.

Joff

Saturday
5th Dec. 1936

Dear Heidi,

Can we take up where we left off before the Opium War of '36? I assume we can, because ill feeling has never claimed more than a fleeting place in our relationship.

Thank you for the cuttings. They arrived the very day I no longer needed them, the same day Fleet Street flooded England with ink about the King's romance. Now everybody knows the name, face and lurid biography of Wallis Simpson. (Who would saddle a girl with the name *Wallis?*) Some of us see the woman as a scarlet adventuress and shameless social-climber. Others insist the King should be able to marry whom he likes. On one aspect we are all agreed ... nobody thinks Mrs. Simpson is attractive. Personally, I think she's hideous. A rail-thin scarecrow with a clenched grimace for a face and grasping talons for hands. I would hate to see her anywhere near the throne.

Most of the newspapers admit they kept silent about the affair out of deference. After the King summoned the Prime Minister to the palace a couple of weeks ago and informed him of his intention to marry Mrs. Simpson, a great deal of thunder and lightning boomed and flashed behind the scenes. Now everything is out in the open and the situation no longer permits censorship.

Mrs. Simpson's second marriage was legally dissolved only weeks ago. Mr. Baldwin told the King his government could not accept the sovereign's marriage to a twice-divorced woman, since the country and the Dominions would never accept her as Queen. The idea of a morganatic marriage has been floated, whereby the King could marry Mrs. Simpson if she renounces all claim to title for herself and any children she might bear. That proposal however, based on a concept unknown to British law, has evidently been rejected. At the moment the King is cloistered in the palace, wrestling with his dilemma. No help is coming to him from Mrs. Simpson, who has scurried off to the south of France. The crisis boils down to a stark choice for poor Eddie. Should he fall to what his critics call a mad infatuation, or should he nobly rise to the call of duty? If he insists on marrying Mrs. Simpson, he will have to give up the throne.

The very idea of abdication shocks most people, including me. It has not fazed my spouse, however. Mary has a single response to the matter which she issues with tight-lipped finality: "If he wishes to marry that woman, the King must go."

Everyone has an opinion, even old Jenkins. He said a way ought to be found to reconcile crown and conscience, which I found poetic and gracious. Ken expressed the hope this might be an opportunity to liberate England from medieval monarchy in favour of a sensible republic. He took offence when I laughed at that daydream. Our hidebound Section Head surprised me. Tremayne supports the King unreservedly, says nobody should dictate whom he can or cannot marry. If Edward does go, many will be saddened. He has created no shortage of goodwill with his visits to distressed villages in Wales and a general attitude that seems caring. I haven't the foggiest idea what his decision will be.

About your letters ... your sudden concern about them intrigues me. Rest easy, they are locked in my desk at the F.O. I have never felt alarm about them falling into the wrong hands, since they contain no scandal. They never reflect (alas!) or even acknowledge my little hymns of adoration. Your letters are totally innocent, unlike my own. Which is why I assume you are seeing to their regular incineration.

Damon left for Berlin with a crate of new canvases. Among them are a batch of oils inspired by the photos I took, but he never showed them to me. He spoke to Vicky on the telephone and promised to be home by Christmas. He also promised not to miss our annual tipple this year. I just hope he doesn't replace our time-honoured *Veuve Cliquot* with shots of *Jägermeister*.

Command me. Should I reduce your letters to ashes? I will do as you wish. Because I am, as always,

Your faithful servant,

Joff

Saturday
12th Dec. 1936

Dear Heidi,

All of us here feel we have taken part in a momentous event simply by virtue of being alive when it happened. Edward's farewell speech was moving. I admit to a surge of emotion as Mary and I sat by the wireless. Mary conceded his choice of words was admirable. None of us will soon forget him saying, "I have found it impossible to carry the heavy burden of responsibility and to discharge my duties as King without the help and support of the woman I love." When the speech ended, Mary and I embraced.

"Nothing flatters his reign," she said, "more than his way of leaving it."

"I daresay that is no compliment."

"I mean him no ill will. My sincere hope is that he never regrets what he has done." At that I took my wife into my arms once again. Then we were able to reach Vicky on the telephone and share a few solemn moments, only a few because all the other girls too were receiving calls from their parents.

People were holding onto one another all over Britain. Many were likely weeping for reasons they could not identify. Edward is a beloved figure for some, but for most this was about our country and what it believes in. On the whole I think the King got it right. I should have said the former King. Curious that he wore the crown for less than a year.

Also curious to think we have had three Kings in the space of a single twelve-month. Now we have Edward's little b-b-b-brother as a consolation. Forgive me, I should resist being crude at such a time. By all accounts Bertie is a serious fellow and will make a solid King, though I wager he will avoid microphones. Have you heard that he prefers to be called George VI rather than Albert the Very First?

Perhaps with his quiet integrity the good George will stop us thinking we have had a sad end to a sad year. He is surely more like his father than his brother could ever claim. Mary supports him wholeheartedly and I wish him all the luck in the world.

My mail has been forlorn of late. Let me know all is well, and please instruct me about your letters. Should I consign them to the fire, or preserve them for the enchantment of my old age?

As ever,

Joff

Saturday
19th Dec. 1936

Dear Heidi,
A disturbing incident at work yesterday. Chilling, actually. I stayed late
to do a rush translation sent down by the Permanent Under-Secretary.
Before leaving I went to say goodnight to Tremayne. He was around
the corner in his broom closet. He must have thought his minions
had gone for the day. He had his legs propped atop his desk. He was
leaning back grandly with a magazine. "Oh, Pearson," he gulped, "still
here!"

He hastily swung down his legs and slipped the magazine into his
briefcase.

"Don't mind me," I said breezily, acting as if I hadn't seen what I saw.
"See you tomorrow."

Hell and damnation. Have you ever stumbled onto something ugly
and wished to hell you hadn't? The magazine looked like *Blackshirt*.
Of course Tremayne might have borrowed the vile thing from the
reading room. He might have been looking at it for a work-related
reason. But then, would he have tucked it away so guiltily?

I have made no mention of this to my colleagues, certainly not Ken.
The suspicion would cast a pall, poison the air further. Our Section
Head a closet fascist? Could he be that far-gone? I shall try to forget
what I saw, or what I think I saw. Maybe the thing was something
other than Mosley's hate-sheet.

Must run to meet Mary. Last minute Christmas shopping!

As always,

Joff

Wednesday
23rd Dec. 1936

Dear Heidi,
Looking at your note of the eleventh, all eight grudging lines of it. Suddenly you sound enormously distant. Is there something preoccupying you? I pray you are well and happy.

I shall do as you say with your letters as soon as possible. In a small reading room next to the lunchroom we traditionally light a wood fire just before Saint Nick arrives. Into that Victorian hearth will go your words. You must tell me about the fireplace where you feed mine and whether a tree drooping with ornaments stands nearby and how deep the snow is outside your window and what gifts you receive from That American. A very merry Christmas to you, great lady. Only your second in Boston, but for this admirer it seems you have been away for eons.

Damon scribbled a note from Berlin to say he returns only in the new year, which saddens Vicky no end because he promised to do a portrait of her as a Christmas present. Have you heard from him, our insane friend balancing on the lip of a volcano? His situation strikes fear into me whenever I think of it.

His postcard says he has established a strong market. He actually uses that phrase, 'strong market'. He annoys me on my own account as well as Vicky's. Our champagne tipple at Christmas has been a ritual forever. But I forgive him. The season of good cheer is no time for annoyance, worry or recrimination. Not even a time to loathe Tremayne who yesterday wished his three charges the best of the season and actually gave each of us a bottle of tolerable port. The wonders He doth perform!

This will arrive long after your celebrations but I wish you and Matt a wonderful Christmas. Will write again before the new year.

Much love,
Joff

Sunday
27th Dec. 1936

Dear Heidi,

This will amuse you. It certainly thrilled Vicky. A wood crate addressed to our darling arrived at the flat the day before Christmas. I guessed instantly what it was when I saw the freight markings in *Deutsch*.

The crate was nailed shut like something hazardous to humanity. It took most of my patience and all of my manual dexterity to pry the thing open. Then Vicky waded through layer after layer of packing to unearth the treasure, a framed watercolour the size of the Mona Lisa but incomparably more valuable.

Imagine Vicky in green tartan sitting on a garden ledge. In her clasped hands bloom a red rose and some deeply purple thistle. The Houses of Parliament and Big Ben lurk in the distance. Her posture implies a pensive scholar while her smile reveals raw childhood. The masterpiece is done in spare broad daubs of paint, probably the work of three or four hours for Damon. The likeness startled us. It captures the precocious depth in Vicky's eyes, yet also evokes a tantalising concealment. She is captured looking into the future and seeing something grand. "Oh, this is sterling," said Mary.

"It *is* good," I said.

Vicky was squealing in a delirium of joy.

"She never sat for him," said Mary. "How did he do it?"

"Photographs I suppose, and memory."

"Magic. Tell Damon he has our sincere thanks." I knew this was heartfelt, because only rarely does Damon's name pass Mary's lips.

Vicky wanted the portrait for her room but Mary insisted we hang it in the entrance hall, another rarity for my spouse. Not often does she expose her inner bourgeois. Henceforth all who enter the Pearson home will immediately notice a Chadwick on the wall, and not only that but a Chadwick of a Pearson. I was delighted. It always does me good to catch Mary acting like everybody else.

We did our Christmas pilgrimage to Bury yesterday. Brought the pater a basket from Fortnum's which cheered him no end. He does adore silly delicacies like candied figs and bottle-shaped chocolates laced with cognac. Have you ever tried mango-flavoured crisps? I myself admit to a weakness for plump prunes from California. But I digress.

Mrs. Stockton has stopped making noises about sending my father away, particularly since I agreed to provide her with an increased retainer. Maybe she will invest some of the blackmail in ventilation of the house, which grows more rancid by the visit. In my father's room Mary had to open the window and sit beside it, otherwise she would have fled from the invading odour of tobacco and boiled cabbage. I blame myself, the fault is mine. I should have forced my father to go elsewhere years ago.

At least he seems to have steadied. He showed impressive vitality when he pushed himself up and wrapped his arms around his granddaughter. Ever since she started trundling about in diapers he has regarded her as his greatest prize in life. Vicky always pays proper awe, and I wager it was her respectful attention that stirred him. For a few minutes the pater emerged from his fog. "Vicky, my sweetheart, you are a true wonder. You have become a lady."

"Grandpapa, you can't call me a lady. Ladies are *adults*."

"Nonsense! I will call you a young lady if I must."

He was so obviously pleased and excited I felt bad for being ungenerous with these visits. He lay back on his cushions and his eyes swung about like spent searchlights, but into his hoarse rasp of a voice came a bit of shine and bounce. "She is you to a 't', Mary," he said. "Look at her. She has your eyes, your alertness. A proud lady like her mother!"

"Victoria is her own self, Edgar, you may be sure of that."

"No, no. Look at her. The very mirror of you, Mary."

I rolled my eyes. My father long ago gave Mary all the credit for our daughter's perfection. I was clearly a bystander during Vicky's creation. Not surprising, though. The pater's initial veneration was for Mary herself. When he first met her she happened to be wearing her Auxiliary uniform and incarnating all the warrior queens of Britain, a heaven-sent compensation for my traitor of a sister, and possibly even a remedy for his erratic low-ambition son. As far as my father is concerned the smartest thing I ever did was marry Mary.

"Vicky, will you enlist like your mother?"

"I beg your pardon, grandpapa?"

"Will you go up in armed aircraft?"

Vicky looked to me for help.

My father croaked insistently, "Vicky, will you fly in the RAF like your mother?"

"Grandpapa, mummy's never even *been* in a plane."

The pater was hearing only himself and his eyes were distracted. "Your country will need you, sweetheart, I would be proud if you joined. Are you planning to join? Sweetheart?"

The cost of exertion. The vitality was gone, leaving space for his senility. Mary smiled wanly and said, "The dear, the dear." Our darling Vicky had mist in her eyes.

Heidi, we must take life in both hands, seize the present moment. I do hope whatever was preoccupying you has passed and you are fully yourself again. Health, happiness, success and prosperity in the new year.

Lots of love,

Joff

PART TWO: 1937

This House will in no circumstances fight for its King and Country.

The Oxford Union

Thursday
7th Jan. 1937

Dearest Heidi,
You mischievous devil, you are a sly one. Now all is explained. How dare you keep it a secret for so long? Sincere congratulations to you and Matt. A more illustrious baby will not be born in Boston or anywhere this year or next.
Max!
A name for a great lady's son. He will make his mother proud a thousand times over. The boy will smite all before him with the elegance of a duke, the intellect of a philosopher, and the charm of a scamp. What's more, the boy is an American! He will fling railroads across rivers. He will champion bold ideas. His countrymen will point at the White House and say, "There is your proper home, take it, lead us." My only troubling thought is that Max may grow up to speak like a Bostonian!
In all seriousness, Heidi, I wish you and your husband infinite joy. You have all our love.
Joff

Saturday
16th Jan. 1937

Dear Heidi,

Missing your letters terribly but I will lodge no complaints, I do have some experience of a baby in the house. How is the little chap doing? Bolted to his feet yet? Started talking? I know the wondrous endowments of his mother, so anything is possible.

The new year has brought an interesting possibility. Could mean the occasional reprieve from Tremayne, maybe permanent escape. The chief assistant to the Permanent Under-Secretary is engaging additional German-to-English interpreters, and he cast his eye first over the F.O.'s own people. Lo and behold, he identified yours truly as a candidate. He must have read the Bristol transcript in my personnel file.

Reg Huntington, the Under-Secretary's man, met with Tremayne and myself, to Tremayne's discomfort I'm delighted to say. "Pearson," said Huntington, "we understand you did courses in interpretation."

I could not contradict him. At the same time I was embarrassed to recall my university years. Bristol educated me in indolence and endowed me with apathy. Enrolled as I was in German literature and translation skills, I came under no pressure. My *Deutsch* matched that of a native. As a son of both English and German, translation between the two seemed as natural to me as walking. I did little studying, yet passed my courses handily. My embarrassment stems from feeling I earned my degree under false pretences.

The only real challenge at university came from courses in interpretation. To those I had to pay serious attention, particularly when translating on the fly from German to English. The order of explanation in a German sentence can be decidedly non-linear. While interpreting you must grasp the whole sentence, analyse the function and relation of the various elements, and re-assemble them into coherent English, all in seconds, while paying heed to how the sentence connects to what precedes and follows.

I remember the shock of discovering that translators and interpreters are as much alike as hedgehogs and eagles. Two different species operating in different environments. For example, translators never have to use their sixth sense, which in the case of interpretation means an inborn grasp of the language being translated. You have to *feel* like a German to interpret it properly. You tackled French when you were a teen, Heidi, so you know very well how different languages come at things in different ways. German is no exception in its seemingly wacky indirection.

I enjoyed the ease of translation from page to page, the straightforward two-dimensional task of replicating prose. Interpretation on the other hand involved multiple dimensions and I mistrusted my ability to deal with the erratic quirks of real life conversation. When I looked for employment it never occurred to me to take up interpretation. My degree after all was in indolence and apathy. I was for the safe place in the underbrush. Soaring was for eagles.

In my defence I should say I am something of a perfectionist. Translation on the page allows for almost relaxed double-checking, whereas interpretation mercilessly exposes initial errors. Notice how I excuse myself for having avoided the peaks of my profession.

Huntington said the F.O. is facing a greater and greater demand for interpreters to handle meetings with German dignitaries. He said Britain's delicate relationship with the Third Reich is well enough known to me; he invited me to imagine the bilateral discussions being engendered by that relationship. He made the prospect of being involved as an interpreter sound genuinely exciting. Would I be interested in undergoing an in-depth departmental assessment? My antennae were finely tuned to Tremayne seething in his chair. Here was the chief assistant to the Under-Secretary encroaching on his turf. You may imagine my gratification. The situation stirred something in me that has not been a nuisance for years … ambition. I heard myself volunteer for the assessment.

Has a beam of light shone into your hedgehog's burrow? Maybe, just maybe, his future is not entirely behind him. You once asked me if I know what I want. I do believe I want this. I think I can do it.

Some unwanted excitement at the flat. Our upstairs neighbours, the luckless Nellis family, had a close brush with tragedy. Their older boy, a wild-haired little terrorist, chased a ball into the street and was hit by a milk van. He took horrific flight and landed with a broken leg, fractured arm, severe concussion and a bruise covering most of his body. Mama-blimp and the former chemical engineer turned former apprentice butcher (the vanishingly thin Mr. Nellis lost his job and is back on the dole) are actually grateful – their son was lucky. The van was slowing when the collision happened, otherwise he could easily have been killed. The boy is in hospital and expected, in the fullness of time, to return to ceiling stomping.

Not a word from Damon, but there has been word about him. The other day Jenkins said, "Look here, something on your famous friend," and he handed me a cutting from the infamous *Völkischer Beobachter*.

"Jesus Christ."

Damon's reputation cannot be helped when a Nazi newspaper considers him *ein willkommener Zerstörer des jüdischen Gebots, dass starke Männer kriechen sollten*, a welcome destroyer of the Jewish commandment that strong men should grovel, whatever the hell that's supposed to mean. The semi-literate article mentions an exhibit of Chadwick's at the Weinhauf, then strays off into Nazi drivel about Aryan beauty. If the article were a dish of food I would be reporting a bad taste in my mouth, because the exhibit most likely involves the works Damon did from my photos.

The bad taste lingers, Heidi.

My vertigo has faded … only the occasional imbalance now. I finished a thriller by Dennis Wheatley last night, *Contraband*, in which the hero deals cunningly with England's enemies while enjoying exotic cuisine, tankards of champagne and splendid girls – a ripping good read.

Our lunch club has suffered postponement after postponement but it seems everyone has now agreed to meet on the first Friday in March, perilously close to when Patty is due to give birth.

My precious daughter won the lead role in her school's Elizabethan pageant. I may be forced to agree with her grandfather. Vicky is increasingly her mother's daughter.

Write soon and tell me all about little Max.

As ever,

Joff

Saturday
6th Feb. 1937

Dear Heidi,
Vicky turned nine last Sunday. Nine! In due course as Max sprouts you will be astounded at the quickening speed of time. We celebrated last night with our traditional dinner and film. Today the ladies are out shopping for a new coat for Vicky. It occurs to me the routine of life is not a bad thing. One can take satisfaction in the humdrum. Should I regret the absence of dash, intrigue, travel and adventure in my everyday? Should I regret not being a buccaneer in a Dennis Wheatley novel? Well ... yes. What man in his heart of hearts does not wish to be a buccaneer in a Dennis Wheatley novel?

Seriously though, as we get older we acknowledge the chief snag of the human condition. Namely that we can never be satisfied. We always feel, rightly or wrongly, that life's great banquet is missing some or other spice. What is the zing I crave right now? I can tell you exactly.

Ten days hence I must deliver a good show for the Secretary's man, Reg Huntington. He has arranged the audition and warned me to be ready for a rigorous test. I could be putting too much emphasis on this opportunity, Heidi, but it looms large. I may yet be lifted from the dull pit of Translation, German Section. A promotion would also honour my mother, who was so diligent in drumming her beloved *Deutsch* into her son.

The film we saw on Vicky's birthday was her choice, a good one and no wonder. Our daughter has taken to pinching *The Spectator* from her mummy's night table and reading Graham Greene's film reviews. Nine years old! If you happen to be in the mood for a female Tarzan, you could do worse than *The Jungle Princess*. Ray Milland might catch your eye. (Dorothy Lamour did mine!) As we were leaving the cinema my precious darling observed, "Americans are so gushy in their films. Are they like that in *real* life?" Excellent question. Would you say Americans are gushy? Please do enlighten us, dear lady.

All my best,
Joff

Saturday
20th Feb. 1937

Dear Heidi,
A pure delight, yours of the ninth, thank you. I can hear the voice I remember so well, still cheeky, restless, defiant, unwavering, but with something additional now that tempers the heat, sheathes all the blades. That added something is not maturity, you were born with that, but something related, like a special wisdom. Elizabeth Heidi Lowell, kindly send me a photo of mother and son. I am certain you have become more beautiful than ever.

All is good here. I had my chance and believe I made the most of it. Took the interpreter's test under what they call frontline conditions and managed to swat away all the slings, arrows and mortar shells they could fire at me. When the barrage was over, the remarks were generous. My mother would be proud.

On one side of the table sat your admirer next to Reg Huntington who pretended to be the Foreign Secretary, Anthony Eden. On the other a German-speaking assistant to the Head of the German desk acted as Konstantin von Neurath, the Foreign Minister of Germany. The fellow playing von Neurath's interpreter was the one real German in the room, though his country no longer regards him as such, a Jew who got out shortly after Hitler came in. Meyer Levinson used to be an accountant in Frankfurt with a large house and two domestics. Here he lives with his wife and children in a basement in Hammersmith. He worked as a dishwasher in a Greek restaurant for two years. Now he is qualifying for accountancy and earning a few extra quid by doing stunts like this at the F.O. He still works where he washed dishes but has since risen to head waiter. I digress.

The test demanded fastidious listening, which is the main key to instant verbal translation. I was reminded of a professor at Bristol who taught us how to "maximise lazy ears". Even if you come with complete knowledge of both languages, the ability to strategically *hear* ultimately governs your effectiveness.

Aside from concisely conveying whatever von Neurath said, my job was to pass notes or whisper discreetly to Eden whenever I detected any *mis*interpretations from my counterpart.

As soon as Levinson opened his mouth I could hear traces of *Frankfurterisch*. Happily he spoke mainly in High German so I had no trouble understanding him. High German is proper German in the same sense the King's English is proper English. We have a host of dialects in the British Isles but they generally share common ground. The same applies to Germany, where the dialects are even more numerous. Introduce a fisherman from Bremen to a street sweeper from Weimar and the result may be a comedy (imagine a Scotsman exchanging small talk with a Cockney), but they will understand each other if they listen hard enough.

The exercise was a simulation to test my ability, but still took the form of a heated exchange. After diplomatic words of greeting and veiled assurances of good faith, the two sides went at it with genuine rancour. Maybe they were testing my *sang-froid* in addition to my *Effizienz im Deutschen*. The pretend von Neurath started with a complaint about the treatment of the National Socialist revolution in the British press.

"Secretary Eden, we sincerely wish to preserve friendship between our two countries," he said. "How do you propose we achieve that objective when vicious charges against the Fatherland appear daily in British newspapers?"

I had no difficulty understanding him. His manner of speaking came straight from a textbook, unpolluted by any regional dialect.

"Minister von Neurath," the pretend Eden replied, "surely you are aware of the tradition and primacy of free speech in Britain. The government never dictates, nor censors, what individuals or privately owned companies choose to say and publish."

Levinson's interpretation of Eden's response failed to convey its full force. He translated 'tradition and primacy of free speech' as *Konzept der offenen Diskussion* (concept of open discussion) and turned 'never dictates' into *sich entscheidet nicht vorzuschreiben* (chooses not to control). I scribbled a note in block letters: HE TONED YOU DOWN!

Von Neurath said, "For the German government the vital interests of the nation as a whole always prevail. We would expect the organs of state in Britain to put a stop to these slanderous rumours, which can only harm the cause of peace."

"If by organs of state you mean the security apparatus of His Majesty's government, Minister von Neurath, then I must say to you again, our law enforcement agencies are constrained by custom and law from interfering with people's opinions."

"So you sit and watch and do nothing? Even when the so-called 'opinions' are totally unacceptable?"

They were testing my composure. When von Neurath reached 'totally unacceptable' he came close to a scream, like his Fuhrer we see in newsreels at torchlight parades. I faithfully expressed von Neurath's meaning, while stifling an impulse to laugh.

"Minister von Neurath," said Eden, "do we burden your government with complaints when German newspapers insult us with descriptions of the Empire as a centuries-old criminal enterprise?"

"You are making a mockery of our concerns, Secretary Eden. There is no basis for legitimate comparison between what appears in the Reich's newspapers and what contaminates the public prints of your country."

"Minister von Neurath, perhaps you have already forgotten the time not so long ago when your own people enjoyed rights and liberties, and were free to write what they wished, without fear of intimidation or arrest."

Levinson's interpretation cut away each and every impact of this statement. He translated 'perhaps you have forgotten' as *Wir alle erinnern uns* (we all remember); omitted entirely the phrase 'enjoyed rights and liberties'; transformed 'without fear' into in *Abwesenheit von* (in the absence of); and drastically reduced 'intimidation or arrest' to *Druck oder Strafe* (pressure or penalty). Either Levinson was brilliantly testing me in his own way, or this whole conversation had been meticulously rehearsed. I assumed the latter and felt comfortable whispering to Eden, "He replaced all your bayonets with bananas!" Which elicited a brief tremor of amusement in the Secretary's face.

The conversation continued for some time, touching on economic and political sore points between the two countries. I began to realise just how well my years in the sunroom have served my German vocabulary and syntax. My confidence grew, and at times I felt I was actually enjoying myself. The exercise came to a close with Eden on the attack:

"Minister von Neurath, countless travellers to Germany have returned with the distinct impression that a martial spirit has overtaken your country. Everywhere in Germany they see new military installations. Barracks, airfields, naval facilities. They see uniformed men marching, drilling. Can it come as a surprise to you when people ask if Germany is preparing for war?"

Von Neurath responded with bluster and dogma: "Secretary Eden, it never surprises us when opponents of the modernisation of Germany choose to distort our objectives. We do not seek conflict with any foreign power. Germany has been reborn and is undergoing a process of restoration. We are rebuilding the Fatherland's strength in the interest of national unity and pride in our destiny."

"You say your movement does not seek conflict, yet it has withdrawn Germany from the League of Nations, has abandoned international efforts in regard to disarmament, and has embarked on a military build-up. Are such actions not deliberate sabotage of the world's means of maintaining peace?"

Listening to Levinson's interpretation of this, I had to scribble another note. The Hammersmith head waiter from Frankfurt translated 'deliberate sabotage' into the thin gruel of *strenge Behandlung* (severe treatment), certainly a deliberate sabotage. My note said, NOW HE'S MASHING THOSE BANANAS!

Huntington dropped his Eden character, favoured me with a grin, and said to his colleague, "We can stop here, I should think."

"Righto," replied the pretend von Neurath, "I believe we have heard enough."

While the two F.O. men took a moment by themselves, I exchanged a few words with Levinson. He remarked in English, "You were very good at catching me out, Mr. Pearson."

"*Danke*, Herr Levinson."

"Clearly you are as German as you are British."

That jarred me, but it was also a welcome compliment in the circumstances. I asked if he was still comfortable calling himself a German. He replied in his mother tongue, "*Nein!* The plague that has infected my country has changed forever who I am."

"Would you go back if conditions allowed?"

"*Nein, nein.*" In English he said, "When Hitler came to power, it was as if masks fell from our neighbours, and even our Christian friends. The rejection we saw in their faces! England gave us a home. We are Englanders now." Then he commented on my accent, saying he had always been fond of the lilting quality of the *Bayerisch* dialect. "You Bavarians, ach, you sing when you speak," he said, causing me to wince again. Did you ever think of your admirer as a Bavarian, dear Heidi, much less a singing Bavarian?

"Thank you on behalf of my late mother," I said. "You have paid her a splendid tribute." Then I wished him the best of luck.

Reg Huntington came over and was good enough to say that he and his colleague would make a positive recommendation. My head has accordingly swelled. I imagine myself in Berlin with the real Anthony Eden, the two of us sitting across the table from that character with the toothbrush moustache.

Thank you again for your wonderful letter. Please be aware that I want more, always more, and I await with impatience a photo of mother and son. Hugs for you and little Max.

Joff

Saturday
27th Feb. 1937

Dear Heidi,

Good things in life always come with a trade-off, it seems. I was riding high for days after the interpreter's test. What made the thing sweeter was that Tremayne got wind of my performance. One morning in passing he said acidly, "I hear you are trying hard to leave us, Pearson."

"Not at all, not at all," I replied cheerfully.

The thing is, Tremayne would like the interpreter's role for himself. It would be a step up from managing the sunroom. His command of German however is not nearly sufficient. Earning academic credentials is one thing, having a German mummy another. Although he can read the language effortlessly and translate tolerably well (his English is precise, but wooden), the nuances and speed of the spoken language would defeat him. Which is why, perhaps, he did his best this week to humiliate me.

I have had my tiffs with Tremayne in the past, but nothing quite like this. When his niggling criticisms occur, like outbreaks of a recurring rash, I apply the necessary balm and keep the annoyance from spreading to my spirit. There are times however when he brings out his sharpest claws and seems determined to flay the skin off me.

He was sitting at his schoolmaster's desk when he said, "This is disgraceful." Which caused his three pupils to look up dutifully and attend to whatever apocalypse he had in mind. "The Schumann memorandum," he said, fixing on me. "You recall it?"

"I translated it months ago. Herr Schumann was upset with Dr. Schacht, the minister for industry."

"Why didn't I see the work before it went upstairs? The Deputy Under-Secretary sent it back."

"Did he find shortcomings in the translation?"

"That isn't the point. He wanted a translation, not ruminations and a lecture from the translator."

"I beg your pardon?"

"Your notes are in front of me, Pearson. Do you really think our people upstairs are interested in your juvenile erudition?"

Hearing my lord and master invoke the ridiculous phrase 'juvenile erudition', I decided to take the Retinger tack. I would simply lie down and let the hailstones hit, and while supine I would secretly laugh at the man.

"No, sir, obviously not," I replied. "Why should anyone upstairs be interested in my juvenile erudition?"

"Don't mock me, Pearson!" he said with considerable force and dignity, which riveted my attention. "You have made an ass of yourself. Kindly don't compound it by acting the clown."

Clearly I lack Ken Retinger's touch. I am unable to simulate toadyism. Tremayne, it turned out, was only getting started. "We pay you to translate, Pearson, but in these shabby notes you imagine yourself an analyst. We call upon you to add notes in regard to idiom and style, but here you presume to read between the lines, you imagine yourself a guide to cause and motive."

You might remember this matter, Heidi, because I scribbled something about it to you. The German minister of industry made a comment about exploiting the skills of Jews, and a demented fellow Nazi accused him, in hilarious language, of heresy. Frankly, that is all that comes back to me. Did I go on to note something *verboten*?

"You act like a peacock when you write," Tremayne went on. "Always trying to impress with your pricey vocabulary and florid prose. And with this you have taken up political instruction."

He must have suffered an earful from someone, maybe the Deputy Under-Secretary himself, heaven forbid. Few things disturb Tremayne more than being held responsible for the blunders of his charges. Jenkins, Ken and myself were in thrall as our master's bitterness poured out.

"For years we have endured your tiresome pretensions, Pearson, your mannered writing. Must you always tart it up? Kindly remember, we require no stand-in for Trollope here."

Game, set and match to Tremayne. I took all the hailstones lying down. A dark day, brightened only by the kindness of Ken Retinger who echoed my suspicions about Tremayne. "The small man is jealous of your potential, Joff. He would like to go where you are going. I will miss you, mate!"

"Not so fast. I have barely left the starting line, so quit counting the proverbial chickens."

Lunch club meets next Friday, dear Heidi. I send you my pricey vocabulary and florid prose.

Your devoted,

Trollope

Saturday
6th March 1937

Dear Heidi,

Met with toute la lunch gang yesterday. We had a proper good time catching up on gossip and finally toasting the new year. Catherine brought the photos you sent her, so little Max held centre stage for a while. Not having received any photos myself I admit to being hurt, but I forgive you. Your son has inherited your noble forehead, the lucky fellow, and I see the influence of That American in his nose, which will do Max no harm, the Yanks do noses well. The photo of both mother and son bears out my thesis incandescently. You have never looked more sublime.

Seamus and Catherine seemed to be hitting it off. In fact I think they were huddling with intent. Is something brewing there after all these years? I was gratified to notice that our heavy friend has shed some serious weight. What's more, I saw unmistakable envy in Catherine as the photos of your little Max went round. Is she ready to call off the search for Mr. Perfect, take an old chum as a husband and start producing the little ones she's always wanted? I think it would be marvellous for both of them, and a fabulous event for our group.

Patty has grown enormous and will probably have her third by the time you read this. Our prolific baby-maker surprised me when she had me alone and started pointing her finger at, of all people, our ambassador in Berlin. Apparently she had dealings with the man in her Balfour Committee days. She found him insufferable then, and she's enraged by him now.

"Sir Eric Phipps," she said scornfully. "You would think they would put a *diplomat* in Berlin."

"What has Sir Eric done?"

"Every time I see his name in the newspapers, *every time*, he's whining and complaining about this or that German policy."

"Patty, sometimes the task of an ambassador is to – "

"His attitude has effectively cut him off from high officials in Germany. How is our ambassador going to promote friendship when no one of rank in the government will talk to him?"

I made no answer because frankly I have never heard so much as a whisper that Phipps might be a liability. Meanwhile Patty was rushing on.

"The mothers of this country are *not* going to send their sons into another war."

On that assertive note she gave me a straight-arm poke in the shoulder. Mercifully at that moment Graham came over and saved me from our over-pregnant friend. He took my arm, said he wanted a word. Safely distant from the table I thanked him. "Good one, Gray. You saved me from a furious lady."

"Pay no attention. At this late stage they grow a bit loony. I say, Joff, when did your friend Chadwick go low rent?"

"What do you mean?"

"I don't suppose you ever come across the magazine *Export Transport*." I looked at him blankly.

He laughed. "I thought not. It appeals strictly to small exporters and lorry operators. Quite useful for identifying opportunities and dealing with cross-border red tape."

"What does it have to do with Damon?"

"The latest edition deals with trade between Britain and Germany. The illustration on the cover was done by your friend."

"Are you pulling my leg?"

"Not a bit of it. The editor's note thanks Chadwick profusely. Is he doing pro bono work now?"

"I have no idea."

"Because if he is, my work with several charities – "

"What does the illustration show?"

"Oh, the thing is clever. He conjures the roadways and train tracks of Britain and Germany into the shape of two hands shaking. You get the impression of connected transport systems. Very clever for the purpose of the magazine of course, which is to promote trade."

I just stared at Graham. I could hardly credit what he had just told me.

"If Chadwick's donating his genius, can you put in a word for my causes? I'm on the board of the Wandsworth orphanage, and I organise fund appeals for a palliative care home in Islington."

"Good for you, Gray. I'll pass on the word."

Right. Like hell. I have long been allergic to asking anybody for anything, so imagine me asking Damon, *Would you do a poster for the orphans in Wandsworth? How about a watercolour for the soon-dead in Islington?* This business of loaning his talent to the cover of an obscure trade magazine strikes me as … inexplicable.

On the career-improvement front, a minor development. Turns out I cannot serve my country as an interpreter until my loyalty to His Majesty has been vetted. Or rather re-vetted. Evidently my service at the F.O. for the last eight years does not speak sufficiently to my reliability. I must submit to an interview with an intelligence specialist from the security apparatus next week. If I survive the grilling I must then spend a full week in Cambridge for a refresher on interpretation techniques. All worthwhile, my dear, all bloody worthwhile if it means escape from the orbit of Tremayne.

Be well and happy, esteemed mummy of Max.

I remain your devoted,

Joff

Saturday
20th March 1937

Dear Heidi,

How perfect that Patty has produced another daughter. I love the little treasure's name, Carolina Isabella! But must it take the birth of a friend's third child to reveal a Spanish grandmother in the family tree? The lunch club conspired mightily but still came up with a rather prosaic gift. Every four months for the next twelve Carolina will be receiving a set of monogrammed togs from Harrods.

My security vetting finally took place a couple of days ago. I met with a long-legged skinny creature named Campion in a drab office block near Regent's Park. The only sign in the building's lobby was for The Trans-Atlantic Export Company and I saw no name-plates on doors, only numbers. The event robbed an hour of my life.

Gerald Campion will forever remain in my mind as the *campion*, a breed of gawky scrounger. He wore rimless spectacles over an expressionless face and his legs stretched out like long rods. Imagine a man who reminds you of a great blue heron but who believes himself a blooming great detective. You would have enjoyed watching my interlocutor going through his paces. He opened my file with the air of Sherlock Holmes about to announce the game was afoot. My irritation was aggravated by a tummy ache that morning, as well as the straight-backed cane chair I was sitting on. Then the silly man rankled me with his first observation. "You were born with the century, I see."

How many times in my life have I heard that tired cliché? "In 1900, yes."

"You are the son of Edgar Pearson and the late Ulli Köhler Pearson?"
"Correct."
"Your place of birth was in Suffolk?"
"The village of Shimpling, yes."
"Your mother took British citizenship?"
"Yes."
"The year of her death was 1923?"
"That is correct."
"Your father left the diplomatic service in 1924?"
"Yes."

Do we ever escape the shadow of our parents? My father had lasted over thirty years in his country's service, moving from minor post to invisible post. He simply did not have it as a diplomat. He could never see any justice in arguments opposed to his own, and his temper came with a short fuse. He also never had a knack for social flummery, so his career was further debilitated. Being taken on by the service in the first place had been his one career triumph. It was almost unheard of in his time for the son of a cabinet maker to join the ranks of the striped pants.

"He then represented the aircraft engine division of Armstrong Siddeley?"

Mr. Campion's habit of framing statements as questions was beginning to annoy me. Why ask something when you already know the answer?

"A short time, yes. A very short time."

The private economy had showed no patience for my father. He was taken on to help open doors abroad for the company's salesmen, but doors had a habit of magically growing locks and shutters at his approach.

"Your father is now living in a private carer's home in Bury?"

"Yes."

"Does your father maintain contact with your mother's relations in Germany? Or with any friends or acquaintances he may have made while he served there?"

"My father's mental capacity is rapidly diminishing. His social circle barely extends to the people who live in the same house."

You could see the signs of sham on my lugubrious investigator as plainly as trousers on an ape. While I answered his questions about my father he invested extraordinary gravity in the act of removing his spectacles and putting them on again. Earlier he had tugged pensively at an earlobe while holding his voice to a sombre, almost hushed monotone. All of it was theatre, counterfeit, stupid and irksome. Comical, really. *The Comical Campion*, a new novel by Joffrey Pearson. What say you, my sweet?

The annoying man turned his probing nose to my file, and shuffled a few pages. "We have no record of your prep school."

"I attended Gresham's."

"Did you ever reside with your father while he was assigned abroad?"

"No. He wanted his two children to grow up British to the bone, so we lived in England with our mother."

Ironic isn't it, Heidi? By leaving us with our mother we were more apt to become German because she spoke hardly any English to us. But my father forestalled that calamity by packing us off to boarding school.

"Did you never join him on his foreign postings?"

"We stayed with him a few summers. Bulgaria, which I hated. Rumania, even worse. Portugal I remember with some fondness, the heat of Lisbon in August was – ."

"Your fluency in German, Mr. Pearson," said the campion, evidently not interested in the vagaries of Portuguese weather, "is the reason behind our meeting today. You say your mother spoke German to you as you were growing up?"

"That's right."

"She took pride in being German?"

"I never heard a word from her to the contrary. She certainly had an attachment to the German language. She insisted my sister and I speak and read it."

"What was her place of birth?"

"Wieden, a small town in Bavaria."

"How did she meet your father?"

"My mother's dream from an early age was to escape her little town. She once saw a photo in a magazine of a typing pool in England. It struck her, that image of … am I boring you, Mr. Campion?" The man's eyes were closed and his lanky frame was hanging on his chair like a drape. He could have been dozing.

"Not at all Mr. Pearson, you have my complete attention. Do go on with your charming reminiscence."

I would have liked to reach forward and seize the lapels of his suitcoat and shake his brains like dice in a cup. However, in the interest of career advancement, I faked a smile and continued my charming reminiscence.

"As I was saying, the image of a regiment of young women behind typewriting machines somehow spoke to my mother. She sensed from it the possibility of independence. She took a course in typing, as well as lessons in English. When she turned eighteen she ran away to Berlin and went straight to the gate of the British embassy."

The campion said dryly, "We take it she was hired as a typist."

"The guard at the gate politely told her to bugger off."

A formidable aptitude of the campion consists of effecting unresponsiveness no matter the stimulus. My interviewer wore an expression very like a yawn, even while no yawn tugged at his face.

He said, "We take it she was eventually hired?"

As you know, Heidi, the cupboard of my family lore is virtually bare, so when the chance comes to share some of its meagre contents ... "She returned the next day and made the same request. Once again the guard sent her packing. This went on for two weeks. Word of it got into the embassy. My mother became 'the waif at the gate'. Our people, including my father who was on his first posting abroad, could set their watches by her arrival. It became a running joke which my father did not find funny. He was the most junior man in the embassy, an assistant attaché sent over to observe, but he decided to go out and meet the girl . . ."

The campion wore his indifference like a turtle its shell.

". . . and the rest, as they say, is what has brought us here today."

"When and where did your parents marry?"

"1898. Bury St Edmunds."

"Did your mother's parents attend the wedding?"

"No, she informed them of it after the fact."

"Did she keep in regular contact with them subsequently?"

"After a long falling-out, yes. She had become a *schlechte Mädchen*, a bad girl, when she ran off to Berlin. Naturally *meine Großeltern*, my grandparents, were humiliated by her behaviour. Things got worse for them when it became known in the little town that their daughter had been carried off by an Englishman."

"What work did your Bavarian grandfather do?"

I found the use of 'Bavarian' as an adjective crudely gratuitous, but then the campion lives to peck and pester, doesn't he?

"He worked in a glassware factory, and my grandmother did seamstress work."

"Did you ever visit Germany with your mother?"

"Twice, when I was quite young. Time had healed the rift between parents and daughter. *Meine Großeltern* wanted to meet their *Enkelkinder*."

"Did your grandparents ever visit England?"

"Once, when I was eleven, at Easter. They brought me *lederhosen*, and my sister a dirndl dress. Are you acquainted with the traditional German shortpant for boys, Mr. Campion? The suspenders and frontflap horrified me. My mother made me wear it with unbearable socks that reached the knee. I was petrified we would run into my chums."

"To what extent do you consider yourself German, Mr. Pearson?"

"My country has always been England."

The campion raised an eyebrow to signal mild impatience. I had not answered his question.

"How German am I? To the same degree I feel Brazilian. Or Chinese."

"Even as you are completely fluent in your mother's tongue?"

"I regard my skill with the language as a lucky accident of birth. As the carpenter might if he were born with a hammer in his hand."

The campion looked upward and surveyed the ceiling with puzzlement. Maybe my metaphor had stymied him.

"How did your mother react to the War?"

"She probably overdid her activities to show her loyalty. I remember she joined the local chapter of the Order of the White Feather."

At that the campion flourished his pencil and made a note in the file.

"My information," he said, "is that your father enlisted at the age of forty-nine."

"Correct."

"I believe the cut-off age for men in the service was forty-five."

"Also correct."

My inquisitor was looking at me. Obviously he was curious to know why my father had volunteered for a ticket to hell. It was a golden opportunity to prove the patriotism of my genes. "My father didn't like being on the sidelines while so many others were making sacrifices," I said solemnly. "You may not know this, Mr. Campion, but some six out of ten Englishmen conscripted during the last two years of the War were found unfit for military duty. My father had his faults, but neglect of his health had never been one of them. On his enlistment papers he cut a few years off his age, and passed the physical with flying colours."

Not a word of a lie in that, Heidi, but still not the entire truth. Just before enlisting my father had suffered one of his career disappointments.

The campion said blankly, "The file indicates your father was wounded at the Second Battle of the Somme."

"He lost his right leg below the knee."

What a needless loss. In deference to his age he had been offered non-combat work in munitions, but he insisted on assignment to the front lines. When he arrived in France his colonel tried to steer him into the ambulance corps, but no, he had to fight the Hun, he had to be a real soldier.

The campion excused himself (he was looking a little puffy) and I seized the chance to get up from that blasted chair. Through the sliver of window giving out on Regent Park I could see cyclists grinding their way round the Outer Circle. My long-limbed interviewer returned in a few minutes with glasses and a pitcher of water, and laboriously folded himself back into his chair. Ignoring my word of thanks for the water he went right back to it.

"When meeting with representatives of the Nazi regime, Mr. Pearson, the role of our diplomats and support personnel is to conduct themselves with unfaltering equanimity. Can we count on you to approach your assignments with dispassion?"

That phrase 'unfaltering equanimity' impressed me. I would not have thought the campion capable of it. Of course he probably pulls out such lines at every interview.

"As I indicated a moment ago," I said, "my fidelity is to Britain and I will perform my duties without regard to any personal views."

For all the interest the campion showed in this answer, you would think he was coming round from an anaesthetic. I was ready to seize those lapels again and box his ears into the bargain.

"There is only a brief mention here about your sister, Mr. Pearson."

"Why should there be any mention at all?" I said.

The campion's nose twitched. He executed a particularly portentous removal of spectacles. "Heretofore, Mr. Pearson, your work has not required a security clearance. My investigation must include your sibling as a matter of course."

"I am estranged from my sister."

"May we ask why?"

"That is a personal matter."

"We understand she has lived in Germany for some years."

"I would be grateful if you came to your point."

"Mr. Pearson, it is not that the circumstances of Anglo-German relations impel His Majesty's security services to take an interest in citizens of Britain who reside in Germany. However, when the brother of such a citizen may be called upon to participate at high diplomatic levels with representatives from Germany, it is only prudent to make inquiries of this nature."

"I understand Irene visited England only once since she left. To the best of my knowledge she made no effort to contact me. Aside from a brief note advising me of the break-up of her marriage, I have received no word from her in four years."

During these last few questions the campion had assumed a demeanour of intense concentration while engineering slow meditative shifts in his chair. Apparently he was unaware of Irene's political foolishness and I had no intention of enlightening him.

"Previous to your employment with the Foreign Office, you worked for six years in the London premises of the Cadbury company?" He was at it again, posing statements as questions to which he already knew the answer.

I nodded.

"You were assistant translator, then chief translator, for the company's German language marketing materials and sales correspondence, were you not?"

I nodded again.

"Did you travel to Germany in the course of this employment?"

"Never."

"Did you form any friendships with German nationals employed by the company?"

"I did not."

Curious, Heidi, how so few memories of the Cadbury years ever cross my mind. Those colourless years have receded into pre-history. My time in the chocolate-sphere seems to belong to another person.

You came once to the little room I had. Remember my precious window not far from Sloane Square?

"Are you, or have you ever been, a member of any political party or movement?"

That brought me back smartly to the present. "Heaven forbid!" I said light-heartedly. "None would accept me at any rate."

You know me, Heidi. I have difficulty bearing a grudge and would try to befriend a rhinoceros if there were no better candidate on offer. Still, this attempt at levity failed to move a muscle on my interrogator's face.

"Do you subscribe, or have you ever subscribed, to any newspapers or journals published by the Communist Party of Great Britain or the British Union of Fascists?"

I laughed out loud and had the satisfaction of seeing a hint of annoyance cross the features of the campion. He said after a moment, "You haven't answered the question."

I laughed again, could hardly help it. "No, I suppose I haven't answered your question. On occasion, Mr. Campion, I have glanced, *in the department's reading room*, at publications put out by both of those organisations. I have never requested the delivery of communist or fascist literature to my home. I don't know which would be more ruinous to the wellbeing of my daughter: the hateful philosophies, or the stilted prose."

The campion made a mark in his file, and resumed his march of questions.

"We understand your wife is an officer in the Women's Police Auxiliary."

"She is Head of Recruitment. I'm very proud of her."

"Does she or any member of her family have relations with anyone in Germany?"

"Her parents have passed on. Her brothers operate a small chain of tobaccanist stalls in Leeds. I expect you already know these things."

The campion wordlessly dismissed the comment. "To your knowledge then, they have no dealings, business or otherwise, in Germany?"

I sighed. "Correct." What next, my daughter's preferred flavour of ice cream?

"Is there anything you can think of in your past or present life, Mr.

Pearson, that a foreign power could use as a lever against you?"

"I cannot."

"Have you ever engaged in homosexual activity?"

That opened my eyes wider. "Of course not."

"Mr. Pearson, I want to assure you of the confidentiality of this interview. The results of our inquiries will have no bearing on your current responsibilities. Department protocol, however, in light of the work you may be called upon to do, requires absolute certainty on this issue."

"What are you saying? That I haven't provided you with certainty?"

"Not to put too fine a point on it, but I must note you hesitated."

"I did not hesitate, Mr. Campion. I was taken aback because the question was alien. You may as well have asked if my parents hail from Mars. I have never engaged in homosexual activity. Is that clear enough?"

"Quite." Then he said, casually, "We understand you have been an acquaintance for many years of Mr. Damon Chadwick."

My dear Heidi, where in heaven's name do these people crawl from? What was this man on about?

"I have been a friend of Damon's since I was seven years old," I replied, calmly enough for a man feeling torpedoed.

"Are you aware that Mr. Chadwick has been spending extended periods of time in Germany?"

"I am. His art has won him some very lucrative business there."

I looked into the campion's eyes which were looking directly into mine. His revealed nothing, and I suspect mine gave away some shock and unease. Curiously he did not follow up on the matter of Damon. I was left to assume our friend's nature is known, and to wonder if the knowers think it reflects on me. The interview resumed.

When the ungainly man with the long legs asked about my hobbies and favourite football side I did not laugh again but answered in a sober daze, still thinking, *They know about Damon.*

He asked about my expectations of the interpreter's role. Did I get on well with my colleagues? Would I be prepared to go abroad? Did I have any qualms about travelling to Germany? Damned if I can remember what else. Suddenly the little man was on his feet dismissing his guest while I was still wondering, *What are they on about?*

Morpheus calls, dearest Heidi. I lost track of time during this long ramble and the hour has grown late.

All my best,

Joff

Saturday
27th March 1937

Dear Heidi,
Rumour has it the Prime Minister is exhausted and thinking of retirement. We hear no debate about his successor. Everyone agrees Chamberlain has done a fine job at the Exchequer while no one else in cabinet has built equal stature. King George is unlikely to rock the boat, so it will almost certainly be turkey-necked Neville summoned to the palace.

Are the Yanks interested in our affairs when we lack an old king being buried or a young king chasing one of their skirts? Let me know if I bore you with the latest from home. You must tell me if you still consider it home!

Reg Huntington called to say my vetting went well. Which means the disquieting Mr. Campion found me no danger to the realm. Curious that I should be relieved by a foregone conclusion. The strange man continues to knock about my head like Banquo's ghost. As best I can recall I wanted to shake and rattle him, not put him in his grave. I suppose I'm as paranoid as Macbeth, though not as homicidal.

Due to the shortage of qualified interpreters the F.O. is now fast-tracking my initiation and arranging for my Cambridge refresher. I asked Huntington if the week in Cambridge is really necessary. He said probably not, given my abilities, but department protocol makes it obligatory. I told him I will happily accept time off from Tremayne even at the cost of enduring a return to school.

"You do sound chuffed, I must say."

"That would be an accurate assessment, Mr. Huntington. Thank you again for the opportunity."

"Keep your expectations in check, Pearson. We shall need to see the highest calibre of performance before we call upon you regularly."

That took some wind out of my sails.

Did have a bit of interesting work this week. Have you ever heard of a vain and stupid fellow named Joachim von Ribbentrop? He was once a champagne salesman, and for the last year or so has been Germany's ambassador to Britain. The man is widely despised. He goes about London in a red Bentley ringing up enormous bills at swank clubs and

183

then neglecting to pay. Apparently he is unable to attend a function without making a nasty fool of himself with the ladies. But I digress …

The ambassador was back in his own country and gave a speech at a trade fair. The transcript landed on my desk the same day it made headlines in Britain. The speech was supposed to be about the German economy and its growing export muscle, but it veered into some serious sabre-rattling. Herr Ribbentoad said prosperity has been bequeathed to all Germans thanks to their beloved Fuhrer, but additional tremendous wealth will come to the Reich once it regains the colonies stolen from it at Versailles.

Since the Nazis came to power, their rhetoric about the German colonies ceded to Britain after the War has been loud, insistent – and ignored. The ambassador said if the colonies are not returned peacefully, they will have to be taken back 'by way of the German people's own power'. This is something new in diplomacy: an ambassador threatening to attack territories of his host country. Maybe that's why my translation of the speech is going straight to Number 10, or at least that's what Tremayne told me. Still, I can't imagine that this particular exercise in sabre-rattling will be treated differently from any other. There will be a few days of fuss in the papers, and then Mr. Baldwin will resume the game of ignoring all such threats from the champagne salesman and his masters.

A single postcard from Damon in the last month. He writes in ever-strengthening German but shares only his adventures in tourism. Of course he cannot possibly hint at what really interests him (and horrifies me).

Weeks have gone by too since any mail has arrived from America. Does my correspondent forget her power to delight? Tell me more about young Max. The thought of him growing up American from head to toe leaves me … I don't know, the thought breeds melancholy. You must provide him with an Englishman's backbone. Give him the British *je ne sais quoi* that the New World lacks. Remind him of his roots! Tell me too, how well is That American taking to fatherhood?

Your faithful admirer,

Joff

Saturday
10th April 1937

Dear Heidi,
This made me laugh … remember Patty kicking up a storm about Sir Eric Phipps, our ambassador in Berlin? Well, I'm thinking our dear Patty must have the ear of the Prime Minister, because Number 10 announced this week that Sir Eric is being replaced by Sir Neville Henderson, who is known for urging a more conciliatory line with the Germans. Rumours say Eden strongly objected to the appointment, but to no avail. Predictably, my Hansard-reading colleague regards Sir Neville as a disaster.

"Hard to believe," Ken said. "Now we have a Hitler-lover as our ambassador."

"I don't know much about Sir Neville, but I know when Professor Retinger is exaggerating."

"The man has said we must find ways to settle our differences without resorting to a belligerent tone and allowing antagonisms to arise."

"Sounds perfectly reasonable."

"Code for, 'Slap us across the face and we shall turn the other cheek.'"

Meanwhile the world is awaiting Elizabeth Lowell's next exhibition. Are you working? You say a nanny has been hired for Max (excuse me, a 'mother's helper'), but I get the impression you're nannying the helper and avoiding the studio.

My darling plum will be home next weekend. Unfortunately, Mary is set on dragging her to a public lecture on Sunday. She announced the sinister plan over breakfast.

"Dearest," I moaned, "spring is arriving. I was looking forward to an afternoon in the park with Vicky. You know how she adores the nutters at Speakers' Corner."

"She can listen to those lunatics any old Sunday. I want her to see Winston speak. He's been invited by the Hackney Women's Institute."

"Churchill's going to berate a bunch of old biddies?"

Mary ignored my comment. She is well practiced at scorning me when I get silly. "Did you say Hackney?" I added. "Is there civilisation there?"

Mary sighed. "Vicky will be thrilled if you come along."

"The biddies allow men in?"

"Do be serious, Joffrey."

"What is the old man going to talk about? Does he plan to apologise for not supporting women's suffrage back in the day?"

Woe unto those who point out imperfections in Mary's hero. With a punitive frown she abandoned the conjugal breakfast table. Later I apologised, hugged her contritely, and added I could not possibly dream of missing a chance to see Churchill among the crones ... at which my policewoman wife rewarded me with a giggle, put me in a headlock, and damn near hurt me.

The destruction of a Sunday afternoon awaits. It will take the form of a hard chair in a stuffy hall in the utopia of Hackney. Still, it might be interesting to watch our precocious Vicky on her first foray into the circus of public affairs.

As for you, *Madame la Sculptrice*, I say again, get thee to the studio!

Your devoted,

Joff

Sunday
18th April 1937

Dear Heidi,

Back safe and sound from the wilds of Hackney. Not a single savage beast was sighted, and the humans appeared evolved. Mr. Churchill too came away in one piece, though not unscathed. As things turned out, our darling Vicky … well, let me tell you things in proper order.

Mary bullied us to the event early and we snared seats in the second row. Mr. Churchill is looking good for a relic in his sixties. The notorious pale blue eyes are still prominent, even youthful. When you think about it the man embodies the last forty years of our history, and here he is kicking and snorting as if in his prime. We should give the old steed credit for his unflagging energy.

The audience numbered in the hundreds and included a group of Fleet Streeters scribbling into their notepads. I was disappointed when Mr. Churchill started his lecture with painful understatement. He seemed distracted, almost subdued. He stood with shoulders hunched, hands gripping the lapels of his coat. In a low drone he paid homage to the volunteer spirit and splendid works of the Women's Institute and sister organisations throughout the Empire. Oh my god, I thought, is he off his game? Are we in for a protracted bore? The spindly fold-up chair was punishing my gluteus maximus, and Vicky's fidgeting started the moment we sat down. The rain beating against the windows was a consolation. At least the afternoon we had travelled halfway across London to destroy wasn't fine.

"Giv' it 'em, Winnie!"

The shout came from a cockney sailor in a bush jacket. He was egging Winnie on, because so far Winnie certainly wasn't givin' it 'em.

Mr. Churchill unbuttoned his suitcoat and hooked his thumbs into the armholes of his waistcoat. An inscrutable smile shivered on his lips. Maybe he was about to share a tease. He looked up at the ceiling, playfully, roguishly, then his expression turned icy. The incorrigible ham. He could have been on a war footing in the Commons, ready to inveigh against his usual foes. His tone remained low, measured, sombre.

"Good citizens of Hackney, I have been invited into your midst to discuss developments in Europe. I shall do so with the aid of vivid facts. Be warned, the details of current reality paint a dire picture. The signals from the continent grow more ominous. They augur little but crisis for our island." His next words came in a sudden growl. "Yet in the face of approaching storm, we are being led by brittle and timid men!"

A scattering of applause triggered a catcall from the back of the room. Mr. Churchill smothered the interruption with an engulfing roar: "THE BRITISH PEOPLE MUST BE TOLD THE TRUTH."

That brought a hush. The master thespian charged in and started telling it as he sees it. The threat to peace in Europe, he said, has been maliciously fired and stoked. Dreams of conflagration prosper in Berlin. The fist of autocracy has cowed and mastered the German people. The productive power of that immensely energetic nation now serves a racist, oppressive, totalitarian regime. The vigorous youth of Germany, increasingly indoctrinated and regimented, are marching in thrall to an odious ideology. The democracies must brand Germany's grievances as fraudulent, indict its goals as abhorrent, and pledge themselves to this truth: that the current predicament in Europe does not stem from the Great War rightly won, but from the Big Lie nurtured in its wake. It is plain deceit to claim the victorious powers imposed a Carthaginian peace on Germany. That is the myth leading Europe to the lip of war. *In fact the German people have not been unjustly punished. It is the Versailles Treaty that has been unjustly condemned.* Twenty years ago the Germans were defeated in a ghastly conflict of their own instigation, yet the victors left them whole, did not divide them, nor break up their state, nor loot them of their lifeblood …

Heidi, you probably remember the gist. We have heard it for years in newspaper articles, wireless interviews, speeches in the Commons. Although Mr. Churchill was saying nothing new, I must admit he has a way of saying it and an uncommon gift for holding your attention. As expected, Mary sat motionless, eyes rapt. Vicky too sat stock-still, her fidgeting banished by the speaker's spell. The hecklers meanwhile seemed content to keep their powder dry.

"Think of the Teutonic might and wrath now glowering over Europe. If we had reduced Germany to a vassal state, would it have possessed the breath and sinews to become the menace it is today? The question answers itself. In violation of its treaty obligations, Germany has rearmed. On land, on the sea, in the air, it flexes the muscles of a malignant war machine. Hitler's factories produce five hundred tanks a month, a fresh U-Boat every ten days. The dictator said he would tear up the Versailles Treaty, and he is keeping his vicious vow, while the democracies stand back, mutely watch, do nothing. Our own factories remain idle and our research goes to rust. The consequence? We have made ourselves mortally vulnerable to Nazi threats and Nazi aggression."

I was irritated by Mr. Churchill's pronunciation of the word Nazi. He rolls the 'z' off his tongue like the mellow 'z' in zipper. It drains the wickedness out of the word, even makes it slightly comical. I must write and tell him!

Mr. Churchill then took up his pet theme of the importance of air power. He said the number of active squadrons and reserves in the Royal Air Force remains dangerously inadequate. He called for the number of aircraft and qualified pilots in the RAF to be doubled, then re-doubled, then doubled again. At this a woman's voice rang out from the row behind us:

"CRAZY MAN!"

Vicky and I turned to see the source of this epithet rise to her feet and brandish her umbrella. "WARMONGER!" she added in a near scream, pointing her brolley at the stage and trembling with fury. This was no practiced firebrand but a nondescript lady in her forties wearing a well-ironed white blouse and modest grey skirt. Reminded me of our dear Patty turning insurgent.

At the lectern Mr. Churchill was patting the air in front of him as if to calm a whimpering dog. "Madame," he said in a tolerant drawl, "thank you for that lively contribution, no matter how imprecise. Be assured of my sole aim. It is to alert the British people to a grave disservice being done them. You should know for yourself, your loved ones, your countrymen, and equally for our cherished traditions of freedom … at the primary and indispensable task of guarding the nation, your government is failing!"

"BOLLOCKS!" The loud vulgarity came from a man as aged as my father. "You are creating panic," the old fellow croaked, as he made his way into the centre aisle. He stayed rooted there after his outburst, shaking a fist at the speaker.

"Sir," said Mr. Churchill, "I salute your spirit. If our country continues down the dark corridor our leaders have chosen, we may need your passion to fuel our survival. For the time being let me say this: do not think that those who back down from the snarl and menace of Hitler have a monopoly on the desire for peace. I am – "

"OLD MOONFACE!"

This comical insult issued from a tall pencil-thin young fellow at the back of the hall. I turned in time to see him follow up his rejoinder with the two-fingered salute.

"Scandalous!" shouted another man, and I could not be sure if he was agreeing with the heckler or rebuking the uncouth gesture. The dam broke then and numerous taunts rose up of *Brandy man*! and *Remember Gallipoli*! Answering cries came from Churchill supporters, including from one livid man who bellowed, "He's the greatest Englishman alive!" So we had a rumpus of boos and retorts as hecklers jeered hecklers and I was confirmed in my view of Hackney as an untamed feral backwoods …

It was at this point when my nine year-old daughter made me feel as if I were in a dream. Responding as she explained later with 'a sort of instinct' to those 'mean shouters', our darling Vicky rose, turned to face the audience, stepped up onto her chair, waved her skinny arms in the air, and screeched:

"Please, *please*! Kindly be *still*! Can't we hear Mr. Churchill *speak?*"

Our little girl's voice, pitched to its uttermost squeak, had the effect of creating a shocked and amused quiet in the hall. Mary and I sat stunned. From one instant to the next a beloved prepubescent daughter can transform into a mysterious stranger and declare astounding independence.

Mr. Churchill rushed into the moment. "From the impulse and courage of our youngest should we take instruction," he said, coming round to the front of the lectern and bowing to Vicky, who had retaken her seat and appeared dazed. "Thank you, my dear brave girl. It will be my honour to shake your hand at the close of these proceedings."

When the lecture ended I dashed out for some fresh air while Mary and Vicky stood in line to meet the speaker. Mr. Churchill did better than shake Vicky's hand. He swept her up and gave her a proper hug.

Then he took both of Mary's hands into his own and complimented her on rearing 'a young lioness'. Imagine the thrill for my spouse. She has only idolised the man forever. She came out of the hall looking nineteen. Vicky said, "You should have been *with* us, Daddy."

"No, my plum, it was your – "

Must run, I just heard Mary's latchkey … I leave on tomorrow's first train for Cambridge. Wish me luck!

Joff

Sunday
25th April 1937

Dear Heidi,

For your amusement, listen to how this rolls off the tongue: *Joffrey Pearson is a graduate of Cambridge.* Sounds perfectly fine, no? In fact it triggers an elevation of the chin. Your admirer took instruction from four eminent professors and strolled the storied quadrangles in discussion with his peers. Granted, he spent only a week there, learned little he did not already know, and his parchment takes the form of a typed letter folded into an envelope. Still, the credulous might fall for it: *Joffrey Pearson is a graduate of Cambridge.*

We were five would-be interpreters of various languages for His Majesty's foreign service. They lodged us in rooms at Selwyn College and drove us every morning to a stuffy little Tudor house off St Tibb's Row. Only one of my fellow refreshees was a German speaker, a cocky young man from a merchant family in Liverpool. He came with good academic credentials but as soon as we exchanged a few words in German I sensed his limitations. He reminded me of Tremayne, full of language but empty of culture. Our Spanish speaker was a roly-poly sunburst of a chap from Central America. He was born in the Canal Zone to a Panamanian mother and British father and might well be the most restless man on the planet. He could be sitting on a bench bolted firmly to the floor but you would swear he was hurtling back and forth in a motorised rocking chair – a jumping bean! The Italian speaker of the group was a former executive at Royal Enfield who recently finished a two-year course in interpretation at London College after spending decades marketing motorcycles in Milan. ("This is my late-life challenge," he told me.) The lone woman among us was the Russian speaker, a bitter daughter of Menshevik refugees who still wears the revolution like a giant chip on her shoulder. She held herself aloof but was otherwise pleasant. Our motley little crew got along tolerably enough.

Three minutes into the first morning's session I felt as if I were back at Bristol. You should have seen the desiccated stick who dragged himself in to deliver the introductory seminar. This was Professor Angus Mallory, long retired, keeping his whistle wet by assisting the

F.O. with these seminars. The man's suit hung on him like flags on a windless day and his voice issued with the authority of a receding murmur. I'm convinced he was half-blind because he could never quite locate whom he was talking to in our little classroom. Furthermore, his bow tie drooped at an obtuse angle and two of the buttons of his shirt were undone.

Professor Mallory told us our work with the foreign office will rarely if ever require simultaneous translation. We will not be decked out in headphones and microphones in multi-participant conferences. Our services will most often be used for private conversations between two speakers. In such instances we will translate consecutively, in stops and starts as it were, giving us sufficient breathing space to grasp and accurately express each semantic constituent of the source speech, as well as the mood and objective of the speaker. We are not to be influenced by the efficiencies of one language over another. Which is to say, if it takes only ten words to express an idea in one language but fifty words in the other, a seemingly inflated interpretation is preferable to an imprecise one. And if source and target are reversed, then a thin rendering is similarly preferred.

My colleagues and I glanced at each other, suppressing various degrees of incredulity. For one thing our creaky professor sounded like a jargon-spouting contraption thirsty for a drop of oil. For another, whom did he think he was addressing? This was baby talk, barely beyond kindergarten material.

Much the same happened when my Liverpool colleague and I met with Professor Konrad Halter in the afternoon. A tall lean man in a houndstooth jacket and baggy black trousers, Halter is reputed to be Cambridge's foremost authority on German-to-English and English-to-German interpretation. In a voice with all the texture of sandpaper that reminded me uncomfortably of my father, he explained German as a gender-based language like French, Spanish and most others besides English. He said you can sound like an illiterate if you don't know whether a word is masculine (*der*), feminine (*die*), or neuter (*das*); and you will be taken for a mental deficient if your case-endings multiply your difficulty with gender. Additionally he drove home the point that the way one articulates words in German can instantly certify or discredit an interpreter, as pronunciation is vital to the cultivation of confidence.

Right. Thank you, Holmes.

I shared a bemused look with the young Liverpudlian. Again, it was as if an earnest mathematician had just informed two highly skilled colleagues that two and two add up to four. What was going on? Probably nothing unusual, it occurred to me. Maybe I have been locked in the sunroom so long as to forget the world outside can be untidy and confused. People will be people, they will mess up a stroll on a beach. The high and mighty F.O., together with the even higher and mightier Cambridge, despite immaculate traditions and starched character, can still stumble and flop like clowns.

In truth the first day was the worst. The rest of the week's lectures proved less pathetic. I picked up some useful knowledge about the F.O.'s protocols for interpreting. For example, certain ground rules are laid down in advance of any meeting so the speakers will adhere to reasonable segmentation of remarks. In German and English, as I remembered well from my Bristol days, three sentences represent the logical limit per segment. We did run-throughs and I found I can still retain the content of three straightforward sentences, but at four the brainpan starts overflowing. I also gathered some helpful tips about dealing with German dialects; we had a full day session on that thorny topic.

The five of us were brought together for lectures on note-taking and memorisation techniques. I found those sessions marginally useful. We spent a whole morning discussing situations where it would be appropriate for the interpreter to ask the speaker for clarification. I found that time largely wasted. You must be bored by all this, dearest Heidi, so I'll stop, but I must confess, for the first time in years, as I await my first assignment, keen anticipation rules my days.

I stopped by the F.O. after returning to London yesterday and found yours of the ninth. You may be right about why the annoying Mr. Campion asked about Damon. If he wanted to test my self-possession, that question did a good job of it. The more I think about it, the more sense you make. Still, such a motive cannot account for them knowing Damon's secret, or why they know about our friendship.

There's Mary on the stairs … Be well.

Joff

Saturday
1st May 1937

Dear Heidi,

Catherine called round this week after little Carolina Isabella was rushed to hospital. Patty had a bad fright when the little treasure would not stop coughing. The fit dragged on and on, shaking her tiny body like a rattle and only growing worse. Patty's no alarmist, she has seen it all with her first two, so this must have been truly new and scary for her. All ended well and the little patient is back home. I dropped by with sweets and found myself knee-deep in children. Three are like a swarm compared to my one. Speaking of the precious One, during our mid-week telephone chat she said a teacher advised her to wait until her teens before attempting Jane Austen. You can probably see the end of this story all the way from America.

"I am finding Mr. Darcy *very* stiff," said my plum.

Refrain from applauding just yet, but my first assignment as an interpreter approaches. A couple of days ago Reg Huntington from the Under-Secretary's office dropped by the sunroom. I do believe Huntington enjoys irritating Tremayne. Either that or he takes pleasure seeing how the lower orders live. He told us in general terms about the assignment. Turns out the refugee flotsam from Germany brings an abundance of gold to our shores in the form of intelligence. Not every runaway from Hitler is a communist, trade unionist, terrified Jew, or unrepentant social democrat. The occasional defector washes up too, pureblood Aryans who have worked for the Nazis, come to loathe them, and are now answering to their better conscience. One of these rare specimens will be debriefed next week and your admirer will be interpreting for him.

Tremayne was seriously put out, to be sure, which delighted me no end. In a tone he vainly tried to keep unpeevish, he said, "This will leave us shorthanded, you understand?"

"Higher priority for Pearson's talents," was the terse reply from Huntington. I could have kissed the man!

Have the American papers been giving you much about the horrors in Spain? The savage slaughter from the air in Guernica has been dominating the news here. Hundreds of defenceless civilians killed by squadrons of the Luftwaffe on loan to Franco. This is something new in warfare. My colleague Ken, as you can imagine, has been up in arms all week. He wonders why others fail to see what he sees. "Spain is a training ground… Guernica's a practice run for Paris and London."

"Oh, come now," I replied, which only made him more livid.

Another tight-lipped postcard from Damon, this one entirely in German and without a shred of real news. *Berlin ist eine Stadt der Wunder und Vergnügungen* (Berlin is a city of wonders and amusements) he writes for the Nazi watchdogs who no doubt inspect every postcard that leaves the country. Funny, Damon, very funny. The lunatic thinks he has immunity from the world's random nooses and snares. *Ich arbeite hart und mache viele ausgezeichnete Kontakte für meine Arbeit.* (I am working hard and making many excellent contacts for my work). Still funnier, Damon, I'm splitting my sides. The German is flawless, his friend must be proofing it. His situation makes me shudder, Heidi. I wish he would come home and stay. I miss him.

I miss you too, great lady. Nineteen months since you left. We adjust, we adjust. These letters are my way of being with you. Must cease our conversation now, and pick up *Pride and Prejudice*. I frankly don't remember much about Mr. Darcy.

All my best and more,
Joff

Sunday
9th May 1937

Dear Heidi,

A surly morning with Tremayne yesterday, followed by a difficult visit with the pater. Today is for convalescence.

Tremayne saw red when I refused to work through the afternoon. He didn't give a tinker's damn about it being Saturday. He has never cared that the vast majority of Whitehall civil servants enjoy all of Saturday off. Weekends are sacrosanct, especially for the bigwigs who have country homes. I have never minded coming in on Saturday mornings, and I would have stayed the full day, but I had planned the trip to Bury for weeks and was damn well not going to miss my train.

The blow-up occurred over a lengthy memorandum that had been left by the White Rose movement at the door of our consulate in Bonn. You may not be aware of it, my dear, but a resistance movement does still exist inside Germany. From what we know, the White Rose is a tiny band of anti-Nazi university students whom Hitler's police state has not yet brainwashed, imprisoned or murdered. These extraordinarily brave young people distribute clandestine memoranda the like of which was dropped at the door of our Bonn consulate. A second typed copy of the same document was similarly left at the French consulate in Leipzig. The anonymous White Rose authors claim to have information about Germany's armaments build-up. Their document puts forth two principal points, both of which are meant to set off alarms in London and Paris.

Point one: the Nazis have created a Spartan war economy. This is an obvious fact, say the writers, yet it has strangely failed to rouse appropriate levels of rejoinder and condemnation in the world. All activities in the Reich – political, economic, cultural – are subordinate to the quest for military dominance. When are the leaders of the democracies going to come awake to this perilous reality? Point two: Germany's generals have developed something new in battlefield doctrine, namely a strategy called 'lightning war' (*Blitzkrieg*), which the German high command is even now putting to the test through its proxy, General Franco, in Spain. Again, how is it that the democracies remain blind to this menace? Should they not suspect and fear that a

Blitzkrieg may soon be turned upon them?

The supporting details in the memorandum indicate the writers have inroads to information in both the Reich hierarchy and German General Staff, and the scholarly discipline of their prose supports the White Rose claim of being a university-based movement. Whoever these rebellious people are, they have certainly taken a massive risk.

"The content of this has already been studied and summarised at our embassy," said Tremayne. "Is it to be taken seriously, and if so how seriously, those are the questions. Secretary Eden thinks it essential to send it further up the line in complete translation. We shall be putting it before the Prime Minister, as well as senior people at Defence. I think it important for the translation to emulate the writers' style as closely as possible, to help in determining validity. With that proviso, Pearson, I am assigning the text to you. Can you have it done by eighteen hundred hours?"

Tremayne is a glove-puppet of habit. Whenever the heat is on he reverts to military time; he also imposes absurd deadlines. It was after ten in the morning. The document looked to be over four thousand words. I was catching my train in a couple of hours.

Unfortunately not possible, I told him. I had an afternoon engagement. In the next ninety minutes however I would be happy to make a start on the document. This was not good enough for Tremayne.

"No," he said, "I need you to stay. I will lend a hand by doing a first draft from the middle on, then you can polish to tally with the writers' style, their mood, their depth." He said this in a tone of definitive pronouncement. What I really heard was a childish settling of scores. He was still in a spiteful lather over my 'posh holiday' in Cambridge.

"I am sorry," I said, "but I must attend to my father in Bury St Edmunds this afternoon. He has been extremely unwell and I am seeing to his arrangements." Not entirely a lie, but if my father had to be on the doorstep of death to preclude debate about my leaving, then so be it.

Harsh colour came into Tremayne's face. He could find no answer to my excuse, which he sensed was bogus. Both Ken and Jenkins volunteered to stay the afternoon. Jenkins of course was quite taken by the document, since every page of it was stamped MOST SECRET.

Tremayne ignored their offer.

"Your cavalier attitude offends me, Pearson. You have begun to look down on your work here. Please leave now."

I stared at him.

"Get out, NOW!" he screamed.

Must tell you, Heidi, I flinched. Ken and Jenkins were equally stunned. The livid Tremayne had his eyes trained on me as if I had just bludgeoned his grandmama. The sunroom stayed quiet while I locked my desk and fetched my coat. Thinking it best not to wish my colleagues a pleasant weekend, I closed the door quietly behind me.

That was my morning yesterday. It was relatively pleasant compared to the afternoon.

When I arrived at Mrs. Stockton's the sun stood at just the right angle to gild her neighbour's flowering dogwoods. I stopped for a long wistful look at the golden blooms before entering my father's mouldy, bleak, cabbage-smelling tomb. He gazes at me through glassy eyes now. I can never be sure if he knows who I am. He began crying a few minutes after my arrival. His lips went sloppily lax and a shadow came over his face. "There's no help for it," he said, "I just have to live with this handicap."

"What's this about a handicap, Dad? When have you ever seen the leg as a handicap."

"You fool! Did you see what the idiot Baldwin said yesterday? And the bleeding *Times* complimented him!"

Oh, shit.

I think it was Goethe who said that error is acceptable as long as we're young, but we should refrain from dragging it into old age. Here was my father merging his mania with senility, creating the saddest of spectacles: a father naked before his son in all his ruin and collapse. He and his mates are also riding a miserable new hobbyhorse in Mrs. Stockton's little corner of Hades. In their moments of lucidity they scan the obituaries with particular zeal. My father brandished the notice for a former colleague, a man younger than himself. There was no mistaking the brief glow that came over him, the triumph of his still-aliveness.

I stayed a few hours and caught only minor glimpses of the man my father once was. He twice mistook me for his doctor and never asked after Vicky. At mention of Mary's latest recruiting drive he shouted, "Too little too late, the cowards, the *traitors!*" On the train home I stared out the window remembering better days. How depressing to think we allowed them to slip away without acknowledging how healthy and good they were.

Today has been restful. I spoke briefly on the telephone with Ken to learn what happened after my exile. He and Tremayne worked through lunch and dinner with sandwiches and finished the Bonn document by seven in the evening. Ken received no thanks, only a perfunctory "Mission accomplished, Retinger," as if he were a foot soldier who had abetted Tremayne's strategic genius.

The Spring Bank Holiday begins tomorrow. Mary has gone to fetch Vicky at the station. Pardon me while I finish up with Mr. Darcy and Elizabeth Bennet. I may be called upon to discuss who was proud, who prejudiced, and why. I send a hug across the ocean. With all my best,

 Joff

Saturday
15th May 1937

Dear Heidi,

When the old fever comes your admirer writes things that are truths, but they are improper truths. Common sense seizes him and he rips the sheet from the pad and tears it into tiny bits. You have a child now. The husband he could pretend to ignore, a child he cannot. Some passions are best strangled and buried.

Vicky was excavating her closet the other day and came across some of her earliest picture books. It made me think of Max growing up on Daniel Boone and other buckskinned Yanks to the exclusion of Sir Lancelot and proper British heroes in metal waistcoats. I asked my darling daughter if she would like to send her baby books to a little boy in America.

"I don't like sending away my books."

"My darling, only *baby* books."

She consented to send five on condition I take her to Foyles and make up the number of surrendered volumes. For starters, she wants *The Secret Garden* and *The Lost Prince* by Frances Burnett.

"But you have read those already."

"I need my own copies, Daddy. Must I trudge to the library every time I want a peek at them."

"Perfectly reasonable."

She then claimed a pressing need for copies of the Just So Stories by Kipling, as well as his *Puck of Pook's Hill*.

"I don't know that second one," I said.

"It is a *very* important book. The stories tell the history of England until the Magna Carta."

"Of course, you must have it. When shall we – ?"

"Wait! I thought we were sending *five* of my books to America."

Like any good extortionist dealing with a pushover, my darling made me feel guilty. Chin on her fist she then looked upward for inspiration, nose quivering like a rabbit's.

"I know! I want *Clive in India*. It's by George. . . George …"

"George Alfred Henty, and the novel is vital for any girl who aims to enlarge the Empire. That's five, my peach. When shall we – ?"

But the extortion did not stop there.

She made me solemnly swear not to call her Vicky even a single time for the next twenty years (I negotiated her down from forty).

Crossing the ocean to your son even as I write are the Knights of the Round Table and selected other champions of the British imagination. It pleases me to think that Vicky's – *Victoria's* – books will be shared with young Max.

My first assignment as an interpreter is nigh. The defector's name is Otto Stroebel. He will be interviewed next Tuesday and Wednesday. I have been told to prepare for long demanding days.

Six months ago the Gestapo arrested Stroebel's brother for belonging to the Communist party. Stroebel claims his brother never even met a communist. His only crime was to antagonise a high Nazi official in the course of an estate transaction. A couple of months after the arrest, Stroebel was summoned to collect his brother's corpse, which was almost unrecognisable. The affair shook Stroebel, and turned him. He took his family on holiday to Switzerland and defected from there.

"He says he did it because he wants revenge," said Huntington, "but we think he also began to fear for himself. That gives you the background."

The event takes place at eight sharp next Tuesday at the F.O. rooms on Downing Street. It represents my chance. If I fail, I suppose I will squirm under the shield of fate and say a career move was never in the cards. Which would be a charade. We have our lives in our own hands. We design our own cards.

Delighted to hear of your return to the studio. No need to reveal a thing about the new project. Your word 'ambitious' says enough. Your admirer is patient, he can wait for great things. He sends you the scents and joy of spring in England.

With love,
Joff

Saturday
22nd May 1937

Dear Heidi,

Applause, please. I was battle-tested for real this time, and have now joined the ranks of the F.O.'s full-fledged interpreters. A few nicks and scratches were suffered during the fray, but nothing fatal to my hopes.

The assignment took me to the highest reaches of the F.O., across from Number 10. The rooms are by no means lavish, but walnut paneled, thickly carpeted, heavy with history. The frames around the portraits are uniformly baroque. You feel the pulse of power in the intense quiet of the place. I passed the Foreign Secretary's room and glimpsed Eden at his desk, reading, forefinger of his right hand worrying the famous moustache.

The debriefing of the defector took place in the grandly named Sedan Clock Hall, which is nothing but a windowless cell next to the Permanent Under-Secretary's room. Present were Huntington, a young Miss Henderson from the steno pool, myself, and the defector Otto Stroebel, lately employed in Germany's foreign affairs ministry. He served in the Near East bureau as the German equivalent of a minister-counselor.

Before the interview began I maintained a stiff outward composure, but my butterflies were in full tumult. I have never known a greater fear of making an ass of myself.

Stroebel had claimed some familiarity with English, but it proved extremely limited. I translated Huntington's questions and every word of Stroebel's answers. We spent two full days taking his statement. I arrived home exhausted both evenings.

Think of a portrait of sloth with a sound track of gasping lungs. That would be Herr Stroebel. Not exactly a model Aryan. The sparse grey hair on his head poked out of the middle of his skull like the spike of a Prussian helmet. He lit one fag after another. A self-absorbed and casually foul-mouthed man. But clever, sharp, articulate. In his late forties, I imagine.

The first day was taken up with the inner workings of the German foreign ministry. Our F.O. is fascinated by how its German counterpart operates. Stroebel and I settled into a pattern. He paused after every two or three sentences and waited for my translation. Otherwise I was invisible to him. He never looked at me. I was largely ignored by Huntington as well. I might have been furniture with vocal chords, but I was contented furniture. My initial fears soon evaporated. I had no difficulty understanding Stroebel. Still, it was a dreary, sluggish day. If I learned anything about the means of policy formulation in the German foreign ministry, I have already forgotten it. Dry stuff! On the second day, however, some damn interesting stuff came out. Stroebel talked about his responsibilities on the Near East file.

"I was given a single task," he said. "It was to further our relations with the Arab on the basis of our common abhorrence of the Jew." As soon as the words were out of his mouth, Stroebel gestured that he wanted them back. He shook his head and waved a forefinger in the air. "Excuse me, Herr Huntington, I have not yet shed the tailored clothing of the propagandist. My role in the Reich's great crusade had nothing to do with furthering German-Arab relations. It was exclusively about introducing additional poison to Arab-Jew relations."

"When you speak of Germany's great crusade, Herr Stroebel, I assume you are referring to its racial policies."

"*Natürlich.*"

"Are we to understand that the ministry of foreign affairs has become a conduit for these policies?"

"Every department of the German government has become an instrument of Nazi policy."

"Does this crusade take precedence over economic and strategic considerations?"

"It ranks among the highest priorities. The principal German aim in the Arab world is to undermine the influence of you British. That aim happens to go hand in hand with the Reich's crusade. In the grand order of things Hitler judges the Arab as barbarian filth, but that verdict is for a later day. Now they can serve as pawns in his war against the Jew."

"You would call Hitler's treatment of the Jewish people a war?"

Stroebel coughed. He hoisted himself out of his chronic slouch, fished a handkerchief from his pocket, and hacked a gob of phlegm into it. "Have you read the Fuhrer's book, Herr Huntington?"

"An abridged version has been required reading in the department for years."

"Then I suggest you have not read it closely enough."

"In your capacity as a foreign service officer," said Huntington, ignoring the unkind remark, "did you consider yourself a soldier in a war against the Jewish people?"

"If I had not accepted my role as a soldier, I would have been relieved of my office long before I deserted it."

"What form did your campaign take, if I may call it that?"

"Your choice of word is accurate. Every action of the Nazis, external or domestic, Jew-related or other, can be regarded as part of a campaign. Organised and deliberate."

Huntington's voice betrayed impatience. "What was your role, Herr Stroebel?"

Our guest put out his cigarette and lit a fresh one. "The office I held was established by order of the Fuhrer in October of 1934. It was named the Bureau for German and Arab Friendship. My predecessor had made his career in the foreign service. He could not, or would not, carry out his assigned duties, and was soon transferred to a minor consulate in Argentina. This – "

"What were the duties of the Bureau?"

"*Wenn ich bitten darf!*"

We had experienced a taste of this the day before: pomposity with a snarl. Our guest was not going to be rushed, prodded or interrupted. He would tell his story in his own good time and in his own ordered manner.

I translated with a lowered voice, "If you don't mind!"

Huntington sat straighter in his chair and took on some hauteur of his own. "Herr Stroebel, I aim to hear without undue delay anything *useful* you can tell me. Meanwhile you will remember that you are in England as a guest of His Majesty."

While I translated, Stroebel ostentatiously licked his lips between puffs on his cigarette. This habit of his had seemed only eccentric the day before, but now it grated. He ignored Huntington's snub and resumed his patronising air. "In general terms my duty was to teach the Arab that the Jew has no respect for Arab tradition, and that the Jew pisses on the Arab holy book."

"I am sure your points can be made without recourse to such

language, Herr Stroebel," said Huntington. He also threw a glare my way. "How did you conduct this ... teaching?"

"My programme involved recruitment. In three stages. First I recruited a cadre of young party members who had already demonstrated an appropriate venom for the Jew. Under my direction they studied the Koran and the sharia. The second stage involved training them to be recruiters themselves. When they were ready, I dispatched them to our Near East embassies as cultural attachés. Stage three involved their recruitment of local people, to spread word of the wickedness of the Jew."

"I would have thought Germany already had allies in the Levant in regard to the Jews," said Huntington. "The Arabs are doing everything they can to keep Jewish refugees out of Palestine."

Stroebel smirked. "Palestine, immigration, these are secondary issues. You must first grasp that from Hitler's perspective the Arab does not properly understand the Jew."

"What do you mean?"

"The Arab abhorrence of the Jew is very different from the European. Remember, the Jew killed Jesus Christ, but the Jew did not kill the Prophet. In fact the Prophet killed the Jew in great number. In Moslem lands the Jew lived for centuries under the Arab thumb. Ask an Arab and he will tell you that the Jew is weak, contemptible, inferior. He will never tell you that the Jew is a danger to world peace!"

Stroebel paused to light yet another cigarette. I was grateful for the breather. Our guest occasionally lapsed into his native Saxonian, a dialect that replaces the sounds of the letters p, t, and k with sounds more related to b, d, and g. It was like listening to a drunkard.

"The Fuhrer's war, remember, starts with the accusation that the Jew is a threat to everything good and noble. Hitler can peddle that lie to Christians, because they secretly want to believe it. They grew up being told the Jew killed their saviour. But the Near East is another market. The Moslems suckled on a view of the Jew as weakling, as underling. My mission was to Europeanise the Arab view. My programme aimed at teaching the Arab to fear the Jew, the better to lead the Arab to eliminate the Jew."

"Tell me about this programme."

"It is not difficult to mislead people who are backward and

superstitious. The Arab lives in spiritual chains from the moment he is born. My boys recruited religious leaders, so-called imams, who exert great authority in the lands of Muhammed. All over the Near East today, thanks to my programme, the Nazis have Moslem preachers in their pay."

Huntington had clapped his eyes on the octagonal clock on the wall and was wearing a look of frank scepticism. The ticking of the antique clock, encased in mahogany, seemed magnified in the momentary silence.

Stroebel added quietly, "Nazi money has built mosques and funded academies for Koran study. Most of the German baksheesh, however, has been funnelled into preachers' pockets."

"Are we to understand the Nazis are bribing Moslem clerics?"

Herr Stroebel appeared amused by my colleague's doubt. These British! Still governing their decadent empire with the rules of that silly game of cricket. "Friendship is always for sale," he said. "Obedience simply commands a higher price. Offer sufficient gratification and you can turn a mother superior into a cock-loving whore."

Almost without thinking I had faithfully idiomised the obscenity, *schwanzlutschende Hure.*

Huntington reacted harshly, "Restrain yourself, Herr Stroebel." He swivelled in my direction. "You can also think before you open your mouth, Pearson." He took a quick look at the stenographer. Miss Henderson was a self-assured young thing in a sternly-ironed white blouse. She appeared unmoved.

"You will remain on point, Herr Stroebel," Huntington said, "or I will adjourn this meeting and make my report to the Secretary."

Our guest made no effort to hide his scorn. These stuffy hunters of foxes and saluters of monarchy. Still prudish and muffled under the tight arse of a dwarf queen from the last century. Besides, he knew Huntington's warning was a non-starter.

Huntington repeated his question about the Moslem clerics.

"They have become dogs on our leash," said Stroebel. "They bark and howl in harmony with our instructions. We have imams in our pay in Egypt, Syria, Transjordan, Saudi Arabia, Iraq and Palestine. These witch doctors in their flowing robes are invited to Berlin and escorted about like visiting royalty. Hitler himself meets with them and pretends to respect their authority. We have allowed them to think *they* are using *us*."

Huntington glanced at me. I sensed my colleague's distaste for our guest's vulgarity was now being trumped by the disclosures he was hearing. I knew from my years in the sunroom that the Nazis were not shy about fanning the flames of anti-Semitism outside Germany. Front groups in scores of countries were receiving money from the Reich to support Hitler's race obsession, just as communist fronts were receiving Soviet money to promote Stalin's class war. Nothing new there. Huntington's glance, however, indicated that the Nazi prostitution of Moslem religious leaders might be credible intelligence.

"Tell me, Herr Stroebel, what are these preachers telling their people?"

"Are you acquainted with the Koran, Herr Huntington?"

"The bible of the Moslems. Only to a limited degree."

"The Moslems believe the Koran is the word of Allah as brought to them by Muhammed. The word Islam means submission. Submission to the laws of Allah. These laws prohibit adultery, fornication, apostasy and many other widely practiced activities. Civilised societies do not obsess themselves with these sins. The law of the Moslems, however, the *sharia*, severely punishes them. In many places of the Near East, for example, women are still stoned to death for adultery."

Our guest stubbed out his cigarette and lit a new one. He adored hearing himself talk. The day he fled Germany must have been heartbreaking. He had built a stage for himself and surrounded it with handpicked listeners. How difficult it must have been to abandon such a limelight.

"Moslem clerics embrace above all a chaste society," said Herr Stroebel, whose German at this point was formal to a fault and giving me little difficulty. He was up on his haunches, *lecturing*. "Accordingly, we taught our Moslem clerics to understand that the cinemas and dancehalls are unmistakable signatures of the impure Jew. The brothels? Look under the bed and there is the Jew pimp. Places of gambling? Look in the cellar and you will find a Jew counting money. Places serving alcohol? Jew-inspired. Every source of corruption, every form of iniquity ... the Jew is always the hidden profiteer."

"And these accusations are taken seriously?"

"How have they fared in the civilised country of Germany, Mr. Huntington? The culture of the Arab – " A tremendous cough erupted from Herr Stroebel. The body-shaking blast did not bother or slow him, however. He treated the eruption like punctuation and hardly missed a beat. "The culture of the Arab has always been strict and merciless. It offers a warm welcome to Hitler's anti-Jew policies. For instance – " Our guest's face abruptly reddened and he launched into a series of ghastly wheezes and hacking coughs. While struggling for breath he was careful to hold his cigarette at arm's length.

Your correspondent, my dear Heidi, had to suppress another tremor of mirth. In front of him was a repulsive carnival in a chair, a gasping troll of a man deftly protecting the cause of his gasps. How could I not want to laugh?

Stroebel settled down, took a huge glug of water, and picked up where he had left off. "For example, the Moslem believes in male supremacy. He accepts that the female is inferior, makes a virtual slave of her in every department of life …" Another attack of hacking and coughing, this one particularly fierce. Stroebel's whole frame shuddered. Huntington rose with some alarm and asked if there was anything we could do. Between gasps the German waved at him to sit down. I could not have cared less if Herr Stroebel met his maker then and there, but who needed the commotion that a sudden corpse would cause? Fortunately for the decorum of our day, no undertaker was required. Stroebel's breath returned and for an unprecedented ten minutes our guest managed to refrain from sucking on a cigarette.

"As I was saying, the Arab attitude toward women is convenient for the introduction of Nazi doctrine. Why? Because the Jew honours his women. We even have our imams claiming the Jew *worships* his women. When you are dealing in lies, it is not a difficult transition to very big lies."

We waited as our guest boisterously deposited additional phlegm into his handkerchief. This was Stroebel in a relatively hale and hearty moment, on the offensive, divesting slime from his throat, as opposed to the gasping Stroebel, defenceless hostage to his gruesome lungs.

Miss Henderson had remained poised throughout. I had been covertly admiring her. She wore a bronze barette in her pinned-back sandy hair. Stroebel's lewd mouth had not unsettled her in the least, but this raucous gobbing into the handkerchief apparently crossed a line. I caught her looking away from the German with barely disguised revulsion.

A noisy finale of throat-clearing and the interview started up again. We had done nearly three hours in the morning and three more in the afternoon. I was beginning to seriously flag. My brain had not endured a workout like this since … well, since ever. We were about to adjourn when Huntington asked Stroebel if there was anything he wished to add.

Stroebel pulled himself up in his chair. "In return for the asylum your government has granted my family, I promised to describe for you the Nazi programme in the Near East. I also promised to share what I know of the Nazi mind. I believe I have failed."

"Why do you say that?"

"I am afraid you have not grasped what I have been trying to tell you. Perhaps I did not make myself clear."

"I think you have been, in your own way, most obliging Herr Stroebel," Huntington replied. "What is it you fear I have misunderstood?"

"Hitler's objective among the Moslems. You should not think the Jew is merely a. . . "

I faltered.

Mark it down to fatigue, but I could not find the word. I surely would have found it at once under less demanding circumstances. While I struggled to remember the English for *Sündenböcke*, I held up a forefinger to indicate I was yet to complete Stroebel's sentence. For several ticks of the historic clock on the wall, I was utterly lost.

"Pearson?"

The word still was not coming, though I knew the word. A panic took hold. My head, instead of working, emptied entirely. I had the sensation of absolutely nothing going on inside my brain. Then came the mocking image of a boat grounded on a beach, the wind full in its sails, driving the boat deeper into the sand. Meanwhile the ticks of the goddamn clock fell on my ears like hammer blows. Huntington threw his pen on the table and that is when the word burst out of me. "Scapegoat!"

With relief I repeated the whole sentence, "You should not think the Jew is merely a scapegoat."

"*Ja, natürlich*," said Stroebel, who evidently recognised the English term.

Huntington appeared confused. "Come again?"

"Do you not see?" said Stroebel. "In one stroke my programme seduced the imams and advanced the Nazi crusade. It was a marriage made in heaven."

It was not until that moment, after all the hours of Stroebel's swagger and bragadoccio, that I was moved to acknowledge, *Yes, this man is a traitor to his former cause*, because something approaching sincerity, even dignity, had entered his voice. Unfortunately, Stroebel found his little play on the words marriage and heaven, which had probably been unintentional, uproariously funny. Along with his sudden guffaw came a spume of saliva and nasal matter that settled like spray on the table. The gravity of the moment was submerged, literally. A convulsion of choking followed as he attempted to regain control of his breathing.

Huntington waited for the spectacle to recede. His growing impatience indicated he was through with Stroebel. Nevertheless he asked, somewhat snidely, "If you're right about the marriage, how would you suggest we arrange a divorce?"

The question hit the wrong chord. Our guest reverted to his sneering self. "There are some games in which you Britishers cannot compete. You are like naïve children. The Nazis regard morality as weakness. They speak only in the language of lies, backed by fists and guns."

Huntington closed his notebook and put down his pen. "Herr Stroebel, is there anything else of a *useful* nature?"

"Hitler does not want the Jew to live in Germany, this you know. He does not want the Jew to live in Palestine, this you have learned. When are you going to see that Hitler does not want the Jew to *live*? If you –"

"I see we have come to the end of useful discussion," said Huntington, and he rose to indicate the session was over. "On the Secretary's behalf let me thank you for your assistance, Herr Stroebel. We await your written recollections. Please make them as comprehensive as possible. Miss Henderson, would you show our guest out once Pearson is done translating these final words of mine?"

Huntington pointedly sat down, reopened his notebook and began writing as if he were alone in the room. Stroebel listened as I conveyed

Huntington's remarks, then he blew a last gasp of smoke at the suffering ceiling and left without further ado. With luck I will never see him again!

"Interesting stuff," I said to Huntington.

"Tons of dirt and fantasy, the odd diamond of truth," he said, as he continued jotting notes. "Not unusual from these characters. They tend to arrive wild-eyed. I found much of his story overdone."

"Oh?"

"For certain. The man was in cuckoo-land at times. I wager he still adores his former causes. Did you hear the 'we' in his voice over and over again? I would not be at all surprised if he still wraps his heart in a brownshirt."

I was almost out the door when Huntington remembered I am not quite furniture. "Thank you, Pearson, and well done. You stumbled for a moment, but my report will remark favourably."

Midnight has struck, Heidi. My memory cells are drained. Must tell you, when done with these marathon scribbles I notice my wrist is close to crippled. Sweet dreams to both of us.

Until soon,

Joff

Friday
28th May 1937

Dear Heidi,
A hasty scribble from the sunroom. Tremayne has been called upstairs. Always a delight to be with you, even momentarily.

The expected change of guard has occurred at last. The king's anointment of the new PM took place at Buckingham Palace this morning. By the time you receive this you will know Mr. Baldwin has stepped down and our former Chancellor of the Exchequer has moved into Number 10. The scuttlebutt says we now have a Prime Minister considerably more interested in foreign policy than his predecessor. This will certainly jangle the nerves of our career people above. They despise interference in their holy work. It will be interesting to see what Mr. Chamberlain gets himself up to.

Ken has kept a stone face since the news came in. "Our new Prime Minister looks like an undertaker-in-chief," he said.

"Give the man a chance, Ken."

"To dig? Chamberlain has said he's a man of peace to the depths of his soul."

"Is that a bad thing?"

"He will bury what's left of Versailles tomorrow if Hitler sends him a dozen roses to spread over the grave. He makes even Baldwin look like a warrior."

"I don't know why you say that."

"Our new Prime Minister has this wacky idea of reaching out to Germany and strengthening its moderate elements. Joff, there are no moderate elements left in Germany!"

Quick hug, Heidi, but by no means a moderate one.
Love you,
Joff

P.S. Telegram yesterday from Damon. He says he will be home in a few days. Bearing what gifts from his mad odyssey who can tell.

Saturday
5th June 1937

Dear Heidi,
Weeks have gone by since your last paltry note. Anxious to hear what is happening in your studio. Tell me too that Max is pleasing his mother with new tricks and making steady progress toward the White House. You must write!

Damon returned and is looking … tired. You might even say haggard, though his capacity for ale remains robust. He kept draining his pint and getting up for another. When I asked him for news he was almost *sullen*. He said he had suffered a disappointment.

"Anything to do with your … friend?"

He drained his pint and went for another.

When he came back he demanded updates on Arsenal's midfielders.

"Can you sit still for two minutes and speak to me calmly? Did the new pieces sell? Are you still a convert to dictatorship?" The jab failed to elicit even a smile of scorn. He looked round the pub. "I have made some progress, but not enough. Things have stalled. I need a thunderclap."

"You need what?"

"Let's top these off with some scotch," he said. "Come to the studio."

Later, sitting at his card table and sipping a fine Glengoyne, I made a comment about a file that came to my desk recently about Nazi race policy. Throughout Germany panels of investigators have been established to look into the Aryan credentials of citizens. "Did you know it is no longer enough these days for old stock Krauts to say they aren't Jews? Now they have to prove it." I was trying to annoy our friend. Imagine my satisfaction in seeing him wince at 'Krauts'.

"Equally questionable offences," he said, "were a regular aspect of British colonial rule."

"You would compare – ?"

"I would. I would also remind you of what Cromwell did to the Irish Catholics."

"That is a specious – "

"We live in a country where the vast majority of people are disadvantaged by the circumstances of their birth. A giant underclass is caught in perpetual servitude so the titled can enjoy lives of privilege. Please do not talk to me about the modern Germany, where a man can rise whether or not his ancestors once lived in a castle."

"You know very well, Dame, I hold no esteem for our class disease, which my mother taught me to loathe. But what of a country that judges a man by his religion? The Jews in your precious Germany are being treated like outlaws in a jeering prison."

"The preoccupation in our press with the Jewish problem is overdone."

"The Jewish 'problem'? Have you adopted the German phrase for their pet hate?"

"The result is, it's done to a crisp, and we have this *ideé fixe* that the Jews are being terribly mistreated."

This was going too far, it could not be our friend speaking, it had to be deliberate blindness. I did something I have never done before in conversation with anybody. I reached across the table and gripped Damon's arm. "What has happened to you? What the devil has happened to you?"

My grip on his arm had only surprised him. Now the tone of my voice – singularly outraged? blackly unforgiving? – did capture his attention. His cigarette stopped halfway to his mouth.

"You have run out of bounds, Dame. You are repulsively out of bounds."

He put down his cigarette, and delicately removed my hand from his arm. Then he rose and pulled a large sketchbook off a shelf. "I was thinking of showing these to my dealer in Munich."

The book contained preliminary studies in pencil for two paintings. The first set showed a standing congregation of bearded men in skullcaps and prayer shawls. The strange thing was, and here was the poke in the eye, the praying men all had guns in their belts. The idea grew sharper as the sketches progressed. The shawls on the bearded men became more identifiable, and the guns grew in size. In the final sketch the sky had become dark with cloud and leafless trees had been added, creating a sense of desolation. The guns of the bearded Jews, now partially concealed but still obvious under their prayer shawls, had been made still larger, and the congregation as a whole gave the impression of a marching regiment …

I closed my eyes and breathed in deeply. I did not look at Damon. In what I can only describe as a kind of revolted trance I turned to the second series of sketches. These drawings imagined a mighty boulevard clogged with motorcars and lined with sky-reaching buildings. The impression was of America and New York City. In succeeding sketches the buildings took on the character of banks, mainly banks, rows of banks, but also film studios and radio stations. A low-slung building, evidently a factory, formed an uninterrupted border around the entire scene. Emerging from it at various points were trains of flatcars bearing new field guns and artillery pieces, or freshly built tanks and fighter aircraft. In the final sketch, corporate insignia had been added above the entrances of many of the buildings. The company emblems, every one, were stylised stars of David.

I closed the sketchbook, and pushed it off me onto the floor. Slumped in my chair I felt strangely beaten, hollowed-out. After a moment I looked at Damon and wondered what on earth he had become. This was not the friend I had known all my life.

"I refuse to believe you drew those things," I said. "They are the ugliest things ever to come out of you. They are also weak, because they are so obvious. Maybe your nastiest critics will be proven right after all, and you will end up as a cheap cartoonist."

He was looking at me with interested eyes. I was satisfied that he at least kept his mouth shut. In for a penny, in for a pound, I let my mouth run on. "You should be ashamed. Turn these atrocities into paintings and your reputation in England will be destroyed. They would be the end of you, and rightly so."

Damon showed no welts or cuts. No embarrassment at all, no, never, but at least he was solemn. Not a word did he utter, sensing I would have shouted him down. He retrieved the book from the floor, turned the pages slowly, studying each sketch, occasionally looking up and gazing inwardly. Finally he said, more to himself than me, "Yes, these go too far."

He went to a shelf and took down an earthen bowl. Then he ripped the sketches out of the book, one by one. Holding them over the bowl he put a match to each, and watched the flame reduce the sketches to coiling ash and black powder. When he was finished he turned to me. "Take a lorry into the country and fill it with manure. Then drive back and dump your cargo in front of my window. It will remind me of what I almost did."

"Amen," I said.

"We will say no more about it."

"Amen to that too."

I may have won only a Pyrrhic victory, however. He left for the continent yesterday. He said the opportunity in Germany is simply too 'attractive' to ignore. Bloody hell. I suspect his Berlin friend has become the main attraction. About whom, by the way, he volunteers nothing and signals he will entertain no questions. I have no idea what the friend does, or his age, or even the damn fairy's name.

I do know this: if no letter arrives soon from Boston I will investigate the cost of a trans-Atlantic telephone call. Consider that a threat. You will write!

All my best,
Joff

Monday
7th June 1937

Dear Heidi,
Two in the morning. Can't sleep. Still disturbed by something I saw in Hyde Park yesterday ... Vicky was home for the weekend. She bounded out of bed early, intent on hearing the Mad Vegetarian. She adores the nutters at Speakers' Corner, especially the ones who bellow and paw the air. I agreed to take her on condition she acknowledge she is nine years old, not nineteen, and cease annoying her mother with demands for lipstick.

"The flat earth man too!" she squealed.

Alas, the flat earth disciple must have fallen over the edge on his way to the park yesterday, but we did catch the richly-bearded animal protector. A worthy spectacle, that bloke. His tattered greatcoat and sweep of grey hair go well with the salt and pepper beard and marvellous baritone. He brings something priestly to his madness, reminds you of mythical characters from the Bible. He delighted my precious darling with a bloodcurdling story about what goes on in 'the animal-murdering places' where they funnel living creatures through horrific chutes and reduce them to sausages. When he started on the benefits of diet without meat, however, the heavens opened and made us flee for cover. But something other than the rain spoiled the day.

Later, near the Victoria Gate, as we were leaving under a clear sky, we chanced on a group of Mosley's men, six or seven of them in those awful black shirts which button on the side. The group may not have been large enough to require an assembly license, but it seemed they had just finished a march. Now they were singing one of their hateful ditties. They wore armbands with that menacing lightning symbol modelled after the swastika. Their raucous singing is what attracted us and other gawkers. When the singing stopped one of the demented hoodlums began shouting hoarsely about the Bolshevik threat and 'Britain for the British!' What they were doing amounted to a demonstration and was therefore illegal. I took Vicky's hand and looked about for a telephone box. I had every intention of calling the police.

That is when I saw Tremayne.

A ways off, but unmistakable, standing by a dustbin. He was wearing a loose windcheater and looking like a boy scout. He had laid his umbrella across the top of the bin to free his hands to applaud. Which he did, in peculiar fashion, smashing his hands together like cymbals. He was the solitary applauder in the crowd, though he may not have realised it. He was absorbed in the speaker and craning his neck. His chin jutted like an accusation.

"My darling, we have to go."

As I sped us away, Vicky trotted to keep up.

"Who were those men, Daddy?"

"They call themselves 'fascists', my sweet. They are not nice men."

"Why do they – ?"

"I have an idea!"

"What?"

"Let's go to Masons' for ice cream."

I am still in some shock at what I saw. I would not have thought it, even on the day I glimpsed him reading the Mosley rag. Tremayne may be an empty, conceited, frustrated little man, but truly malicious? That profoundly dim? It makes me sad. Makes me pity him.

I will try to catch some shut-eye now.

Be well, Heidi. My love as ever,

Joff

Saturday
12th June 1937

Dear Heidi,

Thank you. I needed that. Yours of the twenty-fourth reminds me that life can be care-free, abundant and creative. The Laurentians sound grand. Fourteen bedrooms? This was your first mention of the affluent Montigny family. Does Matt have many friends in Quebec? I was amused to hear your French is still serviceable. I assume by joual you mean the local dialect, but your reference to tabernacle and sacrament as profanity confounds me. Religion-inspired swear words? Kindly enlighten me further.

By now you have received my letter about Damon's sketchbook, so you know how close he came to covering himself in muck. It seems our friend cut short his latest stay in Berlin for some reason. He telephoned a couple of days ago and announced his return. He has started a project here in London, which will occupy him for the next month. I was happy to hear it. "Getting tired of . . . Germany?"

"Not at all. This work has to be done locally."

"What are you working on?"

"Something huge!" Then he bid me good day.

On a cloudless Saturday afternoon in June you might wish for the stompers to be chasing a football in a park, but no, they are *roller-skating* on my ceiling. It sounds like my head is being massaged with gravel ...

Just returned from knocking on the Nellis door. I caught a glimpse of the scoundrels beyond the massive Martha who has only widened since the last time I saw her. She now clogs most of the door frame. The wretched woman had a cigarette dangling from her mouth and said she was honestly sorry but how was she to restrain her older boy who only recently recovered the use of all his limbs after that terrible accident, and the younger one *is* a handful, isn't he?

I am a patsy, Heidi.

Someone with a spine would have turned his fury into a flamethrower and scorched the woman with menacing shouts. Having lodged my protest, however, I found myself at a loss for anything further to say. I actually played the good neighbour and asked after the man of the house. She told me her Martin has been taken on by a carter. Which dumbfounded me, because Martin has the constitution of a twig. Imagine those skinny arms and legs piloting dressers and chesterfields up and down stairs. Maybe he grew some muscle while he was failing as a butcher. As for the spinster, she has no immediate plans to return from Edinburgh.

"We do what we have to do," I said stupidly. Then I retreated from the gloom and din of the Nellis household.

Your admirer, the pathetic pushover, is going to the park for a bit of quiet. His Athena in America will laugh, but he is now seriously considering making a gift of a carpet, a thick one!

As ever,

Joff

Saturday
19th June 1937

Dear Heidi,

I made my debut as an interpreter a month ago, and ... nothing since. My high hopes have descended to a somewhat lower altitude. What did I expect, a deus-ex-machina to lift me from Tremayne's swamp? Come to think of it, that is exactly what I was expecting. Otherwise the whole process, including the miserable Campion and the week in Cambridge, was absurd. I sent a note to Huntington, very carefully phrased (properly solicitous, but not sycophantic), asking if I could anticipate further assignments. He replied with five words: *This is a quiet time.* Meanwhile I bristle with frustration whenever Mary queries me on the matter.

Graham's eldest, Jenny, is marrying a barrister next month. A well-established one I hear. You will be missed awfully at the event. Graham tells me Seamus and Catherine plan to attend as a couple. That is fabulous news. Maybe it augurs another wedding soon.

Vicky's home for the weekend, the last before the hols. Spouse and daughter are out hunting a posh outfit for daughter to wear at the wedding. Vicky demands a floor-length tawny-coloured dress, and heels into the bargain. Mary laughed and told her she's not nearly of age to torture herself, and why a tawny dress?

I asked Mary if she would be buying a new frock for herself and she said the expense can't be justified. She will go in her parade whites, which I rather like. The kit is razor-sharp and frankly hugs her qualities. Striking in a military way, that's my Mary, though I wish she would do more with her hair.

Thought of Damon today when I saw a notice in *The Times* about the Picasso show. The arty set is making a fuss about the opening next month at the Clement. In Green Park we now have a massive human face with the mouth where the nose is supposed to be, and vice versa. Do they deify Picasso in America as they do here?

The memory of Tremayne and the Mosley hoodlums has stuck in my head. I keep remembering the cymbals he made of his hands and how his chin thrust like a cleaver. Maybe he just happened to be in the park that day and got caught up in the excitement. My better reason laughs at that frail notion even as another part of me stupidly clings to it.

Must leave you now for the grocer. The pantry is my responsibility this month. Then my girls will be home and we will set off to the cinema to see *Lost Horizon* on Ken's strong recommendation. Should be a treat, the film is by Frank Capra. Apparently he takes us to a utopia where kind-hearted people lead mellow lives. The utopia part must be why Ken recommended it. Vicky was doubtful, but when I mentioned a hidden valley called Shangri-La our darling granted her blessing. Wish us luck in the land of eternal peace!

As ever,

Joff

Saturday
26th June 1937

Dear Heidi,
I fear another barrage of blows from Boston, so I hesitate to tell you
… I went again with Damon for a pipe.

Keep your hair on. The pillars of civilisation remain secure. Our
friend has been working like a galley slave, he was ready for a night
out. A good number of months had passed since our visit to Edith
Road, so he had no qualms about taking me on another adventure. He
was in such a jovial mood I asked if there was something to celebrate.

"Soon, soon!"

"What is it you're working on?"

"A grand thing," he said, "a fabulous lark," and he flashed a smile the
like of which has been absent for many moons. You know the smile.
The one that says, *I have something outrageous up my sleeve.*

"A new series of oils to attract libel suits?"

"Much more," he shouted. "The stuff of dreams and nightmares. A
beautiful monstrous thing. To come soon enough. Soon!"

I was grateful to have him back, and back in roaring form. This
time he took me to a house in Belgravia, on Eaton Square. "Oh, my,"
I said, "this is above my pay scale." We were standing in front of a
Romanesque mansion. The white marble portico gleamed in the
twilight.

"Be assured," said Damon, "no one will be asking how many thousand
a year you have."

"I suppose they just assume a certain minimum. Who is our host
tonight?"

"Hostess, actually."

"Is she another patron with a vast fortune and decadent soul?"

"No obscure Chadwicks hang here, if that's what you're getting at.
More like Cezannes and Pisarros. The doyenne of the house is not a
collector of mine, only an acquaintance. She offered to be something
more, but I was unable to indulge her."

"Why not?"

"The woman has celebrated her seventieth birthday."

"Ah." But he had avoided my question, and I said so.

"True!" he said cheerfully. "It might interest you to know, W.H. Auden visited this house in 1934. With a good-looking airman on his arm."

"I wasn't aware he – "

"Oh, yes. We shared a pipe. He paid more attention to me than the dashing pilot."

"And … ?"

"I should tell you, Joff, things go on in this house you may not care to know. Offences against nature itself, so it is said, and the law calls it gross indecency."

"Are you dragging me into a den of homosexuals?"

"Not at all. The lady of the house has many uninhibited friends. Some of them do prefer their own gender. Others straddle the fence. There are women who strap on prostheses here, and – ."

"Spare me further details, please."

He laughed at the look on my face and put his arm round me. "These people may be debauched but they remain absolutely discreet. Otherwise our guardians of morality would send in the police."

"You should have told me these things earlier."

"Would you have refused to come?"

"I might have."

He looked at me sharply, "I do apologise then. Please know, the strict rule of the house is privacy."

"I believe you."

"Good! Shall we go in?"

Am I boring you, Heidi? Worse, am I angering you? I hope neither. My only wish is to share, reveal, amuse … *be* with you. The evening at Eaton Square brought the same brief wrenching illness and dizziness of Edith Road, then similar hours of powerful remembering. They were sprints of mental adrenaline not to be denied or opposed but only … appeased. This second pipe was little different from the first, yet no less startling.

I found myself feeling something new for my sister. I had always been fascinated by Irene's anger, the deep anger that had always defined her, but now I felt compassion for the anger, and compassion for her. Felt it like a tide in the blood. The swell lifted me and changed my view of her. I was no longer the pitiless unforgiving brother. I was seeing another side of her, seeing her as a victim. I realised something about poor nasty deluded Irene. She always took an uneducated, perverse delight in denouncing Britain as an imperialist predator, but otherwise showed no interest in politics. Her problems began when politics took an interest in her.

Wait. I wanted to tell you about the lady of the house. I will return to Irene, I promise.

Damon introduced the *grande dame* of the house as 'The Duchess'. He presented me as a dear friend and vital servant of His Majesty. I might have winced at the description had I not been busy containing my dismay. The Duchess was a shrivelled apparition straight out of a child's storybook. Think of what a desiccated elf might look like. I shook her birdlike hand with great care, for fear of crushing it. Damon ceremoniously kissed the leathery claw. He had mentioned she was seventy but she looked eighty or more, and did I say elf? I should have said goblin, the product of a lifetime of dissipation, pallid to the point of ethereal and nicotined to her wrists. From her white robe an elbow poked out like a cardboard stiletto. Ghastly. Frightening at first. Yet I soon found her amiable. Gracious too, despite the alarming squeak of her voice.

The Duchess walked with a cane and took fragile steps nerve-wracking to behold. She led us haltingly through a dining room which could seat a regiment, then sat and chatted in a windowless study lined with three walls of books. The fourth was crowded from floor to ceiling with astounding pictures. Damon had not exaggerated, they were Cezannes and Pisarros with a few pencil works by Degas thrown in for seasoning.

"Who is this woman?" I whispered, as she gave instructions to a liveried servant who was summoned with a single tinkle of a crystal bell.

Damon ignored me. He rose and went to a Cezanne and pointed at three pears lolling on a white tablecloth. "How do you think he made his pears more pear-like than the real thing? It had to be sorcery. The sorcery of the mind convincing itself of something. I'll tell you how he did it. Before he applied a drop of paint, Cezanne gave personalities to his objects. He thought of them as people. He *talked* to his pears and apples. Communed with them. Established an intimacy with them.

He convinced himself they were perceptive. He was painting *life*."

A cackle from our hostess. "He is a bore, isn't he, Mr. Pearson?"

"I'm sure you do not believe that for a moment, Duchess."

"If you are a friend of this bad boy, Mr. Pearson, you are most welcome in my house."

"Thank you, Duchess."

"Are you a bad boy too, Mr. Pearson?"

As I hesitated, Damon came to my rescue. "It will interest you to know, my lady, that Joffrey has made fatherhood an art and raised it to the sublime. His daughter Victoria is intellectually gifted as well as perfectly delicious, and I am honoured to be her godfather."

"I am so glad for you, Mr. Pearson. I myself indulge a beautiful niece, and spoil her terribly." Our hostess leaned forward in her chair, a bit of colour in her face, voice rising like an approaching siren. "Damon is a very bad boy, mean and cruel to me, but he has made us extremely proud hasn't he?"

"May I ask, Duchess, to which of his many accomplishments you are referring?"

"His travels to Germany, of course. The dear sweet thing is like a messenger of peace. Aren't you, my dear sweet Damon?" Just then a light seemed to go out in our hostess. One moment alert as a live electric wire, the next she looked ... lost. Damon reached over and chimed the crystal bell, twice. A girl in nurse's garb materialised and helped The Duchess to her feet. "Goodnight sirs, goodnight," our hostess wheezed, except she had aimed her gasp at the Pisarros and Cezannes. Then she was gone on the arm of her nurse like a relic on a leash.

I had a hundred questions but Damon would hear none of them. The liveried servant soon returned to escort us upstairs. The familiar paraphernalia were laid out in a flower-bedecked room with a lock on the door and the window shuttered. The opium pipes were not museum pieces this time, merely porcelain of no special artistry, but they delivered no less efficiently the expected visions and startling memories. Who would have thought my mind would recapture the day in Shimpling when my sister, dressed in black and clinging unctuously, came home to father with her Kraut boyfriend ...

It will have to wait, dear Heidi, the hour grows late and my eyelids are drooping. Look at my handwriting, my words appear to be shuddering.

Lots of love,

Joff

Saturday
3rd July 1937

Dear Heidi,

Tremayne annoyed me each and every day this week. We think something must be going wrong in his home life. The little we know of his domestic affairs comes from his side of telephone conversations with his wife. On occasion he grows unguarded and raises his voice. More often his tone is artificially gentle, trying to soothe. We take it poor Vera (her name *would* be 'Vera', wouldn't it?) is high-strung and terribly needy. Jenkins met her once, years ago, says she seemed head over heels infatuated with Tremayne. "His looks," I said, "she fell for his looks." "And then went on falling," said Ken, who calls her The Nemesis. After all, she is likely a steady cause of Tremayne's foul temper, which sulks out of him like a trusty gas leak.

He has taken to smirking these days whenever he hands me an assignment. As if to mock, *Still here, Pearson? Haven't managed a ticket out yet?* If truth be told, my impatience is mounting. Mary keeps asking about the same damn ticket.

I was telling you last time about the pipe and my little sister.

The opium brought Irene to me. I saw her in the Shimpling house on the day she arrived with a tall thin reptile on her arm and a look on her face that said the reptile had won her heart. A German reptile no less, attached in some nebulous capacity to his country's trade office in Manchester. He kept his hat and coat on when he came into the house. His eyes darted about and his feet never stopped shuffling. Father was speechless at being introduced, in his own home, in *German*, to a man he forever after referred to as the Hitler arse licker. He addressed him only once, in English. He said "Are you a Nazi?" When Irene hushed the man from answering and announced she was going to marry him – marry this shifty uncouth reptilian spawn of the enemy – our horror-struck father managed four words, "Over my dead body." That was nearly five years ago. Daughter and father have not spoken since.

I was wrong to take my father's side.

All these years I have felt only cold indifference toward Irene, acted as if she were no longer alive. In the house on Eaton Square it came to me that I owe her compassion. My little sister did not wish to estrange the pater. She never hated him. What she hated was herself. More precisely, she hated her lethal unattractiveness to men. Until the German came along no man ever looked twice at her. The birthmark below her right eye made sure of that. The pater had done what he could during her childhood. He spared no expense consulting the best doctors. The medical profession offered a multi-syllable Latin term for the unfortunate blemish and insisted it was too deep to remove. So Irene grew up with a shriek of chocolate on her face no make-up could hide. It masked her with a permanent scowl. The wretched girl never had a boyfriend. She engaged herself to the bottle and drowned her disappointment in gin. She found she could live quite happily in a perpetually drunken state. To hell with all the men who ignored her. To hell with the world that blighted her.

Then the reptile appeared and showered affection on her. Irene eased off the bottle and started practicing a drier devotion. Did she love him? I don't know. Did the German love Irene? I have no idea. She apparently thought he did. She went so far as to adopt his worldview and let the world know it by joining the Mosley movement. This enraged me not simply because Mosley and his thugs are pure shit on legs but because it demonstrated contempt for our father. Her perverse condemnations of imperialist Britain had been juvenile, but now it appeared she was throwing rebellion in our father's face. Never before in her life had Irene demonstrated any interest in organised politics; she couldn't tell a fascist from a Fabian. When the reptile was recalled to Berlin she went with him, thinking good riddance to miserable memories.

One night a year later she staggered into a Wannsee hospital, an arm broken and eyes blackened. The local police were called. When they paid a visit to the matrimonial nest they found Irene's husband nursing a gash in his skull. She had walloped her hubby with a frying pan. A good thing she fled, because the police also found a collection of antique duelling pistols and recent vintage Lugers, several of the latter loaded. The reptile was arrested for possessing unlicensed guns. Who knows what might have happened if he had gotten hold of one of them before the frying pan reached him.

In the fall of '35 a note came from Irene advising me of the end of her marriage and her plan to stay on in Germany. That was my last contact with her. During a brief visit to England the next year she found it the same unwelcoming place she had scornfully abandoned. She swore to a former schoolmate she would never step foot here again. The schoolmate told me Irene had obviously resumed relations with the bottle, and that was the last I heard ... until Gerald Campion resurrected Irene in the vetting. Happily his file contained no mention of the Mosley connection.

My dipsomaniac little sister. Her anger never won my sympathy. The best it did was fascinate me, and then only because angry people always fascinate me.

The pipe brought compassion, then guilt. I saw the poor girl as a victim of circumstance. Maybe I deserved part of the blame, maybe a large part. Had I been a weak selfish failure as a brother, too often the timid abstainer rather than protector? Shame on me.

I dozed on and off in the flower-bedecked room in Eaton Square. Different visions came and went. They seemed urgently profound at the time, yet they escape my recall now. One image did stick. Damon had left the room and when he returned after a long absence his eyes were quiet, reserved, sated, and a private smile played on his lips. I instantly guessed why. That is when the memory came of a pack of boys on a visit to the Fitzwilliam in Cambridge ... an event forgotten for thirty years.

We were barely into prep and this was our first time in a museum. Can you see us? Fresh-faced little lads herded through myriad wonders but not really interested, more caught up in playing pranks or besting our chums in clever disdain of all the arty tosh. None of us took much interest in the life-sized marble of the nude boy standing in an alcove. It was ancient, Greek, polished to a gleam and ... beautiful. The thing probably made us uneasy precisely because it was beautiful. Weren't we all latent footballers and military men? It would never have occurred to us to describe the statue as exquisite. Days later, who knows how the rumour started, who knows if there was any truth to it, word got out that one among us had indeed taken an interest in the statue, a bizarre interest, some whispered, a 'sick, unholy' interest. Word was that he had slipped from the group and made his way back to the alcove. A master found him there with his clothes off; arms and legs and hands encircling, feeling, caressing, connecting. The strangest damn sight the master had seen in all his days. The sight of two boys, one immaculately nude in glistening stone, the other naked in clinging trembling flesh. Eight-year-old Damon in worshipful discovery and embrace …

I dozed and came awake, dozed and came awake. Vaguely noted the restless Damon again leaving the room and soon returning, latching the door behind him. The candlelight was dim and pleasant, the scent of the flowers increasingly poignant. The room was furnished with low couches perfect for loafing. While I was awake my thoughts were not made of words but took the form of visceral streams and tended toward … confession.

My letters to you came to mind, dearest Heidi. I saw them as a vault of feeling, a refuge, a haven. I reached out to you across the ocean, addressed you from my lofty confessional. "I adore you," I said. "Thank you for everything you are to me."

"You're welcome," replied Damon.

I had said it aloud.

My eruptive laugh did not break the spell, only shifted it. The laugh was spontaneous and wonderful, and the spell now hugged Damon. "I am a lucky man," I said, "to have a friend like you."

"I can say the same."

"I'm luckier," I boomed.

"Very good, Joff," he said. "I hear no self-consciousness."

"What do you mean?"

"People go through life with shyness holding them down like an anchor. You are light as air right now."

"You are the greatest man I know, Dame, but at this moment I can make neither head nor tail of what you're saying."

"We should not be afraid," he said, "to say things we don't normally say."

I had the sensation then of listening to our conversation from a distance, as if I were a third party.

Damon said, "I want to tell you, it was not because of The Duchess's age, and not because the woman is hideous, that I refused what she offered."

From somewhere a draft came and all the candles in the room wavered.

"Then why – ?"

"With women, with any woman, I am impotent."

The sensation of distance took on another odd aspect. I was seeing the two of us up close, not through a magnifier as it were, but through a powerful telescope. I asked, "You know this … how?"

"Repeated experience. Eventually I saw it as another evidence of who and what I am."

"Dame, did you fuck someone in this house tonight?"

He was stretched out on one of the low couches. He gathered himself and stood, looking at me intently. He made a motion with both hands as if he were pulling open his chest. The gesture took me back to the studio, the night of photography, his brash nakedness. "Thank you for the honest questions, Joff. May I ask one?"

In the dim light I made out a Damon drawn into himself without his usual worldly might. He seemed to have shed his authority, all the years of his success and celebrity. We were young chums again, both nobodies, almost equal again. "May I speak?" he said.

I nodded, not trusting my voice.

He spoke and what he said was not a question but an admission, a sincerity pulled from a long-hesitant heart. Now that it was in the open I realised I had expected it for years, ever since that day in the glade when he stood with nature and revealed himself. "Please know," he said softly, "this is not the opium talking."

He sat and for a long while in the dim candlelight we held each other's eyes and conversed without a word. He knew he could trust me, that was the great thing, the unique fibre of our friendship. Few men could have this conversation, even silently. Finally I said, "You know I cannot."

"Do you understand my – ?"

"Dame!"

He put up a hand like a stop sign, fingers splayed wide. His authority, the familiar confidence, started flowing back. "It satisfies me to know you are aware," he said, "and that neither of us is uncomfortable. Are you fine?"

"I'm fine."

As I write, Heidi, my thoughts are in no order but neither are they in disarray. My friend spoke an innocent, electrifying truth, one impossible for me to reciprocate, yet no fissure opened between us. That is something we can be proud of. The awkwardness was made small, the potential rupture nullified, by the truth of what I replied to him … I am fine.

Lots of love,
Joff

Saturday
10th July 1937

Dear Heidi,

My ladies are at the hairdresser's, a special treat for Vicky because she insists on appearing totally imperial (her word, not mine) at Jenny's wedding tonight. Graham has spared no expense, the event promises to be grand. Little Jenny! I can remember her fresh from the womb. In a few hours that cute little bundle will be a stunning bride. *Tempus fugit*, Heidi. Before we know it your little Max will be declaring his first candidacy for a seat in Washington and by then Vicky will have conquered … I don't know what she'll have conquered. I only hope to live long enough to see it.

What a treat to see her day after day at breakfast and supper. She holds forth like a budding politician on any number of topics. That comes from religiously devouring the newspapers, a habit she inherited from yours truly. I look at her bent over her books which she regularly brings to the dinner table, my incorrigible plum, and feel as if Mary and I have contributed something special to the species. I look at her and … hear an announcement from Mary today that our darling will be attending a summer tutorial outside of London, starting next week.

I protested. I waved my arms. Vicky is nine years-old! We already send her away for the school year. The summer is for uninterrupted home time, for *fun*. I said I would not hear of it.

I heard of it.

This particular tutorial, Mary patiently enlightened me, is offered to only a handful of gifted students. Our daughter was singled out for her exceptional aptitude in history, and represents an opportunity not to be missed. I was going to say it could very easily be missed, but then Vicky chimed in about how keen she is to go! What remained of my resistance melted away when I heard the venue … Balliol College. Good lord, did you know summer tutorials for prep-school girls exist in such exalted precincts? I surrendered. My little girl at Oxford!

My plum will be home again in two weeks and will be joining us for our August getaway in the Cotswolds. But I am reminded again of a sneaking preference for the way things are done on your side of the pond. Is it true that very few Americans, even among the wealthy, send their children away to school?

Summer has settled in nicely. I actually escaped punishment *twice* last week when I forgot my umbrella. They are calling for a dryer season than normal, thank the gods. The weather in the sunroom has also been temperate, what with the work flow at a low boil and Tremayne acting like a human being. My real hero is Ken. He is increasingly covering for Jenkins, whose inadequacies would otherwise be out in the open. Jenkins has told us, freely admitted to us, he cannot afford the pasture yet. He needs another year of full salary. Ken and I promised to get him there.

I finally received the written statement from the defector Otto Stroebel. What a mess. Reminded me of how otherwise intelligent people can be dunderheads when it comes to putting pen to paper. The statement should have taken me a day, but it took me four to untangle his syntax and straighten out his thoughts. Beneath his layers of repetition and self-glorification, one remark that Huntington had curtly dismissed during the interview seized my attention. It referred to the depth of Jew-hate that obsesses the Nazis and guides their policy. Stroebel baldly asserts that the National Socialist Party supports extinction of the Jewish race, not only in Germany and among the Arabs, but universally. I shaped my translation to reflect as closely as possible his matter-of-fact mention of this fanciful enormity.

The latest news of Damon has left me scratching my head. All the art hacks have been calling him for comment about the ballyhooed Picasso exhibition, since his views on the Spaniard are predictably contrarian. The big event opens at the Clement next week. Here is our friend in full vexation in yesterday's *Telegraph:*

> We asked Mr. Damon Chadwick, England's leading realist painter, if he would be attending the opening of the much-heralded show.
>
> "As a matter of fact I am going to take part," he replied, "but I will not be celebrating."
>
> Asked to explain his remark, Mr. Chadwick said, "Can I be expected to doff my cap to a giant who chooses to act the dwarf?"
>
> The onetime *enfant terrible* of British art went on to

elaborate, "Picasso is one of the most gifted artists of all time. His skills are protean, legendary and unmatched. But look at what he has done with his talent. In Olympian fashion, with the permission of his reputation, he has chosen to paint in the language of bafflement and gibberish. A champion of elocution has reverted to the gruntings and mewlings of illiteracy. I bow to the towering master whom Picasso once was. I turn away from the charlatan he has become."

The Director of the Clement Gallery told the *Telegraph* that to his knowledge no invitation to the opening has been sent to Mr. Chadwick, although of course the distinguished artist would be welcome to attend.

When we asked the painter what role he envisioned for himself at the event, he said heartily, "Do come. I promise you the diametric opposite of disappointment."

I have no idea what he has in store, and he refuses to tell me. When I persisted, he said he could not possibly spoil the surprise and recommended I be outside the Clement a few minutes before eight. "Make sure you're there, Joff. *Outside* the Clement."

Our friend *can* be tiresome. I shall be patient, dutifully guard against being late, and attend as instructed. The whatever-it-is will take place next Thursday evening.

Must receive a letter from you soon or I will jump from a high building. It has been too long. Write! You will be missed at Jenny's wedding tonight.

Your faithful servant,
Joff

Saturday
17th July 1937

Dear Heidi,

One understands now what our friend meant when he mused about a thunderclap. He let one loose two days ago, no mistake. I suppose it was for the edification of his ego because absolutely everybody is talking about Damon Chadwick again. Unfortunately most of the talk is disapproving and a good chunk of it contemptuous. There may not be a single art critic in the country saying a nice word, but so what? The critics are the bastards responsible for his flagging popularity. In his view he has just kicked them in the collective groin. At least I think that's his view.

If you would like some cuttings I could spare a few from the pile collected for Vicky. The bizarre evening made the quality papers, and the low-brows gave it huge play. Damon positively bathed in the uproar. "This should do it," he said on the telephone the next day.

"Do what?"

"Why, attract the proper attention and help me play my historic role."

"Of course, how silly of me."

London has no mural to match it. The tribute of 'monumental' will not appeal to the offended, but the thing certainly merits that description in terms of scale. The thing is eleven feet high and forty-four feet wide. Photos in the newspapers do it little justice.

Shrewd, very shrewd of the bookshop down the road from the Clement to lend the side of its building. Damon's fresco has turned the place into a destination. Traffic on the road comes to a halt as motorists brake for a good gawk. The scandal-smitten are arriving at all hours. Spotlights have been installed for night viewing, and did I mention a bobby patrols the site to discourage vandals?

During the previous two weeks passersby had no inkling what was going on. At no small cost Damon organised the scaffolding and tarpaulins, as well as the kiln and a variety of other props. He hired genuine brickies to come and go with bags of masonry cement. They climbed up and down the scaffolding with trowels, tongs and mortar boards, generally giving the impression a fix-up was underway. Within the tarps a bank of torches lit up the wall while he worked. Damon told me once that painting ceilings was not his style ("There are no Sistine Chapels in my future"), but he never let on about walls. Madness, utter tomfoolery, but the result, my dear Heidi …

Mary joined me for the event, grudgingly. She was at work on a new recruitment manual for the service and wanted to spend the evening with it. We were overdue for a bit of fun, however, so I insisted we make an occasion of it, come what may. We dined on roast beef and triple helpings of asparagus at Henderson's, then strolled over to the Clement. It was ten of eight when we arrived. The vernissage had opened an hour earlier and looked ablaze with festivity. The gallery was well beyond capacity, the overflow still lined up at the door. A large crowd too was milling on the pavement, no doubt attracted by Damon's mysterious summons in the *Telegraph*. Nothing unusual seemed afoot, though I did notice the wall of the bookshop down the street covered with an immense green tarp.

I was checking my watch at five of eight when a chauffered Bentley pulled up in front of the gallery. Damon emerged. He was in black tie and looking his best self. He had clearly visited a competent barber. You might have thought he was a film star arriving for a gala premiere. Following him from the car were two gentlemen in white tie and tails and a young lady in long black chiffon. The chauffeur, an elderly man with a rigid military air, went round to the boot. He retrieved three instrument cases and presented them with theatrical deference to the trio of musicians. I heard myself think, *What in heaven's name are you up to, old friend?*

Damon looked about with satisfaction at the crowd, then led his trio to the empty lot adjacent to the bookshop. The crowd, Mary and I in its midst, drifted along. We watched as the musicians opened their cases. One of the gentlemen took out a trumpet, the other a trombone, the young lady a French horn. Damon was consulting his watch and glancing at the roof of the bookshop.

At a minute of eight Mary alerted me to a young man on the roof. He too was in formal attire and wearing white gloves into the bargain. He took hold of a rope clearly meant to hoist the green tarp, then stood at attention. All about us people were looking up. Everyone now understood what was in the offing. The chatter faded and a sense of imminent revelation overtook the crowd. At eight sharp the trio of musicians raised their instruments and launched the first notes of a shattering fanfare. It was Henry Purcell's *Trumpet Voluntary*, a masterpiece of audacious brass that beats all for sheer pomp. It completely hushed the crowd with the sound of jubilant proclamation.

You are a raving lunatic, old friend, but well done!

A minute into the salute, the white-gloved fellow on the roof began pulling up the green curtain. I caught sight of Damon scanning the crowd, his eyes darting about to collect first impressions as his giant mural came into view. Once the wall was fully unveiled, the musicians ceased playing and a silence of awe settled over the crowd. All eyes were absorbed in the stupendous scene.

The mural transports you to the edge of a battlefield. Above hunkers a grotesque thundercloud, besieging the panorama with a ferocious rain. No combat is evident on the battlefield, no actual grapple between enemy forces, but your immediate sense is of *confrontation*. Your eye is drawn to a great army in ordered ranks emerging from a remote, gloriously sunlit horizon. The army is marching in focused pageant toward a celestial city on a hill. You realise at once the identity, origin and purpose of this army. It is mankind itself, forged in a radiant cradle and bearing courage, defiance, resolve. The march symbolises the relentless advance of humanity, its hard progress and inexorable triumph – its empire of history. Upon this army of civilisation is falling the ferocious rain, a malevolent, tumultuous downpour in the form of watery chunks and globs, some large as hailstones, others tiny as bugs, plunging from the grotesque thundercloud that sprawls across the sky. Mary saw the meaning before I did, and let out a gasp.

"Oh, sterling," she said. *"Sterling!"*

I had only a moment to reflect on this rare instance of Mary expressing approval, however indirectly, of Damon, before I too grasped the significance of what he had painted. "Oh, Jesus Christ."

You find his meaning in the thundercloud, which on close inspection reveals Damon's parody and outrageous slur. He had painted the cloud in the manner of the cubist while cleverly remaining the realist. Taken as a whole it appears a classic swollen mass of pent-up storm, but wait, look carefully, you see a jigsaw at work in the composition, a cloud made of shifting planes and overlapping surfaces, each of which reveals a distinct feature of a most recognisable face. Here you see the dome of the famous forehead, there the renowned pugnacious nose. Those piercing eyes are world-renowned, you know to whom they belong. Suddenly there came a hubbub of provoked, agitated, angry voices confirming, yes, the fragmented pieces of the awful cloud add up to a mocking portrait of the man being fêted down the street at the Clement. And then the crowd recognises among the clefts and fissures of the awful sprawling cloud the pursed lips and heaving mouth of the world's most famous artist, and the inference is unmistakable. The fierce rain pouring down like ordnance is Picasso's awesome spit.

Then it gets worse.

You haven't noticed this yet, Mary hasn't either, but a few in the crowd have their arms lifted and jabbing. They're shouting, alerting you to an obscenity. *Do you see it?* And then you do, everyone sees it now, in the roiling folds of the cloud at the border of the mural, the great artist's bloated manhood, adding its own special stream to the rain …

Well, try to imagine the commotion *that* developed. Once you see it, the outrage is as clear as day. Here is a depiction of the living legend of modern art defiling in the rudest terms the standard-bearers of civilisation. Maybe with reason this moved a good many of the assembled Londoners, normally self-possessed, unflappable, well-mannered citizens, to forget their composure and heckle the mural, jeer and shake their fists at it. We heard angry screams of *Shame! Shame!* A woman crying Wicked!

Did our friend expect otherwise? This was total provocation, an invitation to infamy. Why slander Picasso in such a wanton way? What was there to gain? Damon was nowhere to be seen now, which was perhaps his good fortune because one scandalised boffin very close to us bawled, *Hang the fascist Chadwick!*

Fascist? Hang? Would you believe it came to that in dear old London-town on a warm summer night in the year of our lord 1937? The scene was surreal. I had to restrain my Mary, *my Mary*, from giving the screaming boffin a piece of her mind. What was going on? I steered her away as quickly as I could. There may have been other Damon-supporters in the crowd, but not a single Bravo! did I hear braved. On the contrary, as we fled the area a chant went up of *Tear it down! Tear it down!*

On the telephone the next morning I told Damon he had orchestrated a bedlam. "That crowd you enraged," I said, "became a cartoon in *Punch*."

He pronounced himself delighted, then added, "All in all though I would prefer a leader in *The Economist*."

Madness. Madness multiplied and stirred.

He said he would love to stay in London and enjoy the storm but he absolutely had to be back in Germany and was leaving that very afternoon. What do you make of it all, Heidi? I have ceased trying to understand him.

Have our friends written to tell you Jenny's wedding was a midsummer night's dream, Jenny a goddess, her groom almost worthy? Graham was so pleased he looked as if he were in the captain's chair of an ocean liner and enjoying every bit of the view. A delight to see him getting his money's worth. Our Vicky has grown gregarious. She went about introducing herself to all the guests. I had the feeling it was the mature 'do' of her hair that made her the bold little lady of the ball. The event was almost perfect – you were missed!

My usual forbidden and eternally chaste love,

Joff

Tuesday
20th July 1937

Heidi,
Shame on our friend. Shame!

I assume you know about yesterday's vile event in Germany. Every single London paper reported it today, many on the front page. I know because I bought them all, though I will not be saving any cuttings for Vicky. When I saw Damon's name among the attending dignitaries I wanted to vomit. Thank God there were no photos of him. I *would* have vomited.

The thought occurred of pulling down his portrait of my daughter and taking a scissors to it, then mailing him the shreds wrapped in *Der Sturmer*. I feel he has betrayed her. Lied to his country. Lied to *me*. And for what? To ingratiate himself with his Kraut collectors? Sell a few paintings to the dwarf Goebbels?

It seems most of the reporters covering the vile show had no idea of the proper tone to assume. Should they be outraged and contemptuous? Or should they fall down laughing? I think they chose to be outraged and contemptuous while falling down laughing.

Only the Nazis would be sick enough to mount an exhibit devoted entirely to art they hate. The show consists of paintings and sculptures which Dr. Goebbels's culture police have censored and confiscated. All forms of modern art – from Bauhaus to Dada, from expressionism to surrealism – have been ruled *verboten* in Germany. You cannot put a Matisse or a Van Gogh on the wall of a German museum. And Picasso! He is *the* villain among villains. The works of such 'apes' and 'barbarians' are forbidden, banned, outlawed. Over six hundred of these 'Jew-infected' works are now on display in Munich. The exhibit purports to prove just how degenerate they are by hanging them beside squiggly sketches taken from patients in mental hospitals!

The Nazis think they have orchestrated a giant exercise in ridicule. Which they have, but not in the sense they planned. They come across as comic-opera buffoons. And there was our Damon among them, giving the grotesque spectacle his benediction. My disappointment is … well, how can I express the degree of it? Vicky's portrait is safe, but serious furies are burning deep within me.

All those attention-seeking antics of his, we can understand them now. Spreading his face across acres of newsprint. Ranting on the wireless against modern art. He even stooped to atheism, another means of flattering his Nazi patrons. And then the timing of his giant Picasso circus ... obviously no coincidence. Look at the sub-head in the *Times*: Weinhauf Gallery triples Chadwick's prices. Several of his canvases even made it into the so-called Great German Art Exhibition across the hall from the decadent 'unhealthy' art. They have grouped him with the 'rational' painters, the 'authentically Aryan' painters. Maybe now he will find more ways to pardon National Socialism. Did I already say I want to vomit?

We may be able to defend him against the charge of being a fraud, Heidi, but not against the truth which this monstrous thing in Munich makes plain. Our friend has not merely turned hypocrite and panderer. He is now officially a prostitute.

Nearly midnight. Forgive my venting.

Joff

Friday
23rd July 1937

Dear Heidi,
This day brings a much happier reason to write than what unleashed my spleen a few days ago. We come again to a milestone that glows and pulses on my calendar. Happy birthday, great lady.

Pardon the torn pages from my notepad. I am stuck in the tube at Marble Arch. Motionless for fifteen long minutes. The heat grows awful. Muted grumbling can be heard up and down the carriage. The fidgety shopgirl to my left is appallingly perfumed and making no effort to hide her interest in my scribble. The stolid matron to my right has a grip on her brolley sufficiently tight to choke a horse, and she too is spying on these words …

We are off. Pardon the jar in my scrawl. Will post this at the lunch hour and think good thoughts for you through the day.

Damon telephoned from Berlin two nights ago. He was anxious to tell me the British newspapers had made a mistake. I will tell you about that next time. This note is about YOU.

To a delightful and enchanting birthday, enjoyed in supreme spirits. Hugs and love,
Joff

Saturday
31st July 1937

Dear Heidi,
We met our Balliol alumna off the train yesterday. Should you remain incredulous about Vicky going to an Oxford tutorial, you are not alone. Nine years-old! At that age I wanted to ride my bicycle all summer.

Vicky was thrilled to meet girls like herself from all over Britain. They were eleven in the group, two or three of whom 'might have been smarter' than our darling. She gushed nineteen to the dozen about the professors who spoke to them like equals. The professors were actually graduate students at the College, exercising their lecturing skills and introducing the eager girls to the diverse currents of the human story. Vicky was particularly impatient to tell us about the one and only lady lecturer. "She came in wearing a red beret and *trousers*. She was an *American*. We all adored her *instantly*."

I do believe this was our daughter's first encounter with a denizen of the great Republic. To hear Vicky describe her, the trousered scholar stood out like a bright star among the earnest but relentlessly bland young lecturers. She tossed a single question at the girls and made it the centrepiece of her day with them: *Do events create great men, or do great men create events?*

The brilliant little girls started buzzing but before anyone could respond, the young lady from America said, "Don't answer that yet. First answer this: What is absolutely wrong with the *question* I just asked?"

Vicky looked from Mary to me, then back to Mary. Her lips quivered with the fabulous secret clamouring to fly loose. "I'm stumped," said Vicky's father. "So am I," said Vicky's mother. "The question leaves out great *women!*" Vicky shrieked. "Nobody guessed but me!"

Which prompted my onetime-suffragette spouse to give our darling a hug for the ages. Then I did the same because history is obviously a fraud if it pretends girls like ours cannot shake the world.

"There was one professor I *hated*," she said.

"Victoria!"

"I *am* sorry, but it's true."

Apparently the offending lecturer gave the girls a summary of his

246

doctoral thesis which makes the case that Britain is exhausted, broke, finished as a world power. Vicky had smoke coming out of her ears. "He was wearing thick glasses and first we thought he was *old*," she said, rolling her eyes. "We called him Mr. Goggle Face. He came with a big map and pointed at all the red and said, look girls, it does seem as if the good old British Empire has spread wider than ever since the Great War but what you are looking at is a *mirage*. He said that, Mummy, he said we were looking at a mirage. He said the War made us *poor*. He asked if we knew who came out the real winner from the War? America, that's who. It was the factories of America that turned the tide. Did we girls know how much we owed to America after the War? It was a thousand million pounds, a thousand million. He said our country might still be *pretending* on the world stage but really we are *staggering*. He said that, Daddy. He said Great Britain's time at the top is over. It sounded not right to me. It sounded very wrong to me. I didn't like Mr. Goggle Face *at all*."

I looked at Mary and Mary looked at me, and we were both thinking our daughter had made another of those leaps out of childhood that suddenly ambush parents when their children start relating to the wider world. This was something different from Vicky's outburst at Mr. Churchill's lecture. This was measured independent judgment we were hearing. For now, Heidi, you're safe. Max will remain in complete and exclusive awe of you for at least six or seven years. Then one day, like a lightning strike out of the blue, when he should not know such things or even be thinking about them, he will let loose a learned observation about the price of tea in Ceylon.

I needed to know from our darling what she and her band of underage historians did for *fun* during their weeks at Oxford. She casually mentioned being taken to a bunch of boring landmarks, though she admitted to a good impression of the Bridge of Sighs at Hertford College. Then she glowingly described a tour of the Bodleian Library.

I must go out at once to buy her a bicycle. But first I have to tell you about Damon's telephone call from Germany.

He went to some difficulty and expense to get it through. He wanted me to know – and insisted I let others know, starting with Maddy Kloff – that the British newspapers had made a mistake. He did not attend the Munich exhibit. Nor had he endorsed it. He was invited to the opening but declined to go. Dr. Goebbels however still included his name on the list of attending dignitaries. "I suppose my name on that list disturbed you," he said.

"Disturbed is not the half of it."

"Well, I wasn't there. You know I will have no truck with censorship."

"Your behaviour lately … it made me accept you *were* there."

"That is … hurtful."

"I am also sickened to think you have become a dignitary in Nazi Germany."

"How am I to keep people from calling me names?"

"For some in England you've become a fascist."

"Then I rest my case about name-calling."

"Bollocks. You *created* their case."

"If that is so, I can only say I'm being misjudged."

"True, because I know you're not a fascist."

"Well, thank you for – "

"But the charge of being a whore might be more difficult to disprove."

There is quite a distance between London and Berlin, but the telephone wizards have done an amazing job of shortening it to about six inches. That is how near I felt to Damon. For a moment we were nose to nose and I had just slapped him across the face.

He let out a short laugh with no humour in it. "Well, at least I know how angry this cock-up has made you."

"Why are you surprised? Ten minutes after you slander Picasso in London, you hurry back to Berlin. What is the purpose of the giant mural if not to scream your name all the way to Germany and triple your prices at the Weinhauf?"

"Please never think it was about my prices."

"Let me tell you what else I think. You have an ego with two main features, Dame. One, the thing is huge. Two, it hates being deflated. So you carted your ego to a place more receptive and had it pumped back up. I would have no problem with that, except the place you chose is not one where good men should go."

He spared me a rebuttal. He seemed to have listened respectfully. With some solemnity, he said, "You misjudge me, Joff."

Right, I misjudge him.

The telephone connection weakened and his voice faded, but not before he extracted a pledge from me to exonerate him with Maddy and others. Which I have since done. Our decades of friendship bring me back to lenience, even nudge me towards tolerance. But oh, that slap across the face I gave him felt good.

Mary is out on her Saturday rounds, and Vicky's on the chesterfield with Southey's *Life of Nelson*. I really must do something about that bicycle. For the moment, dear Heidi, I suppose all is well with the world, or at least my corner of it. I send good cheer to you and yours.

Joff

Saturday
14th Aug. 1937

Dear Heidi,
What a magnificent gift from That American. I applaud him again for treating you like royalty. I have no idea what a Studebaker Coupe looks like, and when did you learn to drive? Is it a regular thing for women over there? I can see Her Ladyship motoring about Boston with a dazzling smile and her honey-coloured eyes alight, carefree as a bird. I am feeling rather plebeian now for sending birthday wishes from a stalled tube train on pages torn from a notepad.

Work grinds on as I await more calls from Reg Huntington. This morning I translated an article from a Hanover newspaper that boasts about the complete Nazification of German education. Apparently you can no longer teach in Germany unless certified as unquestioningly loyal to National Socialist doctrine. Thousands of teachers have been dismissed. And that is not the most disturbing thing I learned about Hitler's subjugation of education. The Nazis have declared the triumph of a glorious thing called 'German science', which is opposed to an odious thing called 'Jewish science'. Einstein has thus been branded a villain. Nazi infamy … wearing a clown's nose.

You must update me on what your American friends are saying about Mr. Hitler and his oppressions. Do they care? Do they know?

Meanwhile louder and louder grumblings are being heard in the lunchroom. It seems Mr. Chamberlain has outdone Mr. Baldwin in asserting control over foreign policy. The marching orders for Britain's mission in the world now emanate from Number 10. Our betters upstairs have become note-takers and messengers. The Prime Minister's holy grail is peace, secure and lasting peace, and if the avoidance of conflict requires concessions to the likes of Hitler and Mussolini, then so be it. Talk abounds that the Prime Minister and his Foreign Secretary, Mr. Eden, are seriously clashing.

"Woe unto those who propose standing up to Hitler," says Ken, who claims all his fears about Chamberlain are coming true. "The undertaker has it in his head that Herr Hitler can be reasoned with."

"How do you know what's in his head?" I said, lightheartedly.

He replied fiercely. "I read Hansard. Did you see Chamberlain's latest? Our gutless leader said Germany has legitimate grievances and deserves its rightful place in Europe. In other words, stand back, cease all interference, give free reign to a bloodthirsty dictatorship."

Must bring Ken on my next visit to Bury. My father would adore him.

The Pearson family leaves tomorrow for the Cotswolds, once again to spend a fortnight in the good Mr. Benson's little cottage. My chief aim, aside from enjoying respite from Tremayne (and Ken's righteous indignation), will be to re-acquaint myself with the finest in English goat cheese. Vicky has warned me her trudging over hill and dale will be limited as she will be devoting herself to all three volumes of *A Child's History of England*. Has there ever been such a daughter in the annals of the British Empire?

A second summer holiday, Heidi? Good for you. I am unfamiliar with the Adirondacks. I take it they too are mountains. First the Laurentians, now the Adirondacks. Consider yourself envied, and have a spectacular end of summer. May you loaf in your cherished bare feet to your heart's content.

Joff

Tuesday
24th Aug. 1937

Dear Heidi,
About the London postmark, my holiday has been interrupted. I come
to you from an F.O. conference room. A portrait of Lord Castlereagh
is staring down at me rather glumly. If I remember correctly from
my schoolboy days, he was Foreign Secretary during the wars with
Napoleon. In this painting he appears so mournful you might think
Wellington gave it up at Waterloo.

The summons came yesterday by telegram from Reg Huntington.
REQUIRE YOUR SERVICES TOMORROW. STOP. FOR PERM
UND-SEC. STOP. ARRIVE AT EIGHT FOR BRIEFING. STOP.
I have to say, the telegram sent a few ripples up my spine. It gave Mary
a thrill too. "The Permanent Under-Secretary," she said, eyes alight.
"*There's* a step forward."

Needless to say, I did not dare voice a complaint to her about having
to break off my holiday. I packed some goat cheese and caught the first
train.

I like Sir Robert. A genuinely affable man. He tempers elegance with
humility, like the best of his class. He shook my hand with sincerity,
and afterwards thanked me for a job well done. If I should be struck
dead tomorrow, my daughter will at least be able to claim I once
participated in an affair of state.

I exaggerate. It was no affair of state. The meeting was short, barely a
courtesy call, and a distinctly frosty one at that. Hardly worth suffering
an amputation of my holiday. Sir Robert's visitor was a disagreeable
man by the name of Wolfgang Gebauer. The chubby Herr Gebauer
is leader of something called the Sudetendeutsch Global Friendship
Society. Huntington briefed me before the meeting and said one of
the aims of Herr Gebauer's organisation may be to promote friendship
with Britain and the rest of the world, but its most likely *raison d'être* is
to propagate the grievances of the German minority in Czechoslovakia.

"The Sudetendeutsch form the largest minority of Germans in
any country of Europe," said Huntington. "Before the War the
Sudetenland was part of Austria-Hungary, but in 1919 the Treaty of
Versailles grafted it onto Czechoslovakia. The Sudetendeutsch despise

the Czechs."

"Why?"

"They claim the Czechs are trying to submerge their identity. Our embassy in Prague identifies Herr Gebauer's organisation as a front for the Sudeten Nazi Party, which the Czechs have tried to repress."

"Why meet the man then?"

"Ear to the ground kind of thing."

"Are the Germans actually being oppressed by the Czechs?"

"Not really. Understand, our main concern is Germany's view of the matter. For years Hitler has ranted about protecting German minorities outside the Reich. Lately the sounds coming from Berlin have ratcheted up."

"What is our government's position?"

"We support the unity of Czechoslovakia," said Huntington. "What Sir Robert requires is a faithful rendition of his firmness and resolve. You are not to soften any of his words."

I nodded.

"Our guest will have no interpreter of his own. As you did with the defector Stroebel, you will be doing double duty."

I nodded again.

"One more thing. Give us notes later of any thoughts you might have about our guest's choice of words, habits of language and the like. You might try to discern what he is not saying, what the man is *thinking*. One never knows what might prove useful."

What a flaming joke. You travel to a mountain, prepare to spend hours climbing it, and then find yourself pissing away a few minutes on a tiny hill. Which is precisely how long Herr Gebauer's visit lasted, a few paltry minutes. The notion that he was head of a friendship society was preposterous. He was ungrateful, abrasive and rude. He could hardly say half a dozen polite words in succession, and his tone carried warning and menace. Reminded me of a retired captain of the Guards who frequents The Squire's. Allow him one too many pints and you had better value his wisdom or he'll wreak havoc and mayhem. Same species of truculent ass.

Our chubby guest's suitcoat was too tight and his collar unbuttoned, leaving his necktie askew. He never thanked the Under-Secretary for receiving him. He indulged no preliminaries save for a perfunctory handshake. "Herr Vansittart," he said gruffly, "the people of the Sudetenland will be disappointed to learn Secretary Eden refused to meet their representative."

There were similarities in his German to the Austrian and Silesian, as well as other influences. The traces of dialect that crept in were new to me but comprehensible enough.

"Secretary Eden is away, and you are meeting His Majesty's senior civil servant in the Foreign Office," replied Sir Robert. "Your people should have no cause for disappointment."

"I came here to tell Mr. Eden, in the interest of continued friendship between our peoples, that Britain should assume a hands-off posture as regards the destiny of the Sudetendeutsch."

"Herr Gebauer, His Majesty's government has not interfered in the internal affairs of Czechoslovakia and has no intention of doing so."

Our guest looked up and aimed a rough laugh at the ceiling. "Of course not. Britain has no intention of meddling in Europe. You have only meddled there for three centuries already."

Huntington, sitting at the end of the table taking notes, rose and said, "Shall we show the gentleman the door, Sir Robert?"

This bewildered Gebauer. He had not understood, but he caught the tone. It also surprised your admirer, still a virgin in the waters of state and diplomacy where he assumed all the swimmers would be gentlemen and their behaviour impeccably mannered.

"Sit, Reginald, sit," said Sir Robert, a sad smile on his face. "We learn by listening, even if the offerings make for unpleasant noise." Then he addressed our boorish guest. "Herr Gebauer, it happens that considerable sympathy exists in the Foreign Office for the Sudeten Germans. Many of our people have been sceptical about the efforts by the Czech government to meet your grievances."

Herr Gebauer listened to my translation without a glance in my direction, keeping a sullen stare on the Under-Secretary. I suppose it will take some getting used to, this sense while I interpret of being both a hand puppet *and* invisible.

Gebauer's attitude seemed to relax a tad, but his words still conveyed rancour. "Then you understand we are cut off from our ancestral roots. My people will be relieved to hear you are aware of our predicament. You know that we live as second-class citizens in an artificial country?"

"What we know, Herr Gebauer, is that the German population too could make a greater effort at conciliation. We also know the most divisive voices among your people won support in the last elections by exploiting resentments."

This prompted another rough laugh from our guest. "If you were a German resident of the geographic fiction in which I live, Mr. Vansittart, would you not begrudge the fact that unemployment is much, much greater among your people than among the Czechs or Slovaks? Would you not resent it the more because it is exclusively a product of racial discrimination?"

"I very well might, Herr Gebauer, if what you are saying is true. Even so I would not be looking for succour in an ideology that promotes another form of racial hate. Kindly do not ask us to overlook the connection of your organisation to the government of a neighbouring foreign power."

"You are betraying a traditional British hatred of German unity and self-determination, Mr. Vansittart."

"Your statement is at once inaccurate and offensive, Herr Gebauer. But enough. I agreed to this informal meeting on the understanding you wish to deliver a message directly to my government. May I ask what the message might be?"

"Yes, Mr. Vansittart. We Sudetendeutsche are a proud people and we know our proper affinity. Should we endeavour to alter our circumstances, we sincerely hope no obstacles are placed in our path by the government of Great Britain."

"Thank you very much indeed for taking the time to meet with me," said Sir Robert, rising to his feet and indicating the meeting was over. Heidi, my first thought after they left the room was, *That's it*? I'm sitting here with Lord Castlereagh trying to make it out. I have no yardstick by which to judge what I witnessed. I can understand, however, why both parties agreed beforehand to keep their little get-together private. As for my thoughts about Herr Gebauer, I doubt if Huntington will want to file them. My few notes refer to how the fellow struck me as a gangster; how he spoke lucidly and occasionally cleverly, but invariably in a tone of menace; and how he left the impression, at least with me, that he has no doubt whatsoever that he and his mob are going to get their way ... by hook or by crook.

I will finish up this letter at the flat. Must stop by the sunroom first to see Ken, who has been holding the fort all alone this week. Tremayne and Jenkins too are on vacation …

At my grandfather's desk now. There's something eerie about knocking about in the quiet vacancy of the flat when I should be with Vicky and Mary in the Cotswolds.

Ken was glad to see me. I found him stuck in the doldrums of August, bored and slouched. He grimaced when I mentioned the meeting with Gebauer. "That hoodlum. The man is just a slimy proxy for the Nazis."

"He did give that impression."

"We let Hitler get away with the Rhineland. Now he is looking further afield."

"I found Vansittart quite firm."

"Vansittart is a good man, and so is Eden. You know as well as I do they despise the dictators, but they aren't steering the ship. Chamberlain is at the wheel, the man with no spine. The man who – "

I patted my overwrought friend on the shoulder and told him my anxiety was even greater than his. Only mine was about getting back to the hills of the Cotswolds, which I would do first thing in the morning after a good night's sleep.

Strolling from the tube to the flat I noticed our local library's Union Jack at half-mast. I bought an evening paper to see who has gone to his reward but found no obituary of note. The wireless is similarly without news of a prominent death. Curious …

Are you having a wonderful time at your mountain lake, great lady? You must tell me what new works you have in mind. Or is Max absorbing all your energies?

As ever,

Joff

Saturday
18th Sept. 1937

Dear Heidi,
Thanks for yours of the fourth, I enjoyed it. Reminded me of the follies of Vicky's parents during her nappy years. You must not feel bad, we are all novices at bringing up baby.

Apologies for the long silence. Since returning from the Cotswolds I've been under the weather. Headaches like I have never imagined. Missed two days of work. Those spells of vertigo I had last year were nothing compared to this. Think of the pain of a rotten tooth, throbbing in your mouth. Now think of the same pain in your head, *in your brain*, radiating torment. The first two days were a visit to hell. I met the devil there. Truly. Satan welcomed me to the underworld with an iron bar to the head. Blow after blow to the head. Welcome, welcome, *welcome* to your reward.

Dr. Cooper came to the flat, bless the man. When I told him light acted like a knife through my skull (and soft sounds like sledgehammers!) he instantly diagnosed migraine, but … I wonder. I never had a migraine in my life. The ergotamine he prescribed only made me groggy. Mary was marvellous. She cancelled a recruitment seminar in Hampshire and resolutely donned her nurse's cap. Her cold compresses gave some relief but the only real healer was time, slow time. The hours seemed to be pulling themselves through blinding sun and deafening cannons … the sort of perks and distractions you would expect at Satan's hotel.

Returned to work on Wednesday and sleepwalked through the week. I blame the damn ergotamine which is probably still cruising through my veins. Ken tells me I did an excellent impression, for three days, of a seated shop window mannequin.

I recall something interesting from the haze of those days. A cutting from the *Frankfurter Zeitung* came to my desk. It said the Grand Mufti of Jerusalem has declared war on Jewish immigration to Palestine, but that was not the interesting part. In the last two years, membership in a group called the Moslem Brotherhood in Egypt has shot up from a mere 800 to over 200,000. These Moslem Brothers focus their energy on the global Jewish conspiracy. They hold mass demonstrations in Cairo and march under the slogans SLAUGHTER THE JEWS and

ERADICATE THE DESCENDANTS OF PIGS AND APES. The article reminded me of the defector Stroebel, he of the erupting nasal passages. Seems he was telling the gospel truth about the Nazification of the Arabs.

The week did deliver one satisfaction. A handwritten note on embossed vellum from the Permanent Under-Secretary. *My gratitude for your skilful work. Vansittart.* A proper gentleman, Sir Robert. Maybe now will come a flood of assignments. Must go for a kip. I am still deep under the weather.

All my best to you,
Joff

Saturday
9th Oct. 1937

Dear Heidi,
Pardon my silence. Lethargy's to blame. The mysterious headaches left me a beaten pup. Only in the last little while have I sensed full recovery. Turning my stomach at this moment is the news of our former King. He and his crumple-faced consort dined with Hitler yesterday at the dictator's mountaintop aerie. Apparently Edward gave the Nazi salute. I should never have doubted my Mary about our counterfeit King. He will be remembered as a brainless boor seduced by a painted pirate; a bloodless stick of a man devoured by a vulture. At his side she only makes him look slighter, pitted, used and ashen. A sad relic and his hideous whore. Forgive me, but some things are unforgivable.

Which reminds me of Damon among the Germans, making a home for himself in Hitlerland and that leaves me ... what? Sickened by the choice he has made? Alarmed by the danger he courts with his friend? His last postcard was weeks ago and said nothing of substance.

Aside from my recovery from the mysterious headaches, I have nothing good to report. The lunch club may be dead. The coroner's inquest will probably find death by suicide. We met at The Mandrake and the event turned catastrophic. From what you were telling me about Catherine's letters I thought the group was going to hear a joyous announcement. The very opposite occurred. Catherine and Seamus arrived separately, sat apart, and made no effort to hide their glowers. We were like callow kids back in Middle School. Seamus has regained all his weight and maybe then some. A gloom settled over us. Nobody wanted to linger. Now I must wonder if the club of five will survive. Not to blame you, but we started going downhill when our sculptress sailed for America.

By the way, have you been introducing Max to King Arthur and the Round Table? Your little man may not have reached his first birthday, but we started with Vicky when she was still in the cradle and look how she's turned out. With my usual regards and love, your expert in childhood education,
Joff

Saturday
16th Oct. 1937

Dear Heidi,

My father's situation has seriously deteriorated. Mrs. Stockton tells me there are days he refuses to leave his bed, ignores most of his food, and shuns the newspapers. She said my father's mates have similarly gone downhill and she must hire a young man to help them get about and 'perform their necessaries'. I agreed to pay an additional four quid, what else can I do? Move him from the wretched house? He professes, whenever lucid, to being comfortable there and won't hear of it.

While I take stock of domestic catastrophes I should tell you the latest to afflict our neighbours above. Monsieur caught me on the stair the other day. He has rejoined the ranks of the unemployed. "I'm sorry to hear that, Martin."

"How am I to feed the young ones on thirty shillings a week?"

Unemployment relief amounts to that giant sum, hardly enough to keep Madame in sardines, never mind tinned meats for the stompers. The spinster must be draining her savings. I promised Martin I would keep an eye out for any positions. I can hardly offer to contribute, where would that stop? Besides, the extravagance of Vicky's school leaves us barely coping ourselves.

Are you keeping up on the European situation? Do American newspapers give you a sense of our dread? Tensions are rising over Nazi interference in Austria and Czechoslovakia. We fear a loose spark could set off a general fire. Meanwhile the debate rages about what should be done, or not done. Good friend Ken sees a yellow stripe painted on our foreign policy. He has taken to calling Mr. Chamberlain 'the scarecrow'. Not because of the Prime Minister's scrawny, desiccated, sharp-nosed features, but because of the tatters and rags in which he has clothed our military.

"Britain is officially pacifist now, Joff, which is the polite name for cowardly. The preacher at Number 10 has no belief in guns. No, no, perish the thought, you don't preserve your corn by investing in guns. What if the crows eat the corn? Well, Prime Minister Scarecrow has an answer. You pardon them! You find ways to exonerate them! The crows have to eat!"

"You're gibbering, Ken."

"Am I? Chamberlain will do anything to get an agreement with Germany, a *settlement*. Otherwise the cost is too high for him. There's another of his sacred ideals. Protect our financial standing, *save money*. The turkey-necked bean counter!"

The stompers are at it. The smaller demon has a tricycle now, churning across the ceiling like thunder on rails. Did I say ceiling? I meant my cranium. Goodbye, great lady. In the present circumstance the better part of valour is a brisk walk. It looks chilly but fine out there. I will post this on the way. I also send you, as ever, my faithful adoration,

Joff

Saturday
23rd Oct. 1937

Dear Heidi,
It took considerable doing but a private telephone now sits by my father's bed. I was finding it near impossible to reach him on Mrs. Stockton's line. The telephone has done wonders to alleviate my guilt. I call on Monday and Friday evenings. If I catch him in a lucid moment he reports that he can no longer bear the company of his mates (they are now 'blithering fools'). He tells me too that Mrs. Stockton's cooking has lost every bit of taste.

"You sound terrific, Dad!" A barefaced lie, but anything that further lightens my guilt should also be good for my father's morale.

A serious quarrel with Ken Retinger this week. It stemmed from reports sent by the embassy that suggest the Nazis have begun implementing a eugenics programme to eliminate weaknesses from the Aryan race. Rumours are circulating in Germany that the severely handicapped and mentally deficient have been branded *nutzlosen Esser*, 'useless eaters'. The rumours go on to say that a secret cadre of SS doctors is now quietly visiting nursing institutions throughout the Reich and singling out the *nutzlosen Esser* for… euthanasia.

"Rumours," I said to Ken, as he and I were stretching our legs during the noon hour in St James Park. "I don't believe them."

"Then you are a naïve fool," he replied.

That took me aback. My first impulse was to return the blow. "Furthermore," I said, "an allegation so implausible calls into question the discretion of our embassy. Our people should not be passing on such monstrous rumours."

He stopped on the path and faced me. "Why in hell do you insist on being wilfully blind?"

"Ken, nobody can deny what the Nazis are, but the German people are still the German people. Some charges against them simply do not stick."

"Kindly cease talking to me about the great German people. They thrust their arms out with hysterical joy at the sight of their sun-god. You give them too much credit. Is it because you're half German yourself?"

"Ken, I am as 'half German' as you are."

"Address the point, why don't you?"

"What bloody point?"

"Your precious Germans – "

"My fucking what?"

" – have embraced the devil."

"Agreed!" I shouted. "But that is a long way from treating people like vermin."

He shook his head like someone unable to believe his ears. "Your gullibility disgraces you," he said, and walked on.

I took myself to a bench and sat staring into space for awhile. A strange squall had just passed and I needed respite. When I returned to my desk, Ken ignored me. Silly stuff ... a man acting like a child. Or was it two men acting like children? Curious, but when we mended things later he expressed the same thought. "I acted like a hotheaded boy," he said. "My apologies."

"Blame the times. We get caught up in the times."

"Maybe, but I had no right saying those vicious things to you."

"You made me think," I lied.

The next day at lunch we walked the park without coming to blows. I leave you now, impatient to hear from remote, happy, oblivious America.

Joff

Saturday
6th Nov. 1937

So delighted with your news, Heidi. Truly, my heart is beating quicker for you. Best wishes as well to Matt whom I assume is also walking on air. If the happy event occurs in June, Max will be, what, twenty months older than the baby? Lucky children, to have a sibling so close in age.

Delighted too that you have finally returned to the studio. Your SEVEN MEN project sounds audacious. Pardon my concern, but I have to wonder how you can bring the figures alive if you work only from biographies and photos. Pull this off, great lady, and I guarantee your reputation will be made. Do you have a gallery waiting for the pieces? Should I have a word with Maddy Kloff?

My career as an interpreter leaped onto a rocket this week. I was summoned, hold on to your hat, to an assignment at Number 10. Huntington thought of me when an urgent call came from Chamberlain's people. Some or other mishap befell their usual interpreter. An aide came to fetch and brief me. The morning being fine we walked round by Parliament Street.

The house failed to impress. Beyond the entrance hall and famous black and white marble floor I found it … overdone. Over-decorated, I suppose I mean. Walls lined cheek by jowl with portraits. Busts on pedestals getting in your way. Bleak baroque furniture spread about. A residence trying to act like a museum and ending up a warehouse. The aide briefed me in whispers in a stuffy foyer where a trio of elderly secretaries, one greyer than the next, occupied small desks. Telephones squatted importantly here and there, but none were in use. I will say this: the eerie quiet in the house and aura of power still did their work of intoxication. I had to take special care with my rubbery legs for fear of stumbling, or veering into a grey-haired secretary.

Beside the green baize door to the PM's study hangs a portrait of Disraeli. Shows the wily fox in a relaxed mood, with a mischievous sparkle in his eye and open book in his hands, but he gazes past you to something more intriguing in the distance. Curiously it reminded me of Damon's watercolour of Vicky …

"Sir," said the aide, introducing me to the Prime Minister, "the interpreter Pearson from the Foreign Office." A thrill, Heidi, to be announced on Downing Street: *the interpreter Pearson from the Foreign Office.*

I paid extra attention to the stability of my legs as Neville Chamberlain gave my hand a perfunctory shake. "Sit here please, Mr. Pearson," he said. "Our guest will join us in a moment."

The PM is taller, thinner and paler than his photographs suggest, and his face narrower. Brought to mind Ken demoting him from undertaker to scarecrow, but both descriptions are unfair. Mr. Chamberlain has a studied intensity about him. His outward demeanour may be standoffish but you sense bristling reflection within; he is clearly *earnest.* If I were to see him in the street and guess his occupation, I would call him a vicar. Either that or a professor of medieval history. Something ethereal, no heavy lifting.

I perched on a low backless stool behind Mr. Chamberlain's armchair. He took up a file and I was instantly invisible, a piece of sentient furniture again. Such is the way of these things and understandable, though I'm still adjusting.

The guest was shown in at once. He took the twin armchair across from Mr. Chamberlain. Apparently the introductions had been made and the start of the meeting postponed until my arrival. From my briefing I knew the guest was Wilhelm Bieler, a lawyer from Vienna and personal envoy of the Chancellor of Austria.

"We can begin," said Mr. Chamberlain. "I understand Chancellor Schuschnigg wishes to inform me of certain developments in your country."

Herr Bieler was evidently a neophyte in matters of diplomacy. As I translated he made the mistake of keeping his eyes on me. Mr. Chamberlain shifted in his chair, subtly expressing annoyance. His guest took the hint and thereafter largely succeeded in ignoring me. A quick learner.

"Sir," he said, "I am told you have met Kurt. Pardon me if I refer to him in the familiar. We have been close friends for many years."

Herr Bieler spoke in High German but I could tell his dialect was Viennese. Although similar to the Bavarian, I knew it could rile me with its dropped consonants. More worryingly, it might baffle me with vocabulary borrowed from Hungarian and Czech. I sat up straighter on my stool.

"Yes," said the Prime Minister, "I have had the pleasure of meeting Chancellor Schuschnigg."

"Then you are aware of his deep love for his country?"

Mr. Chamberlain did not recognise this as a question, though I had enunciated it as such. He waited for his guest to go on.

"Sir, as you know, the turmoil in my country grows day by day. The unrest, the violence, the National Socialists have contrived it all. Their purpose is to provoke, so that Adolf Hitler can scream persecution."

"We certainly view with unease the activities of the National Socialists in your country."

"Sir, their activities now consist mainly of intimidation and terror. All Nazi demonstrations turn deliberately riotous. These are not political activities, Mr. Chamberlain, they amount to an insurrection."

"I am certainly aware of the many outrages perpetrated in your country. Many of them have been played up luridly in the British press."

"Sir, this subversion … it is directed from outside our borders."

"We are of course careful in the judgments we make," said Mr. Chamberlain. "The Austro-German agreement was signed eighteen months ago. In that accord Herr Hitler guaranteed the independence of Austria, did he not?"

"He did, sir, but the situation demonstrates that his guarantee is only a piece of paper. The Austrian Nazis march in the streets like a conquering army. Where do their ideas come from? Berlin. Where does their money come from? Berlin. To what master do they bow down? Adolf Hitler."

"Has Chancellor Schuschnigg made his best efforts to address the issues they raise?" said Mr. Chamberlain.

"He has embraced an explicit philosophy of pan-Germanism. Significant elements of the National Socialist agenda have been incorporated into his government's programme. No matter what steps he takes to placate the Nazis, however, their response is the same … Kurt is a betrayer of Austria and enemy of the German Reich."

"Is there not further ground upon which authentic grievances can be conciliated?"

"Kurt has instructed me to speak frankly, sir. No legitimate grievances exist. The Austrian Nazis have invented their so-called grievances, and will invent more as required."

Mr. Chamberlain opened the file on his lap, shuffled through a few pages, and seemed to find what he was looking for. "I would think," he said, reminding me of a headmaster I knew at Gresham's, "there is room for reaching out. Can the ban on the Austrian Nazi party not be lifted?"

"Sir, the – "

"We understand that a number of party members have been dismissed from government posts, and that many Austrian Nazis are in prison. I am told too that the government has banned any wearing of the swastika in public."

"Sir, those measures were properly applied in light of Nazi sedition. None of them can reasonably be regarded as provocations."

"Mr. Bieler, what I am getting at is this: what is the alternative to negotiating with the National Socialists?"

"Sir, they are not interested in negotiation except as a means of achieving the capitulation of the Austrian government and its replacement by a Nazi regime."

Mr. Chamberlain looked away from his guest and fixed his gaze on the corner of the room. He was in profile to me and seemed unconscious of the slight quiver in his lower lip. After a few moments of silent meditation he said, almost accusingly, "I trust there is no question in Chancellor Schuschnigg's mind of a military posture."

Herr Bieler breathed in deeply. "We are a nation of seven million with a tiny army, sir. Germany is eighty million and a military giant. If we stand alone, resistance to German force would be token, and suicidal."

"My officials inform me," said Mr. Chamberlain, "that many Austrians embrace the idea of unification with Germany."

An expression of deep disturbance started in Herr Bieler's eyes and jumped to his hands, which seemed to clench of their own will. Forgetting himself he looked at me, as if seeking help.

Mr. Chamberlain added, "I would think Chancellor Schuschnigg's priority is to prevent such an eventuality."

Herr Bieler's response sounded like, "*i wos a' eh!*" He had slipped deeply into his dialect. I could not make him out. Aggravating my bewilderment was the memory of a blank moment during the Stroebel interview … Within a few seconds, however, I grasped Herr Bieler's meaning from the context. In his agitation, and like a bred-in-the-bone Viennese, he had dropped the consonants and broadened the vowels of *Ich weiss wohl auch*!

"I would probably also!" I almost blurted this to the Prime Minister.

"You understand, I am sure," said Mr. Chamberlain, who seemed not to have noticed my lapse, "our chief concern is to maintain the general peace."

Herr Bieler composed himself. He seemed to gather himself up. "Sir, no one shares your concern more fervently than Kurt. I have come to you directly from his office. Tomorrow I meet in Paris with Monsieur Daladier. Kurt has mandated me to assert Austria's position plainly. He asks that England and France declare unequivocal support for Austrian sovereignty, and state plainly that the threat to the general peace comes from German-inspired sedition."

"My concern is that if we apply inflammatory language, we will only light the fire we are all seeking to avoid."

"Sir, the fire is already raging in my country! A similar fire has been started in the Sudetenland."

"The situation in Czechoslovakia," said Mr. Chamberlain, unmoved by Herr Bieler's emotion, "is another matter entirely."

"Sir, should Austria take a Nazi direction, the position of Czechoslovakia will be jeopardised. The Czechs would be cut off from their partners in the Little Entente. Rumania and Yugoslavia would be weakened in turn. The consequences for stability in eastern Europe would be incalculable."

"Large international issues are of course at play," Mr. Chamberlain replied. "Chancellor Schuschnigg is aware of our guiding principle in dealing with these matters. All of our … calculations, are carefully aimed at preserving the peace. I cannot overstate, this is the primary responsibility of my government."

Herr Bieler kept sending his message and Mr. Chamberlain kept returning it to sender. The pattern finally provoked the messenger.

"Sir, if Hitler's army marches into Austria, will you and your ministers simply write off my country like another Rhineland?"

This too failed to ruffle Mr. Chamberlain. As a man of faith he could ignore a bit of rudeness from a man justifiably anxious for the safety of his native land. The situation called for understanding, even generosity. "Mr. Bieler, the dangers are greater than a parochial view may care to encompass. You may assure your Chancellor we will exert every diplomatic means to safeguard Austrian independence, while resisting temptations to take undue risks."

Herr Bieler and I came out of Number 10 together. A car was waiting to take him to the Croydon aerodrome. "Best of luck," I said.

His eyes had reddened. He gave a bitter laugh and looked at me solemnly. *"Ihr Ministerpräsident ist mutig vom Hals aufwärts. Er bietet jeglichen Beistand bis auf Hilfe an."*

I glanced at the policeman standing at the door of Number 10. His face remained impassive. Then I realised he would not have understood Herr Bieler's comment. *Your Prime Minister is brave from the neck up. He offers all aid short of help.* I bowed my head as the Austrian envoy climbed into the car.

A few minutes later in the sunroom Jenkins greeted me with an effusive, "Well done, Joffrey!" For a moment I thought my old colleague was about to embrace me. "You have reached the summit," he said.

"I guess I am done, then. Nowhere higher to climb."

"Tell me," he said, "were you questioned by a detective before seeing the Prime Minister?"

I had to disappoint Jenkins. He was crestfallen to learn that the lone policeman at the door had given me no more than a good hard look.

"What is it like over there in Neville Neville land?" Ken joined in. "Did Peter Pan fly by? Did the scarecrow offer you a glass of warm fairy milk?" This came in a low voice as he signalled with a thumb that Tremayne was in his broom closet.

Over lunch Ken lost his humour while I related my little adventure. "That bloody weakling," he roared. "That snivelling scrawny *weed* of a man."

"Kenneth, we are not in the park."

He looked round and put a stopper in it. The Prime Minister may not be popular at the F.O., but you still need a grade well above Ken's to get away with abusing him. "Nothing is more obvious than Hitler's plan for Austria," he said in a level, bitter voice. "He put it on the first page, the first *paragraph*, of his monstrous book: the foremost task of the Reich is to restore the Austrian people to the German bosom. Here we are at the testing hour, and our Prime Minister is sending in the striped trousers and top hats."

"I agree, the man is a master ditherer, but what would you have him do?"

"Resign! Get out!"

"Be serious."

"Mobilise the fleet. Recall all men from leave. Send a signal."

"Toward what end?"

"Toward drawing a line, and calling the Nazis what they are. Rouse the world."

"Half the world would ignore him, and the other half would tell him some issues are not worth a war."

"So consign a little issue called Austria to the grave, then? Shame, Joff, shame."

Want to know the most gratifying result of my service for the Prime Minister? It was the gleam that came into Mary's eyes when I told her about it. My darling wife positively glowed. While I enjoy her approval, do I fully deserve it? Should I be proud of my ability to walk and run? No, because walking and running come naturally. As does my fluent bilingualism. When all is said and done, the credit belongs to my mother.

Congratulations again on Max's little … I predict a sister. You have my permission to usurp one of my pet names. You may call her Athena. She will be a princess to rival her mother. Did I say princess? I *am* slipping. I meant goddess.

All my best,

Joff

Saturday
13th Nov. 1937

Dear Heidi,

A grubby day of drizzle and mist. Suits my mood entirely. You should be aware this letter is from a man down in the dumps, a thwarted father. My fast-aging plum, all by herself, cancelled her weekend at home. My melancholy conclusion is that she prefers her studies to her parents.

What is the world coming to when a man's best laid plans bite the dust at the whim of a nine year-old? We were set for her favourite *pappadums* and *chana batura* and my irresistible *rogan josh* at the Bombay Emporium. Then Shirley Temple in *Wee Willie Winkie*, based on a story by her adored Kipling. A proper evening out; an occasion for the whole family; a means for me to forget my father's decline, Tremayne's idiocy, and the nasty drift of the world. But lo! Vicky claims she has piles of reading, and prefers not to deal with the forth and back. My little girl actually used that phrase, 'forth and back', making me realise our customary formulation is in fact the reverse of what we do, but I digress … My little girl also described the American film star as childish! Good lord, Vicky is *younger* than Shirley Temple.

"Let her be," said Mary.

Mummy's sympathy for the precocious darling prevailed over Daddy's sputtering protestations. *I am not happy.*

Damon has also acted up … appallingly. This week I learned from Maddy Kloff that he recently opened a studio on the Kurfürstendamm. She heard this from a German art dealer. "My gentleman in Germany says he's painting portraits and demanding exorbitant fees," Maddy said. "Big-shot industrialists and Nazi Party people are coming to him."

"Jesus Christ," I said.

"Hell and damnation," said Maddy.

Not a crumb of a hint did Damon drop about these plans. Imagine what a favoured pet of the authorities he must be, allowed to wag his tail on the Champs-Élysées of Berlin. Sick and sicker. *I am not happy*!

Did I mention the nasty world? Have you been following the latest from England's corner of it? Despite Mr. Chamberlain's devout wish for an understanding with the Germans, it seems our two countries are increasingly at loggerheads. Lord Halifax is in the air to Berlin at this moment. I don't know much about Halifax except what I hear from Ken, and that is unkind. Air Marshal Goering invited Halifax to a hunting exhibition, the ostensible reason for the trip, but he's expected to see Hitler too. People are hoping the meeting will defuse tensions.

I hear in the lunchroom that Eden is furious. Eden happens to be the Foreign Secretary, after all, and here is a dilettante aristo going over to parley with a head of state. Rather embarrassing, *n'est-ce pas?* The slight comes with purpose, Ken opined in his all-knowing tone. Chamberlain is sticking it to his one quarrelsome minister. The PM and Eden have long disagreed over the best way to deal with Mussolini, and now their differences over Germany and whether we should appease Hitler have come into the open.

From what I see in the Nazi press, Hitler's voice is only growing more shrill. I was struck by a savage anti-British leader in the *Berliner Tageblatt*. Did you know the colonialist, imperialist, Jewish plutocrats of Britain, in their endlessly malign quest for markets and profits, are now designing the means for dragging the world into a general war? Curious, because the *Tageblatt* had been the one newspaper in Germany free from Nazi humbug.

Kindly send good news, I could use a stiff dose. How are your SEVEN MEN coming along?

Good lord, what a challenge you have given yourself. I try to imagine the valiant Heidi opening the door to her studio every morning. She greets her seven charges, then plunges her fingers into their still malleable faces. Four Americans, an Englishman, a German, and a ... hmmm, I guess we can only call him a Jew. Are you devoting yourself to one piece at a time, then going on to the next? Is there, can there be, a common theme among all seven? You have me fascinated, great lady. Eager to hear your progress.

Faithfully as ever,

Joff

Saturday
27th Nov. 1937

Heidi dear,

Seamus is in hospital. Something intestinal. I went to see him and found him in a wretched state. "Never felt worse," he said. "A tearing in the gut, it feels like. What they give me hardly helps." I stupidly asked about Catherine, which sent the wrong colour to his face. I'm a fumbler!

Such a gulf exists between what you read in your newspapers over there and what we read in our newspapers over here, I never know how much you know or don't know about what I think you should know! Did Lord Halifax's visit to Germany make the front page in America? Any page?

He met Hitler in the Bavarian mountains and the two had a long conversation. The newspapers say our man accomplished the Prime Minister's goal of laying the ground for more extensive discussions. Halifax commented to reporters that the German leader is intent on building up his country and has no interest in foreign adventures. You can guess Ken's reaction; he put on a grimace. "Shameful, the spectacle of a representative of the British people begging favours from the leading autocrat of our times."

"Begging?"

"The Germans are so far ahead of us in armaments, we can no longer catch up. Our leaders pretend we have parity, but the lie is for public consumption. So there's Lord Gaunt Fool, representing Prime Minister Turkey Neck, on bended knee to the dictator. Please, Herr Hitler, what must we do to keep any shooting from starting?"

"The German people want peace as much as anybody. I see where Halifax was greeted by cheering crowds."

Ken hooted. "The towering fool did accomplish something with his sordid trip. Hitler now knows we are scared stiff of a fight."

Ken will be Ken. I thought again of dressing him in one of my suits and sending him to Bury. What a tonic he would be for the pater.

Envious of your distance from Europe, and thinking of you in your studio. As ever,

Joff

Saturday
4th Dec. 1937

Heidi dear,
Seamus is out of hospital but still terribly weak. It was a bad bug of some sort, picked up during an exotic eating jag. Silver lining: he lost eighteen pounds. They have given him some strict dietary instructions which he has sworn to follow. Maybe this episode will reform him. Right, and maybe nettles will turn into roses.

After months of silence Damon honours me with nine words and three exclamation points. The message comes on a postcard of the Olympic Village at Garmisch. *Now skiing! Back in London shortly! Champagne to follow!* The champagne refers to our Christmas ritual, which he has trashed the last two years. About the skiing, I suspect that is a joke. Damon has never skied in his life.

Maddy Kloff telephoned again. She hears nothing from Damon, which I find brutally ungrateful of him. Several of her big buyers are prepared to accept he had nothing to do with the disgraceful show in Munich and asked to see his current work. Can we hope for a resurrection of his career in England? Come home and *stay*, Dame, we forgive all your trespasses …

A month has passed since my assignment at Number 10. I think wistfully of the hopes it created, but no follow-up has come from Huntington. So I trudge along, stumble forward. Some interesting shards of our shattering world come my way. I was chatting with Jenkins about the week's workload when he said, "I believe one of our boys at the Berlin embassy is getting sloppy."

"What makes you say that?"

"Look here."

An enlarged photograph of a document lay on his desk. The folder beside it was stamped MOST SECRET. Jenkins, naturally thrilled by the designation, pointed to a smudge of ink in the lower left corner. I asked, "What are you showing me?"

"You want a better look," he said, and held it under the lamp on his desk. I dutifully humoured my aging colleague and stooped for a closer inspection. The smudge was a scribble in which I could make out a capital 'B'. The last letter seemed to be an 'n'.

"Jenkins, my dear fellow, I shall commend your detective work to His Majesty. You have exposed a splotch of ink to be an indecipherable word."

"Ah, but look at this," said Jenkins, retrieving another file from his desk. "A second document, from the same department in the Embassy." Also stamped MOST SECRET, it was not a photograph but an original on headed paper from the *Reichsluftfahrtministerium*, the German Ministry of Aviation. Jenkins pointed to the lower left corner, where a bracketed word in handwriting appeared. It looked like this: [*Bedouin*]

"What exactly is it about your discovery that you find so significant?"

"Evidently our boys have a source by this name. Someone in the Embassy has slipped up, and stupidly jotted it on two different documents and failed to catch the blunder before dumping them in the Bag."

Heidi, from the look on my colleague's face you would think he had just squared the circle, or discovered a cache of gold and diamonds.

"So, on the basis of a splotch and a scribble you have deduced that our boys on Wilhelmstrasse have an Arab agent?"

"Well, Bedouin would be the man's *code* name. These clandestine types adore Russian dolls, you understand."

"Interesting, very interesting," I said, struggling to keep mockery from my voice. The little episode left me downhearted. This is what may come of me if I remain in the sunroom long enough. I will turn into a Jenkins, another dotty greybeard desperate to inject a bit of drama into his dreary days. I was depressed for hours thinking of the wretched smallness of the man's delight. Russian dolls!

Anxious to hear about how your SEVEN MEN are coming along. Tell me too if Max's embryonic sister is yet a bump. Hugs to the three of you!

Joff

Saturday
11th Dec. 1937

Dear Heidi,

Received yours of the twenty-eighth, thank you. I find it interesting that you can work on all the busts simultaneously. Makes me think of a BBC interview not long ago with J.B. Priestly. He said he starts a novel by dabbling in every section, then polishes the ending before he can be sure what works best at the beginning. You artists are odd.

The oddest of the odd is back in London, looking fit as a fiddle. Would you believe Damon has in fact taken up skiing? He declares he was indisputably born to it. "In the course of a single day I was flopping in the morning, and flying in the afternoon!" He claims to have reached speeds of fifty miles per hour, and did I know downhill racers can reach *ninety*?

Not a word about his months of silence. Not a word either about his little enterprise on the Kurfürstendamm. "What comes next," I asked, "application for citizenship in Hitlerland?"

He put down his pint and squinted at me. "What brings this on?"

"Is it true you now have a studio in Berlin?"

"You should see your face, Joff. Have I shat on the King's new rug?"

"Not a bad analogy."

"Just so you know, my little space is not quite a studio, but how did you learn about it?"

"Somebody told Maddy, and Maddy told me. You remain an ungrateful cad when it comes to Maddy."

"Trust me, I will make it up to dear Madeleine."

"With portraits of well-heeled Nazis?"

"That is unfair. You must allow my business to flourish."

"Your art has become a 'business'?"

He gave a great sigh and was about to answer when we were interrupted by that drooling little alligator, Billy Colman, who writes up rumours and other rubbish in the *Evening News*. Damon shouted a welcome, and I excused myself to spend a penny …

I suppose we must indulge our adult baby and keep a stiff upper lip. If he insists on pursuing fortune in Germany and risking the ruin of his name in England, should I care? Well, there it is, I do care. More than he does, it seems.

My telephone calls to Bury ... they grow more difficult. The best that can be said about the pater's condition is that it remains erratic. Some nights he picks up the ringing phone and puts it right back down without a word, or he ignores the bloody thing and I give up after a dozen or so rings.

Not much else to tell. My indomitable Mary soldiers on, always punctual, modestly confident. Our miraculous Vicky reports weekly on her consumption of history. Her other subjects are mere nuisances, she tells us. The Spanish Armada came up again recently. "I am now taking a mature interest in it," she said.

Meanwhile the man in the street talks darkly of another war and in the next breath harbours hopes for his football side or a package holiday in the south of France. We cope. We persevere. We're British. We also long for more letters from across the pond.

Your devoted,

Joff

Saturday
18th Dec. 1937

Dear Heidi,

Another year almost done, Christmas a week away, all gifts miraculously prepared. Not a simple matter, satisfying the requirements of the Pearson offspring. Still harder to come up with a proper gift for an austere wife. And what to do for a senile wreck of a father?

Vicky has never been one for trifles or toys. The only game she plays is chess and she already owns three sets. After some back and forth with our M.P.'s constituency assistant, then with the Member himself, my daughter's heart's desire has been arranged ... a private tour of the Commons and Lords. As for my dependable, stubborn, difficult, wonderful, beloved Mary, I almost asked Damon to do a portrait of her in secret, the way he did Vicky's. I thought better of it at the last moment. (Would I want a friend imposing on me for translations?) I have conspired instead to present my spouse with a hand-tooled, leather-bound copy of Churchill's latest, *Great Contemporaries*. Jenkins recommended a bespoke bookbinder on the Strand and the deed is being done. The goatskin will be tanned to her favourite deep burgundy, and the spine gilt-lettered. The front and back covers will be tooled to harmonise with the spine, and the marbled endpapers will be handmade. The book promises to be luxurious to the touch, durable as a rock, and a treasure to behold. Appropriate, no? Of course if I tell Mary the cost she may take my head off, but I reckon it will be thirty quid magnificently invested. The end result should be an *objet d'art*, a family heirloom born.

Graham called round to gather the five for a Christmas lunch, but only Patty and I agreed to attend. Both Catherine and Seamus demurred. Seems the break between those two might have dealt our little club a mortal blow. It saddens.

The depressing business of visiting my father will be performed tomorrow. Vicky chose this year's assortment of jellied fruits and chocolate covered nuts. I hope he recognises us. The fog in him only grows thicker and more regular. Last night he banged down the receiver after disputing the idea I was his son. He said Joffrey's voice is deeper, and besides his son long ago moved to Canada and works as an engineer in Montreal. *Bang.*

Strange planet.

This week's pint with Damon came and went without a single cross look or mean word. However I did tease him about the trivial hyperbole in Billy Colman's column. See for yourself, I shall slip in the cutting. Renowned painter conquers the ski slopes of Bavaria. Evidently when I abandoned the two of them in The Squire's he filled Colman's head with blather about how to cope with wet snow and negotiate steep moguls. Not a word about painting portraits in Berlin, thank the gods. Happily no one in the press has written about Damon's little outpost on the Kurfürstendamm ... with any luck that madness will stay under wraps. But I must tell you something else, Heidi. This little episode with the scribbler Colman has at long last opened my eyes to something. Look at his writing. Read it closely. Look at the unctuous, fawning way he refers to Damon. Until now the truth about that crawling little bugger never occurred to me. For years I failed to notice. *I was blind.* Is there anything else in my life waving a flag right under my nose that I have somehow failed to see?

Another thing to tell you ... please refrain from cursing. I asked Damon if he would swap our champagne for a pipe this Christmas. He showed no surprise. He looked at me with knowing eyes. Thinking he was about to refuse, I added, "Months have gone by since Eaton Square. Surely enough time has – "

"A capital idea. Hold the bubbly and pass the narcotic. *Passt zu den Zeiten, nicht wahr?*" Impressive, our Damon. His comment popped out in perfect idiomatic German. *Suits the times, right?*

We shall visit Eaton Square again on our pub night next week. Must confess, I do want another experience of ... release. You wrote a long time ago about my crime of 'living unconsciously'. That ironic phrase has stayed with me. Life is speeding by. What we fail to seize now, experience now, value now, is never going to return. Alas, there you have my motive for wanting another go at Eaton Square. Please do not judge me harshly.

My best wishes for a delightful Christmas to you and little Max, his budding sister, and of course That American who stole you from England. Will write again before the new year, I promise.

Joff

PART THREE: 1938

By his father he is English, by his mother American, to my mind the blend which makes the perfect man.

Mark Twain

Saturday
8th Jan. 1938

Heidi,
Your anger has stunned me. And I thought you were burning all my letters. You should not think the pipe was the cause and Damon some kind of predator. If you must pin 'blame' on someone, then pin it on me. I take full responsibility for what happened. I was there. I consented. Maybe some secrets should never be shared. I certainly thought long and hard before telling you this one. Frankly I expected another kind of reaction. Something along the lines of wonder, curiosity, tolerance … not incendiary fury. It amazes me to hear you use the word 'society' in such a way. What has become of your indifference to the old, the common, the ordinary and dull? I know you retired the refrain, but have you now killed and buried it? I will grant you this: you put me in doubt of myself.

Only momentarily.

Your attack is not you, it's not us. Our pact, our history, our intimacy, these should grant me a different response. Where is the woman who ignored every wish of her parents, every prompting of her friends, every custom of her suddenly precious 'society' to enroll in bohemia? Do you think I have forgotten her wild heart? She even ignored her academic genius and a chance at Oxford. Must I conclude no trace of that rebel survives? I do not accept your characterisation of what I allowed. Betrayed my identity? Dynamited my family? (Those short-fused verbs!) At least you stopped before claiming I had exploded *us*.

You may go on condemning me but I will tell you again I experienced no guilt and feel none now. The experience Damon introduced to me was … not wrong. I felt no shame. In fact I felt a liberation of sorts. He took me outside the boundaries of my self. I cannot describe it any better. I celebrate the fact I have a friend, a great enough friend, to have permitted him what I permitted. We simply and profoundly communed, and … shared.

I must say something more. If before the event someone had told me I would stray from what I presumed to be my fixed nature, I would not have believed it. Yet the act did not come over me like a sudden rogue wave, but like a thought that arrived comfortably and took a pre-assigned seat in my mind.

Much to tell you, but not at this moment. I feel we must first right our ship. Do you feel it listing? That is intolerable to me. We must regain our balance, resume course. Until this harsh stinging I never knew how much I feared losing you. I must not lose you. I need you in my thoughts and to be in yours.

Please confirm you are burning these, as I have assumed all along. They are *not* for keeping where your husband or anyone, now or in future, might find them. Burn them. All of them.

Joff

Saturday
22nd Jan. 1938

Dear Heidi,
Nothing from you, only deepening my unease, and we seem to have forgotten to wish each other the world and all we want of it in 1938.

The kettle called Europe seems ready to boil and interesting documents have come from Berlin and my father has taken another turn downward (he began shouting at me the moment I appeared) but you prefer not to hear any of these things right now, am I right? I'm not sure what you want to hear. I told you everything. I left out nothing. I can only tell you the truth, or try to coax out more of it. Imagine falling off a cliff where no bottom exists. You just fall, and keep falling. There is nothing you can do but fall, and soon you realise that you can excuse the falling, you can adjust to it. And justify it. That is what happened to me in that Eaton Square room. I must tell you again, I refuse to feel guilt. Especially here, where our pact, our candour, should make remorse a foreign thing, an unnecessary thing. Please speak your true heart to me. I will feel no comfort until you say nothing between us has changed.

Yours as ever,
Joff

Saturday
29th Jan. 1938

Dearest Heidi,
I don't think I can explain it better than in the letter you called a ...
thank you for taking it back. Thank you. We can smile now as we
recall your arsonist's reaction to the 'abomination'.

Since the event happened I have deeply wondered at society taking
such a brutal interest in it. Has the sky of morality fallen on account of
my behaviour? The thing was private. The intrusion of society, religion,
law, seems to me absurd. No, I have not seen Damon since. He left
two days later. A postcard came from Berlin saying our friendship has
reached beyond life-long and he for one is glad. I value the sentiment
and think it true even if I don't fully grasp it. You ask how I feel toward
him. Nothing has changed. He has always been and always will be my
best friend. We shared a thing of a particular moment. It was. . . alien,
I admit, yet I felt no aversion. The most powerful thing about the
event is that we shared it. We shall go on now as we always have, with
no discomfort, and with even greater trust. I do believe that.

Thrilled to hear your show is at last imminent. Yes, *yes*, send photos
of the SEVEN MEN. Must admit, I still harbour concerns you may
have overstepped with this project. The scale and aim of it always
struck me as intimidating. I only pray your work proves my doubts
daft. In place of myself at the opening, I send you hopes and cheers.

Must rush this and meet up with my girls. Vicky's home for the
weekend and out shopping with Mary. Our darling's birthday (she's
ten!) will be celebrated with a film, then dinner at her latest 'absolutely
most favourite place in the whole world to eat.' That would be
Jasmine's, an unremarkable Chinese restaurant in Soho, but she loves
the pineapple chicken and a wise grizzled waiter named Harry who
dotes on her.

Thank you again for being you, and for upholding *us*.
As always,
Joff

Saturday
12th Feb. 1938

Dear Heidi,
You will laugh. I may be worrying like everybody else about the clouds gathering over Europe, but at least I am no longer obsessing about you and me. An outbreak of shooting on the continent would be one thing but, please God, let us keep the peace between London and Boston. Only to say, it feels tremendously good to have our understanding back.

While we were going through our spot of bother, a major change took place high above me. Alexander Cadogan has taken over as Permanent Under-Secretary. At the same time Sir Robert Vansittart was named Chief Diplomatic Advisor to His Majesty's government. Which was not a promotion. More like a kick in the face. His new post means he will no longer have any say in foreign policy, or any access to inside information.

"Care to know Vansittart's biggest crime, aside from being an articulate foe of the Nazis?" said Ken. "Rumours say he was the source of all the embarrassing information Churchill has been getting over the years. Our vindictive Prime Minister has handed Sir Robert his comeuppance."

"If you ride the bête noir," I said, "watch out for a tumble."

In truth my disappointment matches Ken's, albeit for a selfish reason. After interpreting for the Under-Secretary with the Sudeten thug, I had hoped Sir Robert would become an active patron of my career.

Did you know President Roosevelt offered to involve himself in European affairs? This too happened while you and I were at daggers drawn. Mr. Roosevelt pronounced it necessary to "take some risk out of the prevailing international situation." The White House called for a world conference in Washington, but Mr. Chamberlain stuck his nose up at the idea. Seems the President, dismayed by the disinterest, threw up his hands and let the proposal die. The affair has created tremendous anger here at the F.O., because Chamberlain never conferred with Eden on the matter. The power people upstairs feel an opportunity has been missed.

Speaking of opportunities, thanks to the one and only member of my club of patrons, I was sent on another interpretation assignment this week. It seems I am the player they put on the pitch when the other chap is taken off on a stretcher. In this case the injured party was an American interpreter felled by a loose paving stone outside his flat. He was leaving for work when he took a nasty tumble, shattered an elbow, and created an emergency for his embassy. The Yanks turned to the F.O. for help. Reg Huntington called me off the bench and dispatched me to Grosvenor Square.

"Their ambassador is about to meet the German chargé d'affaires. A car's waiting for you. Go!" That was my briefing.

The ambassador is a new man, Joseph Kennedy, from a powerful Irish family in Boston, you may have heard the name. Could he be one of your Brahmins? Or is that designation off limits to the Irish? You must teach me more about your patricians and how they caste themselves.

Mr. Kennedy arrived in London a few weeks ago with six or seven children in tow, four boys among them. By all accounts they make a handsome set. You would think the father of such a brood would show some camaraderie and smile upon his inferiors now and again. When I was escorted in, however, he kept his eyes fixed on the documents on his desk. I took him for owlish. At one point the ruddy-faced ambassador lifted his head, gazed in my direction through wire-rimmed round spectacles, and took no notice of me. I might have been the porter come to change a light bulb.

While I assumed my accustomed role as the invisible man, he answered one of his telephones. "Kennedy!"

Listening to his caller, telephone wedged between head and shoulder, the ambassador went on shuffling his documents. When he spoke it was in short bursts. "Good, good. We have him by the short hairs. Pull a little harder. Do you hear me, Dean? Drive up the price a notch. Then our bottom line will be solid. If we can trust the son of a bitch."

Ah, I thought, what they call in America a *wheeler-dealer*. Only later did I learn the accuracy of my observation. The new ambassador to the Court of St. James made millions on Wall Street, then a few more of the same in Hollywood.

"Good, good. But hold off for the time being. Do you hear me? My hands are full here. Still getting the lay of the fucking land."

This came in a level everyday tone. Etiquette, I suppose, is not an essential currency on Wall Street or in Hollywood. Why, I wondered, would he have left those capitals of dealmaking for a mere salary and virtual exile in gloomy London? The lure of power, I suppose, the trappings of office. Prominent on his desk was a framed photograph of himself shaking hands with President Roosevelt, and another of him presenting his credentials to the King.

Watching him I saw that owlish was not his true nature at all. More like scowlish, if I may invent an adjective … a mix of instinctive irritation and fierce hauteur; a chap with chips on both shoulders. When Mr. Kennedy grinned, it came as a baring of teeth.

"They have a saying here in England, Dean. They say it while looking down their snobby noses. *Quite amusing*. Put the sheenie straight, by all means. What did you say?" He was obviously hearing something he didn't like, because his expression went from cold indifference to mildly heated frown. When he spoke again his voice was low, curt, menacing. "Maybe you should listen more closely to me, Dean. Not until my say-so. Understood? Good."

Without further ado he put down the telephone and picked up another. Three sat on his desk, like stubby artillery pieces lined up to fire. "Ellen, bring in our guest."

The German chargé d'affaires came with his own interpreter. We had an awkward moment as the ambassador mistook the interpreter for the chargé d'affaires. Once names and faces were sorted out, Mr. Kennedy said to no one in particular, "Why two translators for a fifteen minute courtesy call?"

I almost intervened with a playful comment, but my brain beat my mouth to the finish line and kept me sagely silent. I may be mastering the diplomatic chase!

We took seats at a table. The German chargé d'affaires said, "Welcome to London, Mr. Kennedy. As you may be aware, the Reich's ambassador to Great Britain, Herr Ribbentrop, was very recently promoted to the post of Foreign Minister. Our new ambassador, Herbert von Dirksen, will not arrive in London for some weeks. Herr Dirksen has asked me to pay this visit and congratulate you on your appointment."

The chargé d'affaires, Hans Seibbel, was evidently a Bavarian.

I translated him without difficulty. Mr. Kennedy, who still hadn't acknowledged my presence, cocked his head toward me as he listened. I raised my voice a touch.

"Thanks," he said to Herr Seibbel. "We can dispense with the pleasantries. Let's get down to business."

I thought these remarks would trouble the interpreter across the table, a youngish fellow whose suit was too tight on him, but he proved me wrong. He accurately translated the tactless jab about pleasantries, and skated over the idiomatic 'business' which he turned into *die Grundlagen*, or 'basics'. The look he then shot me had self-satisfaction – and challenge – written all over it. Blimey O'Riley, I thought. Next thing you know the boy will be flinging out his arm in a Nazi salute.

The gauche start to the meeting did it no harm. In fact, Mr. Kennedy and the German chargé d'affaires got along famously, if you can equate 'getting along' with two conceited men talking past each other and enjoying the sound of their own opinions. Neither of them were born to be diplomats, though Herr Seibbel clearly had the benefit of training.

Mr. Kennedy said, "I think it has become crystal clear, my country is staying neutral when it comes to politics in Europe. We don't want to get caught up in your ancient arguments again. It cost us badly in '18."

"We appreciate your clarity, Mr. Ambassador, and agree with you completely. The problems of Europe are for Europeans to solve."

"That is my position, along with my friend Charles Lindbergh."

"A great man! Hugely admired in Germany. Mr. Lindbergh visited with the Fuhrer and they exchanged views with much pleasure."

"One thing you should know. My president must handle a lot of howling. We have many different interests within the United States."

"I understand you perfectly," said Herr Seibbel.

"No matter what differences might stand between us," said Mr. Kennedy, "we should concentrate on expanding our business ties."

"We in the Reich appreciate that the business of America is business," said Herr Seibbel. "We subscribe completely to your objective of greater trade."

Mr. Kennedy then said Americans are hearing a whole lot about what is going on in Germany without necessarily getting to the truth of what they're being told. Would his guest mind if he asked a few frank questions about the Nazi project?

Herr Seibbel said it would be his pleasure. A candid exchange could only be valuable in the interest of building bridges of understanding and cultivating wider fields of cooperation. Herr Seibbel was starting to change my mind about his aptitude for diplomacy, because he said these things without sounding like a greasy hypocrite.

"What you said about my country is correct," said Mr. Kennedy. "We are business people. Our main interest is in building things. How would you describe the purpose of your country?"

An astute question. I was interested to hear how the chargé d'affaires would answer. Herr Seibbel did not hesitate. He launched into a virtual hymn about the agenda of the Third Reich. Five years ago, he said, with the advent of Adolf Hitler as Chancellor, Germany embarked on a path of economic resurgence and cultural renaissance. After the humiliation of the Great War and the treacherous immorality of the Weimar years, Germany embraced its proper purpose. Which is to promote unity among the German people, to build strength to ensure the survival of the German race. That is why the National Socialists have instituted important laws governing blood and ethnicity. "We are dedicated to the preservation of our uniqueness," Herr Seibbel added. "We are single-minded as to the integrity of our identity. All aspects of the National Socialist project take instruction from this central imperative."

I wondered what meaning Mr. Kennedy discerned from Herr Seibbel's hollow rhetoric. The American ambassador's eyes were coolly fixed on his guest, whose own eyes had taken on a shine. Across the table the suitcoat of my young counterpart had come unbuttoned. I noticed his tie clasp was in the shape of a sword with a swastika on the grip.

A telephone rang on Mr. Kennedy's desk.

The ambassador went to it, picked it up and immediately barked into it, "After lunch!" Then he put the telephone back down without determining who the caller was. It was the same telephone he had used earlier with the minion Dean. I made a mental note to tell Jenkins about the three telephones; he delights in such arcane matters.

Mr. Kennedy resumed his seat at the table. Must tell you, Heidi, the American ambassador is a fastidious dresser. His blue pinstriped suit was pure Savile Row, and the sober red necktie and matching pocket handkerchief spoke eloquently of flair and privilege.

"From almost the first moment I arrived in London, Mr. Seibbel," said Mr. Kennedy, "I've been meeting people who hold a negative view of your country. They seem to be persuaded that Germany is hell-bent on pushing its neighbours around and expanding its territory. What do you have to say about that?"

"I can assure you, Mr. Ambassador, one of the most basic aims of the government I represent is to preserve the peace in Europe. The anti-German clique you refer to is expert in the art of defamation. I hope you will not allow wild aspersions to cloud your view of my country."

"I'm not accustomed to having the wool pulled over my eyes," said Mr. Kennedy. "How do you explain the trouble being stirred up in Austria? Ditto for what's happening along your border with Czechoslovakia."

Again I was impressed by Herr Seibbel's young interpreter. Without a moment's hesitation he rendered the colloquial 'having the wool pulled over my eyes' into the equally idiomatic *mich hinters Licht führen*. Just as efficiently, he converted the slangy 'Ditto' into the pedestrian but apt *ebenfalls*. I caught his eye and awarded him a discreet nod.

"Mr. Ambassador, we regard as family the three million German-speakers within Czechoslovakia. At the stroke of a pen in 1919, these blood relatives of Germany were made citizens of a non-Germanic country and found themselves reduced to second-class status within an alien culture. Is the Reich not justified in supporting the Sudetens? If they wish to join hands with the German nation of which they are an ancestral part, must we abstain from welcoming them? I ask you, if there were millions of Americans living under intolerable conditions across your border with Mexico, would you be content if your government ignored their appeals for assistance?"

If this were a game with the objective of talking rings around your opponent and shrouding facts in fog, the American ambassador was clearly out of his league.

"Mr. Seibbel," he said, "You won't find me recommending to my president that Germany be blacklisted for wanting Germans to be part of Germany."

"You will be serving your president well, Mr. Ambassador."

"This military build-up in your country, what does German public opinion say about it?"

Herr Seibbel blinked.

The question flummoxed me too. I should say this in Mr. Kennedy's defence: he is ambassador to Britain, not Germany. Still …

Herr Seibbel recovered quickly. "Ach, of course, Mr. Kennedy, there is total support among the German people for the revival of their country on the world stage. You may be sure the masses stand fully behind their Fuhrer."

"Do they stand behind what he's doing to the Jews?"

Herr Seibbel had probably been asked this question many times in England. His expression and manner changed not a whit. "Mr. Kennedy, the number of Jews in my country is small. The measures affecting them are meant simply to curtail the unwarranted influence of a tiny minority."

"You should know your actions against the Jews create a great deal of bad publicity for Germany in the United States."

"I believe the American people, if properly informed, would understand that the Jews of my country brought this attention upon themselves."

"How's that?" said Mr. Kennedy, sounding friendly, and I caught a hint of sport in this. He was goading his guest.

Herr Seibbel startled me. He took the bait.

"The Jews had begun to treat Berlin as their own," he said in a personal tone, a confiding tone. "Where in the world are the natural people of a land, the true inhabitants of the land, not wary of a tiny minority that seeks to tower above their hosts? The Jews are not of the German soil, but engineers of gain. They are a grasping people. It is in their nature to manipulate and control. They behave similarly wherever they roost, do they not? In my country they took critical positions in commerce and the professions, vital posts in science and the universities … this secretive, clannish minority. What country in the world would tolerate such dominance by a foreign race? We National Socialists are performing our duty to the German people. An alien strain can no longer influence our economic and political life. We have restored our self-respect, Mr. Kennedy."

Must say, Heidi, I impressed myself as I translated this. A mask may have fallen from the face of the German chargé d'affaires, but my own demeanour remained dispassionate, my tone strictly neutral.

Mr. Kennedy sat still during the little lecture, watching Herr Seibbel with interest but giving no hint of a reaction. He looked out the window and seemed engaged in a personal reflection. When he turned back to his guest he said, "I appreciate your coming to meet me. It was interesting to speak with you."

Polite goodbyes were said. As I was taking my leave Mr. Kennedy favoured me with a word. "Turns out we didn't need you," he said.

"I beg your pardon, Mr. Ambassador?"

"That young Fritz with the iron cross on his tie seemed to know his stuff. He could have carried the talk both ways."

"Yes, I suppose he could have."

The ambassador's handshake was brusque. He never thanked me. If you find your Boston Brahmins refuse to mingle with the Boston Irish, I have some inkling why.

Jenkins did enjoy speculating about the uses of Mr. Kennedy's private telephone lines. And of course Mary was thrilled by my latest adventure on the diplomatic heights. "The feathers in your cap are adding up," she said. I refrained from spoiling her delight by asking what they might be adding up to. A ceremonial headdress like those worn by Indians in American western films?

Spotted this little gem in *The Times*, in a list of exhibitions by British artists abroad: "Elizabeth Heidi Lowell's new show of busts, SEVEN MEN, has opened in Boston." Observe how the newspaper, like your admirer, respectfully adhered to your upper-case lettering! Awaiting news of your triumph, and photos of the busts.

Hugs to the famous expatriate,

Joff

Saturday
19th Feb. 1938

Dearest Heidi,
Every day this week I anticipated the arrival of the mail trolley, only to be denied, frustrated – wounded. Such is your power over me, great lady. Must I constantly remind you of my fragile sensitivities?

Lunch with Graham and Seamus on Wednesday was pleasant enough, except for the absence of Patty and Catherine. I guess our little club is extinct, done in by the Seamus and Catherine cock-up. Seamus stayed mum about what happened between them, but admits they never want to lay eyes on each other again. Has Catherine written to you about it?

My week in the sunroom was taken up with documents from our embassy in Vienna. The batch included a frantic letter written to Foreign Secretary Eden by Wilhelm Bieler, the Austrian emissary I met some months ago in Number 10. (His departing remark about Mr. Chamberlain remains vivid in my mind.) Last week Bieler accompanied the Chancellor of Austria to Berchtesgaden for a meeting with Hitler. My poor friend Wilhelm doesn't have much luck with world leaders. Here is part of my translation of his letter:

The behaviour of the Fuhrer toward his guest was that of a master toward his dog. Herr Hitler effectively instructed Kurt to kneel and be whipped for unruly conduct. The contemptuous master will settle for nothing less than the complete Nazification of Austria. We fear for our national existence. Are we to be abandoned by the international community? Is England to remain silent? If so, the wolf in his mountaintop lair will have his prey.

The letter goes on for three pages. It reads like a keyhole look at what happened in Hitler's study. The two principals were alone, but Schuschnigg related the conversation to his advisors immediately after. According to Bieler, Hitler mocked and cursed Schuschnigg, and denounced his regime as treasonous 'in every limb of its pestilent carcass'. Shaking his fist, the dictator accused Schuschnigg of sabotaging the historic German project, and even of 'soiling German blood'. Schuschnigg protested that he harboured only goodwill toward Germany, and was doing everything in his power to foster excellent relations. This only caused Hitler to pound the table, shout louder condemnations – and threaten to march his troops across the border within days.

Interesting work, Heidi. Compensates for the fact I'm still stuck in the sunroom under the thumb of Tremayne. Translating the Bieler letter, I felt myself at the centre of affairs. By writing in such detail to Anthony Eden, Bieler obviously meant to do more than inform. He wrote the letter as a pleading SOS.

Before Chancellor Schuschnigg was allowed to go back down the mountain with his tail between his legs, he was handed a document listing Germany's demands. Hitler's Foreign Minister, Ribbentrop, did the honours. In his pompous fashion, Ribbentrop characterised the document as a fraternal agreement while informing Schuschnigg it had to be accepted in its entirety. Furthermore, the Fuhrer expected Schuschnigg's signature before ten o'clock that night. Bieler writes that when the Chancellor and his advisors retired to a private room to study the fraternal agreement, a terrible silence came over them.

We all went pale and hollow-eyed. Kurt's face seized up into a mask of incredulity. I felt sick to my stomach.

The provisions in the agreement were clearly aimed at erasing Austria's independence. The document demanded the immediate appointment of Arthur Seyss-Inquart, a Nazi puppet, as Interior Minister, and the transfer to him of absolute authority over Austrian law enforcement. Hans Fischboeck, another Nazi, would be named Minister of Finance, to facilitate integration of the Austrian economy into that of the Reich. Yet another Nazi would be appointed supreme commander of the Austrian armed forces. In addition, the document ordered the repeal of all laws pertaining to the repression of the National Socialist Party, and the immediate release of all imprisoned party members. These demands constituted the heavy artillery of the agreement. Numerous subsidiary terms fired more discreet bullets into the body of Austrian sovereignty.

When Kurt returned to Hitler, he requested a number of modifications to the agreeement. The Fuhrer replied icily that not a word, not a comma, of the document would be altered. Then a transformation came over Hitler. Blood rushed into his face. He raised his hands in clenched fists and shrieked for General Keitel. The inference was clear. Would it be Kurt's signature on the agreement, or invasion on the morrow? The outrage was complete.

*The shaming was total. Hitler looked and acted like a madman. Kurt said
he feared being arrested, or even shot. Under a degree of duress no one could
possibly withstand, Kurt signed the death warrant of our country.*

I had to be careful to give exact weight in English to what Bieler
had written in German. When a man cries for help, to what extent is
he exaggerating the cause of his danger? I took care not to paint his
language a single shade lighter or darker.

The events described in the letter took place a week ago.
Developments since then indicate Chancellor Schuschnigg is keeping
his side of the 'fraternal agreement'. Will it mean the end of bombings,
assassinations and torchlight demonstrations? The beginning of a Nazi
millennium in Austria? We wait day by day to see where it all leads.

Do the Yanks give a damn? Do they know the stakes involved? Or is
'Schuschnigg' for them the name of a circus clown?

I also need news of young Max. And let me know what Catherine
is telling you. My demands are benign, n'est-ce pas? Awaiting the
photographs of your SEVEN MEN, I remain,

Your faithful supplicant,

Joff

Saturday
26th Feb. 1938

Dear Heidi,
Your thick blue envelope of the fourteenth arrived, thank you. I am overwhelmed with admiration. I take back all my disgraceful doubts. You have dared and triumphed. These busts should make your name. I wish I could have been at the show but will have to be content with the photographs, which are outstanding in themselves. Is it motherhood and the second life within you that has given your work this vitality, this tremendous confidence? I have to wonder how many portraits of these men you studied, how many biographies you read. These works stand out with a bright sure resolute *knowing*.

The Washington and the Lincoln ... good lord, Heidi. Without sacrificing their eminence you have managed to turn a couple of remote icons into accessible individuals. What these pieces say to me is that you have adopted America with all your heart, and I celebrate your achievement with all of mine. The Roosevelt head is the best, I agree. You have carved his face to catch every bit of light. I can see the aristocrat in him, but more plainly his Americanness, the can-do spirit, the never-say-die, the quick humour he's famous for – you captured his essence.

Were you grappling with the riddle of the infinite as you carved the Einstein? It may be second-best of the lot for quality, but I wager it will be the favourite of the hoi polloi. I have seen only a few photographs of Einstein, but my dominant impression of him looks back at me from your bust. A shambling face rescued by glints of genius in the eyes; that marvellous unkempt hair framing a gaze both mischievous and mysterious; a jolly *homme de science* with the far-reaching vision of a god. My dearest Heidi, *touché*!

Let me know if I have correctly judged your Mussolini ... it makes me happily laugh! You grabbed hold of the peacock in him, and taken us to the realm of comic opera. The belligerent forehead, the conceit of the shiny obstinate football head, these are intimidating, until we notice the cowardice in the eyes. I love the puffy petulant mouth you gave him, and the pathetic blip of a chin. Again, what appears first as bombast we see to be frailty or, better yet, impotence. Thank you,

297

great lady, for making a small man smaller.

The Chamberlain likeness is well realised, but, if I may say, the character in it is incomplete. Madame Lowell's flame of insight burns less intensely here. Maybe she came to the Prime Minister uninspired. Maybe she hasn't seen enough of him in cinema newsreels and caricatures. He is a devoted man, a believer, a preacher. Defiance is not one of his qualities. Neither is magnanimity. I think what propels Chamberlain is *faith*, not in the religious sense, but towards unbending self-confidence. 'I know best,' is his sincere belief. You have caught most of the man, but not his presumption, nor his galling superiority. Forgive me, but the PM's bust must take last place among the seven brothers.

The Hitler head is chilling. That pasty slab of a face with its mat of hair. The snide moustache. First impression is of a vain blockhead, a man we would pass on the street and hardly notice. But you compel us to stop, and here comes the irony. What stops us is a sense of remarkable vacancy, the absence of any sense of individuality. Then we see everything vital in the eyes, the huge contempt and malice. We see there what made his rise possible, the bottomless enabling arrogance. You are a master of men's eyes, Heidi … the telephone.

Evening now. I sat with Mary in hospital and brought the injured dear home. She broke her wrist at the Auxiliary! Silly accident. A slip off a raised platform as she was giving a talk. I just tucked her into bed, cast and all. She says she embarrassed herself in front of a bunch of raw recruits. "Impossible," I said. "Did you cry out when the bone broke?"

"Of course not."

"There you are then. Grace under pressure. Model of fortitude. In adversity, you instruct."

"Fiddlesticks."

She says tomorrow will be quite sufficient for recuperation, thank you very much, and she will take up her duties as usual on Monday morning. Her paperwork is in no danger, as it's the left wrist she broke.

Most of my own paperwork this week originated in Austria again. Piles of cuttings from newspapers. The country's opinion makers, like compliant dominos, are falling in line with the National Socialist agenda. They see the writing on the wall and are trying to save themselves from Nazi revenge.

By all accounts our government has resigned itself to Austria's absorption by the Reich. At the F.O., Eden has voiced deep regret over Mr. Chamberlain's do-nothing policy. He shares Ken Retinger's view, or almost. Friend Ken is not merely regretful. Events have incensed him.

"Chamberlain will go down in infamy for this. He refuses to see how the resources of Austria will only add to Hitler's power lust. *The fool!*"

"Austria is on the other side of Europe," I said. "Even if we were inclined, what could we possibly do to help?"

"You happen to be right. The time has passed when standing up on our hind legs would have made a difference. It's too late now."

We shall see, dear Heidi, we shall see. Most people simply want the tension over Europe to go away. They say if Herr Hitler gobbles up little Austria – which is German anyhow – and the gobbling puts an end to the tension, then let's get on with it.

As for myself, great lady, I cannot possibly say enough about your SEVEN MEN. I fear my stock of glowing words may be inadequate. Let me just say the accomplishment is remarkable and should send your career soaring. You must tell me how many bronzes have been ordered. Any takers for the Mussolini and the Hitler? Art galleries and museums lining up for the presidents? Do tell. I think Elizabeth H. Lowell is going to be a wealthy lady off her own bat. Congratulations again.

Hugs from your admirer,
Joff

Saturday
5th March 1938

Dearest Heidi,

Received yours of the twentieth, many thanks. Thrilled, though not a bit surprised, to hear about the sales. May they continue, and may you enjoy your richly deserved fame.

As you might imagine, we are caught up here with Anthony Eden's resignation. It has rocked the F.O., if not the country, even if we did see it coming. Eden's disagreements with the Prime Minister about how to deal with Hitler and Mussolini were beginning to undermine cabinet solidarity. His departure was inevitable. So was my colleague Ken's reaction: "We had one voice, *one* voice in Cabinet saying no to appeasement. Now that single sane voice is gone. Can you hear the cheering in Berlin?"

Ken despises Eden's successor. He calls Lord Halifax a tall wooden order-taker, a classic head waiter. "We now have a Foreign Secretary," he said, "joined at the hip with Chamberlain. The two of them think of the dictators as men they can deal with. Think about that, Joff. Our leaders think they can trust men who regularly murder their opponents and who have made themselves absolute tyrants."

Listening to others in the F.O., however, I hear the appointment of Lord Halifax to the top job gives hope for meaningful negotiations with Germany. I frankly don't know what to think. Meaningful negotiations seem to be beside the point at the moment. The tension over Austria has only grown. A couple of days ago Hitler delivered one of the most ferocious speeches of his career. Auntie Beeb ran a good minute of his screeching. I wondered if the point was to indicate the man is deranged. Really, Heidi, it was scary. A great nation with a fearsome military is being led by a man who sounds crackers. The speech was a sustained rant about Marxist agitation in Vienna, the breakdown of law and order throughout Austria, and the ongoing sabotage of sacred German culture by the Schuschnigg government. Truth is, Marxist agitators are extinct in Vienna, the breakdown of law and order there is mainly attributable to local Nazis, and traditional German culture is arguably more alive in Schuschsnigg's Austria than in Hitler's Germany!

The cause of Hitler's tantrum was a speech given by Schuschnigg. Apparently the Chancellor of Austria has found defiance in his heart. He dared to assert *Austria will live!* We were all shocked by this development, I can tell you. The meek diffident pushover Schuschnigg throwing egg on the dictator's face? So we remain on edge here. Hitler's tirade, no matter how fraudulent the content, has established pretext. Reliable reports say eight divisions of the army and a dozen squadrons of the Luftwaffe have taken up positions along the Austrian border.

Oh Christ, there's my cross to bear ... the ceiling stompers. The two little hoodlums are only getting older, and heavier – and wilder. Maddening.

Off to do my Saturday errands. How big is your bump now? Kicks from Athena? Be well and happy, great lady.

Joff

Tuesday
15th March 1938

Dear Heidi,

Your correspondent has just emerged from a dreamless well-deserved afternoon nap. He is sitting at his grandfather's desk with a cup of tea, contemplating dark events. We saw all this before, when the Germans occupied the Rhineland. Why else would I be writing you on a Tuesday from the flat? After a couple of hours at the F.O. this morning, my eyes could no longer stay open. We were in full-blown crisis all Sunday and yesterday. The Germans, as your radio must have blared, marched into Austria on Saturday. Packets of material from Berlin and Vienna arrived on special flights, and the tea-leaf readers upstairs demanded the quickest possible translation. The event is being called an *Anschluss*.

Have your Boston newspapers adopted the term? Over here it instantly became common usage and is being bandied about to mean any number of things. An annexation. An invasion. A unification. An atrocity. No matter how you translate it, Austria has ceased to exist. The geography of the extinct country now forms an eastern appendage of the Third Reich. Hitler has accomplished what he called his life dream. Schuschnigg probably overplayed his hand, or maybe the *Anschluss* was going to happen no matter what. By announcing plans last week for a national plebiscite on independence, Schuschnigg only further provoked Hitler. The plebiscite threatened to humiliate the German leader, so he prepared to invade.

At least there was no loss of life. The sea of German tanks on the border did an effective job of intimidation. Schuschnigg cancelled the plebiscite, then resigned his office. The Nazi stooge, Seyss-Inquart, was appointed Chancellor. This all happened on Friday. On Saturday, Hitler's troops marched into Vienna without a shot being fired. They say Schuschnigg is under house-arrest.

On Sunday morning Tremayne arrived with the news that Mr. Chamberlain had convened his cabinet in emergency session. Ken forgot himself and let out a great *Hah*! Tremayne's head shot up but he said nothing. Ken whispered, "Any minute now the British government will send out a stern protest note."

Your correspondent requires additional nap time … the next couple of weeks in the sunroom will be hectic. In touch again soon,
    Joff

Saturday
19th March 1938

Dear Heidi,
Not a pleasant week. Beastly stories out of Vienna, and you know my job ... someone has to translate the gloaters, the prideful champions of the hate and brutality. We thought the anti-Semitic lunacy might have run its course in Germany. Wishful thinking. The Nazis have exported an ugly variant to Austria. Every day of the week the newspapers ran photos of vandalised Jewish shops and paint-splattered synagogues. One report spoke of a rabbi pushed to his knees in a public latrine and forced to wipe toilets with his prayer shawl.

"You would think they're taking revenge for something," I said.

"Don't you know?" said Ken. "All the Jews of Vienna are factory owners strangling the poor workingman. Either that or they're communist plotters threatening to take the factories away from honest business people."

Tremayne was out of earshot in his broom closet. His only comment since the *Anschluss* referred to the prospect that now the confrontation has ended, we can all feel relieved. With Austria out of the way, Europe should be in for a long season of stability. Hardly a consolation for the Austrian Jews.

The incident of the humiliated rabbi was not among the worst. Neither was the spectacle of Jewish industrialists and university professors made to scrub pavements with toothbrushes while crowds jeered. ("The Fuhrer has found work for the Jews!") The loathsome events reached a climax of sorts when brownshirted thugs charged into a sisterhood meeting in a synagogue with whips and snarling dogs. The zealous defenders of Aryan purity dragged the horror-struck Jewish ladies, some of them quite elderly, into the winter streets. They stripped the women naked, made them crawl on all fours, then forced pork chops into their mouths while shrieking "Sarah's hungry! Sarah's hungry!" The Nazis are inventing new lows in human savagery, Heidi. We hear that automobiles, homes, factories have been extorted in return for suddenly precious exit visas. Many who have nothing to trade are taking another way out. Reports say hundreds of Jews, in some instances entire families with hands joined, have committed suicide.

I should have known Tremayne's observation was borrowed from his betters. The idea that stability may take hold, now that Hitler has hammered another nail into the coffin of Versailles, seems to be the general view at the F.O. Our leaders are trimming their sails to the new reality in central Europe. Prime Minister Chamberlain has suggested that conditions are now ripe for a general settlement of differences. Which makes Ken grimace.

"Austria has only further emboldened Hitler, and we have lost another chance to turn his generals against him."

"My friend, you are singing directly from the songbook of Churchill. He wrote the very thing last week in the *Standard*."

"What of it? Facts are facts, no matter who states them. Elements of the old guard in Germany despise the dictator. However, as Churchill says, they need a reason to bring him down."

Ken and Churchill may be right. After the Rhineland, the German people began regarding Hitler as a new Bismarck. From all I read since the *Anschluss*, the masses now see him as a veritable miracle-worker. If he can win victory after victory without shedding a drop of blood, why would his generals topple him?

One threadbare postcard from Damon, the first in ages. His work is thriving, he says, and he has gained weight. That was it, not a word more.

Must run, Heidi. Mary's brothers and their wives have come down to London. Dinner will be at Sebastien's in Covent Garden, and we have tickets for *Idiot's Delight* at the Apollo. That would be Mary's doing. She has a weakness, undeclared but obvious, for Raymond Massey.

Cheers,

Joff

Sunday
27th March 1938

Dear Heidi,
At times the postal system works like a charm. Yours of the sixteenth arrived two days ago, many thanks. I just looked at it again, here on the train returning from Bury. My father did not recognise me today. He hardly acknowledged my presence. At one point he asked if I were the doctor come to examine his leg. He dozed on and off. His life now consists of restless little sleeps during the day and long thrashing ones at night. Or is it the other way round? While semi-awake he mutters and curses. I have the impression his mind is dredging old harbours, stirring up confusion. I sat by his bed for a couple of hours, straightened out some business with Mrs. Stockton, and escaped her fetid little prison with my sanity, I trust, intact.

Your letter gratifies. Then it annoys.

Orders for twenty-three castings … well done. Sounds like you have made a considerable success. Please tell me what it all means in terms of filthy lucre. You are too modest, great lady. Kindly use your biggest fan as a boasting board.

And yes, you have annoyed me … you write how bitter and unforgiving Catherine is, and then you say: 'They were getting along swimmingly, enjoying each other, making plans for the future, but the mask fell off Seamus and the whole thing crashed.' What mask? Never in his life has Seamus worn a mask. He has no secrets. As you well know, he is an unimaginative lab technician with a weight problem, a harmless chap like millions of others. Adding injury to annoyance, you seem to be implying I know what lies beneath the alleged mask! Tell me, what did Catherine say she discovered?

The weeks have flown. Mary's cast comes off on Monday. She never complained, simply accepted the nuisance and soldiered on. It occurs to me she might actually miss the thing. On the second day of the cast, a girl at the Auxiliary painted a Union Jack on it.

Must rush, my train is pulling into the station. Be well and safe for the budding Athena. Why are you sure another boy is on the way? Maternal instinct? Be well. And no speeding in the Studebaker!
Joff

Saturday
9th April 1938

Dear Heidi,
Maddy Kloff took me to lunch this week. She practically begged me to do something about Damon. She has heard an ugly rumour. "It comes from two different gallery owners in Berlin. Decent men I have known for decades. They know all the foreign painters in the city, because these days precious few care to live there."

"What has our boy done now?" I said, fearing she might have heard about Damon's special friend.

"I'm sick at heart about this."

"Maddy, what – ?"

"They say he has been a guest at the home of Hermann Goering. More than once. They say the two get along like chums. Has he lost his mind?"

"Dame has always had a weakness for louche characters, hasn't he?"

"This is no laughing matter."

Maddy could not have guessed what I was thinking. Of course I shared her revulsion about Goering, the obese Air Marshall and purported *Nummer Zwei* in the Third Reich, but a silver lining had instantly occurred to me. If Damon's chummy with one of the most powerful men in Germany, maybe I can stop worrying about the risks he's taking with that other, rather more anonymous, friend of his. The strange webs we mortals weave …

"You do see the scandal, don't you?" Maddy said.

"Of course, this is sickening. Goering's a vile beast."

Maddy, placated, said, "We have to do something."

"What can we possibly do?"

"You must get him back to England."

"Dear lady, how do you suggest I do that?"

"Go to Berlin. The gallery will cover your expenses."

Good, kind, charming Maddy, I have always liked her. She won't see sixty again but remains an imperishable girl. How else wear a purple cardigan jacket and a blood red beret at a precipitous angle and effortlessly carry off the ensemble? I was lunching with an aged bohemian whom circumstances have turned naïve.

"Maddy, as you well know, Dame has never been amenable to people telling him what to do."

She insisted I think of Damon's future. She strongly believes his talent has not yet fully matured. He has it in him to become a giant, but the world's contempt, if this madness should summon it, could kill his name. "He barely escaped drowning in mud with that shameful Munich exhibit last year. Imagine the grime of a connection to the head of the Nazi air force. Damon will be branded the Mosley of British art."

I was very sorry indeed, I said, but any effort to turn Damon from a path of his own choosing would be futile. I also told her I have no intention of ever setting foot in Germany. (Curiously, the moment I made that declaration I realised the truth of it. The idea of going to Hitlerland is repellent.)

A hot colour came into Maddy's face. "You are abandoning your friend to disgrace, then."

"Maddy, I will pretend you never said that."

"This thing has upset me terribly. I *am* sorry."

I urged her to make the trip herself. She has long been a pillar of Damon's career. He might listen to reason if it came from her.

"He would see my motives as mercenary. Which they are not, I promise you. I adore Damon. I revere his talent."

We parted on an upbeat note after agreeing on a plan. We would both write pleading letters to Damon, asking him to come home. Maddy would enlist a few of his collectors, and maybe a critic or two, to write him as well. The letters could cite the growing tension between England and Germany, and argue his career risked irreparable taint by association with an outlaw country. No one is to mention the name of Hermann Goering. Damon is simply meant to hear a choir of friends appealing to his common sense.

I posted my exhortation yesterday, and prefaced it with the latest news of German malevolence. Is he aware that after two months of Nazi rule in Vienna all democratic institutions in the now defunct Austria have been abolished? Has he noticed the *Anschluss* put only a short-term brake on Mr. Hitler's ambitions? Now we are hearing cranked-up demands on behalf of the German minority in Czechoslovakia, and the Leader's heated rhetoric comes with increased troop maneuvers along the border. 'Dame,' I wrote, 'the Czechs are not for buckling. A real fear exists of war breaking out, and France and England being drawn in. Do you care to find yourself on the wrong side of the fence if that happens?'

A long shot, this letter-writing campaign, but at least it will make Damon think. If you have any ideas on the matter, please let me know.

As ever,

Joff

Saturday
16th April 1938

Dear Heidi,
A call from the upper reaches this week. It presented an opportunity, but not the one I have been waiting for. "Pearson," Tremayne announced, "you have an appointment this afternoon at four. The Private Secretary to the Deputy Permanent Under-Secretary wishes to see you."

"That would be Mr. – "

"Samuel Sternthal."

An ever so slight tint in Tremayne's voice coloured the Samuel, then an unmistakable emphasis on the *Stern* of Sternthal. I cannot accuse Tremayne of being an anti-Semite. Clapping for a blackshirt in Hyde Park is insufficient evidence. At any rate Tremayne's bigotry would be genteel, it could never be revealed explicitly, that would be unEnglish of him. His distaste in the case of Mr. Sternthal, as in many cases that involve no Jews or their facsimiles, would most likely proceed from his presumption that the country properly belongs only to those who come from families, homes, schools and religions exactly like his own.

Samuel Sternthal happens to be the highest ranking Jew in the F.O., and probably the *only* Jew in the upper ranks. He came out of the War with a medal on his chest. Then he gained a phenomenal first at LSE in the early '20s. His thesis on Britain's role at Versailles drew wide notice. When he caught the eye of Bonar Law after achieving the year's highest score in the foreign service exam, his career was launched. Sometimes you can't keep them out.

At the moment, appropriately enough, Sternthal is overseeing the F.O.'s role in the reception and assimilation of refugees from Hitler, most of whom are Jews. I wondered what on earth he could want with me.

I met him in his room at the Admiralty. For some reason his refugee project has been tucked away there, maybe to keep it out of sight. First impression was a bit of a shock. Sternthal is a balding little Jew with noticeably feminine hands, dainty things that force a double-take and make you wonder how he won that medal. You would never fear him in a dark alley, but then his people have never been known to be feared in dark alleys, have they? His handshake was neither robust nor reserved, it gave nothing away. Once he began speaking, however, his voice and manner banished the physical impression. I was abruptly in the presence of an authoritative, assertive, compelling individual who wasted no time coming to the point.

"As you know, Pearson, we have been quietly taking in Jews fleeing Germany. Now the Jews of Austria are desperate to find a haven. Many of these refugees come with shocking stories."

"From what I see in the newspapers and my work," I said, "the discrimination against them only grows more ferocious."

"Quite so. When our newspapers report on the persecution, they generally do not conceal the ugly truths, but I fear they have not come near to learning the worst."

"What makes you say that?"

"The file of a refugee named Morris Gelfmann recently came into my hands. It horrified me. I arranged a meeting with Herr Gelfmann and came away believing his story. I am determined to see it told to a wide audience."

Sternthal said Gelfmann had been a Berliner all his life, a success as both a lawyer and municipal politician. He had risen very close to the top of his profession and served for a number of years on the city council. When Hitler came to power Gelfmann was stripped of the right to practice law. He had done nothing wrong, it was enough that he was a Jew. Of course he was also thrown off the city council. That was only the beginning.

"Six months ago," said Sternthal, "he lost his family. Wife and two sons. The incredible thing is how they died. It was difficult to believe at first. He arrived in England a week ago." Sternthal paused. He looked at me intently. "I have asked you to meet with me for a very particular reason, Pearson."

"Sir?"

"I suggest you meet Gelfmann, and listen to the story of what happened to his wife and sons."

"May I ask why?"

"My position has given me access to your translations and notes for years. I saw your work on the memorandum concerning Dr. Schacht. It might interest you to know your comments created something of a flap."

"So I understand, but why are you suggesting I meet Herr Gelfmann?"

"Your fluency in German is total, and your writing shows flair. Many of the refugees from Germany have suffered disturbing and one might say unthinkable experiences. If you hear Gelfmann's story and others like it, you might see the value of doing a book."

I will hand one thing to Mr. Sternthal. He had never pretended our meeting would be related to F.O. business. But neither had he given any sign it would fall so far outside my usual duties. I can sympathise with his concern over the German branch of his tribe, but take on a burden like the one he was proposing? I was less flattered by his suggestion than floored by the potential weight of it.

"Why don't you introduce the man to a journalist?"

"Gelfmann speaks no English. Still, that is not my main reason for bringing this to you. I believe Gelfmann's story would be ill-served if made into something briefly lurid. The same for the stories of his confreres. A sombre book relating their experiences will carry far greater impact, and will endure over time. Additionally, Pearson, your position has given you an understanding of our institutions and the ways of power in England. You know how our decision-makers think and react. If you write this book, it will be noticed by a good many people who can actually do something. You can help open eyes to what is going on in Germany."

I was having difficulty grasping that I was on the receiving end of these remarks. Was he talking about the same Pearson I make fun of every morning when I shave? "You flatter me, Mr. Sternthal, unduly."

"I think not. Be that as it may, I am simply laying before you what I hope you will see as an opportunity."

"No disrespect, sir, but I fear you have misjudged my abilities. I have no special insight of the nature you suggest, and my skill with the pen is not what you imagine."

"Modestly said. Also the response I would expect." Sternthal rose from his chair and leaned across his desk. "Pearson, a barbaric crime is being committed in Germany. Day by day the crime intensifies in concert with the police, all organs of state security and, I am sorry to say, the acquiesence of the vast majority of the German people. The crime has now crossed into Austria. Meanwhile the world is essentially averting its eyes. If the project I propose could shed wider and clearer light on what is happening, you would be doing your duty as an Englishman. I ask simply that you consider it."

My duty as an Englishman.

I knew the comment was calculated, but it still struck a chord. With something of a tremor in my voice, and thinking I would let him down gently in coming days, I agreed to consider it.

He rang the sunroom first thing the next morning. Tremayne called me to his alcove. He was holding the telephone at arm's length. "A highly placed Hebrew for you," he said.

I turned my back as I took the call. Mr. Sternthal thanked me for our meeting and said he had neglected to mention the serious interest of a prominent publishing house in the project we had discussed. Only to say, he could assure me that if the book were written it would find distinguished and prompt publication. After an awkward pause during which I heard myself think, *Right, simple as that*, I thanked him, said I was considering his suggestion, and promised to respond as soon as possible.

"You seem to have a new friend, Pearson," said Tremayne. At least I have friends, is what I should have replied. Instead I tried a taunting smile, but my mouth only quivered idiotically.

Maddy telephoned the other day. She persuaded four of Damon's collectors to join our letter-writing campaign. She also recruited the art critic of the *Manchester Guardian*.

I seem to have lost touch with the calendar. Tell me again when Athena is expected. All my best, and with my customary devotion,

Joff

Saturday
23rd April 1938

Dear Great Lady,
Thanks for yours of the twelfth. Additional congratulations are in order. Having a New York gallery put your busts on display will no doubt multiply sales … but you should stay in the nest and calmly await Athena's arrival. Where is That American when you need someone to police your exertions? Maybe I should slip him a strongly worded note. Loved your description of the city's canyons! I could never look down from the top of the Empire State Building … I would fear the return of Mr. Vertigo.

Spent the week translating leaders from Berlin and Munich newspapers, all citing evidence of violence, looting, rape and other outrages inflicted by evil Czechs on defenceless Germans in the Sudetenland. The verdicts of the newspapers are invariably shrill and call upon the Reich to 'assist our persecuted brothers and sisters' with every means at the Fatherland's disposal, including 'the invincible fist of the Wehrmacht'.

"Recognise the pattern?" Ken said to me. "It worked to perfection in Austria. These stories of atrocities are pure invention."

The level of nervousness at the F.O. is no invention. People are seeing war clouds in the sky. Czechoslovakia is no Austria; it will not be walked over. The country has a well trained army of four hundred thousand men, and a system of fortifications it has spent years building.

The statements out of Downing Street focus principally on the legitimate grievances (a few do exist) of the Sudeten Germans, and the need for the Czechs to make concessions. "Mealy-mouthed Chamberlain and Halifax are so frightened of their own shadows," Ken says contemptuously, "they can't bring themselves to draw a line."

"If they draw a line," I said, "you and I and everybody might have to live with some very grim consequences."

"Such as?"

"Oh, bombs dropping from airplanes over densely populated cities. The newspapers running long lists of dead civilians. Little spots of bother like that."

"Has it ever occurred to you, Joff, that there's also too high a price

314

to pay for peace?"

The war of words goes on, but at least the conflict is still made only of words. Meanwhile I fret over Mr. Sternthal's proposal. If I agree to meet his German Jew he will hear me saying, *I'm grateful for your patronage, the project interests me, show me the way to duty and literary fame* ... and I will have thrust both feet into quicksand. The bait about a prominent publisher must be a carrot of Sternthal's imagination. I don't share his cheery notion that people would be interested. The plague on the Jews of Hitlerland already fills quite a bit of space in the newspapers. For another thing, how would I find the time? Not to speak of the energy. And who is to say my ability as a translator can be converted to writing a book?

The story of Catherine and Seamus ... I am still waiting. What did Catherine say she discovered?

Not a single cheering sign of spring. Dull, cold, remorseless drizzle. Sun missing in action. Grey Britain. Maybe I would prefer the stubborn snow in your garden.

As ever,

Joff

Saturday
30th April 1938

Dear Heidi,
An absent-minded moment at breakfast this week proved fatal. Mary
had returned the night before from Leeds. We were catching up on
Vicky, my father's accelerating decay, the usual goings-on at work,
when I mentioned my meeting with the Private Secretary to the
Deputy Permanent Under-Secretary. I realised my folly the instant
the words left my mouth.

Mary's eyes lit up. "Mr. Sternthal? Samuel Sternthal? I know the
man. We met at a service function once. A decent sort of fellow. Does
he need an interpreter?"

I saw no escape. The trap was of my own making. Still, I tried a
diversion. "You met him? There's a coincidence. Did you speak much?"

"We had a talk about the Auxiliary. He was very solicitous, but with
good reason. He introduced two refugees as potential recruits."

"Really? Did they make it in?"

"One of them joined. What – "

"Is she a Jew?"

"Yes, actually."

"Is that so? How many Jews – "

"What did Mr. Sternthal want, Joff?"

Cornered.

I told her what Sternthal had proposed. Exactly as I feared, Mary
produced a trumpet. "Splendid idea!"

I said something about it being a non-starter, but Mary was off
and running. "Opportunity knocks again, Joff. A perfectly splendid
opportunity. Of course you told him you'll do it?"

I looked at the floor as I made a mumbling remark about workload,
and fixed on the ceiling as I came out with an even more pathetic one
about Tremayne's noose around my neck. Then I said to the coffee
pot on the stove: "Where would I find the time? Can I be expected to
handle two jobs at once?"

My dear wife replied with a deadly silence. She knew that I knew
exactly what she was thinking. Which of the two people sitting at
the table had failed for years to advance his career and bump up his

support of the household? Who had been finding fault those same years with the position he held, the monotonous work he performed, and the tinpot tyrant he laboured under? Did this chance to do a book, *a book*, not offer a potential door to distinction, extra income, a more interesting career? Mary's eyes were unwavering and her lips formed two rigid lines.

Ever felt drawn and quartered, Heidi? I can describe the sensation to you in detail. I am the husband of an officer in the Women's Police Auxiliary, God love her and save me.

The next day, using the telephone on Tremayne's desk, I rang Sternthal and agreed to hear Gelfmann's story. He declared himself most pleased and said he would arrange the meeting. I felt the quicksand tugging at me, pulling me down. My only satisfaction came when I ended the call with a cheerful, "It will be a pleasure seeing you again, Mr. Sternthal" – and saw the look on Tremayne's face blend resentment, misgiving, and a pinch of incredulity.

My spouse should be home from her Saturday rounds any minute now. She will find me … horizontal. I send you the snores of a napping man.

Joff

Tuesday
10th May 1938

Dear Heidi,

Missed writing you on the weekend … rushing this on sunroom time. My precious Vicky was home and we spent a large chunk of Saturday in the National Portrait Gallery. At Vicky's behest, you should know. "Daddy, I must see every portrait *ever* done of the Duke of Wellington."

"Whatever for?" I asked, and she looked at me as if snakes were crawling out of my ears.

"The Duke ended a *terrible* threat to England, Daddy. He *crushed* Napoleon at Waterloo."

I apologised at once for forgetting to wear the empire's history on my sleeve and promised to track down every last image of England's heroic defender in our nation's great repository of portraits. Which turned out to be an unfortunate promise. Do you have any idea how many depictions of Arthur Wellesley, First Duke of Wellington, exist in the gallery? He reigns like a god there in a myriad of oil paintings, engravings, marble busts, and paper medallions. He even bestrides antique cigarette cards preserved under glass. Vicky mercifully called a halt after we stumbled upon a plaster cast of the Duke's death-mask. "We can go home, Daddy. I think I really *know* the Duke now."

As for me, I will soon be getting to know a refugee Jew. The call from Sternthal came yesterday. The meeting with Herr Gelfmann is set for the Admiralty on Friday.

Hurried hugs,
Joff

Saturday
14th May 1938

Dear Heidi,

Must tell you, yesterday was ... grim. Please bear with me because I aim to put it all down. I am keeping a carbon for myself. You will understand why.

Morris Gelfmann was waiting for me in a small conference room at the Admiralty. Sternthal made the introductions and took his leave.

"How do you do," I said in German.

"*Guten Tag,*" said Gelfmann.

Was I with the right person? I had imagined a withered, ragged man, but standing before me was a vigorous looking fellow immaculately clothed and groomed. Every hair on his head was in place and his shoes polished to a gleam. He was tall for a Jew, well over six foot. I asked after his health and how he was coping in London.

In a tone of impatient frustration he almost shouted: "Do not consider my person or current situation of any importance whatsoever!"

Seeing the startled look on my face he immediately apologised. "Mr. Pearson," he said, "you must ... pardon me. I am sorry for my rudeness. Excuse my agitation."

The power of appearance to deceive. Now I saw there was little light in Gelfmann's eyes. They looked incurably tired. The tension in him was palpable, like something contained but impossible to hide. His fine suit, carefully pressed shirt, debonair grooming, these were props. He was presenting a defiant face to the world. I told him he should feel no shame in expressing his emotions.

"I will try to concern you with facts only," he said. "Do you have children, Mr. Pearson?"

"A daughter," I replied, then added foolishly, "whom I love very much."

His face clouded. "I loved my sons, loved them beyond measure. I must tell you, so you can tell others, what the Nazis did to them and my beloved Hannah."

I bowed my head.

"The older of my two sons ... his name was Jacob. After the Nuremberg decrees, the headmaster of my son's school came to his classroom. He pointed at my boy and screamed, *Gelfmann, Jude raus*! My boy was ten years old. He was the only Jewish child in the class. He had done nothing wrong. He could not comprehend what was happening. His teacher stood aside. None of his friends said a word. The headmaster marched to my boy's desk, took him by the ear and hauled him to his feet. My good brave boy did not cry in the school. He gathered his things and came home. There he cried, and kept crying, in his mother's arms." Herr Gelfmann's voice faltered on those last words. He looked away for a few moments.

"Mr. Pearson, I am told you are an informed man. You know of the nightmare that has come upon the Jews of Germany. The laws, the decrees, the endless restrictions ... of these you know. But they are only one side. The other side is more terrible, because it is more personal. Employers dismissing Jews. Jewish children expelled from school. Law-abiding Jews terrified of the police. The Nazis have spread a poison. They have created a hatred in every corner of German life. Libraries and parks are closed to Jews. Hospitals turn away sick Jews. Strangers recoil when they learn you are a Jew. You see revulsion in the eyes of shop girls, postal clerks, bus drivers. Of these personal things you cannot know. The humiliation of being singled out, officially classified as a lower being, something akin to an animal, an enemy – a disease.

"The day my boy cried in his mother's arms was when I realised how foolish I had been to believe Hitler was temporary. Until that day I had believed my fellow Germans would see the evil in the Nazis and push them into the gutter from which they had come. I was worse than mistaken, I was blind. All of Germany has become a gutter. There was no choice but to leave. I began the search for a country that would take us, and that search became my only mission, because I had no work. I was a lawyer and therefore not permitted to work. The system of justice in today's Germany must not be touched by the hands of Jews, lest the system be contaminated. You must pardon me, but no matter how many times I repeat it to you and your countrymen, I fear you will not accept it, I fear you will think me a dealer in drama and exaggeration, but this is how Jews are regarded in Germany today ... as contaminants.

"I will not tell you of the futility of my mission. Not all the walls

320

that surround the Jews of Germany have been put there by the Nazis. Many are the work of the democracies. The democracies condemn the brutality of the Nazis while they close their doors to those who are trying to escape it. But these are things of which you are already aware, surface things, known by those who care to know. I will not speak of them. I am here to tell you things of which you are not aware. Things that are hidden and which are happening in the dark, and which you may not believe."

I doubt if my translation of Herr Gelfmann can capture the manner of his speech. He was speaking with quiet vigour, yet also with great caution. His choice of words was not unlike his bearing … focused, fastidious.

"Hannah and our two boys were in the Friedrichstadt area of Berlin on the day they were taken. They had gone to see our doctor, Dr. Plaut, and had just left his apartment. My younger boy, Bernard, needed attention for his asthma. You may ask why they went to see Dr. Plaut at his apartment. It is because he had been evicted from his rented surgery. One day his landlord simply tore up Dr. Plaut's lease and told him to get out and never to show his Jew face on the landlord's property again. Dr. Plaut did as he was told. If you are a Jew in today's Germany, you do not go to the courts for assistance. You do not appeal to authority. All authority has become Nazi. But again, I am likely telling you things you already know."

As I listened to Herr Gelfmann I felt a weight inside me growing heavier, in both stomach and head. Maybe I should be ashamed to admit this. The weight came not only from revulsion at the story I was hearing, but equally from the expectation the teller was investing in his listener.

"That day in Friedrichstadt when my wife and boys left our doctor's apartment, they happened to encounter a parade of S.A. men on Leipziger Strasse. What I am telling you now is what I was able to learn only days later. The S.A. men were likely marching with their customary swagger and singing their Horst Wessel song. I imagine too that all of the people along the parade route, ordinary people who were going about their daily business and who happened to be there, they surely would have given the Hitler salute to the S.A. men. My wife and boys, who were simply waiting to cross the street, would not have saluted. I am sure you know what kind of beasts the S.A. men are, Mr. Pearson. But do you know how far they will go to exhibit the power they hold?"

I answered Herr Gelfmann by bowing my head again and closing my eyes. The recent outrages in Vienna were likely the work of the Austrian offspring of the *Sturm Abteilung*, the brown-shirted Storm Troopers. The S.A. is the dictator's private army, comprised of soldiers who are no more than bullies in uniform, feral men gorging on a bone of authority. Their only function is to sow terror among enemies of the regime, including communists, trade unionists, democrats of any stripe, gypsies and homosexuals, and above all Jews. The S.A., more than any other depraved Nazi organ, exposes Germany as a place where the rule of law has been supplanted by savage tyranny. I girded myself for whatever Herr Gelfmann was about to tell me.

"People who fail to give the Nazi salute are regularly intimidated and publicly beaten. The S.A. swine choose to interpret any withholding of the salute as impudence and treason. Even visitors to Berlin, unsuspecting travelers or business people from other countries, have been assaulted by these hoodlums. They attacked my family that day. They took away Hannah and my boys – "

His voice tripped. He fidgeted in his chair. He needed a moment to gather himself.

"You must pardon me. I torment myself with imaginations of what occurred. Only after days of anguish did I hear where my family had been taken. A former colleague, a gentile lawyer whom I am privileged to call a friend, agreed to make inquiries. Not all Germans subscribe to the Nazi hysteria, Mr. Pearson, but everyone fears it. This man is a member of the city council, a respected jurist, a religious Christian. Before the Nazis came I had often worked with this man and dined with him. He agreed to learn what he could, on condition I never call or appear at his office or home. He would contact me only from public telephones. Our meetings had to seem like chance encounters on busy streets. I fully understood his caution. I would not have asked him to conduct himself any other way.

"My colleague pieced together what happened. My wife and sons had so 'provoked' the S.A. as to be arrested and taken away. I can imagine it, Mr. Pearson. A pack of gangsters in brown shirts slapping and pushing my family while shrieking *SIE WERDEN DEN DEUTSCHEN GRUSS MACHEN!* The swine might have continued on their way after dispensing their lesson with fists and screams, but one of the S.A. men must have noticed the silver bracelet on my little Bernie ... a bracelet engraved with the star of David. I can see the hoodlum fury reigniting and building into a frenzy. *These filthy traitors are Jews!* They would start kicking my loved ones as they would rebellious dogs ..."

I am transcribing Herr Gelfmann's words as accurately as memory allows, but for the next few minutes he grew almost incoherent. His brave front gave way and he could hardly speak ten words in succession without his train of thought derailing and voice cracking. What I understood was that his family had been taken to a hospital prison near Limburg.

I asked if I had heard correctly. *Hospital prison?*

Herr Gelfmann's voice came in a whisper. "No. It was not a hospital. It was not a prison."

"Was it one of these 'camps' we hear about, where the Nazis imprison their political enemies?"

"You do not understand. It was not a camp."

"Herr Gelfmann, I am not following you. Where – ?"

"They were taken to an asylum ... for the insane."

Herr Gelfmann's lawyer friend was told by a captain of the Berlin police that Hannah and the boys had been turned over to Reich prison authorities. The lawyer friend then contacted a cousin who held a civil service position within the prison system. His cousin was a member of the Nazi Party and had recently been promoted several ranks within the penal bureaucracy. The lawyer asked him if he could look into the disposition of a Jewish family taken by the S.A. The cousin's response came like the sting of a wasp. How dare the lawyer concern himself with such a matter?

In a low tone the lawyer's cousin advised him to cease interfering and forget he even knew the Jew family. Since he and the lawyer happened to be related, he would do him the significant favour of forgetting their conversation ever took place – he should understand that the question of *Lebensunwertes Leben* was for the Reich alone to deal with. This response from the cousin, the reflex ferocity of it, touched something deep in the Christian lawyer. It roused anger and suspicion in him.

Then came the offhand way his cousin had employed the dark phrase, *Lebensunwertes Leben* … life unworthy of life.

The sinister phrase brought back to me the disturbing reference to *nutzlosen Esser*, and the blow-up it had caused between Ken and myself. "Are you referring, Herr Gelfmann, to those whom the Nazis call 'useless eaters'?"

A light flickered in Gelfmann's eyes. "Then you know?"

I shook my head. I felt shame. "I chose not to believe it."

"My colleague did not believe the rumours either. He is a good man, a person of moral conviction. Men like him still exist in the Hitler hell. When he heard the ugly words *Lebensunwertes Leben* slip carelessly, even pridefully, from his cousin … it shook him to his core. Now he needed to learn for himself what had become of my family."

Again, the pain of remembering caused Herr Gelfmann to break down. The rest of his story issued in a random jumble through a choked voice.

His colleague, at mounting risk to his own safety, persisted in his inquiries. He used his influence as a respected lawyer and the prestige of his title as a city councillor. What he learned caused him to grow sick at heart. It could not possibly be, not in his country, not in this century, not in any civilised place. Yet the truth became clear to him. He learned the Nazis are weeding from society whole categories of people regarded as undesirable. Among these are the genetically deformed and mentally retarded. Ken Retinger had not doubted they were capable of it. I owe him an apology. It appears the Nazis are administering euthanasia to thousands of human beings.

Herr Gelfmann's gentile colleague discovered the atrocity goes deeper. Not only the deformed and retarded, but perfectly healthy people in additional hated categories, when caught in the Reich's prison net and transported to lunatic asylums can also be branded *nutzlosen Esser*. Herr Gelfmann's voice issued in a near whisper as he told me of the death certificates he received in the mail.

The official documents, meticulously prepared, engraved with the Reich emblem of eagle and swastika, arrived the same day as a flyer from a grocer and the monthly gas bill. In the large envelope with the three certificates came a letter notifying Herr Gelfmann of the sudden deaths of Frau Hannah Gelfmann, Jacob Gelfmann, and Bernard

Gelfmann. The three unfortunates had been taken to the hospital at Limburg for injuries suffered in a traffic accident. A fire had broken out in the wing where they were held. The conflagration burned their bodies beyond recogniton. Their remains were buried in the cemetary adjacent to the hospital.

I could hardly raise my eyes to meet Herr Gelfmann's. The contemptuous fiction in the letter had added rage to his anguish, yet he dared not express any rage in the new Germany. He had no recourse. His Christian friend warned him against traveling to Limburg, because he would not find the graves of his loved ones there. No cemetary existed adjacent to the Limburg hospital.

It did not occur to me to doubt Herr Gelfmann's story. This was not a man to invent a tale. His life is too clearly one of terminal grief.

"The world thinks it knows what Germany has become," he said. "The world knows only the surface. Others will tell you more. They have fled to Paris, Brussels, Amsterdam. Some are in Denmark and Sweden. A few have begged visas for China. The walls to keep out Jews are high everywhere, Mr. Pearson, even around your noble country. My life is finished but maybe it can still prove useful. Maybe a book can wake a few among the sleeping, reach hearts even in America, where the walls are highest."

He rose, shook my hand, and shuffled off. No, he did not 'shuffle'. He strode manfully from the room. Still, I had the impression he was shuffling.

Last night my eyes grew wet when I spoke the names of the two Gelfmann boys to Mary. Then an urgency seized me and I telephoned Ken Retinger – my apology could not wait. Ken listened in respectful silence. He said no apology was necessary. He urged me to do good by making the most of the opportunity that has come to me.

Maybe a book can wake a few among the sleeping, reach hearts even in America, where the walls are highest.

I don't know if I am up to the task, Heidi, but I can no longer back away from it. All my best,

Joff

Saturday
21st May 1938

Dear Heidi,

Nothing from you in weeks and weeks. Please let me know all is well.

I spoke with Mr. Sternthal first thing Monday morning. I told him the meeting with Herr Gelfmann had shaken my conscience. He replied quietly, "A book of testimonies such as his could shake the conscience of our country." We then shared a moment of silence, and the telephone trembled against my ear. I told him my decision.

"I am very pleased to hear it," he said.

"Of course I will look to you for guidance."

"Allow me time to organise the files. I will arrange for your transfer to my section, as an Executive Assistant. You can then join us in our little department at the Admiralty."

At this, my heart leaped.

"In the interim," he said, "think of the shape you will give to the book."

I may have envisaged a different escape, but I am nonetheless gratified. Executive Assistant in the office of the Private Secretary to the Deputy Permanent Under-Secretary might sound like an amusing mouthful to you, Heidi, but believe me when I say it represents a significant move up from the sunroom where I have no title or standing at all.

My jubilant Mary made reservations at Manfredi's. She is planning on champagne tonight. I tried to warn her about counting chickens etcetera, but she put an end to that by smothering my lips with her own. The passions of Mary Pearson …

Meanwhile the appeals to our friend in Berlin seem to have landed on deaf ears. Neither I nor Maddy have received a reply from Damon. The silence sounds like scorn. *How dare you presume to counsel me?* Next time I have him in front of me, maybe I should ram the story of Morris Gelfmann down his throat.

We all had a bad scare last week over Czechoslovakia, as you surely know. The Germans held a massive military exercise along the border, just as terrorist acts and mob violence intensified within Czechoslovakia itself. Telegrams from our embassy in Prague said the Czechs considered an attack highly possible, and all the country's fortifications were fully manned. This led to our government announcing that any incursion by German troops across the border could only result in the most grievous blow to European peace. "*There's* a serious warning to Hitler," Ken mocked. Anyway, the scare has blown over. When reports came of German tanks pulling back, you could almost hear the continent exhaling.

"Hitler still needs a fig leaf," said Ken. "He wants to be able to say to the world, and to his own people, 'Look, conditions have became absolutely intolerable, we have no choice but to march.' He's waiting for a sufficient provocation, or preparing one himself."

With the tension over Czechoslovakia by turns flaring and merely seething, the sunroom has been busy. This week the embassy sent us a bunch of leaders from provincial German newspapers. I can imagine the instructions coming from the Reichspressekammer, the Nazi Press Chamber, telling writers what to write. Paint the Czechs as rabid animals and their country an intolerable mongrel. Play up the outrage of the typical German at the subjugation of his cousins. Keep spraying petrol on the fire and raise the roar for SOMETHING TO BE DONE.

"What did I tell you?" said Ken, holding up an obscure weekly from a town in Baden-Württemberg. The front page featured a cartoon of rat-faced Czech policemen applying truncheons to Sudeten women in *dirndl* dresses. "Provocation, served as ordered. Right before our eyes, Czechoslovakia is turning into the next Austria."

Your Hitler bronze must be a big-selling item these days, Heidi. His friend Mussolini's as well. Those two popinjays tend to seize the headlines, don't they? Seems like springtime for the dictators. Forgive me, war clouds should not form the stuff of banter. England may not be directly involved, but the feeling is we would be drawn in once the storm starts. We are all very nervous here.

Impatient for your news from a more sensible continent.

Joff

Saturday
28th May 1938

Dear Heidi,
Your correspondent is an idiot. Either that or he was born with a special blindness, the kind that keeps people from seeing the obvious. *How could I have failed to see that Tremayne would throw a spanner in the works?* He is pushing back with all his spite against Sternthal's application for my transfer.

With the consent of my Section Head the file would sail smoothly through official channels. Without it, the process might die a slow death in the bureaucratic quagmire. Tremayne told me I should not take it as a personal matter. "The needs of the Section must take priority," he said, raising his voice for the benefit of our colleagues. "As you well know, we are already understaffed. Why at any rate would you want to throw in with refugee absorption? Sounds a dreary lot."

Jenkins and Ken saw me turn my back on him and dismiss his question with a flick of my wrist. To hell with Tremayne. I am done with him. Done.

Ken said later, "You should have seen the look on his face when you cut him."

"Let the bastard do his worst. I feel a new man." I do feel a change in myself. A note came from Mr. Sternthal which added fuel to my hopes. *I confess surprise at the objection of your Section Head. He cannot however delay us indefinitely. We will sort this out.*

Your letter of the seventh was almost as brief as the note from my new patron, but consider yourself excused. With Max a likely handful now (he nears the terror of two, no?) and Athena soon to pop out, I should be content with whatever attention you can spare. Still, I have to wonder why you continue to keep me in the dark about Seamus. He and I happened to speak on the telephone the other day, organising a little surprise for Graham's fortieth. Seamus may be overweight, lazy, gullible and perilously profligate, but surely those aren't crimes. So please, for heaven's sake, put me out of my suspense. What did Catherine claim she discovered?

Mary and I have no plans for tonight, except to shut out the world and relax with our books. I finally picked up Cronin's *The Citadel*, and

I'm saving *Theatre* for the Cotswolds. No one beats Maugham for holiday reading.

Did I ever tell you about Mary's delight with her leather-bound Churchill? Months have gone by and she still treats it like a newfound treasure. I could tell she was enormously pleased because she never asked about the cost.

Her hero's column in the *Evening Standard* this week set tongues wagging up and down the land. Mr. Churchill took bitter issue with the Prime Minister's sacking of Lord Swinton, the Minister for Air. Swinton had been pushing for emergency expansion of the RAF, and Downing Street responded with a demand for his resignation. This left Mr. Churchill incredulous. He did not restrain himself. He used a jeering phrase I once heard from Ken Retinger. He said Britain has entered 'Neville Neville Land'. He called Chamberlain 'a mouse of a man who mistakes his craven squeak for a moral crusade,' and accused the government of failing to protect the security of the British people. Serious accusations, concluding with an odd literary lapse: 'We need a man at Number 10 with a spine of steel rather than jelly.' A terribly weak metaphor, no? Far short of Winston's usual creative thunder. The backlash against Churchill's 'delirious rant' was so great the *Evening Standard* announced it could no longer see fit to publish the old warrior. Which caused a rumpus in itself because Churchill's column has been a fortnightly feature for years.

Do you catch wind of these goings-on in America? Sometimes I think you might as well be on Mars for all the news you get of home. Speaking of your adopted country, the F.O. lunchroom is now regularly amused by the clumsy meddling of the American ambassador. It seems Mr. Kennedy adores consorting with high society and his mouth goes astray when tippling with the toffs. The latest whispers say he has been trying hard to wangle an invitation to Berlin. Apparently he identifies low regard for Mr. Hitler as a product of the 'Jew media' and thinks he can 'talk turkey' with the Nazis. My less than favourable impression of the Yank may have been too kind!

Right-o, now I want nothing more than to lay my head on a pillow and await the arrival of my spouse so we can spend the evening oblivious to the world. Be healthy and happy. Missing you as always,
     Joff

Saturday
4th June 1938

Dear Heidi,
Glad tidings. Damon is back in London. Very glad tidings, he has grown bored with Germany. He plans one more month in Berlin to wrap things up and, as he put it, 'make a terrific end of it'. It was good to see him swinging about The Squire's as of old, joshing and teasing here, erupting with laughter there, wringing the hands of acquaintances like a man too long absent from home. I postponed my questions about his Berlin friends, Air Marshals or otherwise.

"So," I said, "we had an effect with our letters after all."

"What letters?"

"Come now, are Maddy and I to receive no credit whatsoever?"

"What the hell are you talking about?"

I asked him if his address was still the same hotel on the Unter den Linden. He nodded.

"Weeks ago Maddy and I wrote you, beseeching you to come home. We also prevailed on several of your collectors and even Maddox of the *Guardian* to send similar letters."

He was looking at me hard and not seeing me. His mind was churning. Then he snapped back to himself and gave a wave of his hand. "Watch, they will all be waiting for me in a heap. I've never had a bit of trouble with my mail."

We left it at that. In light of his decision to leave Germany for good, I spared him the Morris Gelfmann story. For his sake I assume he decided to come home because he has finally seen the Nazis for the sinister swine they are.

"What have you been up to in Berlin?"

"The usual. Portraits mainly."

"Who are the people coming to you?"

"People with *money*, Joff." He said a way has been found to repatriate his German earnings. He was seeing his solicitor the next day and would be off again for the continent. A British businessman helped him concoct a scheme whereby Damon is now a nominal employee of a British export firm and his paintings rate as commodities under the terms of an obscure Anglo-German trade accord, which in turn allow his earnings to … I stopped listening. I had a dim strange notion he was making the story up. Besides, there was something else on both our minds.

"We haven't seen each other," I said, "since Eaton Square. Five months, Dame. You've been missed."

"Have I, really?"

"Yes, really. You are the closest thing I have to a brother. Correction, you *are* my brother."

He reached across the table and gripped my wrist. "My dearest friend, I feel the same. I want to say something to you. What we shared at Christmas was … meaningful. I pray you haven't regretted it."

"I haven't."

"Good, *good*. It will always be a thing to cherish, but you should not wonder if – ."

"IS THAT THE ILLUSTRIOUS DAMON CHADWICK?"

The eager shout came from across the pub. We looked up as the shouter ambled over, a flush of excitement in his face, hand extended to the famous painter. An unkind thought occurred. Two unkind thoughts actually, one of them filthy. Damon's avid fan was that belly-dragging little alligator Billy Colman, scandal monger for the *Evening News*. As he pulled out a chair to join us I pushed mine back. "Gentlemen, I must take myself off."

Damon rose and embraced me. "My love to Vicky and Mary. See you in a month's time." He gripped my shoulders and we locked eyes. I felt everything was fine between us.

Colman's column next day mentioned our friend only briefly. "The celebrated artist Damon Chadwick has done his bit for Anglo-German friendship and after a long stay in Berlin will be taking up residence again in London." Luckily nothing about Nazi bigwigs at the studio or friendship with a certain Air Marshal. Of course Colman's discretion may have nothing to do with luck. Remember my theory about that obsequious little man?

A visit to the pater tomorrow. Tending him grows still more burdensome, requiring a fresh round of negotiations with Mrs. Stockton. Wish my stomach well. Missing you as ever,

Joff

Saturday
11th June 1938

Dear Heidi,
Normally I keep your letters for weeks, sometimes months. Yours of the twenty-seventh I tore into little bits the instant after reading it. Not for a moment do I accept what Catherine says. Either she has made a terrible mistake, or she has fabricated an ugly lie. As you know, I recently learned something about where that ancient hate can lead. Seamus would have no truck with it. He is no bigot. The man is utterly empty of malice. Of course you will do as you please, but I may never see or speak to Catherine again. Sorry for my tone but that's the way I feel.

    Joff

Saturday
18th June 1938

Heidi,

God almighty, what kind of world? I can still hardly grasp it. My colleague and friend Ken Retinger ... he died three days ago. There was no warning, no ... point.

I remember feeling shock and grief when my mother passed, but not this profound anger. My mother lived most of a life, saw her children grow into adults. But a man not yet thirty? A life still beginning? He was at his desk when he mentioned a mild pain. He thought it was indigestion and I made a limp joke about constipation. An hour later, less than an hour, he gasped and half-rose from his chair with something savage in his face. He clutched his abdomen, and howled.

I could only gape. He *howled*.

Tremayne reacted. I give Tremayne full credit. Never mind an ambulance, he shouted, we will get our man to hospital faster than the ambulance can get to us. He ran for the telephone and demanded an official car. Jenkins watched, ashen-faced, as Tremayne and I helped Ken hobble out, his arms slung over our shoulders. Tremayne kept up a stream of comforting chatter, told Ken not to worry, it was his appendix, the thing is bursting, they'll take it out, hold on, stay strong.

So horrid, so damn unreal, the rush to the emergency ward of Westminster Hospital, a writhing Ken put on a stretcher, Tremayne behaving nobly, the hard hour of waiting. We assumed it was his appendix, he was having an appendectomy, it was routine, he would be himself again in a few days, at most a week.

Then.

The depleted look of the physician, the light expelled from his eyes, his words coming with practiced sadness. He was sorry, but the patient arrived too late. It was a case of strangulated hernia. An intestinal blood vessel had been squeezed shut and blood flow thereby compromised. With the spread of septicemia, as in this case, death can be extremely rapid. The patient might have ignored early symptoms. By the time he reached the hospital he was beyond the help of surgery. Nothing could be done to save him.

I don't remember saying a word. I remember turning to Tremayne.

He was holding his face in his hands, weeping. Tremayne was weeping. It was strange and dreamlike. And something else was dreamlike, the hospital haste around us, the careless onrush of the world, the nurses and doctors going about their business.

How should one react to a pointless death? A stupid, useless, preventable, small, small death. Argue with God? Send a petition to the human condition? I confess to feeling more rage than grief, still, four days later. And I have not shed a single tear yet, to my shame. To my great shame.

Joff

Wednesday
22nd June 1938

Heidi,

Ken's funeral this morning. Better if I had stayed away. The service was empty, gloomy, pathetic. Creaky chairs in a Watford parlour, the coffin on a metal stand, a token crucifix overhead. Family mourners filled the front pews of the ersatz chapel, Ken's widow with a black veil, her arms sheltering the bewildered little ones. Ken's parents, not old, not nearly old, now broken before their time. Ken's brother, the older brother, the protector, sat dazed, inconsolable. Jesus fucking Christ ...

The eulogist, a hired reverend, intoned some drowsy homilies. The man's clerical collar went askew and his vacant words embarrassed everyone but himself. You know the type, stolid behind his faith, adamantly gazing into infinity. I wanted to leap to my feet and give Ken's people an earthbound memory, something genuine and personal, but the coward in me prevailed, I went on meekly listening, inert like the others. Over the condolence book I stood frozen, couldn't think of what to write, thought stupidly of accusing fate of obscenity. I finally scribbled *Ken was an idealist; he always dreamed of a better world; his goodwill and cheer brought that world nearer.*

We had spoken of getting together, introducing our wives, delegating his little ones to Vicky, opening a bottle of wine in a park, but we never made it happen. Now too many things will never happen. The enormity, the foul enormity of a life never to be lived. In front of me is his desk, his blank vacant chair. I will never again call this place what he dubbed it. The dismal little fleapit has become darker.

Joff

Tuesday
5th July 1938

Dear Heidi,

Duty trumps holiday. Mary was unable to change her holiday time and we had no other arrangements for Vicky. I insisted my ladies go as planned to the Cotswolds ... while I remain at work. The pressure on Translation, German Section has only increased, while Ken's chair remains empty. It will likely stay that way until the autumn when a hire might be made. *Might* be made. Budget restrictions at the F.O., you understand.

Gone is any chance of an early transfer to Sternthal's project. The file was already in limbo, what with Tremayne foursquare opposed and pulling on every available spool of red tape. The loss of Ken has made Tremayne's obstruction easier; he need only point at our diminished ranks. I'm trapped, Heidi. I am also tired and dispirited. Will write again once a better mood arrives.

Joff

P.S. Damon should be returning any day now. That at least will be a relief.

Saturday
9th July 1938

Dear Heidi,
Thank you for the break from the relentless gloom. Sincerest congratulations, great lady. A second son! All my love to Charles Andrew, offspring of Elizabeth Heidi, little brother to Maxwell Brian. You are ever more blessed, which is only your proper due. We shall wait until next time for Athena. Will there be a next time? Strike that question. Nothing matters except the here and now, good health and high hopes. Congratulations again, and lots of love,
    Joff

Saturday
16th July 1938

Dear Heidi,
We envy you in America. You live remote from the shooting if the shooting should start. Over here we live cheek by jowl to a powder keg. People sit by the wireless in the evenings waiting for the latest bulletin. War talk fills the air.

Ken saw Czechoslovakia as the next Austria and he has been proved right; the parallels have become ominous. From the daily drumbeat of grievance out of the Third Reich you would think the Germans of the Sudetenland are being crushed under Czech boots. Hitler's threats grow more menacing and so do his tanks, yet again massing along the Czech border.

The great unknown is France. Will the French fight if Germany invades? France has postured as a guarantor of Czechoslovakia's independence, and Britain is honour-bound by history, friendship and treaty to stand by France. You see the morass into which we may suddenly be pulled. Prime Minister Chamberlain came on the wireless last night and voiced what a great many people are thinking. "How horrible, fantastic, incredible it is," he said, "that we should be fearing imminent involvement in war because of a quarrel in a faraway country between people of whom we know nothing." Next week he flies with senior ministers to Paris for full-dress talks with the French. He says he is ready to fly to Berlin, fly to Prague. He aims to mediate the crisis, seek common ground, hammer out a solution. To keep the peace, he said, no effort, no exertion, no sacrifice will be too great.

My sacrifice of a holiday has taken a toll. Pub fare at The Squire's these two weeks of solitude have played havoc with … you do not wish to know. I leave now for the station to meet my ladies. How I've missed them.

No sign of Damon yet, blast his uncaring ways. He was supposed to be a full-time Londoner again by now. Maddy is particularly put out. Apparently he has missed several promised engagements with collectors.

Proper British hugs to your American sons.
Joff

338

Thursday
21st July 1938

What kind of world, dearest Heidi? Times like these we can only reach for Shakespeare. *When sorrows come, they come not single spies but in battalions.* How are the Americans reacting to our tragedy? You can imagine the shock here. Nobody is walking quite straight.

The first bulletin came before noon yesterday. It said only that the plane had disappeared. Work stopped. Everything stopped. Soon after came the next bulletin, confirming the worst. Within a few hours offices emptied and shops closed. The streets were nearly deserted. People wanted to be in their homes. Mary, Vicky and I stayed glued to the wireless all evening.

The wreckage is strewn over two acres of a barley field near Brighton. This morning's *Times* says body parts are scattered widely, many of them charred. The plane must have exploded on impact with the ground. The cause is not yet known, and may never be. The skies were clear over the Channel and the winds light. Why would a plane go down in perfect weather? Accusations are already circulating. Who was the genius who allowed the PM and his senior ministers to travel in a single aircraft? Rumours too have started. The aircraft was in mint condition, a Lockheed 14 Super Electra, four months in operation and prized as a marvellous machine by all who flew her. It could not have suddenly fallen out of the sky unless … sabotaged.

What bunk. Accidents happen. The high and mighty are not immune. Still, losing half the cabinet and every grandee in it … no wonder the country is in a daze. At times, contemplating the loss of the Prime Minister, Lord Halifax and the rest, I marvel that I am wide awake and not in a dream.

Tremayne has surprised me. Again. Since Ken's death he has been a different man. More prone to chivalry and his better angels. Since the air crash his attitude has been still more solemn, courteous, even solicitous. All of us are staggered and grieving here.

Be well,
Joff

Friday
22nd July 1938

Dear Heidi,
We spent another evening by the wireless. The Beeb assigned the special broadcast to our old friend Tommy Woodrooffe. He did a masterful job conveying the sadness of the nation and the historic scope of the moment. More credit to him, he did not shy away from depicting the horror of the accident. Vicky sat bolt upright and mostly silent the whole evening, staring fiercely into space and gripping Mary's hand. We barely moved from our places as the reports, commentaries, obituaries and tributes went on and on.

Eighteen people perished in the crash. The fourteen passengers were Mr. Chamberlain, Lord Halifax, five ranking cabinet ministers, and a group of top aides. Among the ministers lost were Home Secretary Sir Samuel Hoare; Duff Cooper, First Lord of the Admiralty; and Hore-Belisha, Secretary for War. The others on board were the captain, the first officer, an air hostess, and an RAF lieutenant in charge of the radio.

The enormity of it … the unreality of it.

Mary said, "The country will recover of course, but it will take time." This caused Vicky to pipe up, "Much quicker than you think, Mummy. The entire *world* waits on Britain." At that you may be sure we hugged our precious daughter.

Nothing of substance yet from the salvage team. The head of the Accidents Investigation Branch said it will be impossible in the short term to determine the cause of the crash. Reconstruction of the aircraft may take months. There was no hint of anything amiss before the accident. The plane's last radio communication from over the Channel was routine. No distress call was sent.

The Times today has a story about the American aviator Howard Hughes. He flew an identical Model 14 on an around-the-world flight just two weeks ago. He and a small crew left New York on 10th July, touched down in Paris, Moscow, airfields in Siberia and Alaska, and then Minneapolis before returning to New York. The trip of nearly fifteen thousand miles took only four days and proved the Model 14 one of the most robust and reliable aircraft ever built. Maybe that is why some are blaming the tragedy on human error or foul play. I find those theories equally repulsive, given we have no facts whatever as yet. Meanwhile the grim work of collecting body parts continues. One can only imagine what the men assigned to the task are experiencing.

This comes to you from our bleak little room in the F.O. The whole building feels dark and depressed. Work seems a pathetic thing. Jenkins is burrowing through a stack of newspapers. He has been perversely energised by the tragedy, easily persuaded by the rumours of sabotage. He will soon be breathlessly telling me that a sinister cabal of anarchists placed a bomb in the luggage.

Tremayne has been coming and going importantly, wearing a look of duty. I am not faulting him! He has kept his opinions to himself and hasn't said a nasty word in days.

The King appears in no rush to choose our next Prime Minister. Good for him. Emotions are at fever pitch. Let them cool. We are living through a long solemn hour, Heidi. People feel damaged and oddly threatened.

Still no sign of Damon, not even a postcard. Maddy telephones weekly to ask if I have any news. I suspect our friend is enjoying an extended bacchanal in Paris, but why must he cause us anxiety? Hoping you and yours are well.

Joff

Saturday
23rd July 1938

Dear Heidi,
Third day of what feels like a new era. Yet nothing new has begun.
Funeral preparations overshadow everything. There will be no public
agenda until full homage has been paid to the fallen. We can only
guess whom the King will call to the palace. Meanwhile the chatter
intensifies about what happened in the cockpit during the last minutes
of the doomed flight. The theories are in smallest part informed, and
in largest part ignorant (if not pure poppycock). One substantive thing
we've learned is that initial reports of clear skies over the Channel
were wrong. As the aircraft approached British shores it encountered
a heavy cloud layer, making landmark navigation tricky. Which tells us
precisely nothing about the cause of the crash.

Tremayne said authoritatively this morning that the plane experienced
a complete electrical failure. On what basis Aeronautical Engineer
Tremayne makes such a statement I haven't a clue, but it gives you a
fair idea of the pronouncements being made by completely unqualified
people. As for the latest from my ever more batty colleague Jenkins,
he told me this morning in a low voice that a secret investigation has
started into the pilot's mental health. The implication is the pilot
may have deliberately brought the plane down in a spectacular act of
suicide and mass assassination. Bunk and more bunk. What's the use
of speculation? No matter what we find, it will not turn the clock back.

Reaction in the German press has been surprisingly polite, even
gracious. Messages of condolence have been plentiful, tinted with
something else I can only call ... disappointment. Evidently the
Reichspressekammer has decreed Chamberlain's loss unfortunate.
Dozens of newspapers have run stories identifying him as a champion
of conciliation, and thus a light for peace now cruelly extinguished.

We are gratified to hear how seriously – how massively – the tragedy
is being dealt with on your side. The Americans so often ignore us, but
they properly see this as an earthquake. Still, I do wish your journalists
would learn restraint. We are told that a tabloid in New York finds it
acceptable to report that Prime Minister Chamberlain was decapitated
and his head found thirty yards from his body. What a foul thing to

make public.

Word has come that the King will summon Chamberlain's successor on Monday morning. Good. The guessing game will finally stop. We all trust in the King to name the right man. He must be a leader who can rally the nation at this dark hour, form a government of national unity, and face the tensions that are boiling in Europe.

Mary has booked off Monday to stand vigil with Vicky at the gates of Buckingham Palace. "I think it will be inspiring," she said, "to see the new man go in as the guest of the King and come out as Prime Minister. No matter what storms and trials come, this is the way we do things. Darling, we are going to see history made." "No, Mummy," Vicky corrected, "we will be *part* of history."

After hugging my precious peach I stupidly opened my mouth and acted the wet blanket. "Good luck getting anywhere near the gates. A swarm of newsmen, and thousands of gawkers like yourselves will be there."

"Oh, Daddy, you must stop being such a *pessimist*." At which I grabbed her in another bearhug and apologised.

While we have confidence in the King to choose the right man for Downing Street, the field is wide open and downright mysterious. No obvious candidate has emerged, since all the heavyweights in the cabinet are gone and Sir John Simon, Chancellor of the Exchequer, has ruled himself out. The other surviving ministers resemble a gallery of anonymous hacks. None of them have shown any mettle or earned a name. No less than four newspapers, including the *Telegraph*, have suggested the best pick is not in the cabinet at all. How does Prime Minister Eden sound to you? The more I ponder it, the more I agree, Eden would be a brilliant choice. Yes, I do believe the King will concur. Our next PM will be Anthony Eden.

Ken would be elated. He would hail Eden's appointment as a sign of redemption and buy drinks all round. I miss Ken. His wit and intensity, his youth, even his dogmas! His empty chair strikes me as an obscenity – as unspeakable as the tragedy that has rocked the nation.

My love to you, Heidi.

Joff

Saturday
30th July 1938

Dear Heidi,

My failure as a prognosticator is a good place to start. By the time this letter reaches you, you will have received mine of a week ago and enjoyed a good laugh. I do remember writing with unshakable confidence, 'Yes, it will be Eden'. I offer as my only defence the astonishment of just about everybody at the King's choice. Churchill? Winston S. Churchill?

Prime Minister Churchill?

Tremayne was spitting mad. "The arms merchants have had their way. The bloodsuckers and their bankers reached into the ear of the King. We can be certain of some Hebrew influence behind this too. They have always had a soft spot for the old drum beater, singing his praises in the *News Herald*."

I think Tremayne came within an inch of mimicking Mosley and calling it the *Jews Herald*. The idea rates as vile, that Churchill is anyone but his own man. I have never been a Churchillian, lord knows, but he is now our PM, like it or not. Unless he falls flat on his cherubic growl he deserves our support. As for Jewish money and its power, I wish I could force-feed Tremayne everything I learned from Morris Gelfmann. You may forthwith trash whatever charitable things I have said lately about my Section Head. Refrain from smoothing out any lines on that bust of his. You may keep him looking like the rutted, bigoted snob and failure he has always been.

I assume George is concerned about events in Europe and sees Churchill as the man to stiffen the nation's spine. One thing is true. Churchill may have been a gadfly for years, inflexible in his positions and rambunctious in his pronouncements, but it turns out he has shown greater foresight and more consistency in regard to Hitler's designs than anyone else in British politics. Maybe he does deserve this chance. One more thing: George hasn't forgotten Churchill's support of the wobbly royals during the months before the abdication. The monarchy has had no better friend than Churchill during the last forty years.

Parliament sits again next week and Churchill will rise in the

Commons for the first time as Prime Minister. He has a hard nut to crack. The support of the palace is one thing, but the support of Westminster another, and the support of the country yet another. Many of us are surely recalling his actions during the General Strike of 1926. He took a strong anti-unionist stand. The workers of Britain have not forgotten. They see him as an implacable enemy of their class.

Potential risk for all of us lurks in the simple fact that Churchill has never been one for compromise. He wears a long record of stubborn belligerence towards Nazi Germany. Given the international situation, many people, including me, frankly fear where he might lead us.

We must credit Churchill with at least one rapid miracle. He brought about the Second Coming of my father. "God has saved us! Do you hear me, boy? God has *saved* us!"

"Dad, you sound like your old self."

Alas, the old self promptly faded. His screech of atavistic joy knocked him out, and he soon banged down the telephone after questioning my identity. "My son lives in Canada!"

I was sure my spouse would be equally thrilled by Churchill's appointment, but her attitude has turned cautious. "Winston is a great man, but he may not be the right man."

"Darling, he has been your hero forever!"

"Yes, but he has never been Prime Minister."

"I don't understand."

"Winston's an adventurer. He is prone to being a gambler. Do we want that in a PM?"

There you have it, the mood of the country in a nutshell. If my Mary is suddenly unsure about Churchill after decades of near worship, you have a pretty good idea of the general doubt and unease.

What are your American friends saying? They may be paying extra attention because Churchill is half-Yank. Did you know his mother was born in Brooklyn? Jennie Jerome was her name, a famous beauty in her day. She went through three husbands and had a reputation that was, um, colourful. Interesting times, Heidi.

Trusting all is well with you and yours,

Joff

P.S. Must tell you, when Vicky and Mary left for the palace last week to greet the new Prime Minister, word had already leaked that it would be Mr. Churchill. By the time my ladies arrived at the palace an angry mob had formed, brandishing signs reading NO WINNIE NO WAR! People are convinced Mr. Churchill will trigger a disastrous confrontation with Germany. The catcalls, Mary said, were appalling, and Vicky said, "It was mean, Daddy. They should give Mr. Churchill a *chance*." Despite the jeering crowd, the new Prime Minister insisted his car leave through the palace's front gates. While the car edged its way through the clamour, he waved from his open window with cheerful aplomb. Tremayne made a hideous remark the next day, thinking himself witty. He said the Prime Minister was lucky not to have been dragged from his Bentley and lynched on the Mall.

Sunday
31st July 1938

Dear Heidi,
I plead guilty. Events may have distracted and blinded me, but no excuse will suffice. *I forgot your birthday!* To think I wrote to you about other matters on the very day, the sainted day, and failed to remember. You would be right to disown me. Abject apologies, great lady. I trust the day was bright, long and gratifying. May you celebrate it countless more times.

Anxious to hear how That American topped his gift of last year. You have since presented him with a second heir, after all. But how do you beat a deluxe automobile? Should we await news of the famous sculptress captaining a yacht on Massachusetts Bay?

Hugs to Max and his new mate, Charlie. Awaiting your forgiveness,
As ever,
Joff

Friday
5th Aug. 1938

Dear Heidi,
Rushing this at lunch, excuse the scrawl. Bit of a shock this morning when Maddy Kloff appeared unannounced at the door of Translation, German Section and insisted we take a walk. There was no denying the urgency in her eyes. She has been in touch with art dealer acquaintances in Berlin. No one has seen hide nor hair of Damon in quite some time. She telephoned his hotel on the Unter den Linden and was told he has been absent from his suite for over a month. "I'm dreadfully worried, Joff."

"Our boy is probably in Paris … immersed in one of his escapes."

Maddy dismissed this with a frown. "You must ask the embassy to make inquiries. They should consult the Berlin police."

"Maddy, it's not the business of – "

"Are you not his best friend?"

That shamed me. What with the press of events and my recent workload, I confess to having relegated Damon to the back of my mind. So I have sent off notes to Reg Huntington and Samuel Sternthal, requesting advice and slipping in a suggestion. In light of my close friend Damon Chadwick's public profile and a growing concern about his whereabouts, would it not be appropriate for our people in Berlin to make inquiries?

Will write again tomorrow,
Joff

Saturday
6th Aug. 1938

Dear Heidi,
The world is full of wonders and they crop up at odd moments. Pay heed great lady, I promise you amazement at my dizzying prospects. My note yesterday to Mr. Sternthal went unanswered, I suppose he is away on holiday, but the note to Reg Huntington brought an immediate summons.

"I had no idea you were a friend of Damon Chadwick."

"We go back to childhood. We were seven when we met."

"One hears rumours about Chadwick, mainly that he is ... offside."

I heard no question, so I volunteered no answer.

Huntington squinted at me, then nodded knowingly. "The embassy keeps a file on your friend. He *has* been a concern to us, because he could so easily become an embarrassment."

"Do our people know he's missing?"

"Not to my knowledge. I can find out if you wish, but Chadwick is not the reason I sent for you. Your note arrived just as I was looking at a requisition from Downing Street. The Prime Minister wants a full-time German speaker at Number 10."

There are moments when information enters the brain too fast for it to be processed and one is left a bit confounded. The meaning of what I had just heard seemed plain, but something about it was too remote to grasp.

"Would you be interested in having your name put forward?"

I think I stared at Huntington for a few seconds before replying. "Good lord, yes."

He picked up a telephone and rang Downing Street and booked me to meet an aide of the PM next Thursday afternoon. "Best of luck," he said, "you are now one of three candidates."

"What about my Section Head?"

"What about him?"

"He has been resisting my transfer to Samuel Sternthal's refugee project."

"Forget all that. This is the PM's office. If they offer you the post, there will be no bureaucratic nonsense."

I thanked him for the opportunity, and he shot me a hard look. "I trust, Pearson, that if things work out I can rely upon you in days to come."

My response was a confused and mumbling, "Of course … naturally … you may be sure." At the moment of the mumble I was not at all sure what he meant. I *am* naïve, aren't I?

Can you imagine me at Number 10, which is more than ever the mecca of attention? Barely two weeks in and Churchill has driven a fierce broom through Whitehall. Sackings and demotions wherever his authority can reach. Not a single Chamberlain advisor or assistant has been kept on. Deputy ministers who guided the old cabinet have been shunted into minor roles. Some avenging appointments too: Anthony Eden back as Foreign Secretary, Leo Amery named First Lord of the Admiralty, Harold Nicolson given the Home Office. A cabinet stocked with all the principal foes of appeasement. And then Sir Robert Vansittart named Ambassador to Germany. Vansittart! His anti-Nazi repute is probably second only to Churchill's. Who in Berlin will receive him? Who will even accept his credentials? *The Times* yesterday accused the PM of waving a red flag at the German bull.

Mr. Churchill's speech to the Commons last week came packed with thinly veiled warnings to Hitler. Employing his usual high-flown rhetoric the PM said no one, *no one* should think freedom's torch has ceased burning or that civilised men will fail to preserve its vital glow. Britain, he pledged, will expose and defy the odious racism and dangerous expansionism which are blighting the European horizon. The PM never mentioned Hitler by name but referred scathingly to 'dictators drenched in deceit' and 'strutting corporals in mighty offices'. He said a supine world may have drowsed while the Treaty of Versailles was trampled and gutted, but people should not for a moment think a similar vacancy of vigilance, decay of purpose, or frailty of resolve characterise His Majesty's new government. Nor should anyone underestimate Britain's historic duty and unwavering determination to defend the sovereignty of small democratic states … Does the flag get any redder than that?

It might, it well might. Churchill ended his speech with a promise of emergency measures to ensure the security of the British Isles. An announcement is expected at the start of next week about new and massive programs in military procurement.

The German bull is snorting and pawing, I can tell you. If you read the German press you might be persuaded that an alcoholic madman leads the British people. The honeyed condolences we heard from Berlin on the death of Chamberlain (now seen as a tribune of peace), have turned into rasping complaints about Churchill the wild man, Churchill the intoxicated warmonger, Churchill the Hebrew glove-puppet. Only to be expected, I suppose, given the PM's long record of Nazi-baiting. His enemies at home are hardly less nasty. After the Commons speech the *Daily Mail* published a headline taunting WINSTON WAGES WAR. Following Vansittart's appointment the paper splashed AUF WIEDERSEHEN PEACE above a photo of Sir Neville Henderson, our former ambassador to Berlin, who by all accounts won favour with Hitler. On his second day in office Mr. Churchill re-assigned Henderson to our embassy in Bolivia.

I have not breathed a word to Mary about my new opportunity. The meeting on Downing Street may only end in another letdown. Still, you can imagine my excitement. Please think lucky thoughts for me.

As ever,

Joff

Wednesday
10th Aug. 1938

Heidi,
As I await tomorrow's meeting I find myself on pins and needles,
unable to concentrate on work. My nerves must be showing because
Tremayne has been eyeing me with suspicion and Jenkins asked if I've
developed a rash.

The whole country has gone nervy. The emergency measures
introduced on Monday landed like a giant bomb. Cups and saucers
rattled throughout Britain and clear across Europe. Churchill went
ahead and did exactly what he has always said the government ought
to do. He ordered a quadrupling of the RAF's front line fighters.
Which would be stunning enough, save that he mandated delivery for
the autumn of 1939. People say it simply cannot be done. To which
Mr. Churchill replied it must be done and certainly will be done. He
also revived plans for development of a next generation battle tank
and gave the go-ahead to build eighteen modern destroyers. There is
even talk of blueprints being drawn up for new capital ships. Evidently
the PM aims to launch a military-industrial mobilisation on a scale
never seen before, with a massive dip into the public purse, and on a
schedule tantamount to miraculous.

At the same time, separate ministries have been created for the
army, navy and air force, as well as a new portfolio of national supply
to coordinate what Mr. Churchill calls the 'renovation' of the three
services. For each service a senior acting officer has been named
minister and given a place in cabinet.

If talk in the F.O. lunchroom is any indication, most people regard
Mr. Churchill's proposed spending on armaments as alarmist and
excessive, while parachuting colonels and admirals into the cabinet
strikes them as … deeply troubling. This is not our way, they say,
it's un-British. This is not America where the president can appoint
whom he pleases. Ministers should first be elected as M.P.s, so they
can answer to the Commons. The Daily Mail made its contempt clear
with DOOM MERCHANT PACKS CABINET WITH BRASS
HATS, while the normally sober *Times* decried what it sees as 'a
martial culture seeping into the nation's governance'. Even members

of Churchill's own party have grown alarmed.

"I'm beginning to think the King made a grievous mistake."

Can you guess who said that to me?

My spouse. My very own Mary who has revered Mr. Churchill for twenty years. Gives you an idea of the widespread dismay in the land.

"Darling," I said, amused to find myself defending Mary's hero to her, "the best way to preserve the peace is to prepare for war." As those words marched from my mouth, I realised they were taken straight from the counsel of Ken Retinger.

"When did you – ?"

"Darling, I have no doubt Mr. Churchill abhors the thought of war as much as you or me or the milkman. The point is, he sees a storm gathering and insists on battening down the hatches." Those words were at least partially my own and not because I have an appointment for a job at Number 10. Maybe I have joined the black sheep, Heidi, but I have a hunch the PM is doing the right thing.

Tomorrow's the day. Have you been wishing me luck?

All my best,

Joff

Saturday
13th Aug. 1938

Dear Heidi,
There … a forced landing. My pen was hovering, waiting for a witty thought, but my brain is having none of it. You find me a bit numb actually, knocked about by events, the sudden speed of them. This morning I cleaned out my desk at the F.O. Had something of an emotional moment with Jenkins … but I must tell you what happened on Thursday.

The big day finally came. The morning seemed an eternity. Shortly before two I walked round to Downing Street and gave my name to the policeman at the door. I was fetched by Duncan Bocking-Kerr, a serious young fellow with traces of a Yorkshire accent. He wasn't wearing a uniform but might as well have been. The set of his shoulders and march in his step betrayed drill and discipline. He said he was a special assistant to the Prime Minister and led me to a cubbyhole down the aisle from the PM's room. I would have ventured a peek in, but the green baize door was shut. Instead I winked at Mr. Disraeli whose portrait has survived a thorough house-cleaning.

Number 10 has changed. Many of the antique chairs and needless side tables I remember from my last visit have disappeared. The museum-like pedestals that riddled the corridors are also gone, and the walls are no longer encrusted with heavily framed paintings. Something else too. The solemn muted air is no more. Young secretaries were rushing about with files under their arms. Phones were ringing. I had the impression of spirited *intention.*

Bocking-Kerr's frugal little nook had no proper seat for visitors and my humourless host offered no word of consolation. I perched on a narrow stool and felt like a bird on a wire. The interview was not what I expected. Bocking-Kerr said my qualifications were not in question, there would be no need to probe my language skills. Apart from my presumed talents, Mr. Churchill was principally interested in my discretion. Bocking-Kerr emphasised this with particular force. "The PM will want to know you can be trusted. Absolutely trusted, and then some."

"I understand."

"Do you indeed?"

Just answer his questions, Joffrey. Otherwise keep your mouth shut!

"What I mean is," I said, "my work at Translation, and more recently as an interpreter, has often called for strict confidentiality."

"You will be translating documents and sitting by Mr. Churchill's side when he meets visiting Germans, but that is by the by," said Bocking-Kerr. "This position will involve sensitive matters beyond those activities." Then he came at me like a machine-gun.

"Have you ever written articles for the press?"

"No."

"Letters to the editor?"

"No."

"Do you have journalists among your friends?"

"No."

"Have you provided, at any time, information of any sort to a member of the press?"

"No."

"Do you enjoy lifting a glass, Mr. Pearson?"

"I beg your pardon?"

"Do you *drink*, Mr. Pearson?"

"I have a pint or two on occasion."

"Do you frequent a pub?"

"I have a favourite, but can't say I 'frequent' it."

"You see my point?"

"I do."

"What is my point?"

A crafty lad, this Yorkshireman. He probably strangled his accent at Sandhurst, then polished it at Oxford. "Your point," I replied, straining to keep annoyance out of my voice, "involves the effect of alcohol, specifically as it impacts judgment. I understand you perfectly."

"You did say you lift a pint or *two* on occasion? Could it be three or four?"

"The last time I was intoxicated, Mr. Bocking-Kerr, was while I was a university student, in 1919, in the early morning hours of the first day of that year."

The pokerface gave no indication of being impressed by either my long memory or the embroidered substance of it. He may have inwardly hooted at my barefaced lie.

"How would you rate your ability to guard a confidence?"

"Better than the next man's."

"On what basis?"

"I consider it a matter of integrity on which I could never yield."

This stubborn response seemed to have reached behind Bocking-Kerr's defences. A hint of indulgence sneaked into his eyes.

"Are you familiar with the Official Secrets Act?"

"I attended the standard seminar on the Act when I joined the F.O. Since then I have kept abreast of all memorandums which update the regulations."

"Are you aware that the penalties for breaching the Act include dismissal, fines and imprisonment?"

"I am."

"How often in the last two years have you dealt with classified material?"

"Probably several times a month."

"What was the general nature of the material?"

I raised my eyebrows to show I understood he was testing to see if I was stupid.

"Good, good," he said, with hardly a quiver in his monotone. "What do you consider the principal challenge facing our country?"

I blinked at the abrupt change of tack, but was instantly alert to an opportunity. After all, the new resident of Number 10 has been ringing a loud, persistent, distinct alarm for years.

"The same challenge confronts every country in Europe," I said. "It dwarfs all our domestic issues. We must find a way to deal with the Nazi menace."

Bocking-Kerr stared at me and likely right through me. He asked, "What does the word 'Nazi' mean to you?"

I blinked again, but the question proved my lucky ticket. Maybe the luckiest ticket of my life. "Barbaric hate," I said. "A rejoicing in revenge and murder. The Nazi is a swaggering gangster, really, risen from the gutter and lusting for prestige and plunder."

There was a shuffle of feet behind me. Bocking-Kerr's eyes leaped. "Sir!"

"Duncan, pray introduce me to our guest," said a gruff familiar voice.

I swivelled on my stool. I could not make out if our interloper was wearing a grin or a glare. Maybe it was a blend of both. Countless newspaper photos have acquainted the world with the flamboyant twinkle in those eyes and the stern admonition of those lips.

"I take it," said the Prime Minister, "we have here the number three candidate for the German job."

"I don't know what number I am, Mr. Churchill, but my name is Joffrey Pearson. An honour, sir." I was on my feet and extending my hand. He shook it for only as long as it takes to turn the knob on a door. His expression switched to business and hurry.

"You held up my charge to the lavatory, Mr. Pearson. A formidable accomplishment. Kindly take our guest to my room, Duncan. I shall join you in a little minute."

A short time later I was answering questions from the Prime Minister of England as he paced up and down his study with thumbs lodged in the armholes of his waistcoat and an unlighted cigar in his mouth. I was in the same chair the lawyer Bieler from Vienna had occupied when he met the more sedentary Mr. Chamberlain. During our time together Mr. Churchill never ceased punishing the stretch of carpet between his desk and window with a slow, clumping, back-and-forth prowl.

"I glanced at your file, Mr. Pearson. I understand you interpreted once for my predecessor."

"I did, sir."

"What was your impression of him?"

"I thought he would be well suited as a clergyman."

This won a low chuckle from the Prime Minister. "He did believe all men are brothers, didn't he? In fact, Chamberlain should have remained in commerce. He was perfectly suited as an accountant. He saw his work in government through the lens of a balance sheet and believed rearmament would bankrupt Britain. Still, he did his best by his own lights. We must let the man rest in peace."

"Amen," I said, and realised I was sweating. My armpits were flooding.

"Curious that you met the American ambassador. What did you think of *him*?"

"A man out of his depth, sir. He struck me as unschooled."

"Pray tell, unschooled in what?"

"Diplomacy, sir. The ways of Britain and Europe."

"Your politeness commends you, Mr. Pearson. The man has been trotting about London saying some stupid things."

"He did appear blind, sir, to the nature of the Nazi."

"Ah, the 'swaggering gangster' of overheard character. Do you equate the German with the Nazi, Mr. Pearson?"

"I do not, but the German at this moment is in thrall to the Nazi."

"Why do you think that is?"

"It would probably take a book to provide the full answer, sir."

"Give me your synopsis."

My reply was instinctive. It seemed to emerge from a long tunnel into a moment richly furnished with unrealities, starting with the chair I was implausibly a guest in, and extending to the Prime Minister who was wearing a blue polka-dot bow tie and pacing, pacing, from desk to window and back again while conducting an improbable audition.

"People have a weakness for messiahs, sir. In the case of Germany, the weakness has become a contagion. A whole nation has found what it thinks is a deliverer."

"And what do you make of their messiah with the Charlie Chaplin moustache?"

"There may be no such thing as agents sent to earth by the devil," I said, remembering the wife and sons of Morris Gelfmann, "but if there were, Hitler would be one of them. He has led a great country into monstrous, monstrous shame."

Mr. Churchill scowled impatiently, clearly unimpressed by my trite analogy. "Hitler the man, the individual, what do you think powers him, lifts him?"

Heidi, a well-timed fortunate thing, a truly serendipitous thing … your bust of the German leader came into my mind's eye. "Arrogance, sir," I said. "An immense, enabling, potent arrogance. That is the feature most primal in him. That is his capital. Take away his arrogance and he would be nothing."

Mr. Churchill halted his pacing and fixed me with a look of appraisal. Had I redeemed myself? He took the cigar from his mouth and said, "Thank you, Mr. Pearson. Can you let me have a little minute with Duncan? I will ask Miss Pearman to take you in hand."

Violet Pearman, the Prime Minister's secretary, installed me in a waiting area off the lobby. She sensed my tension and left me with the latest *Punch*. I was unable to look at the thing. I sat bolt upright with an agreeable tremble in my head, imagining my lucky ticket may have been validated.

Soon Bocking-Kerr came out and said in his clipped military fashion, "The German job is yours. I shall let Huntington know. Report here on Monday at seven hundred hours" – and he honoured me with a smile almost civilian.

In a bit of a daze I ambled back round to King Charles Street. Restraining all sense of triumph, I told Tremayne and Jenkins what had just happened. Jenkins, the old dear, at first recoiled, thinking of the implications for the Section and himself. He recovered quickly however, and congratulated me with all his heart. I felt no satisfaction seeing Tremayne's face fall. I understood the blow to him ... a subordinate leaving for a post on Downing Street while his own career remains stuck, likely permanently, in a dismal hole. He said nothing, only flicked his wrist as if to say, "*Go*, if that's what you want," and retreated to his broom closet. I have to say I felt some contrition, however ridiculous that might sound. I went to him and promised to stay late that evening and Friday to finish up my current workload. On Saturday morning I would empty my desk. He nodded without looking up.

I told Mary the news that night. We were alone. Vicky has been away, visiting with a school chum's family in Wiltshire. As you might imagine, my spouse was elated but initially cautious. "Is there any risk of that little man Tremayne – ?"

"Not this time, my darling, none."

She rewarded me with a rare giggle, the gulp of delight which forms one of my favourite sounds in the universe. "Vicky will be over the moon. Her father working with the Prime Minister!"

"Only one pity, darling. With this job there will be no book in my future."

"Who can say?" she replied giddily. Then, "Why do you think the Bocking-Kerr chap put so much stress on secrecy?"

"I have no idea," I said, "but I suspect you have now ditched your doubts about the King's choice for PM."

"Hmmm … I will still worry about where Winnie is taking us, but that is the citizen in me. Right now, the wife in me says a drink is in order."

She rummaged in a cupboard for a neglected bottle of cognac, a gift from her brothers dating back to our fifth anniversary. It needed dusting.

"To Winston S. Churchill," said Mary, raising her glass.

"Let's not forget the King."

"Nor," Mary added with a glint in her eye, "my husband Joffrey Pearson, translator and interpreter for the Prime Minister of England."

"To all of us," I said.

We sipped, and sipped, and savoured the irony of Bocking-Kerr's interrogation about my alcohol intake. Everyone knows of Mr. Churchill's fondness for strong spirits. Mary refilled our glasses. We sipped some more. The evening grew memorable …

This morning at the F.O. was bittersweet. I arrived with a suitcase to clean eight years of detritus from my desk. The only items of value unearthed were some faded photos of Vicky as an infant, and postcards from Spain sent by Damon in 1931 when he revisited his 'true birthplace', the Prado. There was also a letter from Boston, dated early February 1936, asking if I still loved my wife! Mea culpa, the forgotten letter was tucked away carelessly in a yellowed copy of *The Listener*. The envelope fell out as the magazine fluttered toward the dustbin. I dared not bring the letter home, so I reduced it to confetti.

My last task in Translation, German Section was a note to Samuel Sternthal. I thanked him for his efforts on my behalf and informed him of my appointment to Downing Street. *I am obliged to tell you sir,* I concluded, feeling some genuine regret, *that my new position will make it impossible for me to pursue the project we discussed.*

When it came time to say goodbye, Jenkins strove gallantly not to show he was distraught. In the end he surrendered to sentiment, and embraced me. "Do us proud," he said with a leaky eye. "You will be missed."

"My dear friend, I'm not shipping off to Australia. My new salt mine is literally around the corner."

"Might as well be Australia," he grumped.

Tremayne shook my hand with decent grace, but could not help himself. "We will be struggling here, Jenkins and I," he said.

May the lord have mercy on your tiny wretched soul, I thought, but with more pity than rancour. Then I looked sadly at the empty chair of Ken Retinger and thought how his generous heart would celebrate the turn in my fortunes. Which reminds me, I must telephone the pater …

The fog in my father's head has only thickened. "What's that you say?" he shouted. "Churchill at Number 10? Who are YOU?" I must not let the pater's condition dampen my spirits. In a few hours Vicky will be home and we shall be celebrating at Vicky's beloved Jasmine's. Modest fare in the wake of such triumph, wouldn't you say? We Pearsons are humble folk.

Look at these six pages of humility. I have earned my afternoon kip.

Thank you again great lady for the timely help with Herr Hitler. You gave me a moment of conquering clarity. Keep wishing me luck and, please, write soon. All my best,

Joff

Sunday
21st Aug. 1938

Heidi,
I hope this finds you well. Still awaiting your news. This from Huntington: *The embassy knows nothing of Chadwick, save that he's been absent from his hotel.* Which only agitated Maddy the more. Now that I am close and cosy with the high and mighty, she said, I should take the matter to Mr. Eden, or even to Mr. Churchill. She said it so seriously I did not dare laugh. "Maddy, you should take the story to the newspapers. Something will turn up if they report the famous painter missing."

"I can't do that," she said.

"Why not?"

"Once journalists start following Damon's trail, it might lead them to his despicable friend."

"I assume you mean the Air Marshal?"

"Of course. I won't have Damon's name blackened in such a way."

"If Dame is in trouble, Maddy, his reputation should not be the first thing on your mind."

"Hell and damnation," she said, and we ended where we started, without a plan.

A confession: I have spent very little time worrying about Damon, because I haven't had a moment to spare. My first week at Number 10 has left me bleary-eyed. My days end at seven or eight, I stagger into bed around ten, and hoist myself from bed at five. No one told me that twelve and thirteen hour days are routine for Mr. Churchill's staff, I just fell in with it. They say he himself puts in fifteen or sixteen hours, needs only three or four of sleep. My previous view of the man is shamed. If he is indeed a brandy addict, then brandy merits respect as petrol for the human engine. Mr. Churchill engages in unrelenting toil. His midnights are spent with briefing books. Mornings he lies abed dictating memos to a stenographer, then takes his bath with a plank across the tub so he can write notes, an endless stream of which flows to assistants and cabinet members, demanding data, dispensing advice, devising strategy … The staffers who tell me these things regard the PM with affectionate humour and outright awe, but above all loyalty.

They are devoted to him, and not just his person. You would think a colossal mission has been launched with earth-transforming goals to reach, all of which make it easier to accept the gruelling hours. Wives? Children? Other aspects of life come second to the great cause.

I confess to being a little rattled by my new situation. These scribblings will have to be done Sunday mornings while Mary sleeps, though there will be weekends when the Prime Minister decamps to Chartwell or Chequers. Yesterday proved that if a Saturday finds him at Number 10 it may as well be a Monday for his crew.

I lied. I am more than a little rattled. My prized job so far feels like a demotion. Maddy would think a lot less of my influence with the high and mighty if she saw my underground crypt – my room is in the sub-basement. Bocking-Kerr demurred when I asked if this was the bomb shelter. I have no window and the air arrives through a ventilator. My desk is a rickety table with a shuddering lamp, the chair an instrument of torture, and the sole decoration on the walls a mounted brace of medals from the Great War. What at first appears to be a single-drawer filing cabinet squats in a corner. Close inspection reveals it to be an iron safe, much too heavy to budge, and locked two ways: with a dial combination and a bolt secured by a padlock. The thing seems to leer at me.

Five minutes, maybe ten. That is how long I spent with the Prime Minister. He called me in during the lunch hour on Monday while I was enjoying the window in Number 10's canteen. Did you know a quite marvellous garden exists in back of the house?

"Welcome aboard, Joffrey," said Mr. Churchill without looking up.

He was sorting through a heap of scattered documents. On the floor by his desk lay several battered and rusting boxes, the ministerial Boxes. Mr. Churchill was wearing half-moon reading glasses so far down his nose they were almost falling off. I heard no invitation to take a chair so I took notes standing up.

"I shall be very glad to have a daily summary of the German press. Kindly do not belabour what they say but tell me what they are *thinking*. I will need that by eight every morning, on one sheet of paper. Evidently Herr Goebbels sends reams of material to our embassy, yet only a fraction gets forwarded to the F.O., and none to Number 10. I have ordered the lot sent to us. Comb through, would you? Provide me concise summaries. Clues to the beast's Achilles heel can appear in unlikely places. Perhaps too in the books the beasts are publishing. A batch of them have arrived, Miss Pearman has them for you, revisionist works on European history, essays on the new German culture and so forth. Texts for the Reich's cowed and whipped academy. Let me know if they are just bilge … Here! This is a letter sent me by someone in Cloppenburg, a godforsaken little town in Lower Saxony. My primitive German cannot begin to decipher it. Looks real enough, but why would they think I would take such a letter for anything but a silly goad? Give me the gist," he said as he held it out to me, still without looking up, "in two sentences if you please. Ah, before I forget, my note to Ribbentrop, where did it go? You must translate it in the next hour. The buffoon handles English quite well, but I want him assaulted in his own language before the day is out. We shall cable the text to our embassy with instructions for hand delivery. Where is the blasted thing? I just saw it …"

He picked through the papers on his desk while hoarsely humming a vaguely familiar tune. Must tell you, I was startled by Mr. Churchill's lisp. The letter 's' can come out of his mouth terribly exaggerated, like a jeering hiss. When he speaks publicly I suppose he takes extraordinary care to disguise the condition. My dear Heidi, I am doubly shamed. Hearing him on the wireless over the years I thought the slurring in his speech was due to drink!

"Here t'is," he said, finding a scrawled note and holding it out for me, still without an upward glance. "Preserve all the force of it, Joffrey. They already know this chair hosts a different breed, but it will do them good to unwrap a healthy snarl."

"Please call me Joff, sir."

Mr. Churchill looked up. "Good heavens, man, standing? Sit down, Joff, sit, sit." The awkwardness of the moment evaporated instantly. While I pulled up a chair a red file materialised in his hand. "Here is something I would like back first thing next week. I shall be interested in the conclusions you reach."

"What is it, sir?"

"The Blomberg file. Digest it and tell me what it says about the German officer corps."

"Yes, sir," I said, with no idea what he was talking about. Blomberg?

The German officer corps?

As he handed me the file I could sense his mind switching tracks. He asked, "Have you read *Mein Kampf*?"

"Only excerpts, sir."

"When the dictator came to power no book in the world deserved more scrutiny. Did you read it in German?"

"No, sir."

"Translation cannot reveal an author's core. Miss Pearman will give you a copy of the original. We are all acquainted with the dictator's primitive impulses and savage sociology. What I want from you are thoughts on his use of language. Is there a single paragraph in his pretentious scream of a book that rises to the level of literature? Or does he have the brain, as I suspect, of a blustering peasant? Help me know the man better. When can I have your analysis?"

"Give me two nights, sir."

"Done."

He fished another document, mercifully a thin one, from his pile. "Here. Background on a group of loyal Sudetens. Rare, these Germans, they are not cowed, not hiding, not terrified of declaring a desire to remain in Czechoslovakia. We are backing them, quietly of course, with money and counsel. Next month they will be sending a delegation for some jaw-jaw. I shall want you to be my liaison."

"Delighted, sir."

"One thing more … the strongbox in your room."

"Yes, sir, it has two – "

"I have the key and combination numbers. In due course I shall tell you what is inside. That will be all, Joff. Thank you very much." The train switched tracks again. He turned to his papers.

"Thank you, sir," I said, but he was already absorbed in another direction.

On leaving his room, my predominant emotion was not pleasure or enthusiasm. Massive doubt, more like. Had I expected this kind of work? Was I cut out for it? What *had* I expected? Hello twelve hour days and irksome reading at bedtime …

There's Mary up and about. Must put this away and wake Vicky and make breakfast. Have I told you how my precious plum screeched when she heard about my new job? "You are part of *history* now, Daddy!"

Right. As seen from a windowless cellar. Back in it tomorrow. Be well, great lady, and write. All my best,
  Joff

Friday
26th Aug. 1938

Dear Heidi,
Just finished yours of the eighteenth. I am reeling from what you tell me. I now understand your long silence. What puzzles me is how Matt's failure could come as a bolt from the blue. Were there no warning signs? Where is the new house? Far from Beacon Hill? Thank the stars for your own success, your boys will never be in rags, but Jesus Christ this is a shock. What does Matt plan to do? Sorry for the interrogation, Heidi, I don't mean to pry. I am deeply saddened and concerned. Please know you are in my mind. I shall write again tomorrow. The PM goes to Chartwell tonight and most of the staff, including me, are taking the weekend off.

Be strong great lady, the world is still yours, it will always be yours, and I will always be,

Your friend and admirer,
Joff

Saturday
27th Aug. 1938

Dear Heidi,

Your situation kept me up half the night. I was thinking of your adored house, the enjoyment you take in the garden, Max's playroom, your studio in the loft ... how can you bear leaving? Must ask again what the hell happened to Matt. I simply do not understand how he could plunge so rapidly from the heights to penury. Did he make some kind of fatal error? Something to do with the stock market?

Greetings from Graham and Seamus. Of course I told them nothing of your new circumstances. They were eager to see me and came with ridiculous hopes. They thought I would be able to tour them through Number 10, maybe even introduce them to Mr. Churchill. As I say, ridiculous. The policeman at the staff entrance still gravely inspects my identity card before he lets me into the building. Then I vanish into my subterranean galley and spend the days chained to an eccentric oar. Since those few crowded minutes on my first day I haven't had a tick of what the staff calls 'face time' with the Prime Minister. I thought I was taken on as a translator and interpreter. So far I have done very little translation and zero interpretation.

Ask me about the Blomberg file, however, and I can recite it chapter and verse. My summary for the PM ran to four typed pages, but came back defaced by block letters with this instruction: REDUCE TO A SINGLE PAGE! You may be sure this sensitive soul brooded over the exclamation point. For you, Heidi, I will whittle down the summary to a single paragraph. I would be grateful if you can help me guess why Mr. Churchill is interested in a vulgar German scandal long since over and done.

Werner von Blomberg, Field Marshall in the German army, was installed as Minister of Defense by Hitler in 1933. In January of this year the widower Blomberg married a stenographer thirty-five years his junior. Hitler stood as a privileged witness at the wedding. Shortly after, rumours circulated of a police dossier with appalling facts about the bride. It was said she had worked as a prostitute, her mother had operated a brothel, and pornographic photos of her had been taken by a foreign Jew. All the rumours were spot-on. The potential loss of face for Hitler was incalculable. *He had stood in close support while the most senior officer in the nation's military married a whore.* Nazi indoctrination has not erased the aristocratic tendency within the old guard of the German army. The military still regards itself as the keeper of the Fatherland's virtue. The Blomberg affair signified a profound moral failure. Mr. Churchill asked me to tell him what the scandal says about the German officer corps. My conclusion stresses what I see as the scandal's most obvious lesson. Extraordinary sensitivity – a categorical intolerance – exists in the old guard with respect to sexual indiscretion.

All very interesting, Heidi, but I have to say it was also suffocating to delve into old news that has no apparent application to current events. Truly, I am vexed. I see no relevance whatever in the Blomberg file for the Prime Minister of England.

A letter this week from Samuel Sternthal. It seems my credit is still gold with the Private Secretary. From a vineyard in the Dordogne he took time from his holiday to answer my notes. He congratulates me on my new position and laments that it will keep me from joining his refugee project. "Nevertheless," he writes, "I feel certain you will want to pursue the authorship opportunity we discussed. My door remains open to you on the matter." (Right. I will somehow find more hours in the day beyond the twelve I am already working.) The last line in his letter threw me off balance. Responding to my question about Damon, he writes, "As for the Chadwick issue, that is not for me to comment."

Not for him to comment? The Chadwick *issue*?

Vicky is up. Her breakfast cook must run to perform her bidding. You have my thoughts, care and love.

Joff

Wednesday
31st Aug. 1938

Dear Heidi,
Writing this from my catacomb. Vansittart flew in from Berlin yesterday to brief the PM. From what I can gather, after Hitler contemptuously refused to receive him, Vansittart was at last granted an audience with Ribbentrop. The meeting was rimmed with frost. The German Foreign Minister recited a litany of grievances in regard to Britain's new Prime Minister, the malicious posture Churchill is taking toward the Third Reich, and the foolish, menacing, provocative path of rearmament Britain has adopted. Then, almost as an after-thought, Ribbentrop informed our ambassador that Hitler's patience is at an end. The Fuhrer is determined to see the Sudeten problem resolved within the next four weeks. Vansittart would not have hurriedly flown to London unless he sensed Hitler is prepared to order an invasion of Czechoslovakia.

The air upstairs is heavy with dread, though staffers tell me Mr. Churchill seems unperturbed. No one doubts his resolve on Czechosolovakia, and there's the rub. Given fixed attitudes on both sides, the odds favouring conflict have seriously narrowed. I share the general anxiety, but at this moment I am more worried about Damon than about a European war.

The cryptic comment in Samuel Sternthal's letter has been gnawing at me. I kept it from Maddy. She would jump to the same conclusion I have reached. *The F.O. knows something about Damon's disappearance.* Am I wrong, or did the vacationing Mr. Sternthal, writing from a Dordogne chateau, unintentionally reveal as much. He returns to his desk next week. I aim to pay him a visit and make an interrogator of myself.

Not all my news is grim. Arriving home yesterday evening I collided with the Nellis family. Martin the scrawny reed and Martha the ever-expanding blimp make an amusing couple. They were trying to control their little stompers while lugging several suitcases. "Hallo, hallo," Martin trumpeted.

"You've been away, I see."

"We have, we have!"

The power of those lungs. If you weren't clapping your eyes on the emaciated man, you would think his voice had issued from a galloping Goliath. The news he announced was music to my ears. The family will be leaving London. They had been away, staying with Martha's sister in York, no doubt grazing on charity, and lo and behold ... the chemical engineer, pursuing the seemingly hopeless quest for a position in his field, chanced upon an opening for a compound blender in a cosmetics concern.

"Good for you!" I said, perhaps too enthusiastically. "When do you leave?"

Thank heaven they will be gone by the middle of next week, and the lightfooted spinster will be returning from Edinburgh. Now if only the guns stay quiet in Europe and a repentant Damon holds court at The Squire's all will be well in the Pearson universe. It would also be a godsend to hear from Boston that a great lady's capsized husband has righted himself. I seem to recall being an ass in my last letter, nagging you with questions about Matt. You have enough on your mind without me poking and tormenting. I apologise.

You will be pleased to know I have added a touch of green to my catacomb. The plant, one of your favourites, the Saint George's sword, is showing off its spiky leaves on top of the mysterious two-lock safe.

Back to the grind. I am knee deep in the daily press summary, but also thinking good thoughts for you. All my love,

Joff

Saturday
3rd Sept. 1938

Dear Heidi,

To the relief of his staff Mr. Churchill is again weekending at Chartwell. The rumour is he will soon shutter the house. Ironically, as Prime Minister, he can no longer afford to keep it. His income from lecture tours, newspaper columns and book advances has largely dried up. He will have to make do with Chequers, the poor fellow.

Damon's situation, whatever it may be, is preying on my mind. I now fully agree with Maddy. This extended quiet from him feels wrong. I won't speculate on what has happened, but you know my worst fear. Samuel Sternthal returns Monday. He can have the day to gather his legs, but on Tuesday I will be demanding a few minutes of his time.

You doubtless have been reading about British efforts to head off the crisis on the continent. No one knows if the so-called Eden mission can move the Germans a single inch. Mr. Eden will present a plan next week, first in Prague and then in Berlin. From what I hear the proposal focuses on a radical decentralisation of the Czech state, and shows how a federal structure can be designed to satisfy all parties. If the plan is adopted, it will at once preserve the country's unity and provide the Sudeten Germans with a degree of autonomy bordering on independence. Sounds a sensible solution to me, but then my name is not Adolf Hitler. Nor am I the leaders of Czechoslovakia, who could reasonably object to having various limbs of their country's constitution amputated, mutated, and sewn back on by foreign meddlers. Perhaps this is why Mr. Churchill has stressed that for the time being not a word, not a hint, not a *whisper* of the proposed federalist solution should be permitted to reach the press.

Resting my brain today. Donkey work has exhausted it. Every morning a call comes from Miss Pearman, who hands me Mr. Churchill's instructions. The PM dictates terse notes which are typed by his stenographer, then stapled to the files which Miss Pearman summons me to fetch. The pitiless edict ACTION THIS DAY is often stamped in bright red on the notes. My job is to digest, summarise and draw conclusions from the files, as I did with the Blomberg. Many of the files, again like the Blomberg, puzzle me. They often startle me. I have no idea who compiled them, or why. They are also mildly repulsive, as well as beside the point, *any* point. What possible utility can exist in a dossier of reports from throughout Germany on prosecutions of incest, bigamy and bastardy? Why burden me with papers by German psychologists profiling individuals guilty of gross indecency? I came to Number 10 thinking I would sit at Mr. Churchill's elbow interpreting the mannered discourse of visiting Reich dignitaries. Care to know what I have been dealing with the last three days? A file that examines the incidence of male on male rape in the Reich's military ... Enough.

I need rest. I need distraction. The plan is to savour some final summer hours with my plum. Vicky's long holiday has come and gone. Meanwhile she has grown like a nettle in spring rain. She leaves tomorrow for her extortionate school in her absurdly pricey new blazer and skirt. (Did I tell you about my salary bump? It was a brief mirage. The increase in Vicky's costs and fees has devoured it whole.) Enough!

Thinking of you. Hoping and praying your circumstances are on the mend. As ever,

Joff

Tuesday
6th Sept. 1938

A devastating day, Heidi. I am just back from seeing Sternthal. He was evasive at first, pretended to know nothing. "Bollocks," I threw at him.

"My dear Pearson!"

"Please understand, sir, Damon Chadwick has no better friend in the world than myself."

Sternthal sighed. His expression changed. "Your friend's predicament is being kept quiet. The Germans have no interest in telling the world they are holding a famous artist. For the time being, neither does our side care that it be known. That is why the bloodhounds of our press are not yet on to it. Please keep to yourself what I am about to tell you."

I made no such promise. He told me what he knows, which is not much but terrifying enough. A month ago Damon was arrested in a friend's private home in Berlin, and taken to Spandau prison. The charge against him has not been announced. An odd secrecy surrounds the case. Consular assistance has been denied. No one has been permitted to see the prisoner.

"I take it he was arrested on an issue of ... morals?"

Sternthal looked away. "That is one supposition," he said. Turning back to me he added, "Your friend enjoys considerable celebrity. Higher-ups are bringing influence to bear. We must be patient."

I found his manner less than hopeful. Sternthal conceded the Nazi judicial system is transparent as sludge. Rights of the accused, no matter their renown, wealth or nationality, are thin to none. All we can do is wait.

"Must we?" I said. "I have been told that Hermann Goering – "

"The embassy is aware. An approach has been made. It proved a blind alley."

That hit me hard. *Damon's all-powerful chum refusing to pull a simple string?* Heidi, I don't know what to think.

Until soon,
Joff

Wednesday
7th Sept. 1938

Dear One,
Trying to lose myself in work, but relief is fleeting. Damon's situation intrudes … casts a cloud. Yesterday evening was uncomfortable. Mary stayed tight-lipped while her face betrayed her thoughts. Did my friend think his fame would protect him? Every sin brings its comeuppance. Besides, what kind of fool chases the illicit in the most repressive country on earth?

I cast no blame on myself, but Maddy did once implore me to go to Germany and haul Damon out. I almost telephoned her last night but thought better of it. She might revive my earlier counsel and take the story to the press. That would raise an almighty stink, which could end up hurting more than helping. No, Sternthal advised well. Better to keep the thing quiet, let higher-ups discreetly handle it. That was my view last night. This morning I am not so sure. If influence from on high could free Damon, wouldn't the trick have been done by now? It crushed me to hear the embassy has already played his ace. Why would the Goering card achieve nothing? …

Back in my cellar. Lunch was a sandwich of flimsy ham cushioned with wilted lettuce. The canteen tea was tepid. I sat with Bocking-Kerr. He looked terribly gloomy as we discussed the speech Hitler gave in Stuttgart yesterday. Your papers surely reported it. The dictator said the German army was at the Czech frontier and that history-altering events will soon transpire. Bocking-Kerr grew even gloomier when we talked about the leader in today's *Times*. He told me the Prime Minister usually lies abed with the morning papers but today he was early at his desk, and it was there he came across the *Times* leader suggesting the Czechs should give up the Sudetenland. That ignited a Churchillian roar of disgust. Everywhere in the world *The Times* is seen as a mouthpiece for the British government. The PM seized the nearest object, which happened to be a glass paperweight, and blindly hurled it. The tantrum resulted in serious injury to an innocent lamp as well as fatality for the paperweight itself.

Bocking-Kerr did not crack a smile telling me this. He sounded positively mournful over the Eden mission, now entering its third day in Prague. The Czechs, he said, are proving difficult. Today they will no doubt take special umbrage over our foremost newspaper advising the dismemberment of their country. They accept the federal solution in principle but insist on watering it down in practice. Any dilution of the proposed autonomy for the Sudeten Germans will only make it harder for Mr. Eden to sell the plan in Berlin. As we left the lunchroom Bocking-Kerr said, "Have you opened the vault yet?"

"I don't get you."

"The safe in your room."

"Ah, the double-locked little fortress."

"Precisely why we call it 'the vault'."

"Do you know what it contains?"

"Pearson," he snapped, bristling with earnest sobriety, "none of us know."

"The PM told me we would eventually discuss the contents."

"Naturally. That's why you were hired."

I did not ask Bocking-Kerr if my ears had heard right. I suppose one grows accustomed to being startled.

Did you notice what just happened? For a few minutes I stopped thinking about Damon, but the black cloud has come back. Worse, in addition to Damon's plight I now have the contents of 'the vault' to obsess me. If you were the praying type Heidi I would ask you to direct some words upward for our friend. Do it at any rate.

Love you,

Joff

Wednesday
14th Sept. 1938

Heidi,

Sorry, I have not felt like writing. Sternthal promised to share developments and there have been no developments. I sense my fear turning to resignation. I lack the stomach to imagine what has happened to Damon, or to imagine his circumstances. Back soon, must go to a staff meeting …

We were nine in the Cabinet Room. I was the oldest fellow there, save for Sir Robert Walpole who looks dourly out from the only portrait in the room. When I took a place at the table someone said cheerfully, "That's Leo Amery's seat." "Fine," I replied, "you may address me as the First Lord of the Admiralty."

John 'Jock' Colville, principal private secretary to Mr. Churchill, ran the meeting from the PM's chair. A fire crackled in the wide hearth behind him, and the lights shone brightly from the three brass chandeliers in the high-ceilinged room. Colville said the PM was fighting a high fever and would be working from bed all day. Several quips ensued about how productivity would leap. Bocking-Kerr looked fiercely about the room and said, "Decorum, if you please!" which only drew more quips. Your basement dweller stayed mute. The PM's people are brilliant, cocksure, ambitious and, to repeat the most obvious thing about them, *young*. Colville himself (and this to me is astounding) looks in his early twenties. He gently chided Bocking-Kerr, then turned the meeting properly grave.

The whole world knows Hitler pointedly refused to see Eden. What the world does not know is how brief and one-sided Eden's meeting with Ribbentrop was. Fresh off his stony reception in Czechoslovakia, our Foreign Secretary was given a contemptuous half hour in Berlin, and even then shut down by his German counterpart. As Colville put it, Ribbentrop was a brick wall. He came to dispel and instruct, first pouring ice water on Eden's federal plan, then lecturing Eden about the Fuhrer's determination before month's end to 'halt, uproot and annul' the Czech subjugation of his Sudeten brothers and sisters. Go back to Prague, Ribbentrop advised our man, talk sense to the Czechs, and do it quickly. Either they yield the Sudetenland to the Reich or face the Wehrmacht. The former champagne salesman then got to his feet and left the room, making a mockery of diplomatic protocol and leaving the Foreign Secretary of Great Britain grasping in the dark.

Colville summarised our strategy as conveyed to him from the Prime Ministerial bed. Despite Hitler's blatant rebuff and Ribbentrop's sneering dismissal of Eden, we are to proceed as if the Germans have taken the Eden plan under advisement. All comment to the press, including engineered leaks, are to express an upbeat view of behind the scenes negotiations despite the fact no such negotiations are taking place. The German ambassador is to be summoned to the F.O. and steeped in specifics of the federalist solution, just as he would be if his masters in Berlin were signing on and as if the Czechs were fully in accord. Meanwhile, Colville said, Prime Minister Churchill has repeated in the most serious of terms that there can be no public reference to the proposed federalist solution; it must be kept confidential. Colville punctuated this remark with a long silent glare that traveled the room.

He then went on to say that the American ambassador, Joseph Kennedy, is to be invited with his flock of offspring to Sandringham for an extended stay. The purpose is to divert the Yank at this sensitive time and stifle his defeatist pronouncements. Gratitude is owed to the King for his wholehearted endorsement of the 'contain Kennedy' plan. Indeed, it was George's idea to invite additional guests – selected, wealthy, carefully briefed paladins of British industry – to join the party. Business opportunities murmured into Mr. Kennedy's ear will serve to further distract the unhelpful ambassador.

Mr. Eden has left Berlin for Paris. Tonight he flies to Moscow. The mission is to find common ground for supporting the territorial integrity of Czechoslovakia. None of us in the room required a history refresher, Colville said, but we ought to remain aware that Mr. Churchill's government is shouldering the British foreign policy strategy of three centuries vintage. Abandoned by the Baldwins and Chamberlains, the strategy aims to preserve a balance of power on the continent and thereby ensure the security of our island. The vast majority of our fellow citizens are regrettably unschooled in the historical precedents for Mr. Churchill's initiatives. Accordingly, beginning at once, we will make regular use of a new domestic tool. Surveys of public opinion will be conducted every second day throughout Britain. The questions will be slanted toward reminding respondents of our historic national strategy and the results will perforce reflect popular support for the government. Finally, and most critically, the Czechoslovak leadership will be informed of an offer of assistance contingent upon agreement to accept the Eden plan. Once agreement from Prague is secured, and no one should doubt that by hook or by crook Prague will be made to see reason, Mr. Churchill will publicly offer the Czechs a joint exercise in their own airspace involving five squadrons of British warplanes.

A hush came over the room. Someone asked if the cabinet had agreed to that last, um, risky measure. Another wondered aloud if the PM has the authority to make such a decision on his own. A third itchy voice inquired about the probity of 'slanting' the results of opinion polls.

The questioners could not have angered Jock Colville more if they had stomped with muddy boots on the King's portrait. He spoke with controlled fury, his eyes spitting at the sceptics. "How dare you discredit your own boldness which won you a place at this table." Then he pounded the said mahogany and raised his voice to a near shout. "How dare you forget the pathetic caution that disgraced this room prior to Mr. Churchill's arrival. Why do you think the bastard in Berlin has not yet ordered his tanks into Czechoslovakia? Precisely because he thinks he can get what he wants, again, without firing a shot. This room is now disabusing the son of a bitch. We are signalling to his jittery generals, 'Enough'. This is for all of you to understand, or resign. Courage and purpose have finally come to Downing Street and we will act without hesitation in their names!"

One by one my chastened colleagues received their marching orders. When Jock came to the basement dweller he said the F.O.'s translation of German documents has lately slowed to a crawl. My task is to enlarge Mr. Churchill's daily summary of the German press with translations of key passages from prominent newspaper leaders. It may be that Hitler's puppets in the press will provide insights into the dictator's thoughts which are otherwise not perceptible in the frenzy of his speeches. "And, oh yes, Pearson," Jock finished with me, "Mr. Churchill will see you at five-fifty sharp."

Heidi, I should be excited about seeing the Prime Minister, but the overhanging cloud blots out all … Damon's the emergency. You, this, the page under my pen, are more than ever a soothing habit, my relief and refuge.

  With love,
  Joff

Friday
16th Sept. 1938

Heidi,

Thank the good lord, the cloud has lifted. I believe Damon will be coming home. When I was shown into Mr. Churchill's bedroom Wednesday evening I found him deep in pillows, evening newspapers, and files from the Boxes. He was wearing a dressing gown patterned with blue elephants. He did look ill. His eyes were sagging and chin burrowing. He had obviously exerted himself with a stream of visitors. He grunted a greeting and faintly gestured at a cane chair.

I ignored the gesture. I hovered. An impulsive thing happened. "Sir," I flung at the Prime Minister, "are you aware that the painter Damon Chadwick is rotting in a German prison?"

A tremor roiled the sea of papers and pillows. Mr. Churchill heaved himself higher in the bed. A bare pinkish foot, like a strange creature up from the deep, jutted from beneath the covers. I was about to apologise for my presumption. "Sit down, Joff."

I did as I was told.

"How in heaven's name," he said in a croaky voice, "do you know about Chadwick?"

I related my conversation with Samuel Sternthal.

"A lapse on Sternthal's part! What makes you so interested in the painter?"

"Damon and I have been close friends for thirty years."

Mr. Churchill's chin climbed several inches. "I was not aware of that. A curious coincidence."

"Coincidence, sir?"

He waved his hand, which conspicuously held no cigar. "Chadwick has deservedly made a great name. The matter of his arrest is receiving all due attention."

"Can we hope for his freedom, sir?"

Mr. Churchill nodded impatiently. "My aim is to see him back in England within a fortnight."

"That is a tremendous weight off my mind."

"Now, if you are quite done with your interrogation ..."

"Yes, sir, splendidly done. Thank you, sir."

Mr. Churchill did not share my levity. With brisk irritation he wrapped the dressing gown more tightly about himself. A jumble of blue elephants crowded his neck. "It may soon prove necessary," he said in a low growl, taking my attention off the absurd elephants, "for me to deal in statecraft by uncommon means. You will help me prepare."

He scribbled three numbers on a piece of paper. "Commit these to memory. They open the dial lock on the safe in your room. Have you got them?"

I made a mental photo. "Yes, sir."

He tore the paper into tiny bits while explaining how to apply the combination. Then he handed me a brown envelope containing a padlock key. "Inside the safe you will find a file containing personal letters and pieces of a private diary. All of the material is in German. Only three men in England including myself are privy to the existence of the file. You will be the fourth, and the only one intimate with the language the materials are written in. Which makes you my ultimate judge. The contents of the file may or may not reflect the truth. Either way I must know. You will study the file and tell me."

"Who wrote the letters and diary, sir?"

"The writer of the diary is the central figure. He is a … creature, by the name of Anton Kohrbach."

"How am I to judge the truthfulness of the file?"

"From the reliability, the validity, of the voices you hear. Help me answer a single question, taking as your guide the feel and tenor of their writing. *Did the grotesque events these men describe actually take place?* That is all." The Prime Minister fished a file from the valleys on his bed. It took me a moment to grasp I had been dismissed. I rose to my feet on rubbery legs.

Back in my underground room my hands trembled as I opened the safe. The hinges let out a protesting squeak as the heavy door swung open. I imagined finding a bunch of letters still in their envelopes. I also pictured a separate bundle of pages torn from a diary, posh sheets of parchment framed with flowers and vines, my idea of private diary pages.

I can be an idiot.

What I found was a thick file of enlarged photographs. Photographs of personal letters. Photographs of pages from a private diary. Some two hundred photographs in all. Many of them showed only a few scrawled words. The writing in the letters and diary was all in longhand. I identified four different hands. The first dated page was from November 1936, the last from early August of this year. I thought I would dip a toe and return later for a full swim, but I was pulled in, and under. Then deeper. Into behaviours and events the nature of which I doubt you could imagine and which I would not wish you to imagine. I cannot share any specifics of what I read. Even if I could, I would not.

If you are thinking of the horror that befell the family of the Berlin Jew, Morris Gelfmann ... stop. The letters and diary have nothing to do with the Nazi treatment of the Jews. They involve another, very different, realm of sickness. I tried to reject what was before me, tried hard to disbelieve it, but no whiff of artifice rose from what I was reading. The 'feel and tenor' of the writing told me the appalling events being recounted had in fact happened. The sick behaviours were made more sickening by the easy candour, and evident pleasure, of the writers. I went swiftly from one page to the next, no less spellbound for my revulsion. I thought of Jenkins and how his taste for intrigue would be roused by this clandestine trove, this evidence of mucky espionage, and how thrilled he would be by the appearance of prominent names, one of them colossal. When I reached January 1938 I happened to look at my wristwatch. It was nearly eleven. I telephoned Mary and apologised. I told her I had been detained by the PM and would have to work through the night. This gratified her, and I continued to read.

I turned the last page of the file at four this morning, then went to the flat for a bath. Mary fed me an enormous breakfast. I had missed my dinner without realising. An hour of blissful lie-down and here I am, back in my cellar, staring at the double-locked safe. The repellent file inside reminds me of ... this is less strange than it might at first sound ... it reminds me of D'Astou.

Do you remember D'Astou? His Christian name escapes me. He was a friend of Graham's brother. We ran into him from time to time during our wild years, a thin rat-faced fellow with a disdainful snout, always sniffing out schemes too radical even for our trendy set. I think it was '22 when he came home from Paris with the manuscript of the de Sade translation. Do you remember?

Forgive me, I must leave you for the heap of work on my desk. Eden has left Moscow for Prague again, no doubt to dangle carrots and twist arms. I am helping dissect the German press reaction.

Think saving thoughts for Damon, and kindly report the antics of your boys. A tide of cleansing news from America would do me a world of good.

Joff

Monday
19th Sept. 1938

Heidi,
Another Monday and I remain exhausted but to hell with exhaustion. I am coping rather well with the work and despite my place in the basement feel at the centre of things. A seductive gravity grips you at Number 10. The ceaseless pulse of power induces awe and deference. I should marvel, I really should, at the good fortune that has brought me here. The latest bit of luck is grand. I have been invited with wife and daughter to go down to Chartwell next weekend. Who do you think will be more excited, Mary or Vicky? I am pretty damn excited myself.

Violet Pearman negotiated the basement stairs to relay the invitation personally. (Violet and I are getting along famously.) Naturally it will be a working weekend. The invitation has not come by virtue of my parentage, wit or good looks. I must expect to be on call and should not be surprised, said Violet, if Mr. Churchill requires my sharp attention in the wee hours of the morning. As for transport to Chartwell, a government driver will fetch us at the flat on Friday and bring us back Sunday. I feel, Heidi, as if I have joined the elect.

Forgive the abrupt end to my last letter. I dropped the sleazy name of D'Astou and then abandoned you. His Christian name was Peter by the way, it came back to me on the tube this morning when a ratty-snouted fellow sat across from me. Must ask Graham what became of him. D'Astou! It pains me to recall, but our rebellious little set once saw him as a trailblazer. When he came from Paris with the de Sade translation and spoke of having it published, our support sprang from instinct. Goes to show how 'progressive' we were. Of course the book should be published; our duty was to condemn the very idea of censorship. That anybody who dared print or sell de Sade's work in England would promptly be prosecuted only caused us to ask what century we were living in. Surely in the enlightened year of 1922 people should be permitted to decide for themselves what was literature and what obscenity.

Then our turn came to read the thing.

The tatty typescript had probably gone through a hundred hands and after it passed through ours we felt contaminated. We took pride in our boundless tolerance, but this? This went far beyond mere obscenity. It dragged the sexual into the sewer and gloried in brutal filth. It could not be a reflection of anything in reality. It could only have emerged from some profound illness of the spirit, some horrid longing of the deviant. We wondered what kind of mind could produce such implausible vileness. You can now better imagine the nature of the diary and letters in the double-locked safe, that they should remind me of the writing of the Marquis de Sade ...

Tremendous tension this morning at Number 10. Everyone in the building down to the porters and tea girl were anxious about the verdict from Prague. Eden's call to the PM came just before ten. The Foreign Secretary's marathon session with the Czechs had lasted a day and a night. When the PM rang off he ordered the staff into his study. I found myself shoulder to shoulder with Colville on my right and Cadogan from the F.O. on my left. Mr. Churchill gave away nothing as he paced to and fro, a frown of impatience on his face. Once we were all assembled and the room properly attentive, the Prime Minister halted his march and surveyed the troops with a lenient eye.

"Anthony's skills have come full flower. With remarkable persistence and barely a hint of the rough, he has captured the confidence of the Czechs. They have agreed to the federalist solution and will announce it once we signal that the plan can be made public." Mr. Churchill's voice rose and raced with the last few words. Before he was finished everyone in the room was clapping and cheering.

The Prime Minister's snarl – *"We have no cause for jubilation!"* – whipped the room back to silence. "The Czech concession strengthens our case and is manifestly just," he said, wagging an unlighted cigar. "The dictator's objective is not justice however, but expansion. Nothing will deter Hitler unless his generals fear we shall fight. For that the squadrons may serve. The Czechs have our word. The announcement on the squadrons will be made in twenty-four hours. It will be made by myself. With the wireless microphones open and the newsreel cameras rolling."

Mr. Churchill instructed Permanent Under-Secretary Cadogan to summon the German ambassador in advance. ("Do it shortly before I step before the press, and seat him under Nelson's portrait in Anthony's room.") Then he advised on the diplomatic briefs to be prepared, and ended with a theatrical murmur. Joseph Kennedy, he whispered loudly, was thankfully on a short leash up at Sandringham. This impertinent aside eased the tension and sparked some humorous remarks. The Prime Minister promptly turned stern again. He thanked the staff for their dedication and warned of tougher trials ahead. We left the room a solemn lot. Someone said, "Crunch time has arrived." And someone else, "Only a matter of days now."

While I count the days Heidi, the world's urgency worries me less than a single prison cell in Germany and our friend's ordeal in it. Mr. Churchill said a fortnight will bring Damon home. I only fear that larger events may play havoc with that pledge.

Are you thinking good thoughts? Please write. *Tell me good things.*
Joff

Wednesday
21st Sept. 1938

Dearest Lady,

I have yours of the fourteenth. It saddens me. I was hoping to hear of a change in your husband's fortunes. Time will help, Heidi. Give your man time. He is a talented and resourceful individual. His luck will turn. So, as you say, will Damon's. You are perfectly right about our friend, he does have something untouchable in him. He was born with a fence of steel around his core. We can hope and pray he will return to us whole.

The staff gathered in the Cabinet room last night for Hitler's speech. I was tasked with providing the simultaneous translation, and felt more butterflies than if I were on stage at the Apollo ... the brilliant young staffers intimidate me no end. Once the speech started, however, I blotted out their scrutiny and concentrated on Hitler's voice. My eyes were riveted to my hands which I clenched into fists. Hitler came over clearly, at moments sufficiently high-pitched to threaten crystal. I stayed with him and began matching his cadence. He was obviously treating the speech like a theatrical occasion, and had likely rehearsed no less than an actor would for a major role. I felt what he was trying to do with his voice and choice of words – seduce, arouse, incite. Above all incite, and reap at incitement's peak a climactic satisfaction in both himself and the audience. Good lord, Heidi, I understand better now the hypnotic hold the man exerts. In a real sense I have experienced his sorcery from the inside. He does have a gift of oratory, despite how savage his fearsome screaming might sound. Some of his words were lost, engulfed in cheers. They say the Nuremberg pageant numbered thirty thousand. ("Doting robots with vocal chords," Jock Colville interjected.) Through most of the speech Hitler poured contempt on Britain's interference in Czechoslovakia. Drawing his worst bile was Mr. Churchill's announcement yesterday about British fighter squadrons enroute to Prague. His voice rose to a near shriek as he denounced the coming war games in Czech skies as a naked provocation and –

"Trying out for the role, Joff?"

I looked up from my fists. Mr. Churchill had entered the room.

Nervous laughter greeted his remark. Apparently I was imitating Hitler's frenzy!

"Carry on, carry on," said the Prime Minister, beaming. I resumed sheepishly, my fists unclenched.

Hitler lowered his tone, the better to stress his conclusion. He said a thunder of anger is beating in the heart of the Reich. The Wehrmacht stands ready at the Czech frontier, poised to unleash a liberating storm and exalt the German spirit. A glorious event in the history of the German people may very soon transpire.

With the wireless off, the room's attention mercifully shifted from myself to the Prime Minister. The light of good humour had not left him but shone even brighter in a wide smile. "Did you note the conditional 'may'? The dictator has been caught off guard. I believe his generals are edgy. You can all sleep tonight with buoyant hearts. Be assured there will be no bang-bang in coming days."

I trust Mr. Churchill is right. Not just for peace in Europe, but for Damon's sake … my telephone.

It was Violet Pearman. She wanted to confirm that my wife and daughter will accompany me to Chartwell. She said the Prime Minister will be pleased. Then she added, "He asks that you arrive prepared to discuss the – " and she uttered a curious designation, a name for a nomadic people, that rang a distant bell. I begged her pardon.

"The file in your vault. Mr. Churchill requires your analysis."

"Understood, but what did you call the file?"

"Mr. Churchill occasionally refers to it as the 'Bedouin file'," said Violet. "I thought you knew."

A nearly forgotten piece of nonsense from months ago came to mind, Jenkins gleefully pointing at a splotch and scribble on documents from the Berlin embassy. In the thrill of the moment he took them as evidence of espionage and said something about 'Russian dolls'. I remember scornfully dismissing his theory as fantasy.

"Are you there, Joffrey?"

"Yes, Violet! I will be prepared. Thank you."

Prepared also to address a letter from Chartwell for carriage to Boston across this spinning, baffling, dizzying orb. Consider that a promise, dear lady. All my best to you and your three men.

Joff

Saturday
24th Sept. 1938

Dear Heidi,

A long eventful day behind us including a late *late* night for me. We are at Chartwell. Our cup overflows. Mary is fast asleep, sending out some of her squeaky middle-of-the-night sounds. I sit at a battered Chippendale, writing on the drop-front. Can you see me? The lamp over my shoulder is casting a hexagon onto my writing pad. Those squeaky sounds from Mary prove she's content. For my darling spouse this stay in Mr. Churchill's country home could serve as the gift for all her birthdays to come. And my darling daughter! She has been taken in hand by Mr. Churchill's youngest, Mary, who is a dashing sixteen. Vicky is asleep on a sofa in her new friend's room. That is, if she can sleep. Try to imagine my little girl's thrill when the Prime Minister instantly recognised her – "The young lioness of Hackney!" – and swept her up in his arms. To Mary's infinite gratification he remembered the young lioness's mother as well. With both of Mary's hands in his he threw me a glance of mock scorn and pronounced himself betrayed. "A member of my staff has deliberately failed to inform me of a wife and daughter of surpassing allure and courage."

You may add to Mr. Churchill's traits that of incorrigible charmer.

The clock says two-forty. I have just returned from a meeting with the charmer, who can just as easily act the ogre. Whatever role he plays, he is certainly tireless. The Prime Minister says the most productive hours of his day are the four which straddle midnight. He enters them fueled by the dinner conversation, not to mention the champagne, and in the dead of night finds himself more keenly motivated by the implacable brevity of life. Two shorthand-writers are weekending with us. *Two.*

Heidi, I must tell you again … Mr. Churchill has put to rest the rude notions I once had of him. His intake of alcohol may be prodigious, I have now seen it firsthand, but his chief pleasure comes from incessant work. He thinks twenty-four is far, far short of the number of hours a proper day should contain. Meanwhile every waking moment must have a purpose. Gratification for him comes from filling transient time with as much production as possible. Moreover, his religion is Rigour, or perhaps Precision, as the fruits of his work must be without bruise or blemish. I heard him bellow at one of the stenos about a small error in transcription. This was before the guests heard the Prime Minister announce he had decided to steal an hour – "I require just one hour" – at his easel. The man is a fine painter! His canvases dot the house. They range from still-lifes of flowers to charming renditions of English villages and light-filled takes of Mediterranean shores. His works may not belong in museums, but they reveal a definite flair, something singular that announces itself. Did you know he can paint? Mary knew of course. She tells me Mr. Churchill has written beautifully of the repose he finds when sitting with his brush.

He stole two hours.

His wife Clementine (the PM's affection for 'Clemmie' is palpable) has obviously learned to bear his impositions. The day being fine Mrs. Churchill had Sawyers, the PM's valet, set up chairs on the so-called Pink Terrace, from where we had a marvellous view across the Weald of Kent. A platter of assorted breads and caviar materialised, and the maids circulated with trays of beer, gingerale and lemonade. Vicky was spirited off by her new friend to explore the estate, which sprawls with gardens and hilly groves. It must be true, the rumour I once heard, that Mr. Churchill earned twenty thousand quid a year from his writing. Kudos to the power of a fertile pen, that it could turn words and paragraphs into a house with two dozen rooms and grounds covering eighty acres.

Relaxing with the other guests I was amused to hear my spouse tug and stretch her limited French. She was talking with Maryvonne Lagarde, wife of Jacques who heads a Charente winemaking family. Monsieur Lagarde has been a friend of Mr. Churchill's since '16, when the two shared peril in a Belgian village during an enemy barrage. After the armistice Lagarde joined the Quai d'Orsay and made a career as a desk man. In recent years however he could not stomach his country's ostrich-like attitude toward the Nazis, and the final straw was Hitler's unobstructed walk into the Rhineland. He resigned in disgust the day the French army was ordered to keep to its barracks. Or so I understood, because I was excavating my own deeply buried French …

Am I boring you, Heidi? Truth is, I am using a carbon because I will want to recall this weekend in my dotage, this rubbing of shoulders with the titled and mighty. The gentleman in the adjacent bedroom is Lord Beaverbrook. He owns half of Fleet Street, including the *Daily Express*. We gather he is a recent widower. Down the hall we have a General, the much-decorated Hastings Ismay, whom Mr. Churchill calls 'Pug'. The General's wife is a lovely lady with an aristocratic bearing, but she has shown us no airs. All the guests have been unfailingly polite, although we do sense a curiosity as to why a humble staffer and his wife (a policewoman!) should be at Chartwell for the weekend. Not to put too fine a point on it, but the curiosity is one we ourselves share ...

Back from the loo, which I can tell you is freshened uniquely. Hung above the washbasin where one would expect a mirror, one is instead faced with an explosion of white blossom, a magnolia in watercolour dated '31 and signed by our host. I grow almost convinced that if Mr. Churchill had devoted himself exclusively to the easel, he might have jousted on an equal footing with the Manets and Monets.

I must finish telling you about our distinguished company. Alexander Cadogan from the F.O. is here with his wife, and rounding out the company is a loud bumptious bachelor, a professor of physics by the name of Frederick Lindemann. Everybody calls Lindemann 'The Prof'. He strikes me as obnoxiously pompous, but apparently he's a regular at Chartwell. The PM turns to him for counsel on scientific matters.

I once heard a Yank use the phrase 'punching above your weight', which I am happy to steal for Mr. and Mrs. Pearson on this once-in-a-lifetime weekend. We may be doing more listening than talking, but so far have not proven ourselves out of place.

Lunch when it finally came was strictly informal. The Prime Minister's half-finished painting, an oil of Chartwell's pond and surrounding wood, was positioned so he could study it while we helped ourselves to a buffet of smoked salmon, potato salad (strangely but agreeably infiltrated by thinly sliced beetroot), and a whole suckling pig on a silver tray. The PM, oblivious to any hostly duty, was still engaged with his painting. He concentrated on it as he mopped up the remaining caviar with a heel of bread. He said he was having difficulty conquering the perspective and expressed anguish that he would be separated from his easel for a week. In his bow tie, siren suit and zippered shoes (apparently he despises laces!) he appeared the incarnation of an upper-class workingman. Curious how he can instantly, seemingly effortlessly, dominate a gathering even when paying it little attention. The group rose as one when he arrived and always promptly fell silent when he uttered a word. Deference is compelled by something in him. What it is I couldn't say, maybe a quality of mind, a force of will, a kind of ultra self-awareness working outward like magnetism, sending benign hooks when his mood is fair and pelting hurricane-like when he unleashes a temper. He can be totally unconscious of niceties. Once the caviar was mopped clean he closed his eyes and without warning slipped into a nap, causing the party to whisper while the maids, who know the drill, removed the nub of bread from his hand, the napkin from his chin, and tip-toed around like efficient wraiths. I found myself grinning like a fool and quickly put a sock in it ...

Tiring now, but I will go on, must get all this down. I wish I could reproduce the look on Vicky's face when she returned from her roamings. She was wide-eyed over the private expanses, black swans in the pond, a half-built brick wall her friend Mary called her father's 'daft hobby'. What more am I to learn about my new employer? On top of being a soldier, journalist, politician, historian and painter, Mr. Churchill is also an amateur bricklayer.

After lunch my spouse joined the ladies on the croquet lawn, then went off with Madame Lagarde who is an avid bird watcher. Seems Mary has made a new friend. As for me, no mallets or Spotted Sandpipers. Cadogan took me behind closed doors and plied me with questions. Turns out he is one of the three men in England besides myself who know about the file in the basement vault. He wanted my summary of the letters and diary. He demanded my impressions and certainties. He was particularly interested in any of my doubts, no matter how small. When the grilling was done he said, "Get some rest. I know him. You will have to do this all over again, and he will likely call us in at a late hour."

Distinct from luncheon, the atmosphere at dinner was correct, almost painfully so as Mr. Churchill grumbled over his soup, which was not to his liking, but he was too preoccupied to make a point of it. He had spent the afternoon closeted with General Ismay in the library, where

I suspect he suffered a briefing on Britain's military preparedness. Ismay's position as Secretary of the Committee of Imperial Defence makes him as knowledgeable as anyone in the land as to how ready the country is for war. From the look on the PM's face ... dreadfully unready.

Mr. Churchill ignored his guests until the champagne arrived. After his first sip, the lines in his face rearranged themselves and he started hogging the spotlight. To amuse his friend Jacques he launched into a lecture about the mayhem that has characterised public life in France throughout the 1930s. He did it in a childish French with results that were unintentionally funny, almost farcical. Imagine someone speaking a foreign tongue by haltingly reading their lines in phonetic English. Yes, it sounded that laboured. But Mr. Churchill had obviously come back to high spirits and was full of prowling energy.

Must tell you, his monologues do exceed courtesy. People get restless as he goes on, though I confess to fascination myself. The ability to discourse extemporaneously on complex matters, and in structured paragraphs, is not given to many. Did I say paragraphs? Mr. Churchill speaks whole essays. He can also make bewildering leaps in his chains of thought. He was going on about potential breakthroughs in British aircraft production when he abruptly stopped, turned to Cadogan and said, "Alec, when can I have that paper on Turkey?" Then he spoke about the strategic importance of Turkey and the necessity of making that country an ally, which led him to thoughts about Kemal Ataturk and the secular revolution he had wrought, and before we knew it we had been listening to Mr. Churchill go on for ten minutes about Turkish history and culture.

The champagne ... Heidi, the rivers of champagne. I watched in awe the PM's steady consumption and took a few glasses of the very fine Pol Roger myself. In ordinary circumstances I would be snoring like a steam engine by now. It must be the adrenaline. Exhilaration defeats intoxication.

Later the talk turned to Germany and Nazi designs on Europe. Hitler's aim is war, said Cadogan, as a means of complete revenge for Versailles. Cadogan was contradicted by Lord Beaverbrook who said Hitler's aim is a greater Germany but not at the cost of another Great War. Professor Lindemann jumped to Cadogan's defence.

Like a headmaster hectoring a schoolboy he glared, shook his finger, raised his voice at Beaverbrook. "Feeding that line to the dim-witted masses through your lily-livered newspapers has done the country a disservice. Worse, an injury that could prove fatal. Hitler is preparing for war and anyone with eyes in their heads should see it." Lindemann went on to describe Hitler as a ghoul, a mountebank, a repository of all the wrongs in German history and all the diseases of the German psyche. I must confess, Heidi, I took an almost instant dislike of the professor. And not solely because he reminds me of my father's absurd theories about the German people. My father was never a Lindemann, never a loud needling bully.

Mr. Churchill played the host. He interceded and knocked down both his friends. "Prof, how often must I beg you to learn restraint and modesty? But Max, how can you dispute what The Prof says? Hitler has screeched and bellowed that he wants to establish a thousand year Reich and include in it lands that are not today part of Germany, if necessary at the cost of blood. Why do people not take him seriously? For five years we have had highly respected intellectuals, trusting politicans, legions of business leaders, all of whom should know better, telling us, when this man makes a very clear statement, that he actually means something else!"

"They have been telling us," said Lindemann, "to get down on our knees and lick his damn boots."

My spouse and I looked at each other when the professor made this distasteful comment. We usually read each other's thoughts perfectly when in the presence of an unlikable human being. Lindemann is the classic self-made man who worships his creator .... an ego with no bridle and all the answers whatever the subject.

"My dear Lindemann," said Mr. Churchill in his best growly manner, "your colours again careen to the garish." He drained his champagne and turned to Beaverbrook. "Max, your newspapers doubt and dispute me, but look at the monstrous military machine which now exists at the continent's heart. The Rhineland bristles with arms and France feels threatened. Austria is gone. Czechoslovakia trembles. I am taking the dictator, whose intentions I believe I have grasped, at his word. Shall I now do otherwise than my utmost to stop him in his grisly tracks?"

"Oh, but why should you?" Professor Lindemann intruded, this time with dripping sarcasm. He seemed to have it in for Beaverbrook, he was again staring heatedly at him. "Lloyd George wrote that Hitler is the greatest living German. He called him the George Washington of modern Germany. One of the gentlemen at this table will surely remember, because he published the shameful tripe in his very own *Daily Express*."

"Prof, you really must excuse Max," said Mr. Churchill. "He could not be expected back then to censor Lloyd George, and we should recognise that old men sometimes write piffle."

Lord Beaverbrook was taking the conversation good naturedly. There was no lapse in his indulgent smile, even during Lindemann's crude rants. In fact he ignored Lindemann as if the professor didn't exist in the room. "Winston," said Beaverbrook, "you know damn well you can count on my newspapers in a showdown. Meanwhile, for pity's sake, you are not on an election stage. Fill that glass!"

The conversation lightened and someone mentioned Adolf Hitler's private life, concerning which only rumours abound. Naturally the know-it-all Lindemann could not keep his mouth shut, he barged in to inform the room that very few women are invited to Hitler's mountain retreat. "People tell me only Mrs. Goering and Mrs. Goebbels are allowed up, and no females work there. All the servants are male. They are SS men in fact."

Someone said the professor was mistaken. Hitler does have a romantic interest. Eva Braun is her name.

"The Braun woman means nothing to the dictator!" This scornful outburst came from Mr. Churchill, causing all eyes to turn to him. Who would have thought the Prime Minister harboured an interest, much less an insight, into the German leader's love life? Mr. Churchill then seemed to check himself. He said in a tamed voice, a tutor's voice, "You must understand, the dictator's appetites lie elsewhere. The foulness of the man springs from every primitive instinct of the human animal. His hunger is for power. He lusts for power. He lives for nothing else."

Cadogan steered the conversation out of the strange place it had lurched. "Hitler does deserve some credit," he said. "He can be congratulated for proving himself the most effective demagogue of the century."

"He can at that," said Mr. Churchill, seizing the opportunity to change the subject. "Of course the perfect material came to his hand. A smashed spirit in Germany. A huge rabble of ex-soldiers. An immature democracy. Reservoirs of resentment and untapped bigotry. His appeal to the volk is not just a cunning part of his program, it has become his identity, his pathology. A tireless rodent of a man, isn't he? Scurrying, always scurrying. Like the frightened rat that coils round his soul. His cutthroats dressed as stormtroopers toil night and day to keep dissent from his fearful ears, his terrified ears. He knows if dissent spreads the same gutter-thugs in the black uniforms will come to hang *him*."

"An agreeable prospect," said General Ismay. "To see that arrogant neck in a noose."

I was astonished to hear Mr. Churchill reply, "He lives on arrogance, does he not, Pug? Arrogance is primal in him. It's his capital. If it should ever be punctured he'd be finished." The comments were almost verbatim what I had said about Hitler in our first meeting, when the PM was testing me. I wrote you about it, Heidi, how inspiration came from your brilliant clay at the very instant I needed it. Mr. Churchill tossed me a glance of acknowledgement which served better than a wink. Imitation can be the sincerest form of flattery. Up to that moment I had not found a chance to say a word.

"Prime Minister," I ventured, "may I transport the discussion to America?"

"The sea lanes are open!"

"I understand you once met Mark Twain in New York."

"I did indeed, seems like a hundred years ago. He – "

"Did the man reflect the books?"

"Ah, those books. Those marvellous emanations of American humour, and of America's sorrow. Is there, can there be, a better penetration of the American soul than *Huckleberry Finn*? Meeting Twain I felt in the company of a giant. He introduced me to a packed hall in the Waldorf-Astoria in Manhattan. I had recently gotten free of the Boer clutches and written some little things about it, which for some reason strongly impressed the Americans. I was famous. I was also twenty-six. There is nothing quite like being twenty-six and famous, I highly recommend it. The master of wit was kind in his introduction and made a perceptive comment about my parentage. He poked me with only a few needles, and kept his best jabs for Britain which he thought had no business fighting the Boers. But yes, to answer your question, the man gleamed and pulsed with all the authority of his reputation. That swarming shock of white hair, the extraordinary blaze in his voice … you could see in him the fountainhead of all his books, an individual as engaging and memorable as any of his characters. I was sure the larger part of the audience had come to see Mark Twain, not this pup Churchill from across the ocean."

I was satisfied with my one sortie into the dinner talk and thereafter kept my mouth shut. My darling spouse left a better mark. Laura Hastings asked her what physical qualifications were involved in Auxiliary recruitment, and Louisa Cadogan followed up with a question about firearms training. Neither could conceal their doubt as to the suitability of the fairer sex for police work. Mary politely dismantled their qualms, then held the table's attention with some potent arguments for wider participation by women in every aspect of public life. My pride in her must have showed on my face like a waving flag. I saw Clementine Churchill give me an appreciative once-over.

After dinner Mrs. Churchill led the ladies to the sitting room while the men joined the Prime Minister in his study. Brandy and cigars awaited. The conversation was now dominated by General Ismay, to whom even Professor Lindemann paid respectful heed. The General spoke about Britain's lack of preparation for war, the prospect of which seems to him imminent. He recited shocking statistics comparing British and German munitions production. The rearmament programs seeded by Mr. Churchill's government will take many months to bear fruit. Meanwhile our island is exposed. Allowing unmilitary passion into his voice the General said, "Gentlemen, we may face a terrible and protracted ordeal. If war comes, it will be a battle of economies and waged primarily in the factories. It will be a race of our labour against theirs. It will be decided by one side producing more guns, more machines, more vessels than the other. At this moment we cannot compete with Hitler's arsenal, much less his smithy. We have grown soft while Jerry has bulked up."

"The more urgent then," said the Prime Minister, "for me to keep the match from the fuse." During the General's grim sermon a darkness had come into Mr. Churchill's face. His eyes were fixed on Ismay but he wasn't seeing him, he was looking inward. At that moment I felt an inkling of his burden of responsibility.

The group dispersed when Mr. Churchill declared a need to discuss confidential matters with the General. As we were leaving he called out, "Alec and Joff, will you be so kind as to join me here in a couple of hours." He looked at his watch. "Let us say at half past midnight?"

We joined him at that time as requested, and I found myself grateful for the afternoon spent with Cadogan. He had effectively rehearsed me for the exhaustive questions of the Prime Minister, whom we found in a harsh demanding mood, and who took copious notes of my answers. I saw up close that Mr. Churchill has a cold-blooded and ruthless side. He can be unforgiving and quite cruel. Of course the nature of the material we discussed could turn any charmer into a beast. Something happened immediately following our discussion which I am much happier to relate. This heartened me tremendously. As Cadogan and I were taking our leave of the PM, I asked if there had been any progress in the matter of Damon Chadwick.

Mr. Churchill and Cadogan exchanged a glance. "Let me show you something, Joff," said Mr. Churchill, and he took me by the arm. "This will interest you too, Alec."

The Prime Minister led us from the study to a small adjacent room which he called his 'nap room', a private space rarely used by the family and even less often seen by guests. It sported a hard-cushioned sofa, rowdy stacks of books and magazines, and a tank of small tropical fish. The dominant feature of the room, however, seizing the eye as soon as the light went on, was the painting over the sofa, some four feet high and extending nearly the width of the wall.

Once you look at the scene in this picture you cannot look away, you must take it in, you are in. A crowd of roughly dressed men is cheering a speaker on a platform. Each man is standing, cheering, raising a fist or waving a hat, while the totality of men is swaying, swaying, like liquid in a vast shuddering bowl. There is delirium in the scene, and a nameless menace. You sense overwhelming belief and commitment, and yet you know that the belief is a delusion, the speaker a liar, the commitment a crime. You know these things only because of an alchemy, mysteriously achieved, between the painter's intent and your own intuition.

The picture took me back twenty years to the early detonations of Damon's genius, of which this canvas was a prime example. I turned to Mr. Churchill and silently bowed my head. Only then did I notice he had renewed his grip on my arm. He did not have to say he is doing everything in his power to bring my friend home.

The clock says nearly five now. Forgive me, great lady, but the adrenaline has ceased flowing and my eyes can no longer stay aloft. I will come back to you … Soon,

Joff

Monday
26th Sept. 1938

Heidi, my dear, the swiftness of events. My god, the reach and weight of them. I am using a carbon again, to save this for Vicky. Years hence I wonder what she will make of these extraordinary days. The invitation from Berlin has startled all Europe. Every capital is waiting on London's response. Eden strongly doubts the wisdom of accepting, while Vansittart is so fiercely opposed he threatened resignation. He says such a meeting can only end in acrimony, leaving the dictator with a final excuse, his ultimate casus belli.

Mr. Churchill broadcasts to the nation in a few hours. He will ignore the misgivings of his Foreign Secretary and the indignation of his Berlin ambassador. He will publicly accept Hitler's challenge *zum Frieden im Gespräch finden* ... to find peace in talk. The day after tomorrow he will fly to Munich.

"Good lord," I said to Bocking-Kerr, who had come down to my room with the news.

"Let's get on with your paperwork," he said.

I looked at him, not comprehending.

"You are going along as the PM's interpreter."

"Jesus Christ."

He said he envied my front seat at an historic meeting, but pronounced himself in agreement with Eden and Vansittart. "I think the PM is making a mistake. Hitler wants to exhibit himself as a man of peace, so he invites to his table the principal patron of Czech obstinacy. Watch, world, as I parley with the British bulldog. Watch, unbelievers, as I work to reverse the winds of war."

My ears were functioning perfectly, I heard every sardonic word, but my mind was elsewhere, contemplating this latest startling eruption in my life. Bocking-Kerr was going on. "The timid and gullible, eager to grasp at any straw, will applaud the ploy. They will swallow it whole. The PM is playing directly into the dictator's hands. How can he not see?"

All *I* could see was that I would be going up in an aeroplane for the first time in my life, amazingly in the service of my country. I would be sitting at a monumental table as an aide to the Prime Minister and meeting the dictator of Germany. Would I be expected to shake Hitler's hand?

"When the conference crashes, Hitler's tanks and dive bombers will be unleashed with the blessing of failed diplomacy. The PM will have made himself an accomplice to German pretext. Are you listening to me, Pearson?"

I snapped out of my stupid reverie. "Sorry, Duncan, of course. Does anybody upstairs support Mr. Churchill's decision?"

"From what I gather only Cadogan at the F.O. is on side with it."

"Will you be accompanying the PM?"

He gave a short laugh. "Not quite. The delegation will be small. Let's get on with your paperwork, shall we. The Nazis are fanatical bureaucrats."

That was this morning. Now, in the late afternoon, I am just back from a quick meeting with the Prime Minister. He asked for a briefing on Hitler's use of language, said he cannot go to Munich unless armed with insights into the dictator's speech patterns. "Does he drop into the vernacular? Does he use profanity? If so, under what circumstances? How does his choice of words relate to his mood? I need to know, Joff. How do we tell when the man is serious and when bluffing? What do we know of his humour? Does the man ever joke? Go into whatever files we have, and give me the salient points, on one sheet of paper. I will need that in twenty-four hours."

My dear Heidi, I had meant to tell you, and my own posterity, more about Chartwell, our Sunday, Vicky's marvellous thank-you to the PM … forgive me. As ever,

Joff

Tuesday
27th Sept. 1938

Heidi,
The balloon has gone up. The delegation leaves for Munich this evening in the name of peace, but this morning you could see the fear of war on every face in the street. With his BBC broadcast last night the Prime Minister only poured petrol on the fire. He spoke directly to the Czechs, assuring them the territorial integrity of their country is not negotiable. He made special mention of the British aircraft exercising in Sudeten skies. His message to Germany was equally unequivocal. "The predations of the Nazis," he declared, "must cease." Mary looked at me askance as we listened. *Is he spoiling for a fight?* He certainly did not sound like a man on his way to a peace-saving conference.

Be happy you live in America. By order of General Ismay, trenches are being dug in the parks and gas masks are being distributed throughout London. There are vans equipped with loudspeakers on the streets of Westminster urging every citizen to get his mask fitted. I had to see it with my own frightened eyes to believe it, but anti-aircraft batteries have been set up in Horse Guards Parade, and dozens more are lining the Embankment.

In a few hours we drive to Heston aerodrome. Our plane will be a Lockheed 14, identical to the aircraft that carried Chamberlain and his cabinet. In an odd way this reassures me. Lightning does not strike twice. The PM's praetorian guard will be Eden, Vansittart, Cadogan, and Colville. Two career men from the F.O.'s Germany desk will be coming along, as well as Reg Huntington, two stenographers, a couple of Yard detectives as bodyguards, and Mr. Churchill's valet Sawyers.

A strange day, Heidi, exceedingly strange. We know from literature about calms before storms, eyes of hurricanes and such, but can we know how the condition feels until we experience it personally? Let me tell you how it feels: mentally itchy, damned eerie. Reminds me in a twisted way of my old bouts with vertigo. Naturally the staff is … I don't know how to describe what the staff is. 'Nervous' does not begin to tell. My colleagues are walking about as if the floors contain hidden snares. Warily, gingerly. They have no idea what is coming.

They have not yet grasped what *has* come. Mr. Churchill's bellicose performance last night remains a riddle. The newspapers this morning were unanimous in their bewilderment. What was he thinking?

Something else about this strange day ... the gods must have had a pint or two. *Look at all those grey faces in Number 10. Shall we stir in some colour?* The German ambassador, von Dirksen, was scheduled for noon. A courtesy call, simple protocol, to bid the PM well on his journey. Apparently von Dirksen speaks some English, but has trouble understanding it. Finally, my chance to interpret for Mr. Churchill! I was summoned at twenty minutes to the hour. The PM instructed me on the attitude he wished to communicate. "Polite defiance, Joff. Amiable intractability. Not a single severe word, but the ambassador must tell his masters my resolve is explicit, entrenched and adamantine." While we waited for the ambassador he asked for a preview of my findings as to Hitler's habits of language and conduct with foreign leaders. I had just started when Miss Pearman came to the door to announce the arrival of a Mr. Karsh. The Prime Minister, annoyed, said, "Mr. Who?"

"Mr. Karsh, sir. The photographer, Yousuf Karsh."

The Prime Minister waved his cigar. "Certainly not today, Miss Pearman."

"He has an appointment to take your photograph, sir."

"Postpone the matter, Miss Pearman. Tell him to come back when the peace of the world is not hanging by a thread."

"Sir, the appointment was booked shortly after your July visit to the palace. The gentleman has come from Canada."

Mr. Churchill glared at me as if it were my fault, probably because he dared not cast such a look at Miss Pearman. "What is the time, Joff?"

I told him.

"We receive the German ambassador in eleven minutes, Miss Pearman. Tell the man I can spare five."

"I shall tell him, Prime Minister."

"Five minutes!" he roared, and got to his feet. "Bloody pain. Come along, Joff. Take up where you left off."

Waiting in the foyer was a short balding spritely man with a cherubic face and dancing eyes. He wore a black pinstriped suit with a white carnation in his lapel. Mr. Churchill was still glowering as he shook hands with him. The little gnome smiled, said in a thick accent (Hungarian? Bulgarian?), "An honour, sir."

His name came back to me. I once read an article about 'Karsh of Ottawa' in a Sunday paper. The talented little fellow is known for coaxing the famous into revealing their best faces. The article came with arresting photo-portraits of Clark Gable and Ernest Hemingway.

"Sir," said the photographer, "the lights have been arranged in the Cabinet Room. If we may …"

Mr. Churchill, none too pleased, took the cigar from his mouth and said, "We have very little time, Mr. Crash. Kindly do your work here, if you don't mind." The cigar returned to his mouth, the sceptical glower remained on his face. The photographer's astonishment immediately gave way to tolerance, then equally quickly to resolve. He bolted for the Cabinet Room and returned in about thirty seconds, composure unruffled, with a camera in one hand and a flash device in the other. He placed both articles on Miss Pearman's desk and with fastidious elegance connected them with a long-wired plug of a sort I had never seen. He turned and thrust the flash into my hands. "Thank you, sir," he said, ignoring my widened eyes. He maneuvered me into position with a no-nonsense grip on each of my arms. "Please stand here, yes, like that. Hold the flash like this, yes, like that. *Do not move.*"

The little man from Canada was radiating authority like a surgeon in an operating room. His eyes darted about the foyer and stopped on the portrait of Disraeli. He promptly lifted it from the wall and presented it to Miss Pearman, who joined me in dismay. "Mr. Karsh, if you please – !" "Thank you, Madame," he said, then turned his attention to the Prime Minister, who was watching over things like a dyspeptic owl. "I must ask you to stand here, sir," said Mr. Karsh, and he positioned Mr. Churchill (steering him by the shoulders!) to the patch of wall vacated by Mr. Disraeli. "We are ready," he said, taking up his camera. "Can I ask you, sir, to bring your right hand to your hip? Yes, that is you, sir. That is indeed you, sir. That is precisely you. Thank you, sir."

The burst of light from the flash in my hands made me jump. Then another burst came, and another. "Mr Churchill, sir," said Mr. Karsh, "your cigar. May I ask you to put it aside for a moment?"

"You may not," growled the Prime Minister.

A burst of light answered from my hands and in the instant of the flash Mr. Karsh did an inspired thing. He snatched the cigar from the Prime Minister's lips. In the moment of raw Churchillian scowl that followed, the photographer set off another flash and evidently captured what he was seeking. Something near to ecstasy came into his face. "We have it, sir," said Mr. Karsh. "The portrait is done, sir. The portrait is perfect."

How he could know such a thing was beyond me, but so certain was the little man of what he had taken, so vivid the leap in his eyes, I wondered if he wouldn't grab Miss Pearman and start skipping about the room with her. But he remained a picture of dignified satisfaction. "Thank you, sir," he said, calmly returning the cigar to Mr. Churchill. "I believe we have a minute to spare."

"You hail from Armenia, is that right?" rumbled the Prime Minister.

Mr. Karsh beamed. "Armenian by birth, sir, and by luck a citizen of Canada."

"I congratulate you on both counts. Good afternoon."

The German ambassador never arrived. He sent a note of regret, which Mr. Churchill received shortly after the collision with Mr. Crash. The PM intoned the message aloud to me: "'I must inform you that I have been summoned to Berlin on an emergency basis for consultations in regard to the Sudeten annexation conference. My leader and I bid you a safe journey. Kindly accept my sincere and profound etcetera, etcetera.'"

Mr. Churchill swivelled in his chair and looked out the window. "There's a slap in the face," he said, "and us not yet within slapping range. 'Sudeten annexation conference', is it? Like bloody damn hell." He turned back to me. "Thank you, Joff. I will read your findings when our plane takes to the air."

The delegation assembled later in the Cabinet Room. Mr. Churchill arrived last and dressed for bear. With a scarlet handkerchief in his breast pocket, and the chain of his watch like a bracelet on his waistcoat, he looked positively raffish. He briskly questioned Eden and Cadogan about the F.O.'s preparations and satisfied himself that in regard to the federalist solution everyone is on the same page. At that he rose and seemed ready to adjourn, but changed his mind. "A moment," he said, and he scanned the room with chin fiercely lifted.

"You have all read today's newspapers. My remarks of last night appear to have caused some agitation. That was my intent. Despite what you might think, I was not directing my remarks at the Czech people, nor even at the British people. I said what I said for the notice of the military chiefs in Germany. Let them regard me as hot-headed and unpredictable. Let them remember the British squadrons on Czech soil. *Let them think I do not fear war!* Who would gainsay my belief that here lies a means of halting Hitler? Pray, do not forget what Six learned many months after his march into the Rhineland. Namely that he had ordered a withdrawal in the event of French intervention! We must deny the dictator another bloodless victory. The more such success he enjoys, the more uncompromising he becomes – and the less able his generals to restrain him."

"Sir, what of France?" someone asked.

"There is only confusion and fear in France. Daladier and Bonnet crave peace at almost any price. Their refusal to send even a single squadron into Czech skies ratified my doubt of their resolve. That is why I have insisted on a bilateral conference."

"Sir, you speak of the German generals as our hope." This was Bocking-Kerr. "Do you have some private knowledge of their plans?"

"I would be misleading you if I said I did. But I remind you, very few of his generals are Nazis. Many of them despise the little corporal. They could be an ally to reason and the means to exit this crisis. You have read my histories. You all know my abhorrence of the battlefield. The last thing I wish to do is take the British people into another generation-destroying conflict. Having said that, I freely admit we go to Munich at a disadvantage. Germany is stronger militarily. The dictator holds the better strategic cards. The federalist solution is only a uniform of convenience, a proper cap and jacket to wear at the conference. It will not impress Hitler, or deter him. It cannot satisfy his hunger. So I repeat, our aim is to turn his generals. May they take our squadrons, and my refusal to yield, as their counsel."

Mr. Churchill paused and scanned the faces round the table. He stopped briefly on mine, then fixed on Cadogan. "Be assured, however, should the generals fail to restrain the bloodthirsty guttersnipe who leads them" – his eyes and voice, suddenly drained of empathy, sent a chill – "there will be no backing down. I will do whatever is required to save the peace." The room was suspended in silence. Then Mr. Churchill, geniality restored, told us to make our final preparations for the journey and to do so with the faith of the just.

Heidi, I have not taken a sip of alcohol in weeks, so I come by my intoxication honestly. Try to picture your fumbling suitor, the erstwhile Cadbury man and prisoner of Translation, German Section, participating at the sharp end of history's stick. You will be picturing something like a fairy tale turned real, or a folly produced by the distorting mirrors of a funhouse. I am made giddy by the events that have overtaken me, would ravish you like a god if … Forgive me, work awaits. Must focus on it, should excitement allow.

Much love,

Joff

Munich
Tuesday
27th Sept. 1938

11:35 p.m.
Arrived at Oberweisenfeld military airfield, München, after a three-hour flight. Happy to report my knuckles did not stay white the whole way. I found the flying to be comfortable enough, though I could have done with some earplugs for the engine drone.

We disembarked to a row of floodlights illuminating the tarmac. Officials from the German foreign ministry led us between two lines of SS men in black uniforms and white gloves. A formal welcome, certainly not a cordial one. We were whisked to our hotel in black sedans with a formation of motorcycles ahead and a similar phalanx behind.

The German leader has insisted on a brief working lunch as the first meeting tomorrow, just the two principals and their interpreters. It will serve as a get-acquainted meeting, our people have been told. I was in the same sedan as Reg Huntington, who scoffed at the notion. He said Hitler has no interest in a friendly. "The conniving son of a bitch. He will be carefully measuring Winston for the first full dress later."

One of the career men from German Section told us why the schedule is empty tomorrow morning. It may be little known publicly but the German leader is a night person who rises late, and the rumour is he can't think straight before noon.

In the lobby of the Regina Palast Hotel, the barest of ceremony. Foreign Minister Ribbentrop greeted the Prime Minister under a swirl of red banners all screaming with black swastikas. There had been no question of Hitler greeting the delegation. The conference organisers had ensured the Fuhrer and Mr. Churchill would not meet in public. Both leaders have ruled out the idea of appearing in photographs together. I was at the rear of our little pack but heard Ribbentrop say, in his best champagne manner, "Welcome to Munich, Mr. Prime Minister."

"Quite," came a grunt from Mr. Churchill. End of ceremony.

We all gathered briefly in the sitting room of Mr. Churchill's suite.

If I am any judge of anxiety, every member of the delegation, down to the stenos and the PM's valet, are feeling an unbearable tension. The principals around the Prime Minister remain tight-lipped, saying no more than they must, nervous about dropping an inopportune word or appearing defeatist. Only Mr. Churchill maintains a steady aspect of good cheer and confidence. Before we dispersed for the night, he told us a little story.

A man goes to his doctor and says he needs a castration. Would the doctor take him to hospital and perform the castration? The doctor looks at the man as if he's insane. "No, of course not. Impossible. Never!" The man, however, insists. He insists so passionately that the doctor finally agrees to perform the castration. The next day, in hospital, hours after the operation, the man comes awake. In the next bed he sees another patient, moaning in great pain. He asks him, "What are you in for?" The patient replies, "I've had a circumcision." "That's the word I was looking for!"

Most of the laughter was forced. Only the Prime Minister's aide, Jock Colville, gave a great shout of uncontrived mirth. After every member of the delegation received a thank you, handshake and goodnight from Mr. Churchill, we went off to our rooms only a little less burdened.

This little notepad with carbons will remain in my pocket until we leave Germany. We have been told never to leave any conference papers unattended in our rooms. My own documents relate to nothing more earth-shattering than briefing notes on Hitler's conduct in private conversation and lists of his favourite expressions. Apparently he has a tendency to call people *Scheisskerl* … shitheads.

Despite the PM's best effort a few minutes ago, I am not feeling any amusement. Tension rather, like everybody else. And like everybody else I need sleep. The clock is nearing twelve. Goodnight, diary. Goodnight, Heidi.

Munich
Wednesday
28th Sept. 1938

11:30 a.m.

Back in my room after a short meeting in Mr. Churchill's suite. He wanted a final word with the delegation before the talks begin. Eden and Vansittart flanked the PM, Cadogan stood behind. The rest of us took the chairs and couches. Sawyers too was there. He stood with the Yard men and made as if he was guarding the door.

Mr. Churchill showed no sign of the blithe humorist from the night before. "A few words before these deliberations begin," he said, his voice sombre, his jaw set. "Make no mistake about why we are here. We are doing our duty at a cardinal moment in history. We will not abandon a small country to the rape and bite of a savage neighbour. Upon our shoulders rests the fate of an honest, hardy, freedom-loving people. We will not fail the Czechs. Our resolve will be the armour of their independence. Moreover, as you are all aware, we carry with us the hope and trust of much of the world. We face the Nazi in a way no one has hitherto dared. I do not care to think that some of you are harbouring defeatist notions. Be assured, it has never for a moment been the thought of His Majesty's first minister that we will leave this city of hate, this cradle of Nazi venom, except with our heads held high. Indeed, by our toils in Munich may the name of this history-blighted place be restored to esteem and honour. That is all."

The Prime Minister stood rooted. No one in the room moved.

"Here, here," said Eden. "Take no prisoners, sir," said Vansittart. Then we all, as one, put our hands together and applauded.

It's time …

2:18 p.m.

Mr. Churchill and I just emerged from a two hour meeting with Adolf Hitler and his interpreter. You may imagine my condition. Look at the wobble in my handwriting. We were met with anxious looks from our people when we came out, but Mr. Churchill waved them off. He went directly for a nap!

The German leader is a smaller man than you would think, almost slight in a brown tweed suit. I could have taken him for an estate agent in Suffolk save for the abridged moustache which his bearing keeps from being absurd. You soon see he holds himself with authority, and his eyes are commanding. The thing that surprised me most was his voice, which is deeper than I would have guessed, almost hoarse. In the cinema newsreels we often see him screaming in front of giant pageants, so I was expecting a whiny sound out of him, something shrill or tinny. I still have no idea what he looks like when he smiles. He never smiled.

The Prime Minister and I were led to the meeting by his adjutant, whose knock on the PM's door at the appointed minute came like a blow from Thor. The young fellow clicked his heels smartly when the Prime Minister came out. Across from the door stood two SS men at attention in their fearsome black get-ups. Apparently they have been assigned to Mr. Churchill's protection; they silently follow him everywhere with expressionless faces. One of the Yard men muttered, "Jolly chaps, aren't they?"

In the meeting room Hitler and his interpreter were already seated. Hitler half rose, nodded at the Prime Minister, and sat back down. Mr. Churchill stood behind his chair for a moment and slightly inclined his head. There were no handshakes. I suppose the antagonism these men have expressed for each other over the years rules out any familiarity. Hitler offered a bare crumb of reception. "*Im Namen des deutschen Volkes und des Dritten Reiches, Ich heiße den … Vertreter von England in München Willkommen.*"

I was relieved. The files said the German leader's dialect occasionally betrays his Austrian roots. This was textbook speech however and would not trouble me. "In the name of the German people and the Third Reich," I translated, "I welcome the representative of England to Munich." As Hitler had done, I paused slightly before 'representative'.

Mr. Churchill put on his half-moon reading glasses, fished a pen from his pocket, and busied himself with a note. As he scribbled he replied, "Let us strive in these proceedings to vindicate the greatest hope of the German people, which is to preserve the peace" – and he stabbed an end to his note with an audible period.

I recognised Paul Schmidt, Hitler's interpreter. For years he has been a fixture at the German leader's side. He translated Mr. Churchill accurately enough, though I sensed a tone of caution. Schmidt might have thought, as I did, that Mr. Churchill's comment and little flourish were gratuitous.

Nothing in Hitler's gaze, which had disconcertingly settled on *me*, gave the slightest hint of his reaction. I thought of gamblers at cards and their ability to mislead with slight alterations of the facial muscles. Hitler is a proven gambler and at much bigger things than cards.

White-jacketed waiters served lunch on plain wooden trays. Schmidt and I were not included in the lunch. We were served only bottled water. Just as well, because my hands were vibrating and I might have stuck a fork into my chin. The captain of the waiters stood at attention and announced each dish as it arrived. First came barley soup. Then a plate of greens with tomato and leek, followed by a vegetarian lasagna bulging with spinach. Silence lay heavy in the room as the two men ate. Schmidt and I traded uncomfortable glances, but neither Mr. Churchill nor Hitler appeared fazed; they concentrated on their food. The silence was broken when the dessert of apple strudel arrived. Hitler said his guest had surely noted the absence of wine with the lunch. He explained this as a function of his strict rules regarding alcohol at midday. Mr. Churchill made no reply, only a mmmpphhh sound. From where I sat, to the right and slightly behind the PM, it appeared a crabby look had settled on his face.

With the trays cleared and the door closed on the four of us, Hitler spoke in a quiet tone that did little to hide his contempt. "It astounds me," he said, "that an Englishman would come to my table and presume to speak of 'the greatest hope of the German people', as if he could claim knowledge of their hopes. And not just any Englishman, but the champion of those who have urged nothing but shackles upon the German nation since its rebirth."

Hitler did not look at Mr. Churchill as he said this (nor at me, thankfully), but rather at his own hands which fisted and unfisted in an idiom of coiling and warning. When I was done translating, Hitler added in the same freezing tone: "There is only a single matter of substance to be discussed here. We are dealing with the blood of my people, the *life* of the German nation, and no one will ever again dictate terms to it."

Mr. Churchill removed his reading glasses and sat back in his chair.

He had renovated his crabbiness and his voice was sociable. "Surely our task today should be to put aside our rivalry. Can we not give it a seat remote from these deliberations?"

Hitler was looking at his hands again, which were palms up now, fingers enquiring like a devotee's in church. He sounded almost gracious when he said, "A tragedy, the death of Herr Chamberlain. The British people should know their grief is shared by all Germans."

To this snide detour Mr. Churchill replied dryly, "I am sure our officials in Berlin expressed appreciation for such liberal solicitude."

"A sadder and greater tragedy came after Herr Chamberlain's death," Hitler added. "He was not yet cold in his grave when his successor shattered his legacy." The German leader inclined his head slightly to Schmidt. We heard the interpreter whisper *Ja, mein Führer* to confirm my translation had been accurate.

Mr. Churchill smiled. The briefing notes had warned of Hitler's blunt disrespect. The PM was prepared for churlish intolerance and erratic turns. His smile said that now he had seen it, he believed it.

Hitler was not finished. "I am convinced Herr Chamberlain and I would have avoided the precipice to which his successor has led Europe. A man of conciliation is gone. A reckless warrior swaggers in his place."

The PM said, "Most interesting, what you say about my predecessor. People had an impression of Mr. Chamberlain that it would be easy to cheat him at cards, because it would never occur to Mr. Chamberlain that anyone playing cards with him would cheat."

My counterpart across the table hesitated. Before Schmidt spoke he glanced at me and was given a level look back. His translation kept faith with Mr. Churchill's affront. "*Gut!*" said Hitler, whose face remained a blank mask. "Let us speak without chains," and as if to demonstrate he pushed his chair back and rose to his feet. "I wonder if the Englishman at my table who writes books of history remembers the masssacre at Kaaden in 1919. We Germans remember it like yesterday. We remember it as family. A pack of predators at Versailles had just drawn absurd lines on a map and proclaimed the birth of a state. The Germans of the Sudetenland were caught within the absurd boundaries and did not want to be part of an invented country. They saw it as a betrayal, a reprisal. They marched in protest.

Peacefully, calmly, innocently, they marched. The police, every one of them a Czech, opened fire. Ask the schoolchildren of the Sudetenland. They have not forgotten the seventeen killed, the scores maimed and injured. That was the baptismal experience of my people in what you call … *Czechoslovakia*."

Hitler spat out the word as if it were a pulpy maggot in his mouth. He had paced the length of the room and back. Now he halted behind his chair, arms crossed. He did not look at Mr. Churchill. His gaze was fixed on the wall behind us, on a point somewhere above us. He spoke of how the artificial state dominated and oppressed its despised German minority. The tyranny inflicted upon the Sudetendeutsche was calculated, protracted and brutal. Their aspirations were ignored, their culture insulted, their history erased. They formed a quarter of the population yet use of their language in the civil service was strictly forbidden. Political power was denied them; civil liberties stripped from them. How could the greater German nation have allowed the subjugation to continue for two decades? Because the German nation was defeated, weak, defenceless. "*Nicht mehr!*"

The *No more!* issued like a whiplash. A change came into the room, an electricity not unlike the power in a theatre when an actor enthralls. Here was the Hitler we knew from newsreels addressing stormtroopers under torchlight. In that moment I grasped the root of his appeal … a talent to conjure pure ardour; an ability to breathe flame so as to ignite it in those with no ardour of their own.

We watched the German leader pace back and forth, his arms crossing and uncrossing, his voice by turns low, barely audible, then pitched suddenly shrill as if sprung from a trap. Occasionally he beat the fist of his right hand into the palm of his left. We were pupils, Mr. Churchill and I. This was a classroom and Hitler the instructor. Nothing in the instructor's lecture, however, fascinated so much as his self-absorption. The tremendous arrogance you caught in your clay, Heidi, I was seeing it, feeling it, the colossal conceit, the naked narcissism. Do not misunderstand my mention of the theatre. Hitler is not an actor. The superior air he wears is not only conscious and deliberate, he takes as a given that he is superior. The briefing files had warned, repeatedly and vividly, of Hitler's high-strung nature, his tendency to erupt in rage, but that is not what we were seeing. This was not an eruption, nor was it a rage. There was wrath in him certainly, a steady pulse of wrath, but what we were witnessing was more like a controlled tantrum, an adult conniption. He might have been a man inhabiting an hallucination. Perhaps that's why his speech followed no order, meandered into digressions, became a rambling harangue replete with Nazi boilerplate about sinister influences in London, Moscow, New York. He was oblivious to his listeners; they did not seem to matter. What mattered more than his listeners and more even than what he was saying was that he was saying anything at all, because it was him saying it. He, the Fuhrer of all Germans, exposing lies, correcting history, addressing posterity, erecting Truth. If his screed had a theme it was that the world was hostile to his government because the world had always demonised German exceptionalism. The anti-German illness in the world's spirit had only been stoked by the signers at Versailles. The criminal tumour of Czechoslovakia and the oppression of its German minority were conspicuous symptoms of this antique, ever-renewing sickness.

"*Nicht mehr*! Today I speak for the Sudetendeutsche. They are no longer weak and defenceless, precisely because I speak for them. Do you think I will abandon to serfdom members of the German nation, any members *anywhere* of the German nation? Our Sudeten brothers and sisters must be liberated from the yoke of Czechoslovakia. I, Adolf Hitler, will restore them to their proper home." With that the leader of Germany resumed his chair.

I dared not lift my shirtsleeve to peek at my wristwatch, but it felt like twenty minutes or more since Hitler's pacing and arm-crossing began. He now gazed across the table at Mr. Churchill, though I sensed his eyes were still directed inward.

Throughout the diatribe Mr. Churchill had sat with his elbows propped on the table, fists supporting his chin. Crinkles around his eyes occasionally suggested tremors of amusement. I also heard a few intakes of breath articulating revulsion. The Prime Minister took his turn in a slow, measured voice.

"Herr Hitler, you spoke earlier of my predecessor. It happens that the good Mr. Chamberlain, may he rest in peace, inherited much of his attitude to foreign affairs from his predecessor. You remember Mr. Baldwin, of course. Who could forget a Prime Minister of England who so deliberately and supinely turned invisible in the bright light of international events? When your friend in Rome sent his troops into Abyssinia, Mr. Baldwin kept to the wings of the arena and whispered soft words. He also fiddled a conciliatory tune when German troops marched into the Rhineland. It was a heartening day for many when the reticent Mr. Baldwin took his retirement, but into his small shoes stepped a man for whom we soon learned reticence was next to godliness. The good and decent Mr. Chamberlain, whose demise you are certainly right to mourn, held back and did nothing when you helped your friend in Spain bomb and strafe and slaughter his own countrymen at Guernica. The demonstrations of timid and pious statecraft you came to expect from London gave you a free pass into Austria, a proud country which you have since humiliated and erased from the map. Now you propose to dismember another small state, to achieve ends which can easily be imagined. I am here to tell you that the kinfolk of the German people in the Sudetenland deserve the same freedoms of any people anywhere. I am here to tell you I wish to find ways to satisfy their just grievances and provide them a settlement of which they can be proud. I am also here to tell you this … that the representative of His Majesty's government sitting at your table today is not cut from the same timber as his predecessors."

Paul Schmidt's interpretation impressed me. I wrote a note for Mr. Churchill saying he had no cause to fear his words were being misrepresented. The Prime Minister, without a glance at what I had written, picked up the note, crumpled it, and squeezed it into a tiny ball which he deposited in front of me. A reprimand? An unconscious gesture? He had not missed a beat nor taken his eyes off the German leader.

"I listened with great interest to your … presentation, Herr Hitler. I found it enlightening, uniquely so, though not perhaps in the sense you might wish. Yes, of course we should remember history while we conduct our discussions. I am remembering a good bit of history at this very moment. The world was told after the Great War that Germany would be a democracy, with free institutions and civil liberties for its citizens. For over a decade that was the case. Then came the Nazi hurricane. It rained down cruel and deadly reckonings, swept away freedom in Germany, and installed in its place dictatorship, persecution, militarism."

The leader of Germany held up his hand in a fist. "Order. Employment. Pride," said Hitler, unperturbed. "We revived what your masters fear above all: a Germany aware of its destiny. A Germany guided by a single unwavering will."

"Quite," Mr. Churchill grunted. "A Germany that defied the world by building new capital ships and a submarine fleet. A Germany with an airforce which today boasts of being the most lethal machine of destruction ever devised. There is your pride, not to speak of your sources of employment."

"The plutocrats tremble," Hitler replied, "when Germany finds its spirit and flexes its genius. Your masters would prefer we remain defeated and in a thousand broken pieces."

"If only the genius you speak of were aimed at nobler ends. For five years the greatest ally of your subversion has been the spectre of war. You know the people of the democracies fear another conflagration. They will go to enormous lengths to avoid it, even cling to their sleep while fire alarms sound. They hardly stirred when you came to power, stayed asleep as you began arming, and slumbered on when you marched into the Rhineland. The spectre of war has given you a potent lever, which you have used the way Archimedes said it could be used. You know all this cunningly well."

"What I know," Hitler said, "is that while flights of metaphor may entertain your childish House of Commons, with me they fall to earth and break into pieces. Have you finished, or is your pointless rhetoric to continue?"

"Pray, allow me to say my say, Herr Hitler, as I generously allowed you. You insisted we remember history, so I am remembering it. I promise to be brief."

The Prime Minister was not brief. He recounted, from memory, various assurances and guarantees the leader of Germany had pledged over the last five years. Mr. Churchill cited the date and place of specific speeches, and quoted the German leader's precise words. He then showed how those pledges, each involving a solemn disavowal of territorial ambitions beyond the borders of Germany, had subsequently been belied by events orchestrated from Berlin. The PM then turned to Germany's repudiations of its treaty obligations. In a slow and perhaps deliberately infuriating drawl he described in detail the transgressions committed in the service of Germany's rearmament. The exhaustive itemisation showed that the build-up of the German army, navy and air force, together with the far-reaching militarisation of the German economy, could not rationally be regarded as exclusively defensive in nature.

"Meanwhile your words," said Mr. Churchill, "delivered with your customary fervour, and richly scented with peaceful intent, were reported widely and with great hope. Who can forget what you said in ringing tones in the spring of 1935? Namely that Germany had no wish to interfere in the affairs of its fraternal neighbour, Austria. You said this even while interventions of the most lawless and insidious sort were laying the ground for the disintegration of the Austrian state and its eventual annexation."

As the German leader listened to Mr. Churchill he remained nearly motionless, his eyes set in a sourly indifferent gaze. Surely no one had spoken to him like this in years. Still, he seemed to be regarding Mr. Churchill's bill of indictment as he would an unpleasant but anticipated act of nature. Which only made me realise the truth of what Vansittart and the others had predicted. The Germans are hosting this conference for show. The parley is nothing more than temporary window-dressing. Why else would Adolf Hitler subject himself to a taunting prosecution of his years of glory? The world will never know what these two men said to each other. The world will only know that the Prime Minister of England and the Fuhrer of Germany met and sat together in the interest of preserving peace. Should no settlement be reached, the result for the Germans will represent … mission accomplished. The resort to arms will have its pretext and pardon.

"Upon the conclusion of your brutal Anschluss, Herr Hitler, you said that Germany's union with Austria represented your final territorial ambition. Not a month later, however, having achieved what you described as your life's dream, you began telling the world, as you have just told me, that Germany must come to the rescue of the German-speaking people of the Sudetenland. If, tomorrow morning, Germany marches into the Sudetenland and annexes it, will you again announce that Germany's final territorial ambition has been satisfied, only to begin declaring next week or next month that a German minority in *another* country requires your protection? The German minority in, say, Poland?"

Nothing changed in Hitler's steadily impassive face. His tone remained overbearing as he ignored the insolent question. Instead he said, "I congratulate your masters. They have chosen their mouthpiece with great care. They have sent me a well trained messenger, one who could trick fools into imagining he is not a puppet. He might even persuade the world that his masters adore peace. How they kneel and worship at that holy shrine, those hypocrites, those drinkers of the world's blood. Wasn't it your Jew vampire Rothschild who said the greatest fortunes are made when cannonballs fall in the harbour, not when violins play in the ballroom?"

"I am not acquainted with that probable forgery," Mr. Churchill replied. "I do know my Bismarck, however. He said that anyone who has ever looked into the glazed eyes of a soldier dying on the battlefield will think hard before starting a war."

Ah! For once Hitler's imperious demeanour gave way. His lips curled and he lashed back, "From my supreme forebear I take two immortal instructions. It was he who warned the world that no appeal to fear will ever find an echo in German hearts. He also said the prime goal in life is to *make* history, not merely *write* it."

If score were being kept I would have to award that volley to Hitler.

There came a knock at the door. Paul Schmidt went to open it. The captain of the waiters entered and clicked his heels. He begged his Fuhrer's pardon but he had been charged with asking if any refreshments were required. The stony silence in the room prompted him to bow and turn smartly on his well-practiced heel.

I sensed a feeling of unreality take over the room. No, that's not accurate. What I felt was the full brunt of the pretence and posturing that had governed the room since the moment we stepped into it. Who outside in the waiting world would believe what had taken place here? The leaders of two great nations, supposedly meeting as architects of peace, insulting and lecturing each other?

The second hour was dull by comparison. The two men ceased throwing mud and merely vented their views. It was an exercise in talking past each other. Zero progress was made toward resolving the crisis. But why should I be surprised? The proceedings only further confirmed Vansittart's assessment. The conference is an elaborate parody, a Potemkin facade ...

Must run. That was Jock Colville on the telephone, summoning me to the PM's suite. The full-dress meeting of the two delegations begins shortly.

Munich
Thursday
29th Sept. 1938

6:20 a.m.
The afternoon session yesterday dragged on into the evening. The post-mortem and late dinner in Mr. Churchill's suite took us beyond midnight. When I finally reached my room I could not lift a pen. Actually, the pen is still too heavy …

7:35 a.m.
Better, much better. I slept another hour.
Yesterday seemed interminable. It amuses me to wonder if your newspapers in America are reporting that well-meaning people are meeting in Munich, and that negotiations are taking place. *There have been no negotiations*. What I have seen is total make-believe. Our side may have come with serious intent to reach an accord, but that is obviously not the case with the Germans. They conceived this charade in the interest of producing an impasse. So far they have succeeded. The best we have tugged from them has been frigid politeness, and precious little of that.

In the afternoon meeting Mr. Churchill and Hitler yielded the floor to their foreign ministers. I thought Eden and Ribbentrop would finally come to grips over the key issue. Nothing of the sort happened. Eden spoke first and detailed the federalist solution. Under the proposal accepted by the Czechs but carefully kept secret from the press and public, matters of culture, education, employment, and family law in the Sudetenland will fully revert to the jurisdiction of local freely-elected authority. German will be declared an official language of Czechoslovakia as a whole and henceforth treated and used as such in all government communications. Finally, the amended constitution of Czechoslovakia will recognise the Sudeten Germans as a 'founding people' of the state with their own 'distinct society' within it. The political and cultural autonomy thereby gained by the Sudetendeutsche will fully meet, and in some respects surpass, their stated aspirations for self-determination. Moreover, the process will initiate an evolution of the idea of federalism, and serve as a splendid precedent for how different ethnic and language groups around the world can live in dynamic harmony.

Ribbentrop completely ignored Eden's presentation.

From the German minister's performance, none of us could quite forget his former role as a champagne salesman. The fake smile on his lacquered face bared a smarmy man, and the affected opera of his fluttering fingers only added to the impression. He began by repeating a line we first heard from Ambassador Dirksen, describing the talks as the 'Sudeten Annexation Conference'. Then he gave a speech better suited to a Hitler Youth kaffeeklatsch in a provincial village. His remarks dripped with fawning praise for the vision of the Fuhrer and went on euphorically about the preparations being made for the welcome of the Sudetenland into the Reich. This while notes passed back and forth among the aides sitting behind the principals. Later I asked Cadogan if such hectic futility is the norm at international conferences. He only grimaced at me.

Two hours in, Hitler signaled for his adjutant to accompany him out. Not to be bested, Mr. Churchill called for his Yard detective and said the talks should by all means continue but that he was feeling unwell and needed a lie-down. (I have never seen the Prime Minister looking more in the pink!) That left Eden and Ribbentrop in charge. Eden suggested the delegations drop all formality and simply chat. Ribbentrop agreed. He called for Schnaps. Englishmen and Germans clinked glasses and mingled. The two foreign ministers, who have been acquainted for years, put their heads together. So did Vansittart and Dirksen, while Cadogan paired off with his opposite number from the German foreign ministry. I interpreted for a scrum of aides and Paul Schmidt for another. It appeared at last as if there might be some give and take.

Not bloody likely. In Mr. Churchill's suite later all our people testified to an identical finding. On the central issue our hosts have their feet in cement. At every level of interaction between the delegations the Germans put forward a single proposition in axiomatic terms: *the Sudetenland will become part of the Reich*. No other end point will be acceptable. The members of our delegation who cling to the notion that the intractable German stance may be no more than a negotiating strategy … are deluded. Annexation is the incontrovertible policy of the Reich. If not achieved peacefully, it will have to be achieved by the military option, and no German believes the British will go to war over a matter so remote to Britain's interests. Accordingly, Berlin regards the presence of British squadrons in Czechoslovakia as symbolic, foolhardy and strategically worthless. It remains for the British to recognise that *the Sudetenland will become part of the Reich*. Is there no flexibility in the German position? Of course there is. The Germans will bend over backwards to help Britain put the best face on Anglo capitulation.

The post-mortem in Mr. Churchill's suite ended with Eden and Vansittart openly gnashing their teeth. They reminded the PM of their opposition to the very idea of this conference. Day one had taken us nowhere and they predicted the same destination for day two. Unless we go along with their annexation ambition the Germans will equivocate and vacillate, and land us precisely where we started. We will have achieved nothing and will return home with our tails between our legs. Hitler on the other hand will have his propaganda victory. He will tell the world he has done his best to preserve the peace, that deadlock and the status quo are unacceptable, and that he has been left with no choice but to march. By this time next week all of the Sudetenland could be overrun.

"Prime Minister," said Eden, "we believe Hitler means what he says. None of us think he's bluffing."

"Neither do I, Anthony," said Mr. Churchill. "The dictator has grown so confident, he no longer feels the need to bluff."

"Then what do we offer?"

"Would you feed a venomous snake? The Sudeten Germans deserve autonomy under federalism. We will endeavour to achieve it for them. Beyond that, we offer … *nothing*." The PM's response silenced the room for a moment.

"You must pardon our concern, Prime Minister" – this was Vansittart – "but we feel our side has pulled out all the stops, and to no avail. What is your plan? You said Hitler's generals might turn on him, or at least reason with him. Is there any stir in that direction? Do you have any idea what his generals are thinking?"

Mr. Churchill's cigar had gone out. He relit it with impatience, breeding a cloud of pungent smoke. "My dear Robert, I have to admit we are not privy to the deliberations of the German high command. Despite the best efforts of Six we have planted no agents among them."

"Sir, if German tanks cross the Czech border" – Reg Huntington now, surprising me, because it was not his place to speak – "will you order our squadrons into action?"

Mr. Churchill paused before replying. To Vansittart's question he had answered lightheartedly, but now he surveyed the room with a harsh eye. He did not look at Huntington as he said, "I do not believe it will come to that."

"Prime Minister, what is it going to come to then?" Eden again.

"We are proposing the honourable solution," said Mr. Churchill. "The dictator may go on rejecting it, but the right moment will come."

"Can you tell us how or when, sir?" said Vansittart. "Surely you – "

"*Trust the Prime Minister, will you?*" This came from Cadogan. He had remained silent while the sceptics piled on. His little outburst worked like a whiplash. It chastised the room and ended the discussion. Besides, everyone was famished. We helped ourselves to a buffet wheeled in by the white-jacketed waiters.

A long, long day yesterday. I suspect today will be its twin. I am going down now for a bite, and a gallon or two of coffee.

9:30 a.m.

Ran into Jock Colville in the lobby amid the incessant crowd of correspondents, photographers and uniformed men from what seem a dozen different services. You may imagine the iron net of security that has been thrown over this event. Jock had a newspaper under his arm and invited me to join him for breakfast. He has never shown me much warmth, but he was kind enough to say, "Well done, Pearson. I'm told you were a professional in the Hitler meeting." I thanked him and asked what he thought of last night's ganging-up on Mr. Churchill by his own staff. Colville put a forefinger to his lips and pointed with his eyes. The three men at the next table were having an animated discussion in Swedish, or maybe it was Norwegian. They were evidently reporters. One of them had a notebook out. Colville said brightly, "We can expect some glorious sunshine today, though they say the temperature will be plummeting." Unfolding his newspaper he said in a lower voice, "Take a look at this, will you? My German is sketchy at best."

It was the *Völkischer Beobachter.* The headline covered half the front page. *DIE SUDETENDEUTSCHE STEHEN AUF!* I read the first two paragraphs of the story and whispered, "Jesus Christ."

"Does it mean what I think it means?"

"It's not good."

Last night, in towns across the Sudetenland, armed men wearing ski masks and unmarked uniforms seized public buildings, train stations and airfields. They lowered the Czech flag and raised the swastika. Their broadcasts are denouncing the oppressive Czech state and demanding the incorporation of the Sudetenland into the Reich.

Colville gave a grim laugh and said under his breath, "The Nazi shits. Hand it to them for perfect timing," and he took his leave of me at once. I should think Mr. Churchill is holding an emergency huddle. Today's talks with Hitler begin at two p.m.

Something strange is going on outside my window. A dozen or so people in the Platz, civilians, seem to be holding a vigil. At least I thought it strange (civilians demonstrating? in Nazi Germany?) until a car pulled up to the hotel with a Union Jack flying on the bonnet. The arrival of the car prompted a woman in a raggedy brown coat to step forward from the group and angrily wave a small swastika flag. Ah, a government-approved vigil! From where I stood I could not see the woman's face, but from the fierce way she flailed her precious little swastika she was obviously irate. Imagine if the situation were reversed and some loony bitch in Munich waggled a Union Jack at a Nazi.

On my own until lunch in Mr. Churchill's suite. A blessed hour to put my feet up …

2:15 p.m.

The lot of us are waiting in the conference room. The PM is scribbling notes. Hitler and his party are late. "Intentionally keeping us waiting," said Cadogan. Vansittart added sourly, "Putting us in our place. We are after all the weaker party, the nuisance guest."

Mr. Churchill looked up. "The fly in the ointment, Robert," he amended.

Hitler's adjutant, Heinrich Seibbel by name, lieutenant by rank, just came and went. He's a formidable looking tough with a square jaw, steady eyes, not a hair out of place. His face is so closely shaven you might think someone had flayed off the outer layer of skin. A machine of a man. "The Fuhrer will arrive in two minutes," he announced. He said it in a tone you or I would use to herald the coming of Our Lord. Comical and terrifying in equal measure, these Nazi lickspittles.

Must tell you, the wobble in my hand ... I have it under control. You may serve me spinach lasagna in the presence of world leaders and my fork will stay true. Ah, here comes the sun-god of the Third Reich ...

3:30 p.m.

We are taking a breather. Today's meeting has outdone yesterday's for bad blood and invective. A gruelling initiation for Hitler's new interpreter, a young fellow named Franz Stolter. Apparently Paul Schmidt, Hitler's usual interpreter, has been called away on an urgent family matter.

Mr. Churchill began by holding up today's *Völkischer Beobachter*: "Shame!" he said. He then addressed Hitler as he would an errant schoolboy, saying that Germany has fooled no one and that it has acted like a thief in the night. "The sovereignty of Czechoslovakia has been grossly violated," said the Prime Minister. "Two hours ago, I spoke on the telephone with the President of Czechoslovakia. The good Dr. Beneš tells me that the men wearing ski masks in the Sudetenland are frauds. They are provocateurs, masquerading as domestic insurgents. In fact they are foreign agents, members of German elite units, trained to sow unrest by inciting insurrection. Kindly do me this favour, Herr Hitler, do not attempt to deny your cynical and brutal purpose. As you have done in the past, you have created a crisis in order to justify intervention ... to resolve the very crisis you created."

I must hand this to Hitler, he is a genius of hauteur. Much as he did yesterday, the German leader showed no restiveness. He sat like a granite statue through Mr. Churchill's condemnation. Sharp words, no matter how cutting, fail to affect him. His granite skin deflects all. He laced his reply with stinging sarcasm and his customary contempt. He chided Mr. Churchill for his ignorance and gullibility, and excoriated 'the frightened cockroaches in Prague' for spreading lies.

"Baseless slander," he said. "Vicious propaganda. But what else should be expected from the stinking latrine which is the Beneš government? My visitor from London speaks of facts. I will tell him the most important fact of this immortal day. The hearts of the Sudetendeutsche are beating powerfully. The whole world hears the drumbeat of their cause as the hour of their liberation draws near. Since my visitor adores facts, I will tell him another. The men he is talking about are Sudetendeutsche. They are heroes of the Sudeten people. Not a single German soldier has crossed the border! But does the Englishman at my table think the pride of the German people can be withheld if their brothers and sisters are in danger? Has he asked, has he dared ask, why these men have risen up at this moment of all moments? Their message is unmistakable. *They fear this conference in Munich will fail their just demands.* Now the world knows the weight of trust on my back. Now the world sees the burden I carry. So let the world be warned. The Reich will regard as a crime any use of force by the vermin in Prague against the heroic men of the Sudetenland."

Hitler played the role of injured party impeccably. His denials and threats were delivered self-righteously. As the briefing notes had warned, he is not just a talented liar, not just a serial liar, but a pathological liar. Nothing in his demeanour subtracted from the impression that he passionately believed what he was saying. I have to say, I marvelled at …

I just had a conversation with Hitler's adjutant, Lieutenant Seibbel.

He interrupted my scribbling and asked if he might have a word. I invited him to take a seat. Lieutenant Seibbel's posture in the chair made me think of a restless leopard, coiled and ready to leap. I asked what I could do for him. The Fuhrer, he said, had taken notice of my fluency in *Deutsch* and wished to know my ancestry. I hesitated, not knowing if I should be flattered or frightened. Finally I told him my mother's birthplace, the profession of my father, and the circumstances of their meeting. I saw no harm in revealing these things. He stiffly thanked me and was about to go when I mentioned meeting a Hans Seibbel in London while interpreting for the American ambassador. Was the chargé d'affaires of the German embassy a relation, by any chance? "My brother," Lieutenant Seibbel replied curtly.

"There's a coincidence."

"We are not proud of him."

That left me at a loss for words. He added that the Seibbels have been a military family for generations. He, his father and grandfather severely disapproved of Hans for choosing the soft life of diplomacy.

"Ah," I said. "Do you – ?"

"You Englanders fail to see that annexation is inevitable." The unbidden comment came out of the blue, but Lieutenant Seibbel delivered it like a pertinent part of our conversation. They are real charmers, these people. Never, ever, do I think of them as my mother's kinfolk. How could I, as that would make them mine.

We are going back in …

7:50 p.m.

Yeats had it right, good old W.B. *Things fall apart, the centre cannot hold.* When the conference reconvened after my weird encounter with Lieutenant Seibbel, things fell apart almost instantly. Of course the conference never had a centre to begin with.

Hitler began by flatly declaring what tomorrow's communiqué will announce. "The definitive aspect of the statement will calm the world's anxieties," he said. "The wording will leave no room for misinterpretation." He instructed Ribbentrop to read the opening lines.

The former champagne salesman sported a fresh carnation in his lapel. He held a typed sheet in front of him and recited his lines with the comportment of a seasoned butler in a manor house. "'The parties to the meeting at Munich have achieved an historic settlement to abolish conflict in central Europe. The agreement reached by the leaders of Germany and Great Britain answers to natural justice, the logic of geography, and the longstanding aspirations of the German-speaking population of the Sudetenland. In accordance with this covenant to assure everlasting peace, the orderly transition of the Sudetenland to the administrative, legal and political authority of the Reich will commence within forty-eight hours and proceed with all due speed'."

Hitler followed up this outrage with an obscure reference. The meaning of it escaped me, but his tone made it a gibe. "The representative of England is discovering, to his discomfort I think, that Europe is not a house on Sidney Street."

Mr. Churchill's answering laugh made an unkind sound. "Firstly, if I may," he said in a slow drawl which he knew would annoy his host, "I should point out that no meeting of minds has yet occurred in this room. No one can possibly foretell the content of tomorrow's communiqué. On this side we reject the counterfeit assertion put forward by the Foreign Minister. Secondly, I would be inclined to congratulate the German leader's researchers for arming him with history*, if only they armed him more carefully. They might then keep their leader from embarrassing himself with inept analogies."

The hesitant Stolter stumbled briefly. He made too obvious an effort to mitigate 'embarrassing' and 'inept', though his translation was accurate enough. Hitler paid close attention, then pretended he hadn't heard a word.

"The truth must agitate England's masters," he said. "They will never again set a heavy foot on Europe. Their days as the continent's policemen are ... no one smokes in my presence!"

Mr. Churchill had taken a cigar from his pocket and put it in his mouth.

"Pray, do continue, Herr Hitler. I have arrived without a match."

This conference has taught me again, and the lesson always seems learned for the first time, that men in high office, even leaders of countries, can regress and de-evolve ... into schoolboys. I do not acquit Mr. Churchill of the charge. A mischief lives on in him that has never quite transitioned from childhood.

Hitler was not pacified by Mr. Churchill's lack of a match. The German leader's thin lips curled. He was incensed. I thought maybe now we would witness the vile temper, table-pounding and brow-beating of guests that the briefing files had so prominently predicted. But no, Hitler spoke only a single nasty word, and it came out like a casual observation. He said, "*Scheisskerl.*"

"Shithead," I translated.

Mr. Churchill gave a short, genuine laugh. "I am privileged to be the leader of a free society," he said. "My fellow citizens have long

---

Editor's Note: Hitler was referring to an event that had taken place early in 1911 on Sidney Street in the heart of London. A gun battle broke out between a gang of criminals and the Metropolitan police. Winston Churchill was Home Secretary at the time. He rushed to the scene where, it was later claimed by his critics, his trigger-happy manner and interference in operations led to the avoidable death of a policeman and the destruction by fire of a three-storey house. – *Maxwell Lowell* since taught me to endure every manner of insult. Unlike yourself, Corporal Hitler."

Again, I was in a schoolyard. Among juveniles.

Hitler said to Ribbentrop, "*Die Juden in England geben Pisse zu ihren Diener, die es als Wein trinken.*"

Ribbentrop tittered.

"The Jews of England serve piss to their servants," I conveyed, "who drink it like wine."

Eden coughed into his hand. Mr. Churchill took a drink of water and aimed a modest belch at the ceiling. My young counterpart Stolter appeared unnerved.

"Ah, the Jews," said Mr. Churchill. "The sinister plotters responsible for every grievance. Your cruelty toward the Hebrew race has left a stain upon German honour that will take generations to wipe clean."

Eden said, "Gentlemen, I think a short recess may be in order."

"*Natürlich,*" said Ribbentrop.

"No," said Mr. Churchill. "I think not."

Eden had risen halfway from his chair. "Prime Minister?"

Mr. Churchill cleared his throat. He said to Hitler, "We require a private meeting."

Eden said again, "Prime Minister?"

"*Er will ein privates Gespräch,*" Stolter said to Hitler.

"*Nein,*" I intervened, and I addressed Hitler directly, in German: "Mr. Churchill said a private meeting is *required.*"

Stolter's eyes flashed. "*Mein Fuhrer, das ist eine andere Übersetzung.*"

"My leader, that is an alternative translation," I conveyed, now holding Stolter's eyes.

Mr. Churchill spoke again to Hitler, his voice cheerless, stoic, reluctant, as if he were attending to a lamentable task. "A private meeting," he said, "would be most useful."

"*Ein privates Gespräch wäre sehr nützlich sein,*" Stolter translated, correctly.

Hitler waved his hand as if at a fly. "*Ich sehe keinen Sinn.*"

"I see no point."

Mr. Churchill remained impassive. He fished from his pocket a small notepad. Then he patted his suitcoat pockets with some frustration. "I have misplaced my pen," he said. "Anthony, may I borrow your pen?"

Eden could not conceal his surprise. He handed his pen to the Prime Minister. Mr. Churchill swiftly scribbled a single word. He then tore the paper from the pad, folded it in half, then in quarters. He pushed the tiny square of paper across the table to Hitler. "Pray, reconsider," said the Prime Minister.

Hitler muttered something in annoyance, reached for the impudent note and opened it. For a long moment he stared at it. None of the people sitting on our side of the table would later claim to have seen any change come into Hitler's face. If you were to ask me, I would tell you that no change whatever was discernible. He looked up and his eyes betrayed nothing, no unease at all. His hands, his posture, the permanent gash of his thin-lipped mouth ... no change, not a tremor. Yet I was sure that whatever the Prime Minister had scratched onto that piece of paper had indeed triggered something significant inside Hitler, and I say this precisely because the dictator remained undeniably calm. His will is iron, they say, and I believe I was seeing strong evidence at that moment. He was exercising every bit of his mettle to appear self-possessed.

Hitler calmly slipped the little square of paper into a pocket, and said, "Nine o'clock. Interpreters only." Then he rose and left as if summoned by an invisible blaze, his retinue scurrying behind him like a pack of baffled firemen. Ho!

The British delegation kept to their seats. We had silence in the room save for the sound of Mr. Churchill's busy pen. He was scribbling a note to himself. Finally Vansittart went to the door, closed it, and asked: "What just happened, Prime Minister?"

"Surely you noticed. The dictator and I have decided to hold a private conversation."

"Sir, may I ask what you wrote in the note?"

"That must remain a matter between myself and the dictator."

"Sir, – "

"It would be best if you left it there, Robert."

Mr. Churchill made no effort to sort out the confusion. "I have materials to review," he said. "If you please, I must not be interrupted." He called for his Yard man and went alone to his suite. I have glanced at my watch about a hundred times since. Nine o'clock approaches.

The window too keeps drawing my attention. The vigil in the *Platz* goes on. Goebbels, the propaganda minister, came to Munich for the conference and decided to stage a sideshow for the foreign press ... feed the gathered correspondents an extra slice of Potemkin pie, as it were. *Look, free expression in Germany!* The Nazis do not seem to care that their antics deceive no one. The demonstrators have placards now, which they are shouldering like weapons. They may only be Party dupes and hangers-on but they do give the impression of being angry. Angry people have always fascinated me. The private meeting begins in ten minutes ...

11:20 p.m.

We are done. The conference has ended. This evening, in the space of less than an hour, the situation ... turned.

When Mr. Churchill and I entered the meeting room a few minutes late, Hitler was already seated with Stolter at his side. I thought the German leader was now looking a tad older than his forty-nine years. Mr. Churchill nodded briskly. He had obtained a rosebud for his buttonhole. He remained standing as he spoke.

"I am delighted to have your attention, Herr Hitler. I trust it will remain undivided. There should be no doubt in your mind as to the position of His Majesty's government, in the name of which I will now act." The emphasis Mr. Churchill put on the word 'act' made it come down like a hammer. The young Stolter's nerves were showing. Perspiration beaded his forehead though the room was by no means overheated. To his credit, the pressure he was feeling had no effect on his competence. He deftly softened Mr. Churchill's hammer while adhering to its thrust.

Hitler sat absolutely still, eyes fixed on Mr. Churchill. I thought yet again of your bust, Heidi, the obdurate wedge you made of the dictator's face, the sense of absence you caught in his eyes. That absence, I think I know it for what it is. Not a bit of simple human care resides in the man. He has no room for compassion of any kind because he is filled with bile, with a hate deep and potent enough to inspire others to burn books in city squares, unleash dogs on elderly ladies, snuff out the lives of Morris Gelfmann's wife and sons ...

I felt homesick and wanted Mary and Vicky in my arms.

Mr. Churchill stayed on his feet. He hooked his thumbs into the armholes of his waiscoat. He did not promise to be brief. "Before I come to my point, Herr Hitler, let me tell you that I have come to understand your methods. Indeed, it would not be an exaggeration to say I have studied your methods. You have succeeded time after time by making demands which you know to be unacceptable, so that crisis results. At the moment of supreme crisis you engage in brinksmanship, because you are a gambler. But you are a crafty gambler. You fix the deck. Here, in this room, we have reached a moment of supreme crisis. This crisis, however, is different from those you have manipulated earlier. This time you are not dealing the cards."

Mr. Churchill took his seat while Stolter caught up with the translation. The young fellow was doing his job well, though he had to be appalled and frightened by the circumstances. I felt for him. He was probably not long out of university.

"During the years previous to my taking office," Mr. Churchill said, "it can be said with sad truth that the political authorities of my country failed in their duty. They were not alone. The failure was general among the democracies, which watched as the government of a great nation in the centre of Europe ran roughshod over the liberty of its own people. The good and the just stood by while one of the most callous and repressive regimes in history made itself stronger and stronger. The democracies pitifully failed to proclaim and defend the nobler expressions of mankind. This does not mean however that all agencies of the democracies were asleep. Some went on with their proper work. At least one vital branch of His Majesty's government did not reflect the langour and stupor of its political masters. For that the civilised world will, I am sure, give thanks for a long, long time to come."

Mr. Churchill sat back and studied his fingernails. I listened closely to Stolter's interpretation and heard nothing amiss. Hitler had crossed his arms. His eyes were unmoving. My impression was that only a part of him was there and listening. He was commanding himself to ignore the ugly unpleasantness, block it out, treat it like a wound incurred in battle, a transient setback, endurable, survivable.

Mr. Churchill laid both his hands on the table, palms pressed down, fingers splayed, and resumed the narrative he had obviously rehearsed and which he was delivering with muted satisfaction. "The foreign intelligence service of His Majesty's government," he said, "has kept files on the Nazi cancer since the early 1920s. As you can imagine, the files teem with references to yourself, Herr Hitler. For those entrusted with the duty to chart potential danger to His Majesty's interests, how could a malevolent rabble-rouser in Germany not be a focus of fascination? Increasingly so, as his shrill oratory and calls for vengeance won him prominence, and his intrigues – a polite term for lies, intimidation and murder – carried him and his private army of gangsters to supreme power and foul tyranny."

The young Stolter was visibly shaken. For a moment he appeared lost and without a compass. He spoke to his Fuhrer in a low tone which I could not entirely make out. Still, I grasped that he wished to be excused from repeating the unspeakable insults the British visitor had just uttered. Hitler, his voice laced with acid, put the boot to the poor fellow. "'Idiot boy'," I conveyed in a whisper to Mr. Churchill, "you will tell me *exactly* what the British dog-clown is saying'."

Stolter obeyed, faithfully and accurately, through the rest of the meeting. What he was obliged to hear and translate will likely haunt his memory forever.

Mr. Churchill resumed his description of the British government's intelligence files. For years before and after the Nazi imposition of dictatorship, the files grew thick with reports about Hitler the ranting bigot, Hitler the politician on the rise, Hitler the tyrannical leader of his country, Hitler the aggressor on the global stage. Very little information, however, came in about Hitler's personal side, his inner life. Numerous entries said this was so because the lifelong bachelor had ordered his privacy to be guarded assiduously. Furthermore it was speculated that all documents and papers pertaining to his past had been exhaustively ferreted out and destroyed by an elite task force of the SS and Gestapo.

"Sometimes the most interesting thing about a man is not what we know about him," said Mr. Churchill, "but what we do not know about him … and what rumours are spread and believed about him."

Mr. Churchill went on to say that when a man makes a mark on history the like of which Adolf Hitler has made, people are naturally inclined to wonder how he conducts himself when not bathed in public light. What interests does he pursue? Who are his intimate friends?

How does he amuse himself? If answers to these innocent questions remain so scarce as to be non-existent, people might tend to think there are features of his character he prefers to keep concealed. For the intelligence service of His Majesty's government this particular notion in the case of Adolf Hitler opened a potentially useful avenue of investigation.

"After all," said Mr. Churchill, keeping his tone level and understated, "here was a man of whom little was known save that his appetite for power brooked no inhibitions. In view of that, should there be any reason to presume he would act differently in regard to his personal gratifications?"

Mr. Churchill then mentioned a topic that caused the interpreter Stolter to stiffen and go pale. It was only rumour, Mr. Churchill said, but a story had circulated that Hitler once had a romantic obsession for his niece, Geli Raubal. Apparently Hitler could not abide the girl spending time with other men. He held the pretty young Geli so close she felt imprisoned. When the little bird tried to break free of her cage, Hitler's lethal jealousy could not abide it – he had her killed. One bit of gossip said that Hitler himself strangled Geli with a bullwhip during a fit of rage.

"Can the story be fact?" said Mr. Churchill. "I don't know, but I would not hastily disbelieve anything said of the man whose documented list of murdered enemies nominate him to be the Robespierre of our times."

While my counterpart across the table haltingly translated, Hitler held the PM's gaze with aloof contempt. When Stolter came to 'strangled' and stammered over 'bullwhip' I heard for the first time a burst of laughter issue from Adolf Hitler. The eruption was a hoarse guffaw but too quickly followed by a lashing snarl – *"Mein Gast ist ein Kasperl!"* My visitor is a buffoon! – for it to be taken as an authentic reaction.

"What I do know as fact," said Mr. Churchill calmly, "is that one of your closest associates since 1919 was a man named Ernst Röhm. An interesting figure in your life, this Röhm. I would even say towering. He inspired, shaped and built the S.A., your personal army of thugs. The S.A., thanks to your friend Röhm, proved on many occasions indispensable to the success of your vicious schemes. We shall return

436

in a little minute to Ernst Röhm. First, this visiting buffoon from Britain, this unrepentant clown, wishes to make a solemn point."

Mr. Churchill pushed his chair back and rose to his feet. A handkerchief materialised in his hand, which he used to clean and polish his reading glasses. Then he began pacing as he spoke. "Those who study you and the barbarism of Nazism have come to understand your motives. Yesterday in this room I heard you pronounce a fantastic claim as if it were gospel truth. I heard you accuse the world of doing to Germany what in reality the world has always done to the Jews. I recall your words to the letter. You said German exceptionalism has always been demonised, and that this 'antique, ever-renewing sickness' is today prevailing in hostility to your government. What tripe and nonsense. The pronouncement did not surprise me however, because it captures so exactly the unwarranted blame and malicious retribution that you and your henchmen are inflicting upon the Jews. It goes hand in hand with your other inversions of reality. The ferocity, for example, of your persecution of the homosexual … "

Mr. Churchill stopped pacing and stood behind his chair. Across the table, the German leader appeared composed, maintaining an iron serenity, as he inclined his ear to Stolter.

"The homosexual," said Mr. Churchill. "The very word comes freighted with aspersion and evokes the alien. It causes tremors, does it not, Herr Hitler, though the tremors may stay deep and unseen? In my country the word can hardly be mentioned in polite company, and in the Nazi hell it means exile to the camps and hard labour, or worse. Curious then …"

Mr. Churchill's pacing began anew.

"… that your old friend and associate Ernst Röhm was a practitioner of sodomy and pederasty. Röhm, the man who dressed human scum in brown uniforms and taught them to march under your bloodthirsty banner. Curious, that Röhm should have been a notorious lover of well-muscled men and lean young boys. I wonder, does the inclination for which he was so well known put into perspective the brazen incidence of male nudity in Nazi statuary? Forgive my speculation, it is neither here nor there. What is most interesting to me are the events of June, 1934."

Mr. Churchill's voice had shed its understated tone and taken on a hard, prosecutorial edge. His pacing continued. "It was in that month of that year when you ordered the execution of your friend. You had Ernst Röhm and his lieutenants arrested and shackled and shot down like wild dogs. The killing went beyond Röhm's inner circle, far beyond. How many men did you execute during those summer days in 1934? Men who had stood shoulder to shoulder with you when you were nothing, and who helped you climb from nowhere. Was it a hundred men? They were once comrades of yours, but no matter. Friendship, comradeship, fidelity, these are concepts drawn from weakness, are they not? Was it two hundred men, shot and clubbed to death? If it were a thousand I would not disbelieve it. As I have mentioned, Herr Hitler, I would not disbelieve anything said of you. That is because I understand how you regard yourself. When you look in the mirror you see a driving force of history. It was nothing for you to order the deaths of your former comrades, because they were getting in the way of your destiny. They were getting in the way of history. You ordered their deaths not because, as you claimed, the sodomite Röhm and his legions of scum were planning a coup. Not because the pederast and his catamites had conspired against you in any way. You eliminated Röhm for a purely practical reason. You required the loyalty of the regular German army. You had seized power only a year earlier, and your grip on the country remained tenuous. You needed the allegiance of the Prussian officer corps."

As Stolter did his work of interpretion in a voice grown husky from anxiety, Mr. Churchill slowly tramped back and forth on the carpeted floor of the conference room. When he resumed, he said that without an oath of loyalty from the old guard of the German military, Hitler could never have hoped to achieve his totalitarian dream.

"Röhm stood in the way of that oath. The German military symbolised an aristocratic tradition. It embodied a heritage of values and standards. It regarded itself as the ultimate guardian of the Fatherland's morality. You understood that the German military would never swear loyalty to you so long as the scum-filled S.A. represented a competing army, and so long as a proud pervert marched at its head. You well knew that the days of Ernst Röhm's usefulness were over and that he had become a dangerous liability. How right you were, in hindsight, to destroy him. I need only remind you of your almost fatal embarrassment over

438

the Blomberg affair. Or point to the laws on German books governing sexual indiscretions that your government enforces with conspicuous zeal."

Mr. Churchill took to his chair again and scribbled a note while Stolter finished interpreting. My young counterpart had begun translating the PM's harsh expressions into noticeably moderate German, but I saw no reason to intervene. Soften the onslaught as he might, it remained an onslaught.

"Geli Raubal and Ernst Röhm," said Mr. Churchill, "are gone and largely forgotten. They cannot pose any danger to you now. I will delay no longer in introducing the name of a man who can. I turn now to the matter of ... Anton Kohrbach."

At last a movement, a tic, in Hitler's granite exterior. How we forget that while men may command vast armies and whole nations, while they may rise to be colossal in the eyes of the world, they are in the end still frail minuscule flesh in the eyes of God.

"I daresay I could end my presentation at this moment," said Mr. Churchill. "Rather than venture into the muck and stench of depravity, I believe I could proceed at once with your willing consent to a fair settlement of the Sudeten crisis. Is that not so, Mr. Hitler? Is it not so precisely because the name Kohrbach reminds you of events, deeds and unspeakably foul crimes of which you have been surprised to learn I am aware?"

During Stolter's translation, Mr. Churchill sat back with his hands in his lap. He had not expressed himself with undue indignation but with the methodical passion of the prosecutor who was simply attending to his work, the better to impart his deadly resolve. Receiving no answer, Mr. Churchill went on.

"We have come to know the dealings of the man Kohrbach through various channels. Principally we possess pages from his diary, the material of which could never be published under the aegis of civilisation. The diary is, as I am certain you are dreading to learn, a stubborn record of events. It contains dates, places, names. It is a chronicle of descent. I would say of the descent of men to the level of beasts, but I would not want thereby to insult blameless animals. I should rather say of the descent from morality to the most foul pits of obscenity. History has given us pharoahs and tyrants with no affection for simple decency, and God knows literature has given us monsters in human form. Still this diary shocks, because it was written in the twentieth century on the continent of Europe, and it shocks because it concerns men who today guide the destiny of eighty million people. Shall I go on, or can we now agree to implement a federalist solution to the Sudeten crisis?"

Hitler made a steeple of his hands and laid his chin on it. Not a bit of colour enlivened the stubborn anvil of his face. He would not give Mr. Churchill the courtesy of acknowledgment, at least not yet. Rather he looked in my direction and ignored Mr. Churchill's question.

"In addition to Kohrbach's diary," Mr. Churchill continued, "we are in possession of photographs of letters written by people who have … interacted, with this person. We know very little, in fact almost nothing, about the background of Anton Kohrbach. Fortunately this is irrelevant. We have no interest in who Kohrbach is or was, but great and surpassing interest in whom he served, and in what capacity he served them. These things he tells us in stomach-churning detail. He also tells us that the Chancellor of Germany, the mighty Fuhrer of all the Germans … need I go on?"

For Stolter's sake, for the sake of the four of us in the room, I hoped that Hitler would concede he had heard enough, but no, he maintained a clinical gaze that signaled only condescension and imperishable contempt. I can only surmise he wanted to learn the worst. This he did.

Over the next few minutes Mr. Churchill's recitation of events taken from the Kohrbach diary had the effect of causing the young Stolter to fall again into a stammer. Now and then my counterpart had difficulty finding German terms for activities in which very few people of any language have engaged, and from which any honourable mind would recoil.

"I had never felt myself spiral down the circles of an earthly hell," said Mr. Churchill, "before learning of certain events from the Kohrbach diary. You had done well to erase your past, Mr. Hitler. One might wonder how many people you ordered killed to keep it erased, but forgive my aside. You are determined to know all that I know. Very well, I will tell you. I know that never in your years as the supreme leader of the German people did you cease being your essential self. You did not erase the corrupt soul which locates Eros in sadistic adventure, and which drives the sexual impulse to extremes that ordinary men cannot conceive and would never wish to conceive. You did not erase the foul hungers in your soul not only because you could not, and not only because you would not, but because the opportunity for you to indulge those hungers had only grown with your position and authority. On seventeen occasions of which we are aware, on dates and in cities that correspond to your published agenda, you gathered with intimates and participated in activities which did not simply ignore the rules of civilised conduct but which defied and laid waste the idea that rules should exist. I can only gather from the atrocities you committed that literature does not have a monopoly on men who, in the name of a god named Arousal, take pleasure in rituals of flagrant terror inflicted on unwary innocents. You have caused a death of the good, Hitler, a death of the clean. You have degraded humanity. The corruptions which you and your accomplices have performed stink to high heaven."

Mr. Churchill cleared his throat. He took his eyes off Hitler. He turned to the young interpreter, Stolter, and waited as those final blazing remarks were conveyed to the dictator. Then: "I am sorry, Herr Stolter," said the Prime Minister, "that pure chance brought you to this room on this dismal occasion. Thank you for the service you have performed. I pray that destiny will be kind to you. May your career and life take the paths you desire and deserve."

As I translated these remarks for the ears of Adolf Hitler, Mr. Churchill kept a kindly eye on Stolter. Then the Prime Minister turned back to his host. "I am aware," he said, "that revelation of the Kohrbach materials in the foreign press would not achieve my purpose. You would characterise the explosive diary as an obvious counterfeit, a cynical fabrication. I am aware too that your grip on power within Germany is more than sufficient to keep these materials from the attention of the German people. It is not to the German people I am looking for the salvation of peace, however, but to your officer corps. Let me be clear. Unless the British and German delegations at this conference reach an amicable settlement of the Czech crisis on the basis of the federalist structure we have proposed, copies of these materials will be delivered to several score of the highest officers in your military. You have not succeeded, thank God, in annihilating every vestige of honour in the Prussian soul. I invite you to speculate. What do you think will happen when your officers, many of whom remain uncorrupted by Nazi ideology, learn of your ... moral degeneracy?"

The young Stolter was sitting nearly limp in his chair. He translated 'moral degeneracy' as *Indiskretionen*, indiscretions. I could not let that pass. "*Nein, nicht Indiskretionen*," I said directly to Hitler, "*aber moralisches Verfall.*"

The word *Verfall*, degeneracy, hung in the air for a moment. I had broken a cardinal rule of interpretation. I put emphasis on the word though Mr. Churchill had spoken it quite plainly. Meanwhile the steady eyes of Adolf Hitler looked directly into mine.

"I will tell you what your officers will do once they absorb these materials," said the Prime Minister. "They will have seen into the heart and soul of the man who claims the mantle of the supreme German. They will be shamed, and will require expiation of their shame. They will remove a gargoyle from the throne of dictatorship he has constructed on a mountain of lies and corpses. They will similarly dispose of every ranking member of the macabre gang who have their hands round the necks of the German people."

Mr. Churchill paused, the dyed-in-the-wool thespian!

"That would be a happy day for justice. My certainty, however, is that you would lash out at once, while you still could, to save your skin. If finally cornered you would look to Samson for inspiration. You would not hesitate to bring down the temple if you cannot rule it in your brutal way. I believe you would order an immediate invasion of Czechoslovakia to divert attention from the scandal. I am therefore prepared to forgo the incitement of rebellion among your officer corps. In return I must have a bloodless resolution of the Sudeten crisis. Do you think we can agree to achieve that resolution before we leave this room this night?"

I cannot overstate a remarkable feature of the German leader. His sangfroid is incomparable. The control he exerts over the muscles of his face attests to his iron will. The only physical response I saw in him was a slight quiver of his right shoulder. He trained a cold gaze on Mr. Churchill. I felt that he had long since digested and accepted the new reality, and had spent a good portion of his time in this room conducting his calculations. Why fight a doomed battle? Better to

442

limit one's losses. He felt no noose around his neck. *What doesn't kill me makes me stronger.* The fanatical, the messianic, the delusional, the pathological – they will find succour and a way forward in whatever circumstances confront them.

"State your terms," said Hitler, his bravado of disdain yet intact.

"A declaration signed and published by ourselves," said Mr. Churchill, "to the effect that autonomy will be achieved for the Sudeten Germans under the umbrella of the proposed Czechoslovakian federalist structure. I will go so far as to allow the declaration to read *liberating* autonomy."

Stolter winced as he translated the last bit. It was difficult to make Mr. Churchill's offer sound like anything more than a bone thrown to a kicked dog. For a kicked man, Hitler replied with impressive equanimity. "I will accept your terms, with two conditions."

"I am listening."

"You were to remain in Munich until Sunday. You will not remain. You will leave tomorrow immediately after our work is done. Secondly, the text of the declaration will not be released tomorrow. It will be released Monday, at noon."

To my bewilderment Mr. Churchill at once acquiesced to these authoritative pronouncements. "I understand your conditions," he said. "You may consider them accepted."

"The actions of my government in the days and hours leading up to Monday noon," said Hitler, "should not be regarded by yourself as a breach of any commitment I have made."

"I understand you completely," said Mr. Churchill, again to my puzzlement. Then, to my astonished joy, he added, "There is one other matter I wish resolved. Your government is holding an Englishman at Spandau, the painter Damon Chadwick."

"Chadwick is a – "

"We both know what Chadwick is! I must insist upon his release and immediate return to England."

Hitler was containing a seething anger. Not till this moment had we seen him go wobbly. He said in a voice that betrayed a tremor, *"Nicht ohne diese Bedingung: Dann muss ich Baumann, und Vogt ebenfalls."*

I translated, "Not without this condition: I must have Baumann, and Vogt as well."

Mr. Churchill nodded his consent, baffling me yet again.

"Alexander Cadogan will arrange the matter with your Foreign Minister," said Mr. Churchill. "I believe we are now done. I suggest we direct our staffs to meet early in the morning to draft the declaration."

It was Hitler's turn to nod.

"I propose we call it the Munich Agreement," said Mr. Churchill. "Identifying where the peace of Europe was preserved may help salvage the honour of the city where Nazism was born."

Hitler ignored this final knife. He stood, his icy composure seemingly undamaged. As he had done too often for my liking during these two extraordinary days, he fixed on me. "I will instruct my staff," he said. Then he left the room without a sideward glance. The interpreter Stolter looked shellshocked. He dipped his head to us before following his master. He was rickety on his legs, as if he had just run a great distance and was faltering before the finish line.

I looked at my watch. Mr. Churchill pulled out his own from a waistcoat pocket. He gave a grumpy sound. It was shortly after ten p.m. The thought occurred that I had just witnessed the most constructive hour in the history of blackmail.

Mr. Churchill did not get up. He took a cigar from his pocket and put it in his mouth. He said nothing to me. From another pocket he fished a tiny box of matches. He lit the cigar and let out a luxurious plume. Looking up at the ceiling he whispered a few words. I heard them, just barely. *Thank you, Bedouin.*

Shortly after, in his suite, he summoned Eden, Cadogan and Vansittart. To their amazed elation the PM outlined the principal points of the accord. He instructed the three to join their opposite numbers at seven a.m. tomorrow. They are to draft a one-page declaration (Mr. Churchill stressed, "*One* page") summarising the autonomies to be granted to the people of the Sudetenland by means of a federalist structure under an amended Czechoslovakian constitution.

"The text of the declaration will be released at noon on Monday," said Mr. Churchill. "Not a word of its content will be disclosed publicly before that hour. The delay is required. It will allow for … face-saving on the other side. There can be no leaks. Therefore no one else among our group is to be informed. I appreciate how difficult it will be for you to keep this news under your hats, and how maddening for our people. That, however, is how it must be. The dictator's behaviour over the coming days will give you the reason why. Let me repeat myself. Let me underline and emphasise that the dictator will make a show over the weekend. Be assured, his actions will be in the interest of self-preservation, not in cancelling the declaration. Thank you very much, gentlemen. I am sure you are very tired, as am I."

"Prime Minister!" said Vansittart. "You have not told us how this came about."

"Suffice to say," Mr. Churchill replied, "I persuaded the dictator to follow the path of prudence, wisdom and peace."

"Pardon us, Prime Minister," said Eden, "but we can serve you best by knowing the full story."

"Anthony, I do not intend to discuss the nature of my discussion with the dictator, save to assure you I have made no commitments which will in any way oblige His Majesty's government. We leave the matter there. We drop it now and for all time. And I beg of you, please do not stalk and hound Joffrey. He too" – this was accompanied by a glower in my direction – "will be keeping what transpired to himself."

True, so far as it goes. I will not be the one to reveal to the press what happened. That would cost me my place at Number 10, and likely my career. The dirt will somehow come out, though. Doesn't it, in the end, always come out? If I bid my confidante in America to swear eternal secrecy, I would only feel a grown man acting childish. I am tired now, and giddy. Perhaps I am a child …

Those demonstrators in the *Platz* must be getting paid. They continue to shuffle about with their placards. Goodnight, Heidi. Goodnight, diary.

Munich
Friday
30th Sept. 1938

11:20 a.m.

A pity there's no miraculous means by which I can send you my thoughts as soon as I write them. By the time this reaches you in Boston the harebrained attempt on Mr. Churchill's life will be old news. The event is already fading here, helped by a mocking quip from the PM. "There is nothing so exhilarating," he said, "as to be shot at without result."

Early this morning Mr. Churchill was working in his suite with Jock Colville. On the spur of the moment, the day being fine, the PM decided to take some air. He and Colville went down the lift and out the Regina's main entrance. They had a Yard man with them, as well as Mr. Churchill's escort of two SS men. The party of five crossed the street where the PM, unable to restrain his cheeky aplomb, raised his bowler to the demonstrators in the Platz. The answer to the provocation was predictable. The demonstrators set up a chant, *Kriegstreiber Churchill!* Warmonger Churchill!, and shook their placards at the world's foremost anti-Nazi. Nobody was concerned, least of all the SS men, who knew the group enjoyed official sanction. Besides, there were at least as many plain-clothed Gestapo men in the Platz as there were demonstrators.

Colville remembers three things about the instant after the gun was fired. The Yard man shouted "Down!" One of the SS men yelled "*Luger!*" And the Prime Minister muttered, "Bloody nuisance," before his three guardians and Colville bundled him back to the safety of the hotel. There was hardly any need. The shooter was a loopy woman whose bullet went wildly astray and chipped a bronze eagle above the Regina's entrance. After lurching out from among the demonstrators and firing her Luger, the woman screamed "Imperialist bastard!" She was instantly tackled by her horrified associates. Apparently she was the same excitable bitch I saw shake a swastika at the consulate car two days ago, and I'm told her English accent was flawless.

The Germans are mightily embarrassed. If the Regina Palast was previously crawling with Gestapo and SS, the hotel is now veritably drowning in them. The rumour is that Hitler is livid at the lapse and taking it out on that humiliated dwarf, Goebbels, who should be more careful about whom he hires as hecklers.

With the hullabaloo over, Eden, Cadogan and Vansittart are back with their opposite numbers working on the text of the Agreement. Minding the edict from Mr. Churchill, the three have remained tight-lipped. The other members of the delegation have been told only that an announcement is being prepared but that its details must remain under wraps until Monday.

Care to know where I was when the PM took his exhilarating stroll? Sitting in a chair behind a large fern in the hotel library, hiding from my indignant colleagues who naturally want to know what happened in last night's private meeting. Reg Huntington has been a particular pest. He accused me of forgetting that I owe him. I wish I could tell them there will be compensation galore on Monday, when the Agreement is published. Did I say compensation? Of course I mean jubilation, and that goes double for me. My heart is singing not merely for the peace of Europe, but because *Damon will shortly be free!* Cadogan kindly informed me this morning that the Foreign Office has dispatched an unmarked plane to Berlin.

"Chadwick will be taken to Tempelhof," he said. "No public comment will be made. The matter is to remain confidential."

"I can't tell you how relieved I am. Thank you, Alec." Only later did it occur to me that I had addressed the Permanent Under-Secretary by his Christian name. I think my life has changed. I think the world has changed. I will toast Damon's liberty and forgive his trespasses over a bottle of Dom Perignon. Did I say a double dose of jubilation? Make that a triple, or a quadruple. Ach, someone's knocking ...

3:40 p.m.

Feels like days ago, not hours, that I got up to answer my door ... it was Jock Colville. He said, "There's something I must tell you, Pearson."

When he told me the name of the woman who had attempted to murder Mr. Churchill my knees turned to jelly, I had to grope for a chair. Colville said gently, "She is entitled to a consular visit, which the PM has asked me to attend. If you wish to see her ..."

I reacted with disgust, said she does not exist for me, but quickly realised that seeing her was the proper thing to do. A hotel Mercedes took us to Stadelheim prison. Our consul in Munich joined us. He remarked that in 1924 Adolf Hitler had been imprisoned in the very same gaol. Colville and I remained conspicuously silent, so the consul thereafter kept his mouth shut.

A dreadful thing, to regret that one's father is still alive, yet that is my dominant emotion as I write. My father would be better off in his grave than hear about his daughter's unspeakable crime. If the Germans tie a noose around my sister's neck I will not shed a tear. I was almost physically sick when I saw her. It was the response she deserves, that her brother, her one sibling, the single soul in the world who might extend a hand should instead gag at the sight of her … the stupid bitch, the surly *cunt*. Forgive me, but the minute or two I spent with her made for the longest torture of my life. At first I did not recognise her. She was in profile and I entertained a fleeting hope that an error had been made, but no, the woman in the tatty coat looked round and there was the chocolate birthmark. "Irene …"

"Was zum Teufel machst Du denn hier?"

The guttural scrape of her voice, "What the hell are you doing here?", might have come from a demented crone. She looked a wiry ruin, ages older than when I had last seen her, but her shamelessness was brisk, defiant. "Have you got a fag?" she cackled in English, squinting through watery eyes. "Give me a fucking fag, will you?"

The hideous moment determined something for me, namely that my sister would no longer exist for me. I could not allow her to exist for my precious Vicky, who should never have to think of a repulsive traitor as her aunt. I wanted only to escape the wreckage of that alien woman. Colville and the consul were waiting. Seeing my face, neither of them said a word.

If a God exists, then the fog in my father's head will shield him. He no longer reads the newspapers or listens to the wireless, but he still has lucid intervals … someone might tell him of his daughter's infamy. Who would so despicably bring anguish to an old man? Maybe some jackal of a newspaperman … I just realised how very tired I am.

Saturday
8th Oct. 1938

Heidi,

Yours of the nineteenth and twenty-third ... they arrived at a time of need, thank you. I sense a healthy acceptance in your tone. It appears your life remains tolerable after the loss of Beacon Hill. After all, how trying can it be to reside among doctors and lawyers rather than millionaire inheritors? Long live Elizabeth H. Lowell's egalitarian impulses! I am glad too you have softened in regard to Matt. Give him time, he will pull through and renew himself, this is what Americans do – they have second acts.

Now I must tell you, with sadness and gnawing anxiety ... Damon has not yet been returned to us. A week has gone by and the plane sent by the F.O. is still sitting on the tarmac at Tempelhof, waiting. Neither the PM nor Cadogan can explain it. As you know, as the whole relieved world knows, Hitler has honoured his other, much bigger commitments. The end of the Sudeten crisis and the return to barracks of the German troops are testament to that. The dictator may have fumed, raged and threatened over the weekend, but Mr. Churchill predicted such histrionics, didn't he? I remain in awe of the PM's reckoning and prescience. He foresaw how the king rat would navigate the maze. Hitler's menacing gestures over the weekend were all about self-preservation. A mighty shake of the fist to fool people into believing he had conceded nothing at Munich. Then the fist unclenching to reveal an olive branch, followed by both hands extended to introduce the statesman, the compromiser, the peacemaker and saviour. Then the announcement by the consummate liar that he himself had conceived and designed the federalist solution to the crisis. Only a few people know the tremendous depths of Hitler's political deceit, not to speak of his personal depravity. Sooner rather than later, I have no doubt, the true nature of the gutter rat will become known to all.

As for Irene... though my sister no longer exists for me, you can imagine what the brother of the atrocious woman has had to contend with. Most vexing is not the sympathy or suspicion so much as the ... meddling inquiry. People ask, as if I could bloody well tell them, how a daughter of England could have done such a thing. Thankfully her wacky gunshot has been overshadowed by the momentous Agreement. We no longer suffer her name and photograph in the newspapers. I am told a Nazi court may sentence her to death for her crime, though she will more likely spend the rest of her days in prison. I frankly don't give a damn. There are some things in life that can never be forgiven.

I would wager your *Globe* missed some of the details of Mr. Churchill's forty-eight hours after Munich, and his ghastly reception at Heston. Are you aware of how vilified he was prior to the announcement of the Agreement? The wisdom over the weekend, as Hitler jumped through his belligerent hoops, was that the stubborn British bulldog, also known as Warmonger Winnie, had precipitated a catastrophe at Munich. Witness his quick and unceremonious eviction from Germany! I shall slip in some cuttings from *The Times*, two from Tuesday and one from Wednesday. Vicky insisted I purchase a dozen copies of the Wednesday edition. I am not one to boast, so I will simply refer you to the fourth paragraph of the Wednesday cutting. It indicates why Vicky's father can now tell you the colour of the wallpaper at Buckingham Palace, and why he is familiar with the strength of our sovereign's handshake.

My full bearings are yet to be recovered. Consider me buffeted by massive events and wildly clashing emotions. Pardon me if I don't dwell on any of it. Rather pray with me that I will be able to write soon of Damon's deliverance.

Joff

Monday
10th Oct. 1938

Heidi,

Number 10 has gone quiet, everyone has left for the night, save for the duty officer and two Yard men who prowl about up there. I only sense their presence, I don't actually hear them. What I perceive as footfalls is probably my mind playing tricks. I have been sitting, hardly budging, in my windowless cellar for I don't know how long. This is not a day I will remember with pride. It taught me again, *again*, that I am a blind man. I have been wondering, questioning, reproaching myself ... how could I have been so blind for so long?

It was mid-morning when Violet Pearman summoned me upstairs. As I entered the PM's study, he stood. He said he wanted to apologise.

"Sir?"

He gestured me to a chair. The look on his face confounded me. The passions of Winston Churchill do not as a rule spawn contrition. "I have not been fair to you, Joff, and I am sorry for it."

"Why do you say that, sir?"

He came round and took the facing chair. "About your friend Chadwick, I have not been candid with you about his circumstances."

My heart sank. "Sir, please do not tell me his release is in doubt."

"I have to tell you that an impediment has arisen in regard to his release, but that is not why I asked you to see me."

A telephone rang on the Prime Minister's desk. His private telephone. To my knowledge, only a few family members and select intimates can call his private line. Mr. Churchill examined his fingernails as the ringing continued. For a moment as it went on, and on, he bristled. Finally the ringing ceased.

"There are matters of which you are not aware, Joff. They pertain to why the Germans arrested Chadwick."

"I assume they arrested him on a matter of ... morals, sir."

"That has been the assumption of almost everyone who is aware of Chadwick's imprisonment. It is an assumption I have been careful not to disabuse."

"I don't follow you, sir."

"Joff, this is known to only a very few people in England. You deserve to be among them. The fact is, Chadwick has done a vital service for His Majesty and the security of the nation."

Something in me sagged. I stared at the Prime Minister. In the tiny interval before grasping the enormity, I remembered Irene in profile and the fleeting hope a mistake had been made. This was another such hope, instantly doomed.

"Several years ago Chadwick approached MI6," said Mr. Churchill. "He presented an idea. He volunteered his services. Our people saw the potential of his plan. They trained him in the technical requirements. He took on an extremely dangerous mission, as events have alas proved. I do not have to tell you how effectively your friend performed for his country. You saw the evidence of it at Munich. Chadwick was the man who took the photographs in the Kohrbach file."

I have only a vague recollection of what Mr. Churchill said during the next few minutes. I do remember a fever of disjointed thoughts assailing my mind, and a crowd of obscure connections forming in the well of memory. Then Violet Pearman came in to say the Soviet ambassador had arrived.

"Thank you, Miss Pearman," said the Prime Minister. "Joff will be with me one more little minute." He rose and put his hand on my shoulder. "We must adjourn, Joff. You may be sure of our unceasing effort to bring Chadwick home. We don't know what is delaying his release. I doubt the dictator would cross me on this minor matter when he has carried through on the main one. How can he be sure I will not go back on my word? In the meantime we are holding the Nazi spies, Baumann and Vogt. They will not be returned to Germany until Chadwick is again on British soil."

"Thank you, sir," I found my voice, but not much use for it. I rose and shook Mr. Churchill's hand.

"Alec Cadogan is concentrating on the Chadwick matter as his highest priority. You may call upon him at any time."

"Thank you, sir. God bless you, sir."

I will go home now. Do you think, Heidi, I can find my way? Do you think a man who has only lately learned of his complete blindness can find his way home?

Joff

Saturday
15th Oct. 1938

Dear Heidi,

Must tell you, I am beholden to my Mary. I shared Damon's story with her and she has been a great help through the waiting. As the days swiftly pass and he is not restored to us, Damon's sins recede in the eyes of the darling patriot who is my wife. She has become his advocate. She extols Damon's service and laments only that his unique courage can never be made public. "He will return to England very soon, Joff. I believe it with all my heart. Mr. Churchill will bring him home."

I am grateful as well to Alec Cadogan. When I asked to know more about the circumstances behind Damon's arrest, the Permanent Under-Secretary complied in a manner I could not have predicted. Arriving at the F.O. yesterday, I found him sitting with a man who once put me through an irritating hour. A thin man wearing rimless spectacles, whose legs stretched out like long rods …

The nearly two years since my security vetting have not changed him a whit. I remember writing about this man, the *campion*, a species of government agent trained to niggle and peck. Well, here he was in Alec Cadogan's room, with the same expressionless face he had worn during our irksome interview and rising to his feet in the same lugubrious fashion.

"Gerald Campion," I said sourly.

We shook hands perfunctorily.

Our host said, "I was not aware until a few moments ago, Joff, that you and Mr. Campion once met."

"Yes, Alec, our meeting was, shall we say, exhaustive."

"I understand you were not informed at the time of Mr. Campion's actual affiliation."

"My chief memory of the meeting is the sense of having been … ambushed, by Mr. Campion's mention of my friend's name."

"Surely," said Campion, a faint movement of his lips making an attempt at a smile, "you now understand why I found it necessary."

"Sadly," I said, staying grim, "I now understand."

"I need not mince words then," said Cadogan. "Joff, Mr. Campion

453

comes to us from Six. He has played a central role in the Chadwick matter. Other than Chadwick himself, Mr. Campion is the only other Englishman besides myself, the PM, and yourself, who is privy to the Kohrbach file." He turned to Campion. "The Prime Minister and I are of the view that Mr. Pearson merits answers to any questions he may have in regard to Chadwick. We should be grateful if you were to accommodate him."

How the world turns. Cadogan left me with Campion. This time the interview was mine to command. My questions however were more often evaded than answered. Campion treated me with condescension. He was vague and terse at best. He clearly resented having been put at my disposal. At one point I threatened to have the Permanent Under-Secretary rejoin us, to compel the laconic fellow to open up. Be that as it may, Campion did help me see more clearly the design behind Damon's behaviour over the last few years. What I had regarded as erratic conduct was pure sham. Damon's outrageous pronouncements were part and parcel of a concerted strategy. He had play-acted a carefully devised campaign, first to draw attention from, then to ingratiate, and finally to penetrate a particular circle in Berlin. The process started with the photographs in Tatler and the flurry of provocative interviews on the wireless. Here was a celebrated artist in Britain declaring modern art corrupt, even as such art was being outlawed in Germany. Then he revealed his atheism in a national broadcast, even as the Nazis were enshrining their secular creed. Then the same famous painter used the public airwaves to single out Winston Churchill as a villain, when Churchill was the world's leading anti-Nazi voice.

"I see it now," I said. "All for the notice of the German embassy."

"Laying the ground, planting seeds," Campion replied.

A breakthrough came when the German cultural attaché invited Damon to a late-night cocktail in Belgravia. We can easily envision our friend making a success with his wit, budding skills in *Deutsch*, and freely expressed admiration for Germany's rejuvenation. His reward was to be invited back regularly for soirées where he met visiting athletes, dancers, actors, artists – members of an elite in Germany who had the means and sanction to travel abroad. The opportunity arose to exhibit several works in Munich. Then came the invitation from the

Weinhauf gallery and his first trip to Berlin.

Damon's exhibition of male nudes at the Weinhauf brought him the specific notice he was seeking. The paintings were romanticised representations of his own body, inspired by the photographs I had taken. The gallery promoted the event as a celebration of the ideal Aryan physique, and thereby gained him both official approval and entrée into the underground circle he was targeting. On the one hand the nudes, with their glorification of muscle and worship of potency, deliberately imitated the Nazi model of male beauty; they depicted the healthy body as a breeding tool, an instrument for the perpetuation of race superiority and achievement of the Nazi millennium's *Übermensch*. On the other hand, a very different element also existed in the paintings, a more cunning one. Rendered subtly, but discernibly for those meant to perceive it, was a sexual signal, a hyper-masculinity, a species of eroticism that tolerated not only the concealed and forbidden, but the extreme.

Coming from the likes of Gerald Campion this elaborate conceptual language sounded improbable. He sensed what I was thinking, and said I should understand the extent of preparatory work that had been done. The strategy behind the Weinhauf exhibit was scrupulously pondered, debated and calculated. Damon's assignment followed a script as it were.

"As you know from your familiarity with the Kohrbach file," said Campion, "there are men in Berlin, highly placed Nazis among them, who hold, how shall I put it, profoundly unconventional private gatherings. These range from the simply decadent to the grotesquely obscene and, in some instances, the wickedly criminal. During his Paris … exploits, Chadwick caught wind of the depravities taking place in the German capital and the rumour that even the highest of the Nazis were involved. He sensed an opportunity. He came to us with his idea. The path he then followed was shaped here in London by a carefully chosen group of planners."

"Alec mentioned your central role. You were part of this group?"

"I happened to be Chadwick's first point of contact in the service. I coordinated the group."

My power of imagination does not extend to picturing Damon and Campion working together, or even to them sitting in the same room together, but then we have learned about the imperfection of my imagination, haven't we?

The harvest of the Weinhauf exhibit came in the form of invitations. Quite a few Berliners wanted to meet the dashing English painter whose shameless self-reflections had made him a *cause célèbre*. Wives of Reich officials wanted Damon as an ornament at their dinner table, and plenty of *frauleins* dreamed of hosting him in bed. Damon's sole interest however was in the highly placed Nazi men who had taken the hint from his paintings.

"He accepted their invitations," said Campion, "and began putting to use the talents we taught him. I trust you have now sufficiently satisfied your curiosity, Mr. Pearson." Campion rose as if the interview were over.

"I beg your pardon, Mr. Campion, but you cannot leave me just yet. What did you teach him … how to aim a miniature camera at personal letters and a diary?"

Campion sighed. "More importantly, how to search for such materials and how to leave them seemingly undisturbed. Still more critically, how to administer sedatives through drink to eliminate, tenderly, any hindrance to search."

"Jesus Christ."

Campion bowed and turned to leave.

"We are not fucking finished."

I was satisfied to see a crease about the campion's eyes deform his expressionless face, but my outburst certainly did not intimidate him. He sat back down with the air of a man distracted by the antics of a subordinate.

"The mural," I said.

He gazed at me.

"Why did Dame go to such trouble in London? The Picasso madness came long after the Weinhauf exhibit."

Campion answered in a tone suitable for dealing with a thick child. He said that circles exist within circles. Before unveiling his mural in London, Chadwick had not yet come across anything explosive in Berlin. He believed he was still to penetrate an innermost circle of Nazi deviants. The extravagant slander of Picasso was a giant act of attention-grabbing. Timed a few days before the opening of Munich's exhibit of degenerate art, it won massive notice in the Nazi press.

"He did tell me he needed a thunderclap," I said.

"The result exceeded our hopes. Goebbels put Chadwick's name on the list of attending dignitaries. We were jubilant. It led our man to bigger fish."

"Let me guess. To Hermann Goering?"

Campion nodded. "And through Goering ... to Kohrbach."

"It's true, then, that the number two man in Germany patronised Damon?"

Another nod.

I almost shouted. "Why didn't he protect him?" The instant the words left my mouth I realised how foolishly naive I could still be. I waved a hand in the air to dismiss my own question. "Tell me this," I said. "Who was, or is, Anton Kohrbach? His diary gives nothing away about himself."

"I can only tell you what Chadwick told us before his arrest. Kohrbach was Goering's procurer. He satisified Goering's most despicable biddings and was handsomely rewarded for it. If there was a Napoleon of vice in Nazi Germany, it was probably Anton Kohrbach."

"Was?"

"Our information is that Goering has had him killed."

"Why?"

"We believe Chadwick was arrested in Kohrbach's home. He had been a guest there often, and the most recent portions of Kohrbach's diary were on Chadwick's camera. As for Kohrbach, he was probably writing the diary for his own purposes of potential blackmail. We assume the diary, once discovered, brought his quiet murder."

I stared at Campion. He was restlessly rearranging himself in his chair, crossing and uncrossing his legs. I told him I had only one more question, and he did me the honour of feigning alertness. "Why does the Prime Minister call the Kohrbach file the 'Bedouin' file?"

I thought it was an innocuous question, but anger instantly altered the deadpan face of Gerald Campion. He replied with real feeling, which I sensed came from professional pride. "He does it for a trite reason, born in someone's silly head in our Berlin embassy. It could have proved damned dangerous. Think about it in relation to Chadwick's given name, and you will see what I am talking about. Now I will wish you good day."

Something occurred to him before he reached the door. "I should tell you, Pearson. As you are probably aware, Chadwick has no close relatives. He asked me to contact you in case anything happened to him."

"Then why didn't I hear from you when he was arrested?"

"I should be more precise. He asked me to contact you if anything … mortal, happened to him."

I said goodbye to Gerald Campion. Nor was I shy about stating my hope to his face that I would never see him again.

Last night on the telephone with Vicky, I was caught short when she asked about her uncle Damon. Mary and I tremble every morning when we open *The Times*. So far, because neither the Nazis nor ourselves would benefit from revealing his arrest, it has stayed out of the news. Hearing me hesitate, Vicky said, "Wasn't he supposed to be *home* by now, Daddy? Is there anything *wrong?*"

"Nothing wrong at all, my plum. Your uncle is just a little longer coming back from Germany than we expected. We will see him soon."

Pray with me that it's so, Heidi. My love to you and your boys,

Joff

Saturday
22nd Oct. 1938

Dear Heidi,

A wretched week. I spoke with Cadogan daily. The prospect for Damon's release has dimmed. In Berlin, Vansittart finally saw Ribbentrop and came away alarmed. Ribbentrop said the antipathy toward Chadwick in certain quarters is 'oddly poisonous'. Clearly, the real reasons behind Damon's arrest have been kept quiet, even from Ribbentrop. Meanwhile the F.O. is unsure what to make of the purported scheming and manoeuvring within the highest Nazi echelons. From all appearances Hitler remains the undisputed master of Germany, but is he really?

Says Cadogan, "The fact that Chadwick remains behind bars speaks to some kind of internal defiance of Hitler. Already, much sooner than the PM projected, there may be forces plotting to weaken or overthrow him. When we went to Munich, Chadwick had already been arrested. Yet Hitler had no idea we were in possession of the Kohrbach materials. Someone kept that knowledge from him."

"Goering?"

"The fat man had good reason to keep the knowledge among his own sick disciples. He is obviously the one responsible for Chadwick's arrest, and the blanket of silence surrounding it. After Munich, Goering might be in a position to take greater power, or total power."

The little our people have been able to learn about Damon's condition at Spandau is that he's alive and kept in solitary. I can't bear to ponder what he has gone through, Heidi. The arrest, the interrogations, the prison squalor ... I think of little else. Our friends must have wondered at my remoteness when we gathered this week, though I tried to hide how sombre I feel. Graham managed to bring us all together. He is such a good man, Graham, a gentle and good man. The penitent Catherine seems to have realised the magnitude of her stupidity in regard to Seamus. How she could have misread him so badly I can't imagine. They are talking again and I am glad our little lunch club is back in one piece. You were, as always, missed. Love,

Joff

Wednesday
26th Oct. 1938

I don't know how to say it. *I do not know how.* When I heard the slow clump on the stairs, the improbable visitor coming down, I had a grave premonition. My visitor was Mr. Churchill, ashen-faced. Yesterday morning in Berlin a sentence of death was pronounced. In the afternoon, at Spandau, the sentence was carried out.

I covered my face with my hands. I saw a boy in a glade raising his arms in entreaty. Just a boy in a glade, naked and innocent. Then I heard a voice, a croaky voice, say the Germans, every German, all Germans, were to blame. *They should all rot in hell.* It was my voice, muffled … croaky.

I dropped my hands and stared accusingly at Mr. Churchill. What happened to the trade? What became of the trade? Mr. Churchill shook his head. Before Munich, he said, no one would have defied Hitler. Now someone had done so, someone very high, who was no longer quaking before the dictator. Most likely Goering, thinking overthrow, scheming to take Hitler's place, and absolutely unwilling to forgo his pound of flesh from the betrayer Chadwick.

Piece of shit, I heard myself say.

Mr. Churchill said the whole pack of them had crawled from the sewer and would end there. He promised me that. He said the Nazi scum will end as sewage. "Your friend did not sacrifice in vain, Joff. Take some comfort in that."

Right. King and country and bloody empire. Maybe I will be able to take some comfort in that ten years from now, or twenty. Like hell I will. I will never know how to say my friend Damon is gone.

J.

Saturday
29th Oct. 1938

Dear Heidi,
In the mornings I wake to the shock and grief. At night both of those sullen wolves follow me into bed. We have not told Vicky yet. We dread the prospect. We must tell her before the notice is published and the newspapers erupt. That will not happen until our people in Berlin identify the body. We also fear a leak of the news and a lurid scoop in some newspaper. A nightmare. The euphoria following Munich seems like a hundred years ago.

Yesterday, while I was at the flat, a letter arrived by messenger from a Mr. Richard Bentow, solicitor in Kensington, requesting I telephone his office at my earliest convenience. I had never heard of the man and had no idea what he wanted. When I reached Solicitor Bentow, he was the soul of protocol. "Mr. Pearson, I am discharging a mandate on behalf of my late client, Mr. Damon Chadwick. Let me first offer my sincerest condolences on his untimely passing."

"May I ask, Mr. Bentow, how you learned of Damon's death? There has been no formal notification."

"A gentleman by the name of Gerald Campion of the Foreign Office informed me. He too was carrying out a prior instruction from Mr. Chadwick. Mr. Campion authorised me to communicate with you, but demanded that I otherwise remain silent on the matter."

"Mr. Campion told you he is with the Foreign Office?"

"Yes, sir."

I was blindly gazing out the window, imagining the campion as a chameleon, a creature with a cupboard full of hats of convenience. Solicitor Bentow said, "I am aware of the profound friendship you shared with my client. Years ago he named you as his titular first of kin. Some months ago he instructed me to contact you in the event of his death."

The sky was darkening in the late afternoon. I saw a flock of birds alight onto the roof of the adjacent building. "Mr. Chadwick wrote a letter addressed to yourself, sir, and entrusted it to my keeping. I was to release it only in the event of his death."

The blast of a lorry's horn caused the birds to fly off in sudden perfect unison. I came back to myself and asked Solicitor Bentow if he knew what the letter contained. "Assuredly not, sir. I am involved purely as an intermediary. Mr. Chadwick stipulated you as the sole recipient of the letter, and my instructions were to release it directly into your hands."

An hour later I had run the forlorn errand and the letter was in my coat pocket. I kept it sealed and unread, God knows why, until this morning. Not because I feared the contents. I had a rather good idea of what the letter would say. Maybe I was avoiding some kind of finality.

The letter dates from June, when Damon was last in London. I remember him mentioning he had some business with his solicitor. The writing covers two sides of a sheet of yellow paper and looks hurried. He must have dashed off the letter the day he met Bentow, maybe in the minutes before. He would have indulged this little theatric for its own sake, as an amusing exercise or taunting of fate. He had never had any use for intuition or hunches.

My dear kind beautiful Joff,
If this letter is in your hands it can mean only one thing. Rather unimaginable, and I certainly do not expect it, but the thing could happen. If it does, there is much I want you to know. Campion can give you facts, but only I can give you the apology. Let me beg clemency for the vast deceit. It was necessary for me to marry the deception and live with it twenty-four hours a day. I took on my disguise so completely there were moments I myself believed it was real. I can only imagine how you privately judged my behaviour. There were moments when you were aghast and properly harsh with me. Yet you remained kind. Kinder than you ought to have been. For that I credit our long lovely bond.

I have told Campion about Bentow and arrangements for my estate, but not a word about this letter, it would only distress Campion's instinct for secrecy. As for Bentow he knows nothing of my affairs in Germany or what is written here, but he will contact you again about bequests and such. Vicky must go to Cambridge, travel the world at her whim, and damn the expense.

I would have confided in you from the beginning, but the role had to be assumed root and branch. The other side was watching. Even in The Squire's, they watched. The Nazi vermin know only suspicion. They live in constant fear, like a pack of squabbling cannibals. Naturally they hedge all bets, and scrutinise very carefully whom they take into their confidence. Turns out the anti-modernist English artist, the shameless atheist, the brazen Nazi apologist, was too good to be true, though for a long while I have had the rodents lowering their guard.

At the beginning our people put me through a rigorous school. Campion and his team drilled some useful crafts into my head, mainly on the photographic side, with a detour into the chemistry of soporifics. I asked for *mano a mano* combat skills, but they laughed. Their school was also a benign prison. They insisted I prove I could go missing from my life. That was harder than I thought. Three months without a single note or telephone call. You once accused me of spending those months in a Swiss sanitorium! Not far wrong, Joff. I was in a spartan little hideaway in Suffolk, close to your beloved Shimpling. What a man will do for his country. I didn't have a malt, pint or pipe the whole bleeding time. Fortunately one of my well-muscled instructors proved to be, well, let us say, cordial.

Campion will be his careful self and probably not volunteer anything about a man named Anton Kohrbach. In case he does, you should know two things about this man. First, Kohrbach is proving, however unwittingly, to be the key to my success. Second, you should not surmise that Kohrbach is the Berlin 'friend' you think I have made. Please know, I never had such a friend. That was a fable to throw off the scent. The truth is I have made many friends, friends of convenience. They have gained me access. They have taken me into homes. I have been wading through an underworld, my dear Joff. The aim is to unmask, shame, coerce, extort. With luck what I am finding could destroy some lofty Nazis, maybe even the loftiest one. I actually met him once, the monarch of the vermin, just once, under circumstances best left unsaid. I can tell you, he is the distilled essence of human filth. A sadist without conscience. He is the alpha cannibal.

Please, no tears or regrets. I am doing what I am doing for the best reasons in the world, though there's a lark in it too, the grandest caper of my life.

My love to you, Joff. I have adored you as a friend and man for thirty years. I remember with joy our occasion in Eaton Square. Thank you for allowing me to express my devotion. I must say this too one more time: you do not know your own power, your talent, your potential. I pray you will recognise what is in you, and unleash it.

Hug precious Vicky every single day for both of us. Hold tightly to Mary who represents the best in all of us. Remember me for what good I may have done. And stay kind, dearest friend. With my love,

Damon

Copying out those last few sentences has undone me, Heidi. Tears are streaming down my face. Will write again soon.

Joff

Saturday
26th Nov. 1938

Dear Heidi,

Yours of the fourteenth arrived. Thank you for those words. You are so right. We are not supposed to lose our friends in the middle of our lives. We are meant to have them the whole way.

The decision to trade the two German spies for the body caused a stir, but the Prime Minister did not hesitate, he would have traded ten. Meanwhile a pact of silence will be observed. Both sides agreed there was nothing to be gained from revealing Damon's activities in Germany. Mr. Churchill told me he has ordered the destruction of British records pertaining to the matter, including the contents of the vault in my basement room. "I owe Chadwick no less," he said, "and much more." The official story is that Damon was involved in a high speed accident on the autobahn between Berlin and Munich. The German police report reads that the great British painter was, tragically, pronounced dead at the scene.

It pains me to think how few we were at his grave. The burial was a private affair at the Margravine. Damon was laid to rest next to his mother. No announcement was published, no service held. These were his wishes stipulated in his will. Mary and Victoria held tightly to me as the plain pine coffin was lowered into the ground.

Maddy was there. The notary, Bentow. Jock Colville, representing the Prime Minister. Campion, whose presence I did not resent. Somehow that crawler from the *Evening News*, Billy Colman, learned about the burial and showed up in a black Borsalino, the pretentious fool, but I am unfair … he had tears in his eyes the whole time. A young girl unknown to me shyly placed a wreath on the grave. I went to her afterwards and she tripped over her words. She brought condolences from Eaton Square, said she was the niece of Mr. Chadwick's dear friend, the Duchess of Melrose.

You need not take back anything you said about Damon over the last few years. They were thoughts of the moment, justified by the circumstances. You are not the only one feeling guilty. Maddy Kloff could hardly speak. She whimpered about reproaching him for taking canvases to Germany.

I looked at newspapers from New York, Boston and Chicago, gratified to see how the news was treated. Makes me think quite a few Chadwicks hang on walls in America. The obituaries express genuine loss and affection. Your *Globe* mentioned the mighty work he might yet have done.

Victoria asked us to frame the obituary from *The Times*. It stands propped next to her bed with a green jade lion Damon gave her on her fourth birthday. She has not let on how deeply hurt she has been. She never cried in front of us. She looked fierce when she said, "I will never forget Uncle Damon, Daddy. I am especially proud you were his best friend."

I allowed myself a rare early morning drink today. Single malt, neat. The bottle was a gift from Damon years ago and never opened. A bottle of Bowmore, his favourite.

I loved him. It's easy to say now. Or easier. I would not have been able to say it in quite those words before …

Just back from a walk in the park. Went out bundled and scarfed against the chill of the gathering winter. Mary returns from Coventry tonight. By the grove of elms in the park it occurred to me how pleasant it would be, how devoted to memory and feeling if I took her to a candle-lit place and summoned the intimacy we used to share so effortlessly. The summer of '25 was our time. Do you recall how happy we were? I recall how happy *you* were I was off your case.

Does grief bring headaches? I have been having some awful ones. Battling a corker now, in fact, but I should still surprise Mary on the platform. With yellow roses and purple hyacinths, the very flowers I chose when I first came courting. I have something rather important to tell her. Next week I begin the book about refugee Jews.

I telephoned Samuel Sternthal yesterday to revive the project. He declared himself very glad indeed. Then I went to Mr. Churchill, who has given his blessing. The story, he said, is crying out to be told. I will be spending two days a week at the Admiralty. The task will demand every skill I have, and then some. The book's dedication will be to Damon. The acknowledgements will include Ulli and Edgar Pearson … and Ken Retinger.

I go up to Bury tomorrow, but as a matter of form really. My father no longer speaks, and he shows no sign of hearing when spoken to. At least we can thank God he never learned of Irene's infamy.

Victoria asked the other day if additional baby books are needed in America. Her shelves are full and she wants to make room for new, more adult, more important books.

Be well, Heidi. With my love,

Joff

PART FOUR: 1982-2001

We have it in our power to begin the world
over again.

Thomas Paine

Afterword to the Second Edition
by Maxwell Brian Lowell

Since the publication of this book twelve months ago, in September of 1981, a number of historians on both sides of the Atlantic have waged unrelenting war upon it. By various means they have sought to discredit the book's account of the events at Munich in 1938.

Some of the skeptics have questioned the motives of the author as a means of discrediting his observations. They remind the world that Joffrey Pearson was by his own admission a drug-taker and implicit adulterer. They characterise him through his writings as a clever, indeed monumental, deceiver. Their view has it that Pearson was caught up in stimulating the attention of a woman he adored while exercising his perverse talent as a fabricator of history. He therefore invented his own version of the final meeting between Churchill and Hitler.

Other doubters have strenuously mined the historic record, constituted principally of their own works, to allege that Winston Churchill could not have acted as Pearson describes. First they dispute that Churchill could have known the details of Hitler's personal depravity to the extent that Pearson maintains. They point to the absence of documentation in MI6 files in regard to the agent whom Pearson's letters identify as none other than the renowned painter Damon Chadwick, whose death in a car crash on a German highway has never been disputed. Then, arguing that even if Churchill possessed what they choose to call the fictional Kohrbach file, or anything resembling it, they contend it was not in the character of Churchill to employ blackmail as a tool of statecraft.

It is not my intention to engage in detailed debate with the detractors and hecklers of this book. At any rate, others have already taken the book's side with impressive tenacity. The essay by Mr. Garth Evans in the February, 1982 issue of *Harper's*, together with the exhaustive research of Caroline Seto published in the *Sunday Times* of May 9, 1982, answer and defeat the charges levelled against Joffrey Pearson far more effectively than I could hope to do.

Garth Evans draws inescapable inferences from the growing literature on Adolf Hitler's sexual orientation and moral turpitude, which in turn render only too plausible Pearson's account of the Kohrbach file. The German Chancellor was a degenerate erotomaniac. He was a sadist who derived intense sexual pleasure from inflicting pain. Moreover, he was without doubt a practising bisexual, and almost certainly a pederast. The evidence remains uncertain as to whether he engaged in coprophilia.

Evans also dismantles, with some hilarity, the thesis that the British Prime Minister would refrain from threatening the German dictator with targeted disclosure of his perversions. New studies coming to light, based on archives only recently opened to scholars, show that personal files constituted the secret weapon of many of Churchill's successes, before and after Munich. An exhaustive account of the occasions when Churchill used clandestinely acquired personal information to achieve his objectives would fill a volume on its own. Confidential information acted like lethal candy on Churchill's desk. He promised his enemies that he would keep these poisoned sweets concealed, so long as they obeyed his bidding. The great man's merciless application of 'statecraft by uncommon means' as Joffrey Pearson heard him describe it, extended even to onetime close colleagues. Witness the brutal exposure of his Home Secretary in 1947, when photographic evidence of the Minister's extravagant behaviour in a Paris brothel came to Downing Street. Writing for an American audience, no wonder Evans concluded that J. Edgar Hoover, the reptilian and infamous Director of the FBI, known for his leveraging of confidential files, might well have learned his ways at Churchill's knee.

In addition, Evans burnishes the standard explanation for why Churchill's own writings do not corroborate Pearson. Churchill did not inform posterity about the Kohrbach file, or indeed about any of his other invocations of hidden smut, for a simple reason. As Evans sensibly notes, "He wanted history to show him as the knight on the white horse, not as the gumshoe in the cathouse."

For her part, Caroline Seto performed a masterwork of research. Her principal finding precipitated a sensation of its own. She uncovered a sinister and tragic facet of the Munich story which powerfully corroborates Pearson's account. Seto learned the fate of Franz Stolter.

The circumstances that make Franz Stolter a key figure in this controversy are detailed in the memoirs of many of the key participants in the Munich Conference. At noon on the second day of the negotiations, September 29, 1938, Paul Schmidt, the affable gentleman who normally translated for Hitler, was called away on a family emergency. The man who substituted for Schmidt that afternoon, and during the private meeting that evening, was Franz Stolter. The multi-talented Stolter, an assistant and protégé of Joseph Goebbels, was a rising star in the Propaganda Ministry. He was the scion of a wealthy family in the metals industry which had profited immensely from the rise of the Nazis. Stolter studied English literature in America at Princeton, and then psychology at McGill University in Canada. His command of idiomatic English had made him a favourite of Goebbels, who often received English-speaking visitors. The thirty year-old Stolter had accompanied the Propaganda Minister to Munich. On the recommendation of Goebbels, Hitler accepted him as a stand-in for Paul Schmidt.

When Caroline Seto took an interest in the controversy surrounding *Churchill At Munich*, she posed the obvious question: what did Franz Stolter have to say? He was the only other person in the room with the two leaders and Joffrey Pearson during the private meeting of September 29, 1938. If still alive, he would be in his late sixties and could verify, or debunk, Pearson's account of what transpired.

Seto's article in the *Sunday Times* traces her months of investigative digging in Germany through Nazi archives in Munich, the files of a provincial Bavarian weekly newspaper, a coroner's report in the town of Langenfeld, and finally an unmarked pauper's grave outside Dusseldorf. Seto ascertained to her satisfaction that Stolter was never seen alive after the evening of September 29, 1938. She also concluded that a body matching his general description, found two weeks after that date in a ravine near Monheim, was the corpse of Franz Stolter. The dead man had a small tidy bullet hole in the back of the neck. The timing of Stolter's disappearance and the manner of his death told Seto everything she needed to know. She ended her article with, "Case closed."

The objective approach of Garth Evans and Caroline Seto, together with similar articles by other writers in the United Kingdom and the United States, as well as a curiously impassioned defence of Pearson by Angela Tranter in *Der Spiegel* (the German translation of *Churchill*

At Munich will appear only next spring) provide unbiased analyses for which I am immensely grateful. I should note too that each and every commentator writing in support of this book has decried the fantastic notion that Joffrey Pearson could have gone to the trouble of creating such a detailed account merely to impress a woman whom he had not seen in years, whom he had little likelihood of seeing again, and whom he assumed to be burning his letters once she had read them!

Still, I am compelled in light of persistent charges against the book and insinuations against its author to divulge more than I have hitherto done as to what my mother, Elizabeth Heidi Lowell, said to me upon revealing the existence of Pearson's letters. This disclosure is owed to the hundreds of thousands of readers throughout the world whose interest in the book have helped make it a focus of controversy.

My mother spoke to me only briefly about Mr. Pearson, but with a keen lucidity drawn from the passion of memory. She said that he had been a dear friend and good man. Pearson had loved and revered her, and he had gone on loving and revering her long after both of them were married to others. My mother made a point of asserting that Pearson would never have dishonoured her with deception; he would never have lied to her. On reflection I have grown convinced that she sensed the importance of emphasizing to me her belief in Pearson's veracity, in light of the extraordinary material I was to find in his letters.

She had begun saving Pearson's letters because she believed the human foibles and quirky observations in them merited preservation. So she ignored Pearson's wishes and secretly collected the letters, considering them keepsakes of a turbulent period. My mother had always planned to leave them to her three sons at a point in her life and theirs when the revelation of Pearson's devotion to her would cause no great embarrassment. She sensed her sons would value the letters for both the light they cast on history and on her own journey through life. She was equally sure her sons would overlook or forgive her morally questionable involvement in the correspondence.

At the point when Pearson began meeting prominent public figures and taking part in behind-the-scenes diplomatic meetings, my mother felt that something unique was coming into her hands. Later, after a number of histories of the Munich conference had been written, she realized the letters in her possession spoke of things of which the world might never be made aware.

"Max," she said to me, "after I'm gone, I trust you to do the right thing with the letters. My wish is that they be published as they were written. Preserve them and take every precaution with them. At the appropriate time, find the most suitable publisher."

Of course she regretted having concealed from my father the liaison with Pearson, but she did not consider her participation in the correspondence to have been a betrayal of her marriage. "I encouraged Joffrey in every instance to be candid, but I did not reciprocate his countless tokens of affection," she said to me. "We were close, very close, but I did not share his feelings. There were no declarations of an intimate nature in my letters. If it turns out Joffrey did not burn them and they are found, don't worry, they will not reveal a scarlet woman. I can look at myself in the mirror with no guilt or shame." My mother told me these things when she knew her life was nearing its end.

I am satisfied that she had provided a willing ear to a friend for whatever he wished to say, and that this proffer of free rein formed her *raison d'être* from the start. On the basis of what she told me I have accepted as true and accurate Joffrey Pearson's account of the final meeting between Adolf Hitler and Winston Churchill at Munich in 1938.

It may be difficult for some to accept that a batch of personal letters from the pen of an obscure translator could trump and neuter the scholarly writings of a brigade of historians. My trust in my mother's judgment, however, and in the corroborating work of Evans, Seto et al, convinces me that this is the case.

Boston, Massachusetts
September 1982

Afterword to the Third Edition
by Maxwell Brian Lowell

On the occasion of the third printing of *Churchill At Munich*, it is necessary once again to answer unprecedented attacks upon this book's integrity. When accusations that involve details of the historical record are directed against the book, it is reasonable for people of good faith to entertain doubt about the author's veracity. When vicious innuendo is levelled in regard to the book's very provenance, however, there can be no polite reasoning with the perpetrators. The vendors of slander deserve only angry contempt.

I refer to the criminal clowns in the guise of amateur 'truth-finders' and newspaper reporters who have alleged a conspiracy and peddled the theory that *Churchill At Munich* is a massive literary fraud. The sad circus began when an otherwise reputable history professor suggested in *The Guardian* that the entire content of the book is a forgery. He asserted that no actual letters addressed to Elizabeth Heidi Lowell were ever written by Joffrey Pearson; that Joffrey Pearson may very well have been a real person but that his name, identity and profession were appropriated for this comprehensive invention. He accused the undersigned and the publishers of the book of having engineered a fraud. The tabloid press in the United Kingdom instantly scented an opportunity.

Consequently a scandal, or rather the fervent appetite for scandal, with all the tawdry speculation and sordid nonsense attendant upon same, was born. The notorious series of 'investigative' articles in *News of the World* formed the most egregious of the attacks upon the book's fundamental honor. These articles put forward the notion that the letters of Joffrey Pearson are imaginative creations, and that they were concocted by a swindler with the talent of a novelist. Like other libels, the articles were ultimately shown to be groundless, serving only random malice in the pursuit of squalid entertainment.

No hard evidence whatsoever was brought forward to challenge the authenticity of the letters published in *Churchill At Munich*. Moreover, in April of this year I made available the original letters and commissioned an analysis by independent forensic experts in Washington, D.C., and London, England. In a fully transparent process over a period of three weeks, they conducted tests upon the letters and surviving envelopes.

In June of this year the panel of investigators declared the handwriting in the letters to be that of the late Joffrey Pearson, employed as a translator at the Foreign Office from October 1927 to August 1938, and thereafter employed in similar capacity at 10 Downing Street until December 3, 1938, on which date he died at his desk from a cerebral hemorrhage. The experts also declared beyond any shadow of a doubt that the paper, ink, stamps and postal markings are genuine to the 1930s.

Boston, Massachusetts
September 1983

Epilogue to the Twentieth Edition
by Victoria Pearson

I extend my profound gratitude to Maxwell Lowell for the opportunity to contribute the Epilogue to this twentieth anniversary edition of *Churchill At Munich*. When my late father began writing the letters collected in this book, I was eight years old. Today I am Professor Emeritus of Modern History at King's College, Cambridge.

My father authored this book, yet did not intend it. Never did he suspect, or even begin to imagine, that his letters to Mrs. Elizabeth Heidi Lowell would one day be read by countless people around the world. *Churchill At Munich* has been translated into eighteen languages. My father would be astounded still further to know his unintended book now acts as primary source material for students of the Munich Conference.

Historians identify that meeting as the first in a series of events that gave shape to today's world. All roads of inquiry lead back to the confrontation between Adolf Hitler and Winston Churchill in the autumn of 1938. The showdown in the Bavarian city provides above all the master key to understanding the main feature of the modern age, namely Britain's position as the world's pre-eminent economic, cultural and military power.

....

Adolf Hitler entered the Munich Conference a determined warrior and emerged a professed peacekeeper. His about-face was shocking, inexplicable and unconvincing. It robbed him of his aura of invincibility, and marked the beginning of the end of the Third Reich.

In the days leading up to the meeting between the Fuhrer and the Prime Minister, the German people expected Hitler's demands, prosecuted with his usual intimidation and bluster, to grant him yet another bloodless victory. Moreover, in this case, should a resort to force have proven necessary, the German military held the strategic upper hand.

During the weekend following the conference, Hitler feigned both deep reflection and preparation for battle. All of Europe held its breath, swaying on a knife's edge between peace and war.

On the evidence of the dictator's threats, an invasion of Czechoslovakia appeared inevitable. In reality, as we now know, and as history has likely concealed in many similar instances, the axes of this monumental decision turned on a depraved secret and the calculation of a power-drunken man's wicked ambition.*

The implications of the Kohrbach** file were potentially dire for Adolf Hitler. He left the conference resolved to shield his personal perversities from exposure to the Prussian old guard, no matter how great a turnaround in policy would be involved. He therefore embraced the option most likely to deliver him from accusations of reversal. He would posture as a saviour of world peace.

At noon on October 3rd, 1938, as the Munich Agreement's provisions were published in Berlin and London, Hitler went on radio to address the German people. He summoned all the reserves of his guile, and proceeded to play the conciliatory statesman.

He insisted that only his, Adolf Hitler's, talent for compromise had avoided a confrontation in Czechoslovakia and a consequent general

---

*The exposure of Hitler's degeneracy and the role played in it by Damon Chadwick has of course drawn enormous attention. In the years following publication of *Churchill At Munich* I received countless requests to speak about the dear man I knew as a child and whom I called uncle. I declined them all and continue to decline them. I resent the deceptive 'research' and repulsive imaginings in regard to my godfather's activities in Nazi Germany. They do a disservice to his memory. Damon Chadwick would not wish to be remembered as a spy, no matter how successful a spy. He belongs in the history books as one of the great painters of the twentieth century, tragically cut down in his prime. Full stop.

**At the request of Maxwell Lowell I have agreed to comment on a lingering mystery of the Munich Conference. What did Winston Churchill write on the scrap of paper he slid across the table to Hitler? The memoirs of those present have given us only the barest of clues. Sir Robert Vansittart said in his autobiography that it appeared to be a single word written in cursive script. Anthony Eden recalled, "The Prime Minister rapidly wrote two short words; I say two because I saw his hand pause for a speck in mid-moment." Joffrey Pearson, who was the closest witness, observed that Churchill "swiftly scribbled a single word". Since *Churchill At Munich* was published twenty years ago, a number of commentators have renewed speculation about that little scrap of paper and what it contained. In my capacity as an historian I normally shun speculation of any kind. However, in this instance I would point out that the name Kohrbach is composed of two syllables, and when the word is written in a cursive hand the tendency exists to pause 'for a speck' at the junction of the two.

war. He outlined the Agreement's terms for the Sudeten Germans, and described the federalist provisions for an autonomous Sudetenland – provisions devised and drafted by himself – as a total victory.

Voice quivering with passion, he claimed that the powers he, Hitler, had gained for his brothers and sisters in Czechoslovakia met and surpassed the Reich's fundamental demands. He characterised Winston Churchill as a terrorist whose warmongering instincts he had tamed. Then, for the first time in his political career and maybe the first time in his life, he spoke a sentence in English. It was a strange and foolish little gambit, indicating how rattled he must have been. Hitler said, "I now address myself to the people of Britain."

The dictator had not adequately rehearsed. Each word came out tortured, as if dragged through oily muck and then strangled. He spoke only the one sentence in English, but it was enough to strike all ears like a comedian's gag.

Reverting to German, Hitler appealed to the better instincts of the British public. He spoke of a potential new era of cooperation between Germans and the noble race of the British Isles. Were they not after all Aryan cousins destined for common greatness? He concluded by hinting at a possible alliance between the principal European powers that would satisfy Germany's long-term demands without a need for recourse to arms.

The reaction almost everywhere in the world to Hitler's speech was one of surprise and grateful relief. People soon forgot their surprise, but they gave permanent thanks for the preservation of peace. In Germany however relief was tempered by incredulity, and the surprise blighted by disillusionment. This was not the promised outcome. The Reich's would-be messiah had proved mortal. Here apparently was one performance too demanding even for Hitler. He could not disguise backing away as moving forward, and the garments of the peacemaker looked hurriedly borrowed. Across Germany people asked themselves how Winston Churchill, a man who had been relentlessly portrayed as a *Schwätzer und Trunkenbold*, a windbag and a drunkard, inherently corrupt and vain, corpulent and decadent, could have stared down German arms and bested their Fuhrer. The only logical answer was that Hitler had quailed before the prospect of a fight.

Hitler's generals at first reacted in disbelief. Then they laughed behind their hands as they renewed their impression of the 'little bohemian corporal' as a strutting imposter, a charlatan in oversized boots. They were not strong enough to depose the poltroon immediately, but they set plans in motion. Hard core Nazis as well, dumbfounded by Hitler's *volte-face*, took to whispering and scheming, observing bitterly that Germany's strategic advantage had been squandered, the Reich's momentum halted, dreams of expansion effectively betrayed.

For all intents and purposes, it was as if the German dictator had indeed lost a decisive battle. His hypnotic hold over the German people came undone. Abroad, the visceral fear of Adolf Hitler transmuted into cheerful derision. Cartoonists drew him shame-faced or with a tail between his legs. On the cover of *The Economist* he was depicted shorn of moustache.

Bells began tolling for the Nazi tyranny.

The German economy had geared for war. It waited on annexation of territory and the spoils of conquest. No war was being waged, however, and armies in barracks gather no booty. Military spending in Germany plummeted, munitions plants closed, unemployment soared. The elites who had supported Hitler began looking beyond him. They found eager and motivated partners among the German officer corps, which was largely composed of the Prussian old guard. These professional soldiers and proud aristocrats had always regarded Hitler as an upstart vagabond, and their world view did not include an egomaniacal claim to global conquest.

Eleven months after Munich, in August 1939, the assassination of Adolf Hitler signalled a coup d'etat led by a group of Wehrmacht generals. The summary execution of Goering, Himmler, Ribbentrop, Hess, and Goebbels put a seal on the Nazi era and set the stage for decades of revolving door tyranny in Germany. Infected by a deeply rooted culture of autocracy, the country endured one military ruler after another, each less forgiving than the last. Meanwhile, underground remnants of Hitler's brownshirt rabble, dreaming of a Nazi resurrection, invented the car-bomb, subway explosion, airline hijack, mass hostage-taking, suicide vest and schoolroom massacre. As internecine conflict tormented the country, the annual number of civilian casualties numbered in the thousands. Germany's economy withered, its influence in the world dissolved.

In early 1951 a broad-based popular revolt delivered an unplanned effect. The revived Communist party seized power, and a Soviet-backed regime became the latest predator of the Fatherland. The dictatorship of the proletariat only exacerbated the despair of the German people and decline of German industry. For forty years the communists held sway over a sullen, alienated, frustrated once-mighty people. Germany was Europe's uber-Argentina.

In 1991, when the Soviet Union collapsed, communism also imploded in Germany. The failed system was replaced, albeit tenuously, by a social democratic system. Although autocracy has proved no easy mantle to shed, we are entitled to hope that representative government, respect for human rights and the rule of law have taken enduring hold. Free markets, individual initiative and a new outreach to the international community have unleashed the productivity of the German people. Their economy today is volcanic, as catch-up wealth creation forms the national credo. From light years behind, the country now generates the equivalent of roughly eighty percent of the gross domestic product of Italy. Given current growth rates, the size of the German economy may rival Britain's within twenty years.

....

The fruits of the Munich Conference proved quite different for Britain.

The denouement at the Regina Palast hotel was initially understood as an unmitigated catastrophe. With the British delegation abruptly sent home and Hitler in high dudgeon, a Nazi invasion of Czechoslovakia seemed imminent. The preponderance of blame was laid at the Prime Minister's door. Surly headlines in London spoke of leopard's spots and tiger's stripes. It was generally accepted that a naturally bellicose Churchill had goaded the German leader, insulted him, dared him to the brink. Rumours swirled that Hitler was about to order full mobilisation.

Churchill did not return directly to England, but stopped for two nights in Paris for talks with the leaders of France and Czechosolovakia. More rumours sprang up. One absurd story, taken seriously by many during those fearful days, had it that the Prime Minister could not yet face the King or Parliament with this fatal fiasco. He had failed his sovereign who had entrusted him with the future of the nation, and he had let down his beloved Commons where he had long thundered for a tough hand with Hitler. Well, he had applied the tough hand, and look where it had led the nation.

The appeasers had a field day, and Churchill haters a red-letter day. The cartoonist Low in the *Evening Standard* drew Churchill as a deflated balloon leaking his last gasps over countries called Shameland, Defeatium and Warmania. A photo taken in Chicago years earlier of Churchill dressed like a gangster and aiming a machine-gun appeared on the front page of *The Manchester Guardian*. The caption said, 'He fires blanks!'

Meanwhile, Churchill adhered to his pledge of silence. His office released a brief announcement disclosing that the communiqué of the Munich talks would be published at noon on October 3rd. Otherwise the Prime Minister uttered no public word for two days. An unconfirmed story had him stealing out of Paris to visit a favourite spa near Drancy, where he enjoyed a Swedish massage and spent hours dozing and reading the latest Agatha Christie in a mineral bath. The rumour, even if disbelieved, appalled his supporters and turned his critics apoplectic. The complete blackout on news raised public anxiety to a fever pitch, and only stoked anti-Churchill passions the higher.

When the Prime Minister arrived home from Germany the morning of Monday, October 3rd, the threat of war hung thick. Panzers and infantry were reported massing along the Czech border, and German radio had announced the Fuhrer would deliver 'a momentous statement' to the German people at noon. Landing at Heston Aerodrome, Churchill was greeted by students from nearby colleges waving placards depicting him in horns and a spikey tail. The labour unions brought hundreds of their members with banners reading WINSTON ASS CHURCHILL and MILITARIST WAR DOG. One demonstrator took rage to an extreme with DROWN HIM IN HIS TUB! A regiment of aggressive ladies from the League of Women Pacifists carried signs that more leniently demanded, RESIGN!

"Churchill out! Churchill out!" was the chant that went up as the Prime Minister emerged from his plane, eyes alight, cigar firmly attached to the cherubic face, bowler slightly askew. When he waved his stick in a jaunty fashion a chorus of boos answered and the police were put to severe test restraining the livid mob. In his memoirs Churchill wrote of these moments:

> Here was irony of the first order, at once delicious and disheartening. We were returning with peace in our pocket, an honourable peace, a victorious peace, a permanent peace, only to be accosted with calumny. A pity I could not for some hours yet publish the proof and brandish it like a prize. So I raised my arm and with ebony stick mocked the heaving sea of ignorance and discourtesy. The police performed admirably, and did the favour of preserving the body and soul of His Majesty's proud servant.

A *Times* report about that day discloses that Joffrey Pearson accompanied Churchill from Heston and stayed by his side in the palace. As Hitler's speech came live over the shortwave, my father interpreted for King George and the Prime Minister. A minor detail of history perhaps, but one I cannot forbear from sharing now. And, if a septuagenarian historian may be permitted the indulgence of a crystalline memory from her childhood, here is one more detail, perhaps not so minor: my father told me that same evening, after sharing a startlingly warm embrace with my mother, that King George had gone to a window overlooking the Mall after the broadcast from Germany and said while looking out, "One c-c-can almost hear. . . a g-g-general sigh of relief."

Churchill went from Buckingham Palace to the House of Commons. A special session awaited him. If he had arrived a few hours earlier he would have been greeted by a rumpus of jeers, brays and calls for his resignation. But now, on both sides of the aisle, members were euphoric with the news from Germany. Immense relief had given way to noisy jubilation. Hitler's claim to have been the originator of the federalist solution could only be taken as acceptance of the right of Czechoslovakia to pursue its course as an independent country. The release of the central terms of the Munich Agreement confirmed Germany's compliance with international law. There would be no mobilisation. There would be no military incursion. The crisis was over.

The Prime Minister rose with a solemn air. He felt he was in league with destiny. He had not only curtailed the Nazi menace, but foresaw that he had strangled it. In hushed tones he began, "Mr. Speaker, I have the honour of confirming to the House that the government of Germany, through hitherto unpublished undertakings and now public pronouncement of its Chancellor, has committed itself to a path of peace."

As a pandemonium of applause washed over him, Churchill looked up at the public gallery and fixed an adoring smile on his wife, Clementine. The Prime Minister then kept his remarks brief. He summed up the general terms of the Munich Agreement, and took pointed pleasure in proclaiming the continued sovereignty and territorial integrity of the Republic of Czechoslovakia. He concluded in grand forthright terms, famously telling his countrymen, "The Anglo-Saxon peoples have preserved the flame of freedom. We have once again met our historic task. In civilisation's name His Majesty's government goes forward, principled in means, unwavering in purpose, resolute upon triumph in our time."

Triumph in our time.

Churchill's adversaries soon recovered from the shock of his Munich achievement and began ridiculing his pomposity. They identified the real meaning of his new motto as 'Imperialism, Part Two', and in this assumption they were, for once and for all time forward, spot on.

....

By the end of 1939, with the threat of war a receding memory and Hitler in an unmarked grave, Winston Churchill's tough hand at Munich had long since been vindicated. His government was re-elected in the fall of that year, then twice more, in 1944 and 1949. It spanned fourteen years in office, and achieved most of the colossal aims envisioned by its architect.

Triumph in our time: the phrase became the leitmotif of Churchill's tenure. After Munich he employed all his geopolitical genius in the interest of Britain's global dominance. He paid no heed to his island nation's disadvantages of size, population and resources in comparison to such giants as the United States and the Soviet Union. He blithely moved forward in his determination to assert British exceptionalism and its role as icon of freedom and democracy. He believed it was *necessary* to perpetuate Britain as the world's leading power.

"Only in this way can we ensure containment of the Soviets and the uninterrupted march of Western values," he said to his Secretary of Foreign Affairs, Anthony Eden, who later quoted many of Churchill's private remarks in his own memoirs. "Otherwise who knows from what quarter will come the next challenge to the Judeo-Christian tradition. If we must, from time to time, dispense with the pleasantries of diplomacy to hasten our march, so be it. Do not expect me to shrink from the opportunity that history and God have given me. We will do what we have to do."

Using the immense political capital he had acquired at Munich, Churchill performed what he deemed his duty. The weapon of coldblooded ruthlessness that had won the day at Munich became the very quality that helped him win the century for Britain. Churchill's first major act after Munich was to make his government the majority shareholder in British Petroleum. His second was to put in motion the vast project that would yield the world's first atomic bomb. His third was to establish a United Nations of exclusively democratic states. Let us look at each of these crucial achievements in turn.

Throughout the year following Munich, Churchill focused on the linchpin of his grand strategy: the takeover, by peaceful means if possible, by whatever means if necessary, of the oilfields in Saudi Arabia, Iraq and Iran. As Eden recounts:

> Winston foresaw the long-term implications of the control of this resource, not only for the benefit of Britain but to the detriment of the Soviet Union. The Soviets had plenty of oil for export, but if Britain could flood the world with Middle-Eastern oil, that would deny the markets to the Soviets and deprive them of desperately needed hard currency. So under no circumstances was Winston going to allow the oceans of oil under the Arabian desert to remain the swag of what he called a menagerie of despotic camel jockeys. He whispered to me in the House of Commons at the height of the Allan Moffatt debate, "There can be no giving in. If we refrain from

controlling the oil, there's no telling what mischief the Arabs would get up to with that wealth. We shall allow them a fair royalty so long as they spend it on the good of their people – and on goods from British factories."

The Allan Moffatt debate was named after the Scotsman who headed British Petroleum and whom Churchill appointed as his special envoy to the Middle East. In a series of transactions that have gone down as the most one-sided in history, the redoubtable Mr. Moffatt negotiated the 'understandings' that placed in BP's hands the world's largest oil reserves. It was revealed later how Moffatt had earned his reputation as a fearsome presence at the bargaining table. The negotiations were conducted for all intents and purposes under the aegis of the Royal Navy and Royal Air Force.

The debate in the Commons had many Labour members shrieking about a new colonialism, which Churchill shrugged off as praise! One MP accused the Prime Minister of giving real meaning to the phrase 'perfidious Albion', while another coined the term 'the Churchill doctrine' to define his foreign policy. More than a few critics suggested that Britain was embracing fascism and imitating Nazi skullduggery. Said Clement Atlee, Leader of the Opposition, wagging his finger at Churchill and bringing a rare fever and shrill decibel level to his tone, "This is *Lebensraum* and *Raubgier* in English translation. Shame! This government ought to hang its head in infamy."

Churchill instead raised his chin, looked down his nose, hooked his thumbs in his waistcoat, and recited his mantras. To Atlee he intoned quietly, "The cause of civilisation goes hand in hand with development of the British Empire." On another heated occasion he parried gently, "Pray, do tell, do show, do demonstrate to the British people where His Majesty's government has done harm." On another, meditatively, he looked upward and said, "Power in the hands of the just, is just." It was around this time too that Churchill, in a discerning moment of impatience with the cynical buzzing swarm, invented the phrase 'ankle-biters'.

Graham Greene's satirical 1942 novel, *The Good Emperor,* captures better than any history book the background and flavour of the notorious Allan Moffatt affair. In Greene's imaginative rendition, Churchill's 'statecraft by uncommon means' becomes an ironic caricature of Machiavellian intrigue. Tremendous benefits for the human race can come by way of grand deception. Honourable disregard for probity in international dealings can prove instrumental for world peace. 'Britain knows best' was the motto of Greene's not so fictional Prime Minister.

By 1943, British Petroleum was the largest and most powerful company on the globe. It gushed wealth into the British Isles. The enormous dividends paid to Churchill's government were re-invested in education, medical science, industrial research and military supremacy. Britain was the engine of world growth, easily outpacing, out-inventing and out-maneuvering its slumbering cousin, the United States. The Americans were still struggling to emerge from the Great Depression. Their troubles were largely self-imposed; they had weighed down their economy with the sandbags of protectionism. In 1939 they failed to reach a free trade agreement with Britain because they refused to dismantle selected tariff barriers. Churchill believed in wholly open markets; he was the first true globalist. He walked away from the trade pact negotiations rather than accept less than he demanded, knowing that eventually the Americans would beg him to come back. Writing in his diary after meeting the British Prime Minister, Franklin Roosevelt noted:

> If I had spent two hours in the company of a nasty madman poking me in the eye with a sharp stick, it would have been preferable to sitting with this jolly sphinx and trying to get him to change his mind. He is a brandy-loving cheerful troll and my candidate for history's most stubborn son-of-a-bitch, but no one can fault him for ever letting down his side.

In the presidential election of 1940 Roosevelt himself, after two terms in office, was faulted for failing to pull America out of the economic doldrums. The working people of the country, dispirited and desperate, voted in massive majority for the Socialist Party candidate, Norman Thomas. The great prize of the White House fell to the siren call of the Left. In the days following his inauguration, Thomas proved faithful to his campaign promises. He promptly nationalised vast swathes of America's anemic industry, including the railroads and energy sector, and erected still higher protective fences around domestic manufacture. Fortunately he kept government hands off the family farm. America thus remained an agricultural power and progressively acted as the breadbasket of the world. But for nearly thirty years after the Thomas tsunami, American enterprise and industrial prowess struggled to recover.

The United States finally began to mend after the presidential election of 1968, when the political pendulum swung decisively to the right. In that year the White House was won by a conservative firebrand and former actor from California, Ronald Reagan. His two terms of unapologetic de-nationalisation, de-socialisation and de-regulation restored the American spirit of self-reliance and innovation. The sleeping giant lurched awake. The unleashed entrepreneurial genius of its people transformed the American economy. During the fourth year of President Reagan's first term, in 1972, the U.S. at long last signed a free trade agreement with Britain. The pact abolished all commercial barriers between the two countries, and has since been responsible for the largest eruption of bilateral business activity in the history of the world. Today the vast natural resources of the United States, twinned with the ingenuity and productivity of the American people, have brought the country very near the level of Britain as a creator of wealth and guarantor of global stability.

Britain unveiled its atomic capability in 1944.

The thermonuclear blast above Christmas Island in the Pacific Ocean astounded the international community. No one had anticipated it. Britain's years of research and preparation for the detonation were even kept secret from half of Churchill's own Cabinet. Churchill had created the program on his second day in office, fearing that the Germans enjoyed a head start. In fact, Hitler had shunned atomic power as a chimera derived from 'Jewish science'. The United States was the only other country to undertake the enormous outlay of resources required to achieve the splitting of the atom. The American effort, however, launched by Franklin Roosevelt, was abandoned during the presidency of Norman Thomas.

Accordingly, as the world's only member of the nuclear club, Britain's opportunities to secure its strategic goals … multiplied. It now bestrode the globe, impregnable, dauntless, venturesome, magnanimous and generous. The island nation chose to be the enforcer of the general peace. Its capital city, already the financial, technological and corporate headquarters of the world, was soon to become its political epicentre as well.

In 1946, in London, Churchill presided over the first plenum of the United Nations. The British government had designated a vast tract of land at Canary Wharf for the United Nations Plaza. The architecture of the complex, awe-inspiring for the time, pointedly included the world's two tallest towers at 114 floors and 108 floors. A third tower of forty-four floors, sheathed in green glass and copper, stood at water's edge and transformed into golden arrows of light the rays of both the rising and setting sun. This glittering firework of a structure housed at its base the hall of the General Assembly.

A distinct minority of the world's states, mostly European, attended the first plenum, since Churchill had invited only those countries with democratic systems of governance. "You don't invite arsonists into the ranks of firemen," he said. "If we let them in, the dictators will only confuse and stymie every effort to stamp out the flames of repression."

With membership restricted to free countries, the initial delegates to the General Assembly were therefore predominantly white, northern, and Christian. Not a single Arab state had qualified for entry. India and Thailand were alone in representing Asia. The only Latin American participants were Chile, Costa Rica, and Panama. From Africa, tiny Senegal was the solitary invitee.

The most significant members of the 'snubbed club' were of course China and the Soviet Union. True to its sardonic form, *The Economist* created a sensation when it published a new map of the world as a wall poster. It showed members of the United Nations in vibrant red and blue, with the vast territories outside their borders covered in menacing hues of murky grey and captioned HERE BE BEARS AND DRAGONS.

Since that first plenum over half a century ago the complexion of the United Nations has changed radically. Membership has quadrupled to include virtually all countries, which was precisely the organisation's objective. In Churchill's address inaugurating the proceedings of the General Assembly, he called for the universal overthrow of tyrants:

This great institution of democratic countries has but one aim and one irrevocable purpose, and that is to bring the light and succour of freedom to every corner of the globe. We will not rest from winning that prize, nor accept too long a delay in its capture. Let our adversaries know: we will not initiate military action to achieve our ends, but we are nevertheless in battle. We are advancing to the borders of enslaved nations with the most compelling weapon ever conceived – the ideal of human liberty. This is a cry no tyrant can silence. From this day forward we shall use every lever of persuasion, every means of communication, every tool of trade and diplomacy to make outcasts of hateful regimes. Soon enough we will isolate them. Eventually we will bring them down. Ultimately we will pulverise their legacy. So let us at once cease all business with the self-appointed guardians, messiahs and odious 'strong men' of the world. On every continent where they rule by terror and feast on fear we shall choke and suffocate them until the boots of subjugation are at last lifted from the necks of men!

How else could it have been done peacefully, if not through ruinous quarantine? For Churchill this was the sensible path. Segregate the despots, render them lepers. Make no deals with them, buy nothing from them, sell them nothing. At the same time challenge their grip, appeal to their people, sow subversion, exhort rebellion.

Prodded by Britain, increasingly the prime mover of the affairs of humanity, Resolution 0001 was introduced in the General Assembly of the United Nations on July 11, 1946. The resolution proposed that members engage in concerted action to universalise Western values. It asked them to adopt a policy of exclusion whereby all repressive and single-party states, no matter their particular creed, were to be regarded as pariahs and treated as adversaries. Accordingly all trade ties were to be discontinued, aid programs abolished, diplomatic relations severed, tourism halted.

The sweeping resolution came under attack from diverse quarters, chiefly in regard to the harm it would inflict on countless innocents. The dictators had their apologists and they made use of lobbyists. Relativists in Western universities sent up a hue and cry of their own.

How dare the egomaniac Churchill act as the world's policeman and take it upon himself to lay down the law for all governments. Different cultures, different sets of mores, could result in systems that were different from democracy, and different did not necessarily mean inferior. Familiar insults evoking colonialism, jingoism, imperialism and especially fascism were hurled at Churchill. Some of his enemies branded him Herr Absolutist; others called him *El Caudillo Britannico*. The newspaper of the Communist Party in Britain, the *Daily Worker*, asked on its front page in towering type:

ARE WE SHEEP?
ARE WE TO GO MEEKLY
TO THE SLAUGHTER
PLANNED FOR US BY
GENERALISSIMO CHURCHILL
AND HIS TOADIES?

In the Commons that day Churchill rose with the grin of a Cheshire cat. He held up the *Daily Worker*, flapped it languidly at the Labour benches as if he were dispersing an unpleasant odour, and said, "Mr. Speaker, if I may answer in one word on behalf of my toadies who go by the names of Justice, Liberty, Compassion and Truth … Ba-a-a-a-a-a-a!"

No one quite believed that the unprecedented step would be taken, yet the General Assembly of the United Nations passed Resolution 0001 in the autumn of 1946. The significance of the day occasioned more Churchillian rhetoric at Canary Wharf:

Of such events as this are bold milestones constructed along the hard road of human progress. In unison we have declared that no one will be permitted to crush the yearning for freedom that rises up from the hopes and dreams of striving mankind. With certainty in the integrity of our cause we will now go forward and kindle regime change wherever regimes must be changed. With all the strength of our common determination, we have announced to the wicked and malicious who cling to ill-gotten power: YOUR TIME IS UP!

History took a turn. The United Nations represented something more than a club of dithering diplomats. Its bite now sported teeth. By virtue of the broad commercial injunction in tandem with targeted education and incitement, the democratic states achieved their openly seditious purpose in the span of a single generation. Assisted by UN machinations, peoples throughout the world deposed their unelected masters. As soon as they embraced democratic forms of government they were welcomed to United Nations membership and the family of the free.

Malcolm Tatemichi's magisterial book, *The Artillery of Ideas*, has become the standard text for students of the era. Tatemichi is particularly perceptive in regard to the factors behind the demise of the juntas and brutal systems of Italy, Spain, China and the Soviet Union. Alicia Laur's *The Ethiopian Domino* gives us perhaps the best insight into the virus of 'individual emancipation' which began in Ethiopia and toppled dictatorships and oligarchies throughout Africa. A similar dynamic created a cultural earthquake across the Arab and Muslim world when a remarkable movement rose up to abolish male dominance. The best accounts of how UN operatives trained cadres of female insurgents, who in turn incited the masses of Islamic women to rise up and execute The Gender Revolution, can be found in L. Ian Murray's *Exit Hijab* and Marco R. Steven's *Patricide in Mecca*.

By the mid-1970s the world was at last sanitised of medieval theocracies and grotesque kleptocracies. Weaned from war, nurtured by unprecedented stability, unhindered by the artificial barriers of national borders, humanity entered a new era of development. The global common market created unprecedented trade and prosperity. By the turn of the millennium, sprawling populations that had subsisted in poverty were lifted into dignity.

Scores of books have chronicled the astonishing wealth creation that took place during the last three decades of the twentieth century. The most insightful general narrative of the period may be Nathaniel David's *The New Industrial Revolution*. The book includes a masterful analysis of the competition that now shapes global destiny, producing creative destructions that progressively deliver wave upon wave of market-altering, life-improving innovations. I must also mention Professor Leah Kristi's international bestseller, *Silicon Vistula*, a book that stands out for the specific lesson it teaches about recent history. Along the banks of the Vistula River in Poland occurred one of the greatest flowerings of ingenuity in human history. Starting in the late 1980s, the children of a traditionally spiritual culture turned their attention to the silicon chip and the semi-conductor. They launched electronic start-ups in abandoned stables. They wrote reams of computer code in tool sheds. They tinkered with cybernetic prototypes in garages. Did they suspect, even in their wildest imaginations, that they were inventing the foundation stones of whole new industries? Their companies, kindled by little more than brainwaves, emerged from the stables, sheds and garages to become some of the largest corporations in the world. Vast new fortunes materialised in the hands of singularly untraditional young Jews in Warsaw, Cracow, Sandomiersz, Bydgoszcz, and Gdansk. In a world reliant upon information technology and the software that pumps the blood of business, the sons and daughters of generations of rabbis and talmudic scholars became vital power-brokers of innovation. Professor Kristi can boast a signal achievement in *Silicon Vistula*. She persuasively traces the roots of the Polish miracle to the ground laid by the elimination of international conflict. Uproot the weed of hate, banish the battlefield from human affairs, let people live and flourish, and who knows what gardens of creativity will spring up from where.

Looking back at the 20th century, which suffered the unspeakable cataclysm of the Great War of 1914 - 1918, it might appear natural that the better lions of the human race would finally come awake and coalesce; that they would gaze about their domain and institute proper authority; that they would mercilessly isolate and extirpate the jackals in their midst. From the perspective of today it seems only apt, if not inevitable, for the asphyxiation of fascism, communism, and all forms of despotism to have been performed by a compact of free nations acting in the interests of humanity. Yet none of this occurred or was even conceived until a single determined man ignited the process. As my American friends would say of this man's advent, "We got lucky!" It took a rare flash of lightning in the fog of history – the career of Winston Churchill – to spark the unity and wrath of the good.

All the more curious then that a certain hypothetical scenario has intrigued many writers of late, and exerted a fascination on members of my profession. Dozens of popular and scholarly speculations have been written about what might have happened had Churchill's career been denied its apogee and had he never taken office in Downing Street. If, in July 1938, the Lockheed Model 14 Super Electra had survived its flight from Paris to London, what posture would Neville Chamberlain have assumed two months later at Munich? If Hitler had marched into the Sudetenland and gotten away with his aggression, would he have been emboldened next to look east? How would history have subsequently unfolded? Would the world today enjoy the bounty of a uniquely British determination to teach, spread and entrench the tenets of a universal Magna Carta? Might the supremacy of individual rights, the democratic process and plain old obdurate *civility* still have become the pillars of our common cause?

You will not find answers to those questions anywhere in my writings. This is one historian who refuses to ponder the opaque repercussions of events that never took place. I prefer reality. Give me facts. The lessons of our time are transparent. Sixty-three years after the Munich Conference the world wholly embraces democracy, individual liberty, borderless trade and boundless wealth creation. Conflict between countries has essentially been abolished. Sectarian animosities have diminished to the vanishing point. The outlook for perpetual peace strengthens with every passing year. Thus does Winston Churchill's stand against Adolf Hitler continue to deliver incalculable service. Let us take inspiration from that truth, and instruction.

Cambridge, England
September 12, 2001

494